PHILIP R. JORDAN & DAVID A. PALLISER

STONES
OF
CONSCIENCE

Matador
9 De Montfort Mews
Leicester LE1 7FW, UK
Tel: (+44) 116 255 9311 / 9312
Email: books@troubador.co.uk
Web: www.troubador.co.uk/matador

ISBN 978-1906510-886

A Cataloguing-in-Publication (CIP) catalogue record for this book is
available from the British Library.

Typeset in 11pt Bembo by Troubador Publishing Ltd, Leicester, UK
Printed in the UK by The Cromwell Press Ltd, Trowbridge, Wilts, UK

Matador is an imprint of Troubador Publishing Ltd

To our wives

*All the characters in this book are fictitious and any resemblance
to actual persons, live or dead, is purely coincidental*

And yet some of the episodes in this book actually took place…

Chapter 1

The heavily panelled room was dark; faint odours of stale tobacco mingled with the heady smell of fresh polish. The loud, slow methodic tick from a grandfather clock was all that broke the intense silence. Candle flames danced on their wicks, caught in a draught, sending eerie shadows upon the polished wood grain. The Tsar was dressed in full military uniform, having just returned from a visit to his de-moralised army who were now quelling a rebellion against him. The Russian Emperor slumped in a heavily built leather chair at his writing desk. He gazed at a painting, resplendent in a rococo gold frame, which was propped up against a chair near the forlorn looking empty fireplace. His thoughts were on the young woman in the portrait: he could not come to terms that she had been born in sin and now she had died in sin. In the Tsar's mind however she was, and always would be, as innocent as a lamb. He seemed oblivious to the Englishman sitting opposite him.

Sir Wesley Henshaw was not sure what to do. He shuffled nervously in his seat; the shame of his actions was already weighing heavily on him. The life he had known was about to come to an ignominious end: if not by the man in front of him, then by his wife back at his new home on the Isle of Rhum.

The Tsar continued to mutter to himself and shake his head. A devastating defeat at the hands of the Japanese was humiliating enough, but the knowledge that his beautiful Xenia had been de-flowered by this arrogant Englishman, and a commoner at that, hurt even more than his recent military disasters. Finally the Tsar rose from his chair and laboured over to a large, heavily carved walnut chest of drawers. He opened one of the drawers and extracted a casket. Turning he returned to the desk and gently laid the box down.

Wesley had never seen anything quite like it, his eyes widened as he took in its breathtaking beauty. The lid and front facia had dark wooden panels which separated the gold and silver craft work of acanthus leaves and rose buds. Within the panels lay gold monograms woven into letters that Wesley could not make out and he could only speculate they must have been Russian. On the front of the box, which was the size of a musical box, silver Doric columns rose from a silver plinth. Wesley felt an urge to reach out and touch the box but then he noticed the Tsar fumble in his pocket pulling out a delicate silver key and, tenderly turning the lock, he barked a sentence to a plump, slightly balding man, perched nervously on a sofa in the corner of the room.

'Sir Wesley, His Excellency wishes to know,' translated the formally dressed man, 'if you have anything to say for yourself?'

Sir Wesley's whole body had started to shake as he heard the Tsar's deep resonating voice fill the room; the words almost suffocating him as he sensed the hatred within them. Wesley tried to speak, but coherent speech failed him and he meekly shook his head. His entire life's work and labours were to be destroyed by a moment of madness. A few nights of stolen, forbidden love with a young Russian girl should have been, and were for a time, forgotten. Then came her letter informing him of his condition; he would never forget that moment as he read it, his legs became so weak they gave way beneath him. He had spent weeks considering how to rectify the situation only to receive a royal summons from the Emperor's private secretary to come urgently to Russia. How could this young Russian girl have anything to do with the Romanov dynasty?

The Tsar had turned and his gaze went back to the portrait. Sir Wesley followed the Tsar's look away from the magnificent box in front of him to the woman's eyes which were so intense; he felt himself flush. It was as if she was there with him, holding his gaze. Her beauty was startling and, despite her formal pose and expression, in her face there lay a hint of a mischievous smile as if she had a secret and was teasing them. The jewels she wore looked exquisite and Wesley wondered how the artist had managed to capture the jewel's light with such perfection. Wesley looked into her brown eyes and recalled how they had once shown to him a fiery passion, which he had not been able to resist. Wesley's reverie was broken when the Tsar turned his gaze away from the portrait and focused on him. The expression on the Emperor's face caused his stomach to tighten. Wesley desperately tried to read the Tsar's expression. The Russian's countenance confused him as he could see the anger, hatred, and sorrow, but there was also something else etched on his face. Could it be a desire for retribution or did Wesley see guilt? The Tsar broke the Englishman's train of thought, and hissed a short sentence, and then with a brief flick of his hand gestured towards the translator.

'His Excellency wonders if you know what has happened to Lady Xenia?'

The Tsar raised his eyebrows questioningly, but with a steely menace, as the translator finished. Sir Wesley had heard a rumour on his journey to Russia, a terrible rumour.

'I have heard that, that she has, she has…,' Wesley could not finish the sentence; the Tsar did it for him.

'*That she died.*'

The Tsar started to move towards Sir Wesley and the Englishman felt his body shrinking back into his chair, he had no idea what to expect; Russian Tsars had a reputation for brutality. The Emperor halted and remained standing, his eyes having been drawn back to the portrait. Then stooping forward he opened the casket in front of him and swivelled it around, revealing its contents. Wesley's fear waned for a moment as his curiosity grew; he lent slightly forward. His intrigue turned to surprise as he saw the shoulders of the man in front of him make a small but noticeable shudder. The Tsar spoke again but this time his voice was hoarse and a tear ran down his cheek. On one occasion the man in the corner started to translate, but the Tsar flashed him an angry glance, silencing the minion instantly. The Emperor continued until he had finished, then he returned to the other side of the desk and sat down heavily, fixing his eyes on Wesley, his hands wrapped tightly around the arms of the chair.

'His Excellency has said,' the translator coughed a little and he looked upwards as he tried to re-call the exact words the Tsar had spoken. 'Lady Xenia died during child birth. His Excellency knows the baby girl is your bastard child.' The small man re-adjusted his position after making this statement and pulled at his starched collar. 'His Excellency is, however, inclined to be gracious and lenient. Despite the terrible deed that you have done, he cannot ignore your efforts and good office during the recent war with Japan, especially at the Treaty of Portsmouth...' The Tsar raised his arm to silence his servant.

'You, Sir Wesley, of all men, should know my intense hatred of the Japanese and your efforts alleviated some of the ignominy of the defeat.' The Tsar's face was pale and shallow as he spoke a language he had always struggled to master. Wesley could not help himself but quickly looked at the scar on the Emperor's forehead and recalled the assassination attempt of the Tsar's life on a state visit to Japan. The Tsar noticed Wesley's glance. The tension in the room momentarily relaxed as the Tsar instinctively touched his forelock and Wesley thought, or rather he hoped, the darkness in the Emperor's eyes had faded. He was wrong.

'You will name the child Olga, after my sister. When she is old enough you will give her the painting of her beautiful mother, and tell her, yes Sir Wesley, you must tell her, who her mother was and *what you did to her.*' The Tsar's hands were gripping the arms of the chair so tightly Wesley could hear the creak of leather and saw the Emperor's white knuckles protruding out of his hands.

Sir Wesley nodded obediently and unable to hold the Tsar's look he lent forward to see inside the box and he tried to stretch his back to see as he started to speak, 'But Your Excellency how am I to…'

The Tsar closed his eyes and releasing the chair he raised both his hands. 'My poor Xenia, she was so ashamed of what you had done to her; she withdrew into herself, she couldn't face me or her mother. She never told anyone she had gone into labour and unfortunately for young Xenia the baby was a breech birth. If the maid had not heard her screams it would have been too late to save the baby. Fortunately my physician performed a caesarean section, but my poor girl...' The Tsar's eyes became dark and glazed and he once again slowly stood up steadying himself by leaning on the desk. 'You had better know that Xenia, her mother and grandmother before her carried haemophilia, an unfortunate illness, but very common in the royal households of the crowned heads of Europe. May Our Lord take pity on my poor girl's wretched soul.' The Tsar cast his eyes back to the picture by the fireplace.

Wesley became light headed, and for a brief moment the room seemed to spin as the realisation that he was facing not only the Emperor of Russia but also Xenia's father dawned on him. The ringing in his ears was followed by his vision becoming blurred; now it was his turn to grab hold of the arms on his chair. One indiscretion would mar his entire life and to have undertaken such an act with the Russian Emperor's illegitimate daughter... His mind raced as to the events unfolding around him and it now felt as if his very life blood was running out of his body; he felt himself become faint. The Tsar watched the highly agitated man squirming in front of him and continued only when the realisation of what he had said had been fully absorbed by the Englishman. The Tsar pushed the casket forward allowing Wesley to see inside; curiosity forcing away his faintness.

'In this box are a few of my family's finest jewels, which have been gifted to Lady Xenia by many within my family, except these…' The Emperor lifted out a deep tray, laden with jewels, and underneath, laid out neatly, were a necklace, bracelet, earrings and a large sapphire and diamond ring; all with a similar styling.

Wesley immediately recognised them from the portrait. 'This is a suite of jewels I had specially made for my beautiful Xenia. I tried to give them to my sister but she wouldn't take them calling them the *Stones of Conscience*.' The Tsar ran his fingers over the gems and became still and thoughtful for a few moments.

Sir Wesley leant fully forward and his eyes widened as he was memorised by the dazzling contents of the casket. He started to reach forward but a withering look from the Tsar made him recoil back and he felt his fear return.

'I have decided that you will take these jewels with Olga. You will use them for the sole purpose of ensuring this young girl is properly brought up, do you understand? You may also use them for her dowry to a suitable man. I give you my solemn word Sir Wesley, that unless you carry out my wishes, I will…' The Tsar whispered a few words to his translator.

'Enact a most terrible revenge, Your Excellency,' answered the suited man.

'I will enact the most terrible revenge on not only you, but your entire family.' The Tsar finished by brushing his moustache with the back of his hand and slowly stroked his beard in a lavish and grand gesture that made the finery of his uniform quiver.

'Your Excellency, I truly share your remorse for Xenia and of course my role in her terrible and tragic fate, but…' The Tsar tried to stop Henshaw by raising his hand, but this time it was Sir Wesley, whose fear had now turned to panic as he realised his predicament, felt compelled to say something in his defence. 'Sorry, Your Excellency, but my shame necessities me having my say.' The Tsar seemed bemused by Sir Wesley's insolence, and not fully comprehending the Englishman's words allowed him to continue. 'I know what I did was wrong and I have no excuses, save to say I am just an ordinary man and at times, like all men, make foolish mistakes. I give you my word that this baby will be cared for in the most proper manner…'

'Enough! You took a young girl, my young daughter, who had barely reached womanhood, into your bed. I believe you are a married man, did you forget your vows…?' The Tsar drew in a large breath and exhaled noisily realising the hypocrisy of his own words. Hadn't he done exactly what this man had done? Didn't Jesus once said "Let those without sin cast the first stone…"?

Emperor Nicholas took another long breath and continued. 'Yes, you *will* care for this child, but do not forget one thing Sir Wesley.' The Tsar's words came out slowly and were measured while he replaced the tray, closed and locked the casket gently. 'Nobody, and I mean nobody, must ever know the identity of Olga. If her fraternal parentage ever becomes known it could put her, and all those around her, in a difficult position. However, there is one, and only one, exception. If you, or the young child, should ever get into difficulties that might endanger her life, or her well being in any way, then you will contact my embassy in London and give the Ambassador this note.' The Tsar opened a drawer of the desk and pulled out a folded piece of parchment tied tightly with a red ribbon and the Tsar's waxed seal entrapping the knot. 'You will only use this in the most dire of circumstances. Do I make myself clear?' Sir Wesley's eyes narrowed as he focused on the note. 'Finally, it must never be opened by anyone other than my ambassador. Do you understand?'

Sir Wesley nodded as he tried to hazard a guess as to the content of the letter and what the consequences would be if he did actually open it. He took the parchment carefully and slid it into his inside jacket pocket. Sir Wesley's mind was confused as he became aware he would be able to walk away from this meeting without any serious repercussions. He started to feel a sense of relief as the meeting was clearly coming to an end and, although he knew he had many problems ahead, he was already planning how he was going to rid himself of his new issue; especially as he now had the jewels to assist him. They must be worth a fortune, he pondered. Maybe, just maybe, he could keep his life as it had been and return to his beloved Kinlock Castle on Rhum and his loved ones. The Tsar continued to watch the man in front of him, disdain and loathing once again consumed him. Emperor

Nicholas ll clicked his fingers at the servant who instantly stood and trotted over gathering up the portrait and the jewellery box and led Wesley away.

'Sir Wesley,' bellowed the Tsar as Wesley was about to exit the room. 'I think you have forgotten something.' The Tsar held up the silver key. Sir Wesley shuffled reluctantly back towards the Emperor and opened his hand to accept the key. 'I truly despise you Henshaw but you can thank the Lord that I have decided to take the Christian way and forgive you, for Olga's sake.' Sir Wesley bowed as the Tsar dropped the key into his hand and returned to the waiting translator. 'Do not forget Sir Wesley, if you do not carry out my instructions to the very letter, or if I find out the jewels have been used for anything other than for Olga's sole interests… I think you can guess the outcome. I do not make idle threats.'

Sir Wesley Henshaw bowed his head again and hurried from the room. Relief, fused with trepidation, cascading through his veins.

Chapter 2

Tobermory, Isle of Mull, June-1997

Marcus lent on the cold damp railings of the harbour wall. Rain had finally given way to a fine evening and clouds were scurrying eastwards lit up by the setting sun. The small fishing port, with its surrounding hills seemed calmed as they basked in the evening sunlight. The dark, oily water was being disturbed by his old friend, valiantly trying to rescue an inflatable tender that was about to be dragged out of the water by its own painter; the tide was now on the ebb. Just into the bay the water swirled and occasionally a large smooth seal's head would surface, its nostrils flaring and whiskers twitching as it curiously watched the man perched precariously on the ladder. Marcus watched as the creature ducked out of sight and he scanned the bay for over a minute but the seal's curiosity had been sated; it must have moved on. Seagulls swirled above him honing in on a few fishing vessels moored a hundred yards to his left, squawking noisily at each other and fighting over the scraps the fishermen threw into the sea.

Marcus shook his head as his gaze slowly turned towards the Sound of Mull, the thick blankets of purple heather, interjected by dark green and yellow gorse, were highlighted in the evening light. The majestic cone of Ben Nevis was just visible in the distance. The outgoing tide could be seen rushing out towards the Atlantic taking with it flotsam and other debris. The strength of the sun on his face warmed his entire body and he made an involuntary shiver. He ran his hand through his dark mop of hair and, in his usual manner, smoothed his face with his hand.

'If only this place had the weather…,' he muttered to himself looking down at the still struggling crew mate. 'Come on Charles, for pity sake. The others are going to be totally pissed before we even get there.'

'Well,' shouted up the skipper of the chartered yacht, 'a little help from you and I would have had this done ages ago.' Charles Ashford finally tied the dinghy's painter onto the harbour wall's ladder close to the water line and hauled himself up, his longish blond hair flopping unruly over his forehead.

'It's not even our bloody tender,' said Marcus taking one of the lapels on his friend's sailing jacket and helping him up onto the roadway.

'That's not the point. It will be my good deed for the day…' Charles adjusted his sailing jacket and briefly looking towards the sun he smiled at the man in front of him. 'If everyone helped each other a little…'

'You're a ruddy hero Charlie, a ruddy hero. Now if they had put their tender on the top of the slipway, like us, then they wouldn't have to worry about the tide,' said Marcus turning and quickly stepping out of the way of an old battered pickup truck, laden with dirty, fishy smelling boxes, which narrowly missed him by inches. '*Watch it!*' he screamed at the passing truck. 'Come on, I need a drink.'

The two men walked purposefully towards the yellow painted building on the other side of the road. The Mishnish Hotel nestled in between two other vividly painted buildings, on one side red, the other blue.

'What a cracking name for a pub,' whispered Charles. 'The Mishnish. It beats The Chelsea Potter. Well, we had better see what condition the other two are in and you can buy your potential future son-in-law a drink.' Charles ducked the playful punch directed at him. 'Really Marcus, he's a great lad. Your Dawn could do a lot worse, and I mean a lot worse.'

'Yes, yes, but anyone who wears an earring, and a diamond one at that, *has* to be of questionable character.' Marcus stopped at the door to the pub. 'Your kids are years away from all this mating malarkey; I know what goes on in young men's minds at his age. I was young once.'

'Yeah, and a long time ago,' said Charles once again avoiding another swipe at him. 'Toby is very level headed, and as a couple they seem absolutely natural together. Toby is not like you at all; he hasn't got Dawn pregnant on their first night together…'

'OK, OK, let's change the subject. I still don't like the earring though.' Marcus pushed open the door and a warm snug aroma made him check for a moment as his eyes grew accustomed to the gloomy light. A thin haze of blue smoke hung in the air occasionally stirred by the draught from the open door behind them. Marcus saw the other two members of the crew over in a corner. Douglas Campbell was holding court with a few people on the next table, while his daughter's boyfriend looked on with a slightly bemused smile. Marcus was astonished by the number of empty glasses on their table. Marcus waved to Toby gesturing to ask if he wanted another drink. The young man shook his head but pointed at the Scotsman sitting next to him and nodded.

Marcus and Charles went to the bar and ordered two beers with chasers. When the drinks arrived Marcus picked up one of the chasers and nodding at his friend downed the whisky in one.

'Beautiful,' he whispered slightly choking and brushing his hair back with his free hand. 'I have to say this island malt stuff is much better than the fire water I'm used to drinking. Charles, get it down you.'

Charles picked up the other small glass and sipped it, but seeing a frown form on Marcus' brow, he emptied the glass.

'Two more please,' Charles croaked at the landlord, and continued. 'Look, I found a tender very nearly dangling on the wall of the harbour. It was white with orange flashes on the side. Do you happen to know who it belongs to?'

The landlord placed two further whiskeys on the bar.

'If they're that stupid not to realise the tide is going out then that's their problem. I'm no nursemaid to a bunch of yachties.' The landlord's Glaswegian accent and withering stare stunned the Englishman.

'I told you Charles, we're not all of a saintly disposition,' laughed Marcus sipping his pint.

'Look Marcus,' whispered Charles, 'before we join the others I think we should plan a visit to a place a little more lively.' Marcus took a gulp of his beer and gave his friend a puzzled look. 'Toby is being very patient and I don't think he can understand a word Douglas says when he's had a few…' They both looked towards the Scot who was animatedly waving his hands around. 'You're also being a bit off hand with Toby and…'

'Rubbish, I'm not. It is just that I can't be my usual self,' defended Marcus. 'I can't say some things in front of him like, well you know, it is a bit embarrassing…'

'At times you are a real prig… It is so unlike you of all people, Marcus'

'Look what if I tell a saucy joke or talk about sex,' pleaded Marcus dropping his voice. 'What if he starts talking about *it*, then I'll *know* he and Dawn are, well, are at *it*.'

Charles lent back and laughed out loud. 'They've been going out for months and, by all accounts, very much in love. Of course they're at *it!'* The pub seemed to go quiet just as Charles bellowed out his last phrase.

'Oh! You two,' came a loud, deep Scottish accent from the corner. The two men turned to see their Ayrshire crewmate standing waving an empty glass. They had met him on another sailing trip several years ago and ever since then he had become a regular member of the crew. They watched as he gestured towards them, his wiry long hair and full beard, which nearly obscured all his face, could not hide his bright green eyes which shone like beacons. 'Are you two southern nancies going to come and join us or not; if you are bring a pint of heavy for me?' The two men at the bar exchanged a smile and bought another beer then joined the rest of the crew.

'When you said we were to have a week's sailing in Scotland,' continued Douglas, 'I didn't realise you weren't going to have a dram or two. Hell, I've had to find new friends…' he waved his hand over to the neighbouring table. Charles noticed they all had white sailing jackets and a distinctive orange flash on the lapels and cuffs. He decided not to say anything.

'Yes, sorry about that,' answered Charles. 'We were checking the anchor and the tender.'

'Charles wasn't only checking our tender but everyone else's,' smiled Marcus.

'For heaven's sake Charles,' shouted the Scotsman. 'You'll be needing a few bevies if you want to sleep tonight. Anyway, my friends here are from Sweden and are interested in buying antiques.' Douglas turned to the next table where the three men and two women were smiling politely, but clearly they were struggling to comprehend Douglas's words. 'These are my two buddies I was telling yer about. Here we 'ave *Captain Bligh,* alias Charles Ashford. *He* works for the Victoria and Albert Museum, no less. He researches old relics and antiques, a very intellectual sort.' Douglas smiled as he tried to pronounce the last word. 'While next to him,' he pointed at the hapless Marcus, 'is the first mate, the right horrible Marcus Chapman. Now he goes round making lots of money out of old bits of furniture and artefacts.' Douglas again struggled to pronounce the last word and leant forward taking a large mouthful of beer. 'So if you want to know anything about old junk, these are your men. Me, I prefer MFI myself.' Douglas bowed, made a loud laugh, and sat down banging the table and disturbing the beer causing it to slop onto the table.

A pregnant pause filled the corner of the pub, Charles nodded politely at the crew on the next table and turned to his friends, looking at Toby he asked, 'Look Toby, Marcus and I were wondering if we should sail up to Mallaig tomorrow? It may have a little more life for you. It's a bit dull here, don't you think?'

'Dull? What rubbish is that,' demanded Douglas leaning forward banging the table again. 'This lad doesn't need to be pampered by ye two; do you Tobs?' Douglas didn't wait for a reply. 'Let's go and have a sail around to Muck and then to Eigg. If we get to Eigg at around 3 o'clock in the afternoon the ferry pulls in and everyone and their dog on the island goes down and has a few drams in the boat's bar. They don't have a pub on the island, ye see. It's a great atmosphere, so I hear. He doesn't want to go to Mallaig. There's girls there, you know that Marcus.' Douglas had a mischievous twinkle in his eye. 'We don't want your Dawn finding out we led the young lad astray, do we, eh?'

Charles looked at Toby questioningly. 'I'll get some more drinks,' said the young man. 'You lot decide, but I am enjoying it, seriously.' Toby looked sideways at Marcus and gave a little smile. Marcus smiled back and nodded. He watched the young undergraduate going to the bar and he had to concur with Charles, he wasn't such a bad lad. He just couldn't help a fatherly protective urge towards his daughter. The irony of it all made him smile. He had only just started to get to know his daughter properly since her move to university in London and now he may lose her again,; he just wished she hadn't met Toby so young.

'Penny for them,' said Charles quietly leaning forward and eyeing Douglas as he continued to torment the Swedish crew.

'You're right, Toby is a good lad. But you see I have just got to know Dawn, and I'm frightened I'll lose her again, this time to him.' Marcus finished his drink, his old friend watching him. 'Getting Linda pregnant when I was eighteen, and the bloody awful mess that followed… Can't you understand my protectiveness?'

'Marcus I've known you since the age of seven. I have rarely offered advice but tonight I will.' Charles quickly glanced towards the bar and continued. 'If you carry on being protective you will force Dawn away. Embrace Toby, he's a smart lad. Next year he'll have his law degree and who knows what next…' Charles lifted his pint. 'To Toby and Dawn. I wish them every happiness.'

'Yes Charlie; I guess you're right. Let's get some drinking done.' Marcus said eyeing his empty glass and he swivelled round to see Toby tottering over to the table laden with a tray full of drinks. 'Well done Toby, you've passed the first test as a future son-in-law by carrying eight drinks and not spilling a drop!'

The Swedes' politeness had started to wane and even Douglas realised his audience was tiring of his constant chatter, so he turned and spoke to the rest of the crew.

'So Charlie, what do you say about Eigg then?' Douglas said taking his drink. 'Then we could go to Rum. Do you know it has been spelt with an 'h' in the past? Rhum.' Douglas emphasised the 'Rh' in his last word. 'Apparently some Sassenach, who once owned it was abstemious,' Douglas looked pleased he managed the last word, 'and he didn't want to live on an island named after a liquor. Crazy, eh?'

'Well actually I was hoping we would try to get to Iona, south of here. It is the burial ground of the Kings and Chieftains of Scotland. It is meant to be stunningly beautiful,' said Charles rummaging for some notes he had made that afternoon.

'I hope it's got a pub like this Charlie,' interjected Marcus. Charles lent back and rolled his eyes to the ceiling, the other three laughing at Charles's apparent frustration.

Several more rounds later and the four men were not in a state to discuss anything rationally. Marcus did make a point of talking to his potential son-in-law; Charles' advice had hit a chord with him.

'Time, Ladies and Gentlemen, *please*,' cried the landlord placing a tea-towel over the beer pumps.

'Good God, it can't be that time already?' Charles checked his watch and looked through the window to see the remains of a sunset casting long shadows across the bay. 'Actually fellas, I'm hungry.'

'That's the first sensible thing you've said all night, Charlie,' said Douglas standing and stretching. The five Swedes had already left some time before. 'How far out are we anchored?'

'Not too far, a hundred yards or so. Why?' said Charles gathering his belongings.

'Well I don't think we brought any life jackets, and it's a well known fact that most sailing accidents happen when ferrying to and from the boat.' Charles frowned for a second while Douglas looked quite pleased that he had managed to wrong foot Charles.

'Oh, stop your harping Doug,' said Marcus as they all piled out of the pub into the crisp, cool island air. 'Charles and I have done this a hundred times before. Oh ye of little faith!'

Marcus and Charles walked ahead making for the slipway and, taking a rope on either side of their tender, hoisted it onto their shoulders and started to pick their way down the slipway avoiding the seaweed. Suddenly both men were flat on their backs the tender's small outboard engine making a worrying crack against the concrete. The taut painter to their tender still fastened securely to the railing on the harbour wall. The noise of their fall echoed around the hills of the cove and was quickly followed by the hysterical roars of laughter of the other two crew members standing at the top of the slipway, watching the pitiful scene.

Douglas was laughing so much he was doubled up holding his stomach. 'A hundred times before, eh? Oh ye of little faith, eh?' He walked over to the railing and untied the painter throwing it to his two friends, who were still struggling to stand up on the slippery surface.

'I'll be back in a few minutes,' shouted the humiliated Charles tersely to the two spectators.

'Aye, but don't forget to bring back life jackets, *my* faith has just run out,' cried Douglas whose voice was drowned by Charles starting the outboard motor.

Charles took two trips to ferry all of them back to the yacht; it was decided that cheese and wine was the order of the day. Charles went down below and started to prepare the evening snack when two large explosions ripped through the still night air; their echoes could be heard resonating up distant valleys. Charles quickly put on the VHF radio.

'What was that?' asked Toby watching the two bursts of bright light above the small cove.

'Lifeboat!' cried Charles coming on deck with a pair of

binoculars. The blue and orange lifeboat was moored only a few yards away. A couple of minutes later two tenders were racing towards them from the jetty. Marcus and Charles brought the food and wine to the outside table and the four men watched the RNLI crew prepare for a rescue.

'It seems someone has gone missing in a rowing boat down the Sound of Mull,' said Charles craning his neck to listen to the radio.

'Oh, it's not the two goons who couldn't untie their tender then?' Douglas didn't manage to avoid a cheese biscuit which hit him firmly on the side of the head. He laughed and threw it over the side and watched several seagulls dive towards it squawking and stabbing at it as it floated away. 'Listen lads, I'm beached. I'll see you all in the morning,' he continued, and without waiting to hear the insults about his stamina, and the lack of other manly attributes, Douglas slipped down the stairs and staggered forward to his berth in the bow.

'I think its perfect conditions for a night sail...' said Charles, who watched for Marcus' reaction. Marcus munched on some cheese and looked up at the darkening sky.

'I would, but Charles we have had an awful lot to drink.' Marcus stole a quick glance at Toby whose eyes had noticeably widened.

'We'll show that Scottish landlubber, hey Marcus,' said Charles his speech slightly slurred and already starting to tidy up. 'I'll get the charts out and you two clear and stow everything, OK?'

'I don't want to sound a bit of an old woman,' started Toby, 'but wouldn't we be better doing a night sail when we were sober?'

'Tell him Marcus.' Charles dropped down into the salon and took the seat by the navigation table.

'Well, we have always done night sails when we have had a few drinks. Makes the night go quicker...' Marcus tried to keep his voice firm and calm as he stacked the plates; Toby wasn't fooled.

'Marcus? This is madness...'

'Toby, don't worry. You go and bunk down and you'll wake up moored off… Where are we heading Charlie?' Marcus said shoving his head through the hatchway.

'Iona. Thirty five to forty miles, perfect for a full night sail. I'll sign up your log book, Toby. You'll need it for a Coastal Skipper.' Charles was now studying the charts and tide tables and occasionally scratching his head and pushing back his blond locks.

Charles made some notes and stumbled up the steps. 'Are you ready Marcus?' Not waiting for an answer he fired up the diesel inboard engine and letting it warm up he went forward to examine the anchor windlass. Marcus eventually joined Charles and after a brief discussion Charles went onto the helm. Within a few minutes, with the anchor stowed, they were gliding gracefully out of the harbour. Tobermory's twinkling lights were reflected in the still water and as Marcus joined the skipper they both felt that tinge of excitement on leaving a port. The only noise was the throbbing chug of the Penta engine below their feet, the bubbling sound of the engine exhaust and the slap of the sea on the bow. Unnoticed they slipped out into the Sound of Mull.

'Could you take over Marcus?' asked Charles. Marcus nodded and slid in behind the wheel of the 34 foot yacht. 'Take a North Westerly course and when you get to Ardmore Point,' Charles pointed to a headland in the distance, 'go virtually due west.' Charles had had to raise his voice as the wind had started to increase as soon as they had left Tobermory.

'Charles, look,' said Marcus pointing forward. Ahead of them the sea was still relatively calm, but in the distance on the other side of the headland, white horses could be seen running furiously to their right; fine spray was being whipped of the top of the waves by the wind and clouding the view of the island of Coll.

Charles slapped the coach roof and shouted to his friend. 'This is British made, it can take anything the sea can throw at us, don't worry.' Charles, however, gave a wary look at the seas ahead; a momentary doubt flashed through his mind. Why hasn't the tide turned, he thought? For a moment he considered calling the coast guard to inform them of their passage but he feared they might tell he was slurring his words and thought better of it. Anyway the night's excesses were now being cleared by the sea air and he shuddered at what the Scotsman would say if he turned back now; there had always been quite a competition between the two men. 'Come on Marcus it's like the old days,' shouted Charles stepping out of the cockpit onto the deck. 'Let's get the sails up; turn her into the wind.' Marcus put his thumbs up and turned the boat as instructed. He took out a woollen bobble hat from his pocket pulling it tightly over his head. He struggled to zip up his sailing jacket but finally he managed it and clipped his collar across his face. The boat rose and fell as the increasingly larger waves passed underneath; they had just passed Ardmore Point.

Charles struggled to raise the mainsail as the boat was pitching badly in the seas and several times he lost his footing, hanging on desperately to the rigging. He could see Marcus was shouting at him but the wind was too strong and carried the helmsman's voice out to sea. Then he saw Toby raise his head out of the hatchway for a moment; his expression full of confusion and fear. Finally Charles managed to hoist the main sail and put one slab reef in to compensate for the freshening wind. Tottering back towards the rear, clutching the hand rails tightly, he dropped back into the cockpit gasping with exhaustion.

'Dear Lord, I'm not as young as I was,' he said to the helmsman. Marcus was looking ahead with a deep scowl and he didn't answer. 'What's up, Marcus?'

'I don't want to sound like a girl's blouse, Charlie, but you haven't got a life jacket or harness on. This is very unlike you and Toby is genuinely concerned; don't forget he's never been sailing before.' Marcus finished by bringing the nose of the boat away from the wind and he pulled in the sheets as tight as he could. The wind immediately caught the sail making the boat heel over around fifteen degrees and the heavy slapping of the oncoming waves ceased as the boat now seemed to cut through them more efficiently.

'Do you want to turn back?' enquired the skipper.

'No, it's not that. I just don't want Dawn to hear from Toby that we acted recklessly. Let's play by the book on this trip and make sure we are using all the safety equipment.' Marcus had to shout to Charles as the wind had now started to howl. 'Believe me if Dawn thinks we are a pair of idiots in a boat, she'll stop me coming again.'

'*She'll* stop you…'

'You wait Charlie old boy, when those daughters of yours grow up, they'll be bossier than any wife.' Marcus turned to see Charles still panting and looking incredulously at him.

'Never,' he said as he furled in some of the Genoa, tightened the sheets on the winch and cut the engine. The two men looked at each other; no further words were necessary, they knew their actions were at best foolhardy, at worst down right dangerous. Despite Charles bravado he was considering heading back when the wind seemed to slacken as they had now passed the headland; neither man was prepared to discuss the subject any further. Male ego is a powerful force.

'Marcus can you see that lighthouse in the far distance?' Charles said standing and pointing through the spray and mist. Marcus narrowed his eyes and eventually nodded. 'That is Eilean Mor and is the north end of Coll. Get as closed hauled as you can and try and get as far south of the lighthouse as possible.' Marcus nodded. 'This tide will change shortly, I'm surprised it hasn't already.' Charles said swinging himself down into the salon, wedging himself into the navigation table and brushing back his wet hair. He looked up to see Toby sitting bolt upright on one of the bench seats clutching his life jacket with one hand and gripping a hand rail with the other. His face was ashen and his look was enough to let Charles know he wouldn't be taking Toby on any more sailing trips. Charles threw him a weak smile but Toby's expression could have been etched in stone.

Charles recalculated his tides and realised he had omitted the British Summer Time alteration. He shook his head in disbelief and cursed to himself; he had never made such an error before.

The problem he now faced was the south westerly winds, which meant a long and very uncomfortable sail to Iona. Even if they motored, although it would be quicker, it would not be a pleasant experience even for the hardiest of sailors.

'Seen anything of Doug?' Charles said to the man on the opposite side of the salon. Toby slowly shook his head and continued to gaze towards the hatchway. The skipper sat back and pushing his hair from his brow, he rubbed his chin and made a decision. Charles took out his parallel rules and poured over the chart. Several minutes later with a relieved smile on his face he slid out of his seat, checking the chart for a final time, ascended the steps and told Marcus to bear away.

Marcus gave his friend a puzzled look. 'Bear away? I'll be going almost due north if I do.'

'Yes, that's exactly the course I want you to take,' screamed Charles over the wind, which had now started to strengthen again. 'We would be tacking down to Iona for days with this wind and Toby is looking pretty poorly.' Marcus nodded and the two men released sheets as the helm turned the Westerly yacht to starboard. The incessant thumping of the bows crashing into the waves stopped; the boat took on a different aspect. Marcus struggled to steer as waves went under the boat causing the boat to speed up and then almost have a sensation of stopping as the wave lifted the bow upwards. The boat corkscrewed on the top of the wave and then the same process was repeated. Marcus looked at his friend and he shouted to Charles. 'If this doesn't make Toby sick, nothing will.' Charles shrugged his shoulders; he knew there was nothing else he could do.

Although the wind was stronger the effect of running with it dispelled some of its force and apart from the corkscrewing it was a more comfortable sail. Charles nodded to himself and raising his binoculars could see the distant silhouette of the Isle of Rum.

'We will make Mallaig in four to five hours,' said Charles adjusting the Genoa's sheets. The boom was being tugged and pulled back by the heavy seas and when a wave went under the boat it would crash down sending a deafening clanking of the kicking strap. After an hour Charles could not stand the noise anymore. He put on a harness and, clipping it onto the lifeline, went onto the coach roof to adjust the strap. Without warning the wind changed direction just as Charles was tightening the kicking strap.

'Watch out… Gybe-ho!' screamed Marcus with all his might and spun the wheel to try and correct the boat. The boom flung itself across the boat catching the ducking skipper on the shoulder, sending him sprawling on the deck. A loud metallic snap, indicated the demise of the kicking strap and sending the aft of the boom upward. The wind shifted again and the boom once more careered across the boat for another gybe, but this time it was too high to trouble Charles who was on his knees clutching his shoulder and cursing loudly.

Marcus was also cursing as he desperately tried to steady the boat but then the nose of the boat went into a wave sending down a wall of dark green water towards the struggling skipper. Charles let out a loud scream as the wave swept him against the spray hood and his arms flailed out trying to grab anything secure. Marcus couldn't prevent the yacht slapping into another wave and more water drenched Charles dragging him further down the deck, sending him helplessly towards the aft. Charles made a grab for the railings but his arm crunched into a winch and he howled in agony. Marcus let go of the helm and started towards his friend, but the wheel span round causing the boat to lurch further to starboard as the bow veered to port. Marcus turned and grabbed the wheel as another wave washed over the decks pushing Charles further aft and perilously close to the transom and gunwale.

Charles had been stunned and let out a weak cry as he realised he could not manage to grab anything with his damaged arm. Then he felt a vice like grip on his ankle and the majority of the water engulfing him continued on its way. He lay there perched on the gunwale partly through the railings; the sea skidding along only a few feet below him. Charles turned to see Douglas holding onto his leg with one hand whilst his other arm was gripped tightly around a winch.

'Pull yourself back towards me,' said a deep Scottish accent. Marcus turned the engine on and releasing the sheets, tried to keep the boat steady. Charles inched himself along the deck and, with Douglas' aid, he dropped back down into the cockpit.

'Thanks Doug,' Charles gasped, finally mustering some energy to sit up. He could hear the kicking strap being slapped around frantically on the coach roof.

'What the hell are you two doing?' Douglas shouted standing up and surveying the dark pitching scene in front of him and trying to orientate himself. He took Charles' binoculars and looked north. 'I suggest you get to safety pretty quickly before that bloody kicking strap takes the entire gel coat off. Plus poor Toby is beside himself with worry down there.' Douglas pointed towards the hatchway and turned to Charles. 'You won't be able to run without a kicking strap so look in your pilot and get into Rum. There's a good loch on the East side and will be perfect shelter with this wind and sea.' Douglas pointed towards Charles' damaged shoulder. 'Are you alright?'

Charles let out a muffled wince. 'Yes, I'm just a bit shaken. Thanks again Doug, I could have gone over. I should have clipped myself on the other side, but I wasn't expecting a gybe.' He threw Marcus a sideways glance, but immediately felt guilty that he was trying to shift the blame to his old friend; the responsibility was his alone.

'Yes, sorry about that Charles but the wind shifted; there was nothing I could do.' Marcus stammered still trying to keep the pitching boat on course.

Douglas looked between the two of them. 'It's still a long hard sail and if you want me I'll be down below. Now for Christ sake you two grow up and let's do our sailing when we are fit and able.' Douglas didn't wait for a reply and descended the stairs still muttering to himself. Charles followed him down to find the pilot and, seeing Toby, he avoided the young law student's glaring look. Charles flicked through the pilot and studied it for a few moments and went back up telling the helmsman the new course.

Charles adjusted the sails in silence while Marcus cut the engine as the yacht steadied on a broad reach, which pushed the boat effortless through the waves.

'I'll go and make some tea,' said Charles eventually as an aching pain was becoming more noticeable in his shoulder and ribs. 'Sorry about this Marcus. It's my fault, bloody foolhardy idea.' Marcus nodded, straining his eyes as he tried to make out the shape of Isle of Rum in the distance. They gave each other a quick glance; nothing else needed to be said.

Charles made the tea and put plenty of sugar in for everyone. Even Toby gave a weary smile when Charles handed him the mug. Picking his way forward Charles took Douglas his mug of steaming hot tea, but the Scotsman was back in his berth snoring heavily. 'How can he do that?' Charles said to himself and went back on deck giving Marcus the spare tea and indicating to him that he'd take the helm for a while.

'How long before we get to Rum?' Marcus said wrapping his hands around the mugs and steadying himself from the pitching boat.

'A couple of hours max. We'll sail into Loch Scresort. At the top end of the loch there are some reasonable anchorages. We need to get in quite close though as there is a lot of kelp apparently.' Charles had one hand on the wheel while he drank his tea with the other. 'There is a place called Kinloch Castle, I'm not talking Knights of the Round Table here, it was only built at the beginning of this century.'

Charles' shoulder was stiffening up and he became aware that he was trembling. 'Bloody hell Marcus, that was the closest call I've ever experienced. I feel a bit of an idiot if you want to know the truth.' He glanced towards Marcus who nodded at him and threw him a wry smile.

'Strange isn't it, Charles. As we get older we should become wiser, but this was total madness; quite out of character for you: Captain Sensible. I suppose we should reflect on this and ask why we put ourselves in danger; still trying to be a reckless youth? We would seriously let down our loved ones…' Marcus finished by raising his eyebrows and looked at Charles.

'Oh don't. My daughters flashed in front of my eyes when that wave nearly took me over the side. No more idiotic stunts like that, I promise.' Charles downed the remains of his tea and passed the mug to Marcus.

Charles saw Marcus' face soften into a smile. 'It wasn't all your fault; I was up for it as well. It was a ruddy stupid thing to go and do; it all seemed quite a laugh at the time. You'll not get Toby back on this boat when he reaches dry land, you know that don't you?'

Charles nodded. 'Look this Kinloch Castle does, apparently, bed and breakfast, and on certain evenings, dinner. Why don't we stay tomorrow night?' He looked at his watch. 'We should be in at around five o'clock this morning and hopefully we'll have some light as sunrise is just after 4 o'clock. We can rest all day and stay in the castle for a night, what do you think?'

'I don't think Doug and Toby will want to lash out on a hotel room.' Marcus wedged the tea mugs under the canopy. He didn't fancy going below.

'Yes, you're right. It will be my treat then; it is the least I can do.' Charles said studying the sea ahead of him.

'Well if you're paying then I am up for it,' said a pale faced man in the hatchway still clasping his life jacket. 'Anything to get off this…' Toby checked himself. 'Damn boat.'

'Ah Toby, in hindsight it wasn't the best idea I've ever had,' said Charles relieved that Toby was now at least talking to him.

'Well that's going down as the understatement of the year,' Toby shouted back as a glimmer of a smile formed on his face and he disappeared back down below.

'Opps, I think my Dawn is going to hear about this,' moaned Marcus frowning. 'Come on let's get this tub moored up,' he said gently pushing Charles out from behind the wheel. 'Can you manage to go and drop the sails and we'll motor in; I can't stand the kicking strap flapping around anymore.' Charles nodded as he

25

rubbed his shoulder and considered for a moment trying to persuade Marcus to go forward. He thought better of it.

Charles waited until Marcus had started the engine and headed into wind he quickly furled the genoa, and, picking his way gingerly forward, raised the topping lift and pulled down the mainsail, finally taking off the disabled kicking strap. He carefully picked his way back into the cockpit and tightened all the sheets, making the riggings as secure as he could in the weather conditions. Marcus noticed Charles was holding his left arm.

'Charles, you're struggling with your shoulder, aren't you?'

'It'll be fine. The boom gave it quite a clout, and then I bashed my ribs on that winch,' Charles said pointing towards the innocent piece of steel. 'I'm going to need a holiday to get over this one.'

'Well I wouldn't mention that as soon as you get home…' Both men gave out a short laugh.

The sea subsided a little when they were in the lee of the Isle of Rum and Charles brought up the pilot as Marcus turned the boat to port. The dawn had broken and dark menacing shadows now started to reveal themselves as headlands covered in heather, gorse and bracken. Motoring down Loch Scresort, Marcus caught site of Kinloch Castle. It was a long, low sandstone building with a large tower offset to the left with a further smaller one guarding the end of the building. Low misty clouds were hiding the hills on the island; shags skimmed the water in front of them as they went out towards the headland to fish, and seagulls cried into the wind, circling above, eyeing the boat below for food.

'For the moment, Marcus, aim for the two white crofts to the right of the castle.' Charles said checking the chart.

Marcus nodded to his skipper and taking a large breath, took in the whole scene. There was a ruggedness that excited him. The cold and wind was not an issue as it was in London. You dressed for these conditions, he thought to himself and he wondered if he could live here; leave the turmoil of London behind him. He found islands romantic in a mystic sort of way; maybe one day…

'How in god's name did they manage to bring all that stone

up here?' finally muttered Marcus almost to himself. 'What a stunning looking place. Who owns it?'

'The pilot says it is now part of the Nature Conservancy, although I think it's now called Scottish Natural Heritage, but it used to be owned by a Lancashire mill owner.' Charles flicked back a page in the pilot. 'Sir Wesley Henshaw had it built when he bought the whole island from some Scottish laird. Not a bad weekend retreat?' Charles looked towards the castle and eyed a couple of boats anchored to the left of the loch. 'Let me take over, Marcus and you go and prepare the anchor. I can't see any moorings so it's anchoring time again.'

Marcus went to the bow and laid out 20 yards of chain on the deck. Annoyingly this boat did not have depth markers on the chain. The noise of the chain rattling on the decks bought the other two crew members out.

'You found it then,' yawned Douglas stretching. 'Fine looking building isn't it?' he said nodding at the castle. All four men sat and gazed at the building as the skipper manoeuvred the yacht slowly towards the other boats. It took several attempts to lay the anchor as the kelp prevented the anchor from taking a good hold. Despite the sheltered position the wind was still gusting and swirling down the loch.

When Charles was confident the boat was secure, he untied the dinghy and fastened the small outboard to its transom. 'Right let's all have a few hours rest and then we'll do some exploring,' said Charles making the dinghy fast, his voice showing his relief that they were now safe.

'Do you mind if you take me ashore,' asked Douglas. 'I actually slept quite well last night and feel like a walk on terra firma.' Douglas looked towards Toby and raised his eyebrows questioningly. Toby shook his head.

'OK, Douglas, but how you could sleep through all that is beyond me.'

'Ay, but I did get interrupted in the middle of the night if you remember…'

'OK, OK, It won't happen again, I promise. Right, I'll take you ashore and if you take the handheld radio you can call me when you want to come back.' Charles climbed down the transom ladder and jumped into the tender. 'Go and get your stuff,' he continued looking back at the Scot. A few minutes later Douglas was walking down a track towards the castle, quite pleased to be off the pitching boat. By the time Charles had returned the other two were already on their berths and settling down for some sleep. Charles sat down and opened the yacht's logbook. He started to write but his shoulder ached and his tiredness was finally demanding some response. Charles edged into his aft cabin and fell into his berth where sleep overtook him before he had time to mull over the night's events.

Chapter 3

The rhythmic metallic slapping of a halyard against the aluminium mast woke Charles and for a few seconds he lay there blinking his eyes and trying to remember where he was. Slowly the recollection of the previous night seeped back into his conscious memory; he inwardly cringed at how stupid he had been. Charles dragged himself out of his berth, wincing as pain from both his ribs and shoulder reminded him of his close escape. He fumbled as he dressed, struggling with the buttons and went into the main salon and galley area.

'Anyone for tea,' he shouted filling the kettle. A mumbled reply came from a pile of bed clothes on one of the salon seats.

'Ruddy hell,' came a cry from the fore-cabin. 'Look at the time.' Marcus entered the salon his black hair ruffled and a dark unshaven shadow on his face. 'Charles its gone twelve o'clock. What about poor old Douglas?'

'Oh shit,' uttered Charles and pulling on his sailing jacket he climbed the stairs grabbing the binoculars and shouting back at Marcus to make the tea and prepare some breakfast. Charles winced from a sharp pain in his shoulder as he scanned the shoreline through the glasses; nobody seemed to be about. The weather had calmed from the previous night and a gusting breeze brought the scent of gorse across the loch. Charles put the strap of the binoculars over his neck and lent against the bulkhead absorbing the sight in front of him. He continued to scan the shoreline as well as checking the slipway to the right of the Kinloch Castle.

'Damn, he'll be furious being left out for nearly six hours,' he muttered to himself. He started to go down when something white caught his eye on top of the colonnaded verandas that encircled the castle. Quickly he raised his binoculars, causing another twinge of pain, but the sun came out and the reflection from the castle windows obscured his view. 'Dear god,' he whispered, squinting into the sunlight.

Charles came down the stairs carefully, still pondering on what he had just seen. Marcus noticed the worried frown on the skipper's face.

'Everything alright?' asked Marcus as he laid out some bacon on the grill.

Charles watched Toby make his way to one of the heads. The young lawyer looked pale and the thought of the salon being full of the smell of cooking bacon was clearly not to his liking. Charles waited until Toby had closed the head door then he turned to his friend. 'I think I've just seen a ghost.'

Marcus lent back and roared with laughter. 'Are you sure the boom didn't hit your head and not your shoulder? Come on Charles, if there is one person in this world I would have put money on *not* claiming to have seen a ghost; it is you.'

Charles stirred the tea in the pot and cleaned out three mugs in the sink, his long blond hair falling forward, not answering the barracking from Marcus who was now buttering some bread. Marcus glanced towards the skipper again.

'Ruddy hell Charles, you're not joking are you?' Marcus' eyes searching his friend's face.

'I'm telling you I saw a white figure walking along the first floor colonnade or whatever it's called; I'll swear to it. As I put the binoculars up the sun dazzled me and then it had gone.' Charles shook his head. 'Oh my god I'm going mad; what am I saying. Forget it Marcus, it must have been a trick of the light.'

Marcus finished preparing breakfast and shouted forward to Toby. 'Grub up Toby.'

'You have got to be joking,' came a muffled reply.

Marcus and Charles gave each other a wry smile then a

subdued quietness filled the salon as the two men ladened their bacon sandwiches with tomato sauce and began to eat. The head door suddenly crashed open and Toby rushed past them scaling the stairs and disappeared towards the rear of the boat. The other two men gave each other another knowing glance. 'Not quite got his sea legs,' Charles said forcing a smile but he was worried about the young man. 'I wonder where Douglas has gone?' he continued to Marcus as he finished his breakfast.

'I think he may have gone for a walk on the other side of the island,' said a pale looking Toby as he gingerly re-entered the salon. 'He was telling me there are lots of deer on the island and despite his apparent bravado towards sailing, I don't think he actually likes being on the sea.' Toby stopped as he watched Marcus wipe his plate with a piece of thickly buttered bread. He looked towards Charles and Marcus. 'I know how he feels.'

'Look Toby,' started Charles. 'I fully apologise for last night, it was unbelievably stupid, but you know how it is…'

'I would appreciate if this didn't get back to my Dawn,' interjected Marcus, giving Toby a disarming smile. 'She'll have my guts for garters if she hears what happened last night.' Marcus finished by raising his eyebrows questionably towards his potential son-in-law.

'You could have been killed,' said Toby looking at Charles.

'Yes, I know. Thank heavens Doug came up in the nick of time.' Charles started to clear up the dishes and the silence was only broken by the continuing clatter of the halyard on the mast and the rhythmic slap of small waves against the bow.

"Rascal of Mull, Rascal of Mull; Shore party, Shore party, over." All three men looked towards the radio.

'It's Dougie,' cried Charles clearly pleased that the fourth member of the crew was OK and sounded in good spirits. Charles grabbed the microphone of the radio.

'Shore party, this is Rascal of Mull, where are you? Over.' Charles looked at the radio expectantly.

"Waiting for you lot, over"

'We're ready. Do you want picking up or shall we come to you. I repeat, where are you? Over.' Charles turned and looked at the other two.

"Just get your southern nancy arses over to the castle. I've got something to show yer. Out"

Charles considered trying to raise him again but knew once Douglas had said "Out", he meant it.

'Right, come on you two. You finish clearing up here and I'll sort out that blasted halyard and check the anchor,' said Charles putting a few plates into the sink. 'The forecast is blustery showers so you'd better put something warm on.'

Charles climbed the steps into the cockpit, his ribs now really starting to ache, and tentatively inched his way forward to the mast. He could just manage to raise his arms to secure the flapping halyard and then returned to the cockpit calling the other two men. Dropping into the tender he felt a sharp pain from his shoulder and massaging it, still chastising himself at his own stupidity.

Five minutes later the three men were in the tender heading towards a muddy looking slipway just to the left of the castle. Charles had decided not to use the small jetty on the other side of the bay as it was too far away in the strong wind. They pulled the dinghy well up onto a grassy bank and secured the painter to a tree. All three stood for a moment and absorbed the scene in front of them. To their left was the long, low castle and to its right, two white crofts were nestled down by a shingle beach. The loch looked blue and inviting as a rare glimpse of the sun light danced on the water. Above them, the tops of the trees rustled in the wind; Charles took in a deep breath, turned and headed up the track towards the castle, rubbing his aching shoulder. Marcus stood for a while longer with Toby taking in the scents of bracken, heather and gorse; it made him feel light headed.

Marcus looked at Toby and smiled. 'Wow, what a place!' he said. 'It sure beats London. Mind you anything beats London.'

'You really don't like the smoke do you Marcus?' Toby asked with a touch of surprise. Marcus nodded.

'I just sort of drifted towards London, it has a magnetic pull of its own. The problem is once you're there it's not easy to leave. Remember that.' Toby listened and nodded slowly. Marcus looked up the track. 'Come on, Charles is marching ahead as if he was on military manoeuvres'. The two men strode out after Charles, trudging through the puddles on the path and reached an impressive looking bridge, which forded a small river.

'This doesn't look like local stone,' said Charles who had stopped to inspect the rampart of the bridge. 'I wonder where it came from?'

'Never mind where it came from, how on earth did they get it here?' Marcus continued picking his way round a couple of large pools. They moved on bearing round to the right and coming out of the trees they found themselves on a shale drive with the castle in front of them, majestically standing on a large grassy embankment. All three men stopped and gazed in disbelief at the building.

'You're right Marcus how could you get all this amount of stone transported here? Amazing, truly amazing.' Charles was standing gazing at the building in front of him when he straightened up. 'Look there it is, up there on the left,' cried Charles.

'What?' yelled back Toby taken by surprise at Charles' anxious tone.

'There on that glass covered balcony. The ghost!' Charles was pointing frantically towards the left side of the house where a white figure was standing and holding a large book.

'Ghost, what do you mean, ghost?' shouted Toby taking a small pace back scanning the castle nervously.

Marcus raised his binoculars calmly and a broad smile could be made out below the glasses. He slipped the strap off his head and handed them to his skipper. 'Ghost indeed. You're ruddy well cracking up Charlie Boy.'

Charles grabbed the binoculars and quickly adjusting them and looked up at the castle, ignoring the continual stabs of pain.

There standing, resplendent in a white dressing gown, stood their Scotsman. Douglas looked up from his reading matter and waved at his fellow crew members. He shouted to the three men but the wind carried his words out towards the loch. Marcus pointed at the front door under the tower and, when Douglas nodded, headed over to the wide stone steps leading to large double doors underneath the main tower.

'Come on you two, there isn't any ghost busting to be done here,' laughed Marcus, shaking his head.

'Gee, Charles you really had me there,' said Toby slapping Charles on the back, and the two men followed Marcus.

Marcus had reached the front archway and had to push hard to open the large wooden door, which entered into a small entrance hallway. Coat and hat stands were lined up on his left and umbrellas were scattered all around. Long chapel hat pegs were perched high on the wall, but most were empty. To his right was a small table with some brochures of Kinloch Castle, some post cards and a few leaflets on the Scottish Natural Heritage. There was no other sign of this being in anyway a commercial establishment. Marcus continued through an inner arched doorway on his right.

'Oh my… Charles come and look at this.' Marcus stood turning round on the spot not believing his own eyes. It was as if he had entered a time warp. Before them lay a grand oak panelled trophy room, crammed with period antiques. Along the right hand side stood a large inglenook fireplace, its dark oak lintel twisted as it defied the load it endured. Stretched out in front of the hearth, lay a lion skin; its head, with bared teeth and glassy eyes glaring up from the floor. Hanging from oak plinths under the roof trusses were numerous animal heads. Antelope, bear, lion and local deer all looked mournfully down at them. Marcus shook involuntarily at so much carnage to satisfy man's vanity. Marcus was angered by the sight of the portraits, with the arrogantly posed hunters, adorning the walls. Toby was less impressed and sauntered off to try and find someone. The other two men slowly circled the room examining and gently caressing the artefacts.

'Have you ever seen such a selection of stuff, or should I say collection.' Charles had stopped at two large blue and white vases, standing nearly five feet tall, on the other side of a large panelled door. 'I am sure this is Hirado…'

Marcus continued to scan around the room and he now saw the wide banisters of the stair case which led to a balcony encircling two sides of the room. 'It's positively an Aladdin's cave, but I still can't understand why people of this age undertook so much carnage.' Marcus wandered over to the fireplace gingerly stepping over the lion's head and examined two late 17th century oak Waincot chairs. Everywhere he looked he saw porcelain, glassware, furniture and fine art. It was a strange mix of periods and cultures but Marcus knew this was typical of the aristocracy's 'Grand Tour' type collection, where items were brought back from Europe and the dark continents. He sighed and imagined them in his shop on the King's Road. What a killing he would make.

'Marcus come and look at this,' whispered Charles who had found an open cupboard door under the stairs. 'It's an 'Orchestrion'!' he continued and Marcus frowned at him. 'It can produce a number of instruments to make it sound like an orchestra…'

'I believe it is forty instruments,' said a voice from the landing above them.

Charles and Marcus bumped into each other in their rush to withdraw from the cupboard. Charles making a small cry as Marcus bumped into his left and still tender shoulder. 'Sorry, but I, we, couldn't resist taking a peek,' stammered Marcus.

The man came down the stairs, his shirt was stained and the buttons bulged around his ample belly. He had a round white face, damp with sweat, while his thinning black hair was greased back and shiny. 'I apologise for my appearance,' said Pat Malone seeing the tinge of disgust in Charles' eyes. 'I am trying to prepare tonight's dinner and get your rooms ready. You *are* the rest of the crew from Rascal of Mull, Douglas' friends?'

Marcus nodded and caught his first, and rather unpleasant, whiff of the man now standing in front of them. 'Yes, so has Douglas booked us all in?'

'He sure has, *and* for dinner tonight. I'm a bit short of staff at the moment and I've only got some old local crone who does nothing but whinge. However, if you're patient I can cook, serve on, make beds and pour drinks.' Malone's voice had a weary sarcasm in it and both men felt a little uneasy in his presence.

'Douglas tells me you're both into antiques?' Malone started to make his way towards a door on the far side of the hallway. 'Well, you'll be in heaven in this room. Follow me, this one is especially stuffed with them.'

'There's more? This hallway alone is mind boggling,' said Charles motioning his hand towards the room they were already in.

Malone beckoned them to follow him and opening the door went inside. They entered what could initially be taken for a drawing room. However, over to their left was a full size billiards table built into an impressive anti-room. An alcove window housed a large leather bench, set upon a plinth, to enable ease in watching a game.

Malone turned to Charles. 'Are you Marcus?'

No I'm not; this is Marcus,' he said quickly pointing to the other man and trying to manoeuvre away from the man and his repugnant odours.

'So you're the one that just reads about antiquities,' he barely whispered at Charles and then turned his attention to Marcus, who was already studying a fine example of a Davenport desk just behind the door. Malone came towards Marcus and made a polite cough. 'You, so Douglas says, wheel and deal in antiques.'

'Chapman Antiques, at your service,' he replied, spotting a Regency Cabinet in the corner of the room. Marcus pulled out a small, slim silver case and extracted one of his calling cards and handed it to Malone. 'I normally specialise in the very unusual, but I'm not averse to a bit of day to day bartering. Something has to pay the rent.' Marcus saw Charles raise his eyes to the ceiling.

'Mmm, I would like to know what you think some of the pieces around here are worth.' Malone stood watching Marcus struggling to take his eyes away from the furniture in the room. Charles went over to a small cabinet and made a small gasp as he realised it was full of medicines, a beautiful selection of glass bottles and jars housed various powders and liquids. 'Would you value them for me?' continued Malone. Charles turned quickly sensing this man may have ulterior motives other than just a valuation.

'So Mr. Err,' Charles interjected waiting for the man to answer.

'Pat Malone, caretaker and dogsbody of Kinloch Castle,' he replied a coolness and tinge of self pity in his voice.

'So Mr. Malone, who owns all this fine furniture and porcelain?' Charles now started to come back towards Malone.

'The Scottish Natural Heritage. I've been asked to get some valuations of the contents for insurance purposes. Don't worry, I couldn't sell it even if I wanted to; how on earth could anyone get anything off this god forsaken place?' Malone had turned to face Charles. The skipper saw the look of greed and disillusionment and decided, there and then, to make sure his friend didn't get persuaded to do anything rash. Charles had bailed his friend out before when buying 'dodgy', or as Marcus preferred to call them, 'specially acquired antiques'.

Malone felt uncomfortable in Charles' presence and, making his excuses to leave, he told them how to find their rooms and also invited them to wander around the house at their leisure.

Charles waited until the sound of Malone's footsteps receded into the back of the building. 'That man gives me the creeps and he really stinks. Is it me, or does he smell of steak and kidney pie?' Charles had picked up a billiard cue and practised a shot on the table. 'Marcus, just be very careful…' Charles stopped as they heard a faint female cry from the rear of the building, and then a yelp of anguish from a dog. 'Odd, it sounded like someone being hit and a dog getting a leathering.'

'Possibly Mooney's assistant that he mentioned has just taken a whiff of him.' Marcus turned holding a fine humidor in both hands. 'Look at the inlay on this…'

'Mooney, where did that come from?' Charles asked taking the beautiful box back to where Marcus had found it.

'Oh, his rather round pale, pitted face reminded me of the moon. You're right though, the guy does really smell of food,' he said grinning to his friend and pointing towards fine carved chair nestling in-between two grandfather clocks.

'Look Marcus, I can see in your eyes you're already planning something. Don't forget I've known you a long time and when your mind starts whirling… I bet you're thinking how much a few of these pieces would fetch back in Chelsea. I am right, aren't I?' Charles had turned to face Marcus, his countenance now quite stern.

'Even if I wanted to, we would never get this lot back to the boat. I can't see this clock; my god, this is an Archibald Coats,' whispered Marcus his fingers gracefully sliding down the side of the large clock. 'As I say I can't see us strapping this to the deck for the trip home, especially the way you plan voyages.' Marcus gave his friend one of his full broad smiles as he saw Charles begin to protest.

'Come on let's go and find the others,' continued Marcus tugging Charles' jacket by the shoulder but stopped as he saw Charles' face grimace. 'Sorry Charles, I forgot, anyway I want to know what the hell Douglas was up to.'

The two men finally pulled themselves out of the room back into the hallway and climbed the stairs. They turned a corner to be met head on by a man, in his mid-fifties, striding towards them at a fast pace. Almost colliding with Marcus he made a hurried apology. The man's grey wiry hair was dishevelled, his clothes slightly soiled and he was followed by a younger woman.

'I'm so sorry, we are in a bit of a hurry.' He said smiling but for a moment he stopped and looked hard at Charles.

Marcus couldn't take his eyes of the young woman who he noticed had started to blush as their eyes met.

'Are you here for dinner?' asked the man. Charles nodded. 'Good we'll introduce ourselves then but we must dash. Come on Tamara.'

The couple went on their way, the man striding out, while the woman almost ran along behind him.

'Dear god, this place is…' Marcus cast a glance back at the disappearing couple and made a quick study of the woman's rear end as she started to descend the stairs.

'I know him, Marcus,' whispered Charles grabbing the back of his friend's coat. 'I can't place him, but I know that guy, I'm sure of it. He's out of context here, but I have met him before. There is something not quite right about him, for I am sure he recognised me as well; although he didn't want to let on.'

'Ghosts, mysterious men, screwing up the tide times; I am getting more and more worried about you Charlie. Seriously, are you sure that boom didn't clout your head? Lighten up Charles, if he wasn't so old I'd say they had been up to no good.' Marcus made a mischievous giggle; but a pang of envy caught him by surprise.

'Ah, Captain Bligh and his merry mate have arrived,' boomed a voice from behind them. 'It's about time. I'm getting hungry.' Douglas was still adorned in a full length towelling bath robe. 'I have found the wine list, and there are a couple of good bottles here, but at highway robbery prices. Our host had better come up with a deal, or we're drinking God's wine tonight, unless you're paying Charles; you're the only one here who can afford such extortionate prices.'

Marcus looked Douglas up and down. 'You look as if you've come out of a suite in the Ritz. Relaxing are we? What happened to stalking the local deer then?'

Douglas closed the wine list with a loud slap and, grinning, beckoned the two men to follow him. 'I tell you what fellas the plumbing in this place has to be seen to be believed.'

'Plumbing,' yelled Marcus at the man in front of him. 'You're going on about plumbing when the house is stuffed to the gunwales with antiques…' Marcus stopped beside a long Adam sideboard made of satinwood and heavily inlaid. 'Charles, take a look…' Marcus was alone in the corridor and stepping forward quickly saw the men going through a twin bedded room on his right.

'Come on, Charles. The shower is a piece of art,' chattered the Scotsman. 'You're in the next room and I think you've got one too.'

Marcus followed them into the bathroom. At the end of a grand bath stood what could only be described as a sentry box. The side panel had been removed and large, thick lead pipes filled the space. 'Not only is the pressure amazing,' continued Douglas, 'but there are huge taps, no, they're more like bloody handles, and you can direct the water from any angle. You can even douche yourself!' Douglas stepped into the bath and pulling back his sleeve on his robe he demonstrated the shower.

Marcus looked incredulously at Charles as he too was taking a lot of interest in the shower. 'My God, I've seen everything now, two grown men getting worked up about a ruddy shower. Marcus turned exasperated and for a moment caught the view from the window. Three yachts were straining on their anchor chains as the loch seemed to roll on forever into the greyness. It took Marcus' breath away and, forgetting the two budding plumbers, he marvelled at the rugged and mystical beauty of this part of the world. He turned to his friends. 'Look guys, I'll leave you two in your plumbing paradise. I'm going for a little wander.'

'OK, but I think I'll go back to the boat and get some decent clothes. Do you want me to bring anything back for you,' asked Charles, who had now joined Douglas inside the shower cubicle to inspect the taps.

'Yes, throw a pair of slacks and a shirt into my sailing bag would you?' Marcus heard a muffled response as he left the room; anticipation flowing through him at the thought of some time alone in the castle. He went back downstairs and, after surveying the hallway and drawing room again, stumbled into the dining room. The length of the table took him quite by surprise. Marcus was astonished at how many ornaments were left out on display; some were clearly valuable even to the untrained eye. One particular piece caught his attention on a window sill. He went to it and looking outside saw Charles and Toby trudging down the pathway towards the tender, straining against the strengthening wind, Charles still massaging his shoulder. A pang of guilt held Marcus for a moment, but then he saw what he thought was a fine example of Wemyss porcelain and he was soon concentrating on the vase, studying the markings on its underside.

The sound of a creaking floorboard behind him made Marcus turn. Malone stood in a far doorway his shirt even more stained with food. 'I don't think your friend likes me,' he said edging forward.

'Charles? Oh, he's OK but sometimes he can be so straight laced it really does beggar belief.' laughed Marcus placing the Wemyss down gently. 'He works for an extremely prestigious organisation, you have to understand. I on the other hand…' Marcus looked and smiled at the plump man standing in front of him with the look of hope in the man's eye. Marcus' stomach turned as he caught a whiff of Malone. 'Oh, we heard a scream before and then some yelping. Everything alright?'

'What? Oh yes, the old crone dropped something but never mind that.' Malone looked agitated but edged closer. 'I was wondering if we could have a chat about the…' Malone's face broke into a sneer and he took another pace towards Marcus '… *valuation* I was talking about. If you get my drift.'

'Oh, I think I understand your drift, Pat. I'll be honest with you if I could bring a Bedford van here I could fill it three times over and still leave enough so it wouldn't be noticed.' Marcus noticed Malone was watching him closely.

'That's just the point, everything here; well almost everything here has been audited.' Malone sighed, who had now come up almost in front of Marcus.

Marcus couldn't help himself, took a step back and turned slightly. 'I do admire the fact that everything is out on display and not locked away or kept behind large red ropes with the punters herded along like untrustworthy animals. There is a lot of trust going on here.' Marcus could see his skipper out of the window passing some bags to Toby; who was still in the tender bobbing beside the yacht. Malone repulsed him and he certainly wasn't trustworthy, but he could not resist the idea of taking a piece or two. He made an effort to turn back towards Malone and forced himself to look him in the eye. 'Anyway, who polishes and dusts all this lot?'

Malone now edged forward further and stood only inches in front of Marcus watching him intently. 'You are looking at the man for all seasons,' said Malone and feigned a small bow. 'It isn't however strictly true, I do get some help, for what she is worth…'

Marcus shuddered at the thought of working with this man in such a remote place. 'What brings you here? You're not local, you don't even sound Scottish by your accent.' Marcus waited for a reply but Malone was still staring at him and in deep thought, he hardly seemed to hear Marcus. 'Malone, sorry Malone, are you all right?' Marcus had noticed the man was sweating profusely and he wished he could find a way to distance himself from the acrid odours of the caretaker.

'Never mind my role or how I ended up here…' Malone looked round and eyed the open door into the main hallway. 'Are you up for buying a few bits of *really* tasty stuff?' Marcus couldn't help himself and nodded at Malone while he made a questioning gesture with his hands. 'I'm not talking a few hundred quid here, I'm talking mega bucks,' continued Malone, still watching Marcus closely. 'The beauty is that,' Malone once again glanced around the room, 'that I don't think anybody knows *they* even exist.'

'*They*…?'

'Yes, *they*. The old crone…' Malone stopped and again looked around the room. '*I* found them in a very unusual place; a place that was built to house, or more accurately, hide them.' Malone had now come up very close to Marcus, but Marcus resisted backing off, he didn't want to cause offence. His instincts sensed that he just might have stumbled onto something rather unusual.

'So what are these, *'they'*?' Marcus jumped a little as he heard the main front door slam.

'Bugger, it's that friend of yours,' said Malone taking a few steps back. 'Listen, do you want to talk business or not? I'm talking thousands of pounds for them.' he said quickly under his breath. Marcus now nodded enthusiastically.

'OK Pat, but I need to know exactly what *'they' are?*' hissed Marcus this time it was he who glanced warily at the door and took a pace towards Malone.

'Some absolutely exquisite…'

Charles' head popped round the door. 'They're you are, Marcus.' Both men standing on the far side of the room took a couple of quick paces away from each other. Charles noted it and felt a tinge of exasperation as to what Marcus and Malone were up to. Watching his friend closely he continued. 'I've brought everyone's clothes and as this is such a grand place, I've put some of my ties in.' Marcus grimaced and shrugged his shoulders. 'We were going to take a walk up to Coire Dubh, which is the reservoir for this place. It also generates the hydro-electric power. Hey, self sufficiency Marcus, are you impressed? You're always harping on about being self sufficient, so I've thrown your walking boots in your bag as well. OK?'

Marcus rolled his eyes to the ceiling and gestured to the gods for patience. 'Plumbing, wearing ties and now electricity? Charles have you seen the amount of antiques we have here? What's up with you? I was just discussing this with Pat, here.' Marcus pointed out a few ornaments behind him.

'Yes, I do appreciate them but I also can't get over how impressive the building is. It is a treasure in itself.' Charles caught sight of a George I bracket clock on a desk in the corner; he started to approach it, but Malone was in the way and he thought better of it. 'Well, I'm going and so is Douglas, so it's up to you.

Oh, Toby is still a bit knackered so he's going to rest.' Charles turned and made his way out of the room.

'I'll be up in a minute,' shouted Marcus after him and turned to the waiting caretaker. 'I *will* be back down when they've gone for their walk. Where will you be?'

'In the kitchen sorting out dinner, but I won't have time to speak to you: I do have a lot to do. Listen go with them on the walk, that Charles fella is a bit suspicious of me. I'll meet you...' Malone took Marcus' arm and the antique dealer had to use all his self control not to cringe away from the foul smelling caretaker. They waited for the other men to climb the stairs and disappear towards their rooms. Malone then led him into the hallway and pointed to a corridor on the other side of the staircase. 'Down there at the bottom of the corridor,' he whispered barely audibly, 'is a small anti-room. I'll be waiting for you around six o'clock. OK?' Marcus nodded and Malone turned and waddled off towards the kitchens.

Marcus gave a sigh of relief the man had gone and decided that he would never get that fat. He started for the stairs when he caught site of the grey haired man, who had nearly knocked him over before, crouched under the stairwell examining the musical instrument.

'Fascinating isn't it?' said the man running his hand through his wiry hair. 'I've never quite seen such a thing before.'

'Oh, yes it's an orchestra making thingy-me-jig...' Marcus' mind raced. Had this chap heard anything? Had he been lurking there on purpose?

'An Orchastrion, I believe it's called. My name is Julian Appleforth.' He stretched out his hand.

'Yes, I believe we briefly met before on the landing?'

'Ah yes, sorry about that. I'm here with my, err, niece, Tamara. We're studying the bat population and we had inadvertently disturbed a few so needed to get out and see how many there were.' Julian stooped down and came out from under the stairs.

Marcus for moment could not help but smile. Niece indeed, studying bats indeed, he thought to himself. The guy is having a randy weekend and again he experienced another bout of jealousy. 'Marcus Chapman.' They shook hands. 'Yes, Malone said he had a couple of batty people staying here,' laughed Marcus, but realised his humour had not been appreciated.

'Yes, very good,' said Julian with a frown. 'You're here on holiday?'

'Yes, sailing, and we were heading for Mallaig but got caught in a storm last night. A bit of a hairy crossing from Mull, I can tell you.' Marcus shuffled a little uncomfortably. Charles was right this guy is a bit weird, he thought.

'Anyway, it's been nice to meet you. Are you here for dinner?' asked Julian.

'Yes, but after seeing the state of the chef's top, my appetite has waned a little.' Marcus again laughed but it sounded hollow. Nodding a farewell at Julian he continued towards the stairs.

'Oh, what's the name of the man that was with you?'

Marcus was so taken by the strength and deliverance of the question he answered instinctively.

'Charles Ashford, may I ask…' Marcus stopped as the man had already turned and was heading at an astonishing pace towards the front door. Marcus shook his head in disbelief and contemplated how many rude people there were in the world.

Sauntering towards the bedroom he studied every piece of furniture he passed. 'I'm in heaven,' he hummed. 'I could make a fortune here.'

Entering the room he saw Charles preparing for the walk. 'Coming?' the skipper asked.

'Yes, why not, the air will do me good,' Marcus answered taking out a jumper from his sail bag.

'I see you were getting on admirably with our moon faced friend…' Charles said not looking up from tying his boot laces.

'Charles, just leave it. He genuinely wants to get some valuations, that *is* all.' Marcus felt a slight flush to his cheeks. 'I met that chap you thought recognised you,' he continued quickly changing the subject. Charles immediately stopped tying his laces and looked up. 'His name is Julian something and he is here with his, yes wait for it, *niece*. Oh, and he's watching the local bat population. I tell you he must think we were born yesterday. I told him I thought he was batty. Didn't go down too well...'

'You didn't? Marcus one day someone is going to turn round and land you one,' said Charles unable to resist a chuckle.

'Actually Charles, I'm a touch envious. There is something about her...'

'Even on a nearly deserted island you find a girl you fancy. Marcus it is about time you stopped romping through women like changing your underwear and settle down. You've been divorced from Linda for years now.' Charles finished tying the laces to his highly polished boots and gave Marcus a hard look.

'That's just it, I've never found anyone that *really* takes my fancy, but this woman...'

'Marcus you've only seen her for a few seconds for pity's sake. Don't tell me you believe in that love at first sight rubbish. Come on let's get going.'

Marcus made a weak smile and pulled on his grubby boots, clumps of mud still left on the soles. 'Lecture finished now?'

The two men laughed and went and knocked on Douglas' door and the three men left the castle and walked up the hill behind it. The men talked for awhile but Douglas started to brief them on the history of the island and Kinloch Castle. Charles noticed how quiet Marcus had become, he hoped it was tiredness from the night sail, but he sensed he had something on his mind.

'It seems the man who built this place,' started Douglas striding on while the two Englishmen struggled, panting behind him. 'His name was Sir Wesley Henshaw, now that's a good Methodist name! Anyway he presided over a treaty to stop the Russo-Japanese war in 1905. You guys said there are a lot of items from Japan and Russia, that explains it, I suppose.'

Douglas continued to chatter and his dialogue was interspersed with constant complaints about how hungry he was and how he couldn't wait for dinner. The two men following him could hardly make out his chatter in the wind. The walk seemed to soothe the aches that Charles had been experiencing all day and he was relieved that it appeared he hadn't done any permanent damage. Marcus kept his thoughts on the chef's attire to himself; just the thought of the quality of the food Malone would produce was causing his appetite to dissolve.

Two hours later they returned to the hill top above the castle. All three men stopped and took in the view. The hill swept down to the castle and the loch stretched out before them, waves rushing along being chased by the ever present wind. They heard barking and saw a small border collie inside a court yard at the back of the castle.

'I hadn't heard a dog before,' said Douglas. 'Great dogs those Collies. I had one once...'

Douglas stopped as he watched a door open and the large frame of the caretaker came out and started to kick the dog. Malone continued to kick it repetitively, ignoring the pitiful yelps of the dog, finally picking up the cowering animal and threw it through a door. An old woman came out and started to shout at Malone but he just pushed her aside and walked back through the door leaving the woman languishing on the cobbled courtyard.

'Oh!' screamed Douglas and started to run down towards the castle.

'Bastard,' cried Marcus and followed the Scotsman, with Charles close on his heels. All three men arrived at the courtyard door panting but found it locked.

'Malone,' bellowed Douglas. 'By god, I'm going to have words with that over sized bully. I'll give him a kicking and see how he likes it.'

The three men went round and entered the castle by the front door but, despite a thorough search, there was no sign of Malone nor the old woman. They did find the dog in an out house and Douglas was pleased it didn't seem to have suffered any major injuries but whined softly, looked up at him and seeing his eyes wagged his tail expectantly.

Charles was the first to speak as they went back into the castle and ascended the stairs. 'OK, Douglas calm down, we don't want an incident here and end up being thrown out…'

'Charles,' interrupted Marcus, 'we can't let him get away with kicking a dog senseless and pushing an old woman around.'

'Too right Marcus. I'm surprised at you Charles…' Douglas stood with his hands on his hips and his chest puffed out.

'No, I'm not saying we don't do anything but let me handle this. You know what you're like Douglas, you'll punch the man and then we will have the police on our backs…' Charles pleaded.

'Punch him; I'm going to kick him where it hurts…'

'Just a minute Dougie, leave him to me.' Marcus had stopped on the stairs a bit below the other two and they both turned towards him. 'Don't say anything. He didn't see us, and I think I may have a way of getting our own back that will make him rue the day he ever kicked that dog or pushed the old lady.'

'Bloody hell Marcus, you look positively scary,' whispered Douglas. 'What's your plan?'

'I'll let you know later. But don't approach him either of you. Agreed?'

Both men nodded and they all continued to their rooms. Marcus was relieved when Charles crawled onto his single bed and a few minutes later a low gentle snore drifted towards him. Marcus checked his watch and slipping off his bed he quietly put on his shoes and made for the door. A floorboard creaked loudly causing a brief interruption to Charles' snoring; he muttered in his sleep but continued sleeping.

The antique dealer crept stealthily to the landing and, keeping to the side of the stairs, tiptoed quietly down. He was thinking how he was going to get his hands on some of the antiques when the pitiful yelps of the dog and the crumpled figure of the woman returned to him. Malone will pay, he thought. He made his way tentatively down the corridor stumbling in the gloom. At the end of the corridor another passageway veered off to his right and he was in a small wooden panelled anti-room. Several hunting trophies adorned the walls but the main feature was a large tapestry hanging from a thick, black metal pole. Marcus checked his watch and straining to see in the dark could just make out it was now past six o'clock.

'That bastard has possibly sent me on a wild goose chase,' he hissed to himself.

'Is that you Marcus?'

Marcus actually jumped a little and his heart thumped loudly in his chest. 'Where are you for god's sake?'

The tapestry moved slowly and Malone's greasy white face poked out. 'In here. Watch the step and mind your head, you'll find it a bit of a squeeze.' Marcus had to put himself sideways to manage to get through and he noticed one of the panels was hinged back. A short passage led into a dark and musty smelling room. The only light was from a thin, slit window and Marcus realised he must be in the base of one of the towers. The sunlight highlighted the freshly disturbed dust and on the far wall the shadows of tree branches mottled the stone wall.

'How did you find this place?' Marcus asked in a hush voice.

'By accident. I was taking the tapestry down for a dusting and when I was trying to take it off the pole I slipped and crashed into the panel, which gave way. The old woman went hysterical when I found it and I knew she must know something, so… Anyway we're not here to discuss the past.' Malone was sneering and fumbling around in his pockets.

'Haven't you any light Malone, I'm not an owl you know.'

Malone extracted a lighter and lit two candles. 'Let there be light!'

Marcus' eyes became accustomed to the flickering light and around him were a confusion of boxes scattered around the floor; some were open revealing books, porcelain and other ornaments. A small stone fireplace was the only sign that it had another purpose other than a hidden store room.

'This can't be a priest hole. The castle is far too new for that,' mused Marcus. 'Why the fireplace, you can barely stand up in here?'

Malone smiled and began to kneel down when he noticed Marcus' gaze falling on the portrait hung above the fireplace. Marcus took a pace forward towards it. Even in the shadows the presence of the young woman in the portrait took Marcus by surprise. The frame was a fine rococo gold but the detail of the painting captivated him.

'Wouldn't have minded giving her a good shafting in her time,' sneered Malone. Marcus felt a shot of anger go through him but he bit his tongue. 'Shift out of the way and go across the room, I've got to get to *them.*'

Marcus backed away but continued to study the beautiful features of the woman. She looked so majestic and yet despite the formal pose Marcus felt that it was as if she had just been laughing. A diamond necklace lay resplendent on her high laced bodice; Marcus marvelled at how the painter had managed to highlight their sparkle even on her pale skin tone. Marcus spotted the earring and the broach and realised she was wearing the classic suite of jewels which were common in the aristocracy of this period. Marcus was so taken by the portrait he had not noticed what Malone was up to, only that he was rummaging inside the fireplace.

Marcus stepped forward again to look for a signature on the paintings but could only make out a few unrecognisable letters, which could have been Greek, Russian or from somewhere in Eastern Europe. Marcus couldn't help but feel as if this woman also had a secret and was challenging the onlooker to guess what it was. Her eyes started to make him feel uneasy; it was if she was looking through him into his soul.

'Ruddy hell, no wonder they put her in here. She seems to be reading your secret thoughts.'

'What?' Malone had now scrambled to his feet and he cradled a canvas bag, soiled with cobwebs and bits of masonry. 'What are you jabbering on about Chapman? It's just a picture of a girl. I bet she liked a bit of rough, hey? Now come on, I haven't got all day. I've got much better pictures of girls in my bedroom if you're that desperate.' He turned and placed the bag on a box besides him.

'How the hell did you find these in the back of a chimney place?' Marcus asked.

'Ha, *she* eventually told me...'

'She? Is this the old woman you have been talking about...?'

'Do you want to see the jewels or not?' Malone barked becoming defensive.

Marcus sensed that he had to play this man very cautiously and nodded at him watching as Malone untied the string of the canvas bag; his hands shaking.

'Never mind how I came by them, that's no business of yours,' Malone laughed to himself as he eased out a book from the bag. Then he extracted a casket and placed it on one of the packing boxes. Marcus gasped as he saw the casket and felt a rush of adrenalin through his veins which made him dizzy. The casket before him, even in the darkness of the room, was magnificent. It was the size of a shoe box, the front was split into three dark wood panels each separated by silver arched Doric columns rising from a matching silver plinth. Marcus went to touch the carved gold acanthus leafs and monograms intertwined with Greek looking letters. For a moment he stopped and thought they were similar letters to those he had seen on the painting. Then his eyes caught the splintered gash around the keyhole.

'You ignorant moron,' blurted Marcus, his patience with this man finally snapped.

'Hold on Chapman, I couldn't find the key. If I hadn't opened it then I wouldn't have found *them,*' said Malone pulling away a splinter of wood.

Marcus went to pick up the box but Malone pushed his hand away and grabbed the box cradling it in his lap. Marcus realised he was holding his breath in anticipation making him a little light-headed.

'I'm not sure I like you Chapman, in fact I don't think I can trust you.' Malone sat their nursing the box and eyeing Marcus.

'OK, I was a little out of order before. Sorry Pat, I just hate to see things damaged, especially things of such beauty. I have a real thing about things being damaged so if you want me to go…'

Marcus started to stand and he felt his heart pounding as he tried to assess how Malone would react.

'Sit down Marcus. I accept your apology,' he smiled smugly at Marcus. 'Behold the secret jewels of Kinloch Castle!' Malone opened the box slowly and, despite the little amount of light from the candles and small window, the room came alive with flickering beams of light bouncing from the gems.

Marcus lent forward to pick up a gold bracelet encrusted in diamonds and rubies which lay on the top of a pile of jewels. Malone withdrew the box and shook his head. 'Oh no you don't, you're just window shopping at this stage.'

'Dear god man! Do you know where they came from?' Marcus did not know what else to say. 'Look Pat, you'll have to let me have a proper examination…'

'Yes, but only when we have had further discussions.' Malone turned the box towards him and carefully pulled out a tray with the jewels in. Placing this down on the other side of him he moved some jewels around inside. Satisfied with his handy work and knowing that Marcus was still watching him, he turned the box around and stretched out his arms towards Marcus. Marcus craned his head forward and his eyes widened as he saw a suite of jewels. Two diamond and sapphire drop earrings were in the top two corners; a bracelet encrusted in diamonds and sapphires, a large ring matching the bracelet and a Collette necklace consisting of over a hundred stones, again mainly diamonds, but in the centre an enormous sapphire. Marcus let out a long breath and sat back pushing his fingers through his hair, he nodded at Malone.

'So I ask again, where are these from?'

'Not really sure and I'm not about to give you a bloody certificate with them.' Malone gently moved one of the earrings to be in line with the set. Marcus looked up at the portrait and realised they were the ones in the picture. Malone followed his gaze.

'Before I found them I was in a pub in Mallaig and got talking to a few locals.' Malone took the ring from the box and handed it to Marcus. 'I told them my job here and some old codger was going on about there being a rumour, or more of a legend really, that the guy who built this place had disgraced himself with a well to do woman.' Malone pointed a chubby figure at the portrait. 'Well I knew the old crone would be full of any gossip that was going, so I persuaded her to tell me all she knew… She put up quite a fight though; I'll give her that.

'This woman,' Malone jabbed a picture at the portrait, 'wasn't short of a bob or two and had a mysterious past. It seems that the old crone had been entrusted to protect them and I still think she knows a lot more about these than she'll ever let on. You should have heard her when I finally got it out of her where they were from, what a wailing she made… But who cares so long as they fetch me a bob or two.'

Malone smiled and took back the ring. 'If the old woman was right these jewels were hers, but if she was his mistress then I bet, as he couldn't give them away, he must have hid them. Lucky bastard with a tasty bit like that on the side, no wonder he showered her with jewels.' Malone took the book and handed it to Marcus. 'Finally there is this. It was in with the jewels. No idea why, it just looks like a musty old book to me.'

Marcus picked up the book and was surprised by its title. Malone took it back and then carefully picking up the tray he slid it back into the box and slammed it shut. He placed them both back into the bag, turned and as he knelt again he puffed and snorted. He put the bag and its precious contents back into the chimney place finally replacing the brick.

Malone stood up and brushed his hands on the back of his trousers. 'So how much will you give me for them?' He blew out the candle and picked the other one up holding it so they could see each others faces. 'They must be worth a small fortune?'

Marcus tried to go into his normal bartering mode, but the

whole situation had taken him off guard. He had dealt with jewels before, but nothing like this. His mind raced as another and more sinister plan started to develop in his mind. It wasn't just revenge for clearly hurting the old woman or the kicking of the helpless dog; this could be a life changing find for him. 'Well, I need to check them,' he finally said. 'I have barely had a chance to see them…' Malone snorted and stared at Marcus. Marcus made a small cough and continued, 'Second hand jewellery in today's market, I'm afraid they don't fetch much…'

'Stop jerking me about for Christ's sake Chapman. We both know they are pukka, and if you're not prepared to make me a reasonable offer…well I'll go elsewhere.' Marcus noticed the caretaker seemed agitated and sweat stains were now revealing themselves from under his arms. He chided himself to think clearly.

'Well they certainly look the genuine article, that I grant you, but what if they are stolen or if I were to sell them on and it came to light that…'

'Forget it,' spat out Malone and thrust his porky finger into Marcus' chest. 'I thought you were a man who would know about this sort of thing. You're as bad as that poncy mate of yours.' Malone blew out the remaining candle and a blue swirl of smoke snaked past Marcus, who didn't move. The smell of the extinguished candle alleviated the stench from the caretaker and the musty smell of the storeroom.

'OK, how much do you want for them?' Marcus' eyes adjusted to the remaining light.

'Twenty five grand, and don't bother trying to barter me down, for I won't take a penny less.' Malone took a step towards Marcus, his puffy eyes glinting in the remaining light. Marcus sensed desperation despite his bravado.

'OK, twenty five grand. What about a few of these antiques thrown in?' Marcus stretched out his hand.

'No, only the jewels. I told you The Scottish Natural Heritage undertake thorough audits here. They even check the bloody bed linen. So do you want the jewels at twenty five grand or not?'

Marcus nodded and Malone shook his outstretched hand.

'Deal, but it has to be cash. Fifty pound notes.'

'What! Where am I going to get that sort of cash?' Marcus followed the caretaker outside into the corridor.

'I have to go, the dinner will get ruined if that dozy old crone is left to her own devices. If you want the jewels it's cash or nothing. There is a bank in Mallaig so use your bloody initiative Chapman.' The caretaker shut the panel door and pulled the tapestry across then he started to walk away but Marcus detected a sense of relief from Malone.

'I'll get you the money, but this is strictly between the two of us.'

The caretaker turned. 'Too bloody right it is. Marcus, when this is over I'll deny I ever saw you. Oh, and don't get any ideas about them,' he nodded towards the tapestry, 'they won't be there next time we meet.'

Marcus watched the fat caretaker continue on towards the rear of the building and taking a deep breath he started down the corridor purposefully but paused as he heard the faint howl of a dog. 'Bastard,' he muttered and entered the hallway to see the couple he had encountered earlier on the landing, sitting on one of the large sofas. He briefly smiled to himself as he recalled they had been christened Mr. & Mrs. Bat on the walk earlier.

Marcus decided not to be drawn into a conversation, despite a quick glance towards the woman, he took the stairs two at a time. He felt the grey haired man's eyes boring into him; he did not turn to meet his stare.

'See you later at dinner,' he shouted as he rounded onto the landing, his heart pounding with the exertion and excitement. He walked briskly to his room hoping Charles was still asleep.

Chapter 4

Marcus slowed his pace as he came to the bedroom door and pushed it ajar quietly. There didn't appear to be any key despite the large brass keyhole embedded in the thick wooden door. He heard the sound of rushing water and could just make out Charles humming in the adjoining bathroom. Marcus saw his sail bag that Charles had fetched from the yacht on one of the single beds and he went over to the bathroom door, banging on it, to let his friend know he was there.

'Where on earth have you been?' Charles shouted through the noise of cascading water. 'Doug and I came looking for you but couldn't find you, nor that Mooney fellow, anywhere.'

'I'll tell you about it later,' he replied racking his brains for a credible story that would be plausible to Charles' inquisitive mind. Marcus flung his bag into a corner and threw himself on his bed, which made a rather alarming creaking noise. You wouldn't want a night of passion in this bed, he thought to himself. For a moment he imagined the shapely body of the assistant bat researcher; he didn't think there would be much chance of tapping onto her tonight. Marcus noticed his heart was still beating quickly and his clothes and hands were covered in dust and cobwebs. He quickly stood up and stripped off as he had spied a long white dressing gown hanging behind the door. Wrapping the large garment around him he suddenly had an idea, and rummaging through his bag he took out his clothes for the night and hung them up. Then he went and searched in the side pockets and found the two miniature bottles of vodka and hearing the water ceasing in the next room he slipped them into his trouser pocket.

'That'll sort you out, Mooney,' he whispered and as he turned he saw himself in the mirror. He was startled the sinister grin on his face. 'People like that just bring the worst out in me,' he continued muttering to himself.

'What's that?' came a bellow from the bathroom.

'Nothing, I'm just talking to myself…'

'Well you know what they say about that, don't you,' said Charles opening the door, attired with the now customary white dressing gown. He entered the room followed by a billowing cloud of steam. 'Marcus, seriously, you have to try the shower.' Charles laughed almost to himself, rubbing his hair with a large towel. 'Don't put the bottom tap onto douche though, not if you value your manhood,' he was now laughing hard to himself. 'It does seem to have done the trick on my shoulder…' Charles was swinging his left arm round in circular movements. 'What a find, Marcus. I can't believe this place. It is like living in a museum; I feel as if I'm in a time warp.'

'I'm surprised you like it. Working in the V&A I thought you would want a rest from museums. Sometimes this place gives me the creeps.' Marcus heard an intonation in his own voice that even surprised himself.

Charles stopped rubbing his hair and lifted his head, a worried frown formed by his friends intonation. 'Marcus are you alright?'

'Yes, sorry Charles, I should have caught some shut eye when you did, I'm knackered.'

Charles checked his watch. 'Well you could grab a few minutes now. We're meant to be meeting the other two downstairs shortly, but…'

'I'll be fine. You should bring the current Mrs. Ashford here.' Marcus said as he started to make his way towards the bathroom. 'She would love it.'

'You're right of course, but I would never bring the kids here, can you imagine the breakages!' Charles turned and dropping his robe started to dress. 'You wouldn't do yourself any harm by finding a good woman and bring her up here to this area. My father used to call the Scottish islands and highlands, "God's country".' Charles turned and buttoning up his shirt gave his old friend another quizzical look. 'So Marcus, where the devil did you get to?'

'Oh, I've been concocting a plan for our dog and woman beating friend. I'll tell you about it later. All I want now is a shower and from what you're telling me it will either kill or cure…' Marcus turned and went into the bathroom, gently closing the door behind him.

Charles stood watching as Marcus disappeared. The problem he faced was that he knew Marcus too well. His old friend had never been able to resist a deal or a quick buck. It was no coincidence that he had been unable to find him and Malone half an hour ago. He knew Marcus was up to something and a feeling of frustration went surging through him. He had bailed out his friend several times before and ever since they had been young he had had been protective of him. Charles pulled on his trousers and noticed Marcus' discarded pile of clothes on the floor. Hearing a shriek of alarm, and the thunder of water, from next door, Charles smiled to himself and zipping up his trousers went over to the garments. A few seconds later his suspicions were intensified by the state of his friend's clothes. He hadn't been wandering around the house at all, he had been in a dirty and dusty place, considering the soiled condition of the garments. The cobwebs were the biggest give away. Further shouts came from the bathroom. Charles opened the door a fraction.

'The top tap is for temperature and is a little sensitive; the bottom directs the water flow.' Charles had started chuckling to himself at his friend's squeals.

'A little sensitive! Ruddy hell Charles, this thing has a mind of its own. Ahh…'

'I'll see you downstairs,' laughed Charles. 'We've agreed to meet in the main hallway and let's see if this Malone guy has any beer in the place. See you; happy ablutions!' Another yell echoed in the room as Charles shut the door and went downstairs. He planned to question Malone while Marcus was out of the way. He was determined that Marcus wouldn't be led astray this time, plus he had his own position to consider; he had worked with the Scottish Natural Heritage in the past.

Charles was greeted by three pleasantly surprising sights. First was their host who had clearly washed and changed and actually looked quite presentable, although he was still sweating a little. Second, the sight of beer cans laid out on one of the sideboards which looked inviting. Finally he noticed a rather pretty blond girl he hadn't seen before; although to Charles' disappointment she was standing very close to a tall man, also very fair. Douglas, as usual, was holding centre stage talking loudly while waving his arms about and sending disdainful looks towards the caretaker. Malone saw Charles descending the stairs and pointed towards the beer cans.

'Yes thank you, I could do with one,' he said approaching Malone and the sideboard.

'We have an honesty policy here,' said Malone. He pointed at the book opened on the end of the sideboard. 'Just put down what ever you take.'

That's a joke, thought Marcus.

'What about wine?' interrupted Douglas harshly and glared at Malone as he approached the two men.

'I will put a bottle of the house wine on the table for every room, and if you want anything else, just ask for the wine list.' Malone answered taken slightly aback by the Scotsman's hostility.

Charles was now inspecting the cans of beer. 'Good, but Douglas says you are a little pricy.' Charles continued to examine the beer and he wrinkled his nose in disappointment. 'Don't you have anything else other than these?' he asked. Malone shook his head. 'Beggars can't be choosers, I suppose,' finished the skipper, picking up a can and cracking it open took a gulp, grimacing at the warm metallic flavour in his mouth.

'We do have glasses,' blurted Malone, seeing Charles' expression and pointed towards one of the cupboard doors.

'Oh yes. Becoming too used to life on a yacht.' said Charles stooping and extracting a large glass. Douglas was still standing close to Malone staring at him. 'Douglas, Marcus will be down shortly and he has something to tell you which I think should be pleasing to your ear.' Charles finished by giving the Scotsman a searching glance.

'Aye, well the wine and food had better be good,' answered Douglas and giving the caretaker another withering look, marched back into the centre of the room.

'What have I done to upset him?' Malone threw a wary glace back towards Douglas.

'It's a long story, but dear old Dougie gets very tetchy when he is hungry. You'd better make sure he gets plenty of food and, of course, wine.' Charles laugh sounded forced. 'I tried to find you before. I understand you were with my good friend.'

Malone threw an edgy glance at Charles but sensed the uncertainty in his voice. 'Yes, yes, I was showing him around a little. I don't think he was impressed though.' Charles sensed Malone's unease. 'I took him to the old cellar, not that it was designed for wine…' Charles inclined his head in surprise. 'Yes, the old man who built this place, Wesley Henshaw, was a strict Methodist. No booze. I also showed him a few outbuildings and where there used to be a magnificent conservatory. The contents of which were incredible, are now stored in various outhouses, you see.' Malone shuffled a little and turned to hand his guest another can. Charles cursed under his breath Malone had cottoned on that he was fishing for information. Charles did see a flush in the caretaker's face and he wouldn't meet his eyes. He now knew the two of them were up to something so decided to speak to Marcus and tell him in no uncertain terms that he would not tolerate any antiques been taken from the castle.

'Oh I see, I'm not surprised he headed for a cellar. I am astonished though, that he had any interest in architecture, normally he doesn't take much and notice of such things.' Charles poured the rest of his beer once the froth had subsided.

'Well to be honest, and I don't mean any disrespect to your friend, he didn't show much inclination to me either,' said Malone giving a nervous titter. 'Sorry Charles, but I had better go and prepare your food.' Malone turned and announced to the room that dinner would be ready in ten to fifteen minutes, and disappeared through the door on the far side. Charles looked across the room to get another look at the young woman, but instead his eyes met 'Mr. Bat'.

'Oh, hello,' said Charles putting out his hand. 'Julian wasn't it. Do you want a beer? You apparently help yourself and fill in the book over there,' he said pointing towards the dark ragged looking book. Charles tried to get a close look at the man without appearing to stare.

'Yes, I know. How did you know my name, Charles?'

'Oh, the same way you know mine, Marcus told me you two had met again earlier.' Charles was infuriated with himself as he could still not recall where he had met this man; he felt that it could have something to do with his work. There were aspects of his job that nobody else knew about, not even his beloved wife; normally he would never have forgotten a face or a name. Why was his memory failing him now? 'And may I ask who this young lady is?' Charles asked smiling at the woman standing beside the bat researcher. Her clothes were plain and slightly baggy on her; concealing most of her figure.

'Yes, this is my niece and partner in crime for my project here, Tamara.' Charles shook the woman's hand and was immediately smitten as her face changed when she smiled. She had long light brown hair and wore no make-up, but she was attractive in a non-sensual way. Her eyes were quite piercing but there was a hint of sadness in them. He placed her in about mid to late thirties; she wore no ring, nor any other jewellery.

'Project? What project is this?' he asked already knowing the answer.

'We are studying the local bat population. There are not many houses like this where they have been undisturbed for decades,' answered the woman. She had a faint accent that Charles could not place. 'Do you know much about bats, Charles?'

'Not a lot, except they can see in the dark and they are rather partial to a drop of the old blood.' Charles now had a sensation he had also met this woman before.

'That, unfortunately, is the vast majority of the public's perception of the poor bat. There are only a tiny number of vampire bats…' She saw Charles shudder. 'They are beautiful creatures, really.'

'I'm sure you're right but…'

'May I have a private word with you Charles?' interjected Julian casting a stern glance towards his assistant, who took a step back.

'Yes of course,' said Charles feeling unease. 'Oh sorry, it will have to be another time; look here's Marcus. Excuse me, but I had better fetch my friend a drink, he looks as if he needs one. We'll try and catch up later, OK?' Charles picked up a glass and a can of beer, trying to get as far away from the bat professor as possible. He didn't want to engage in conversation with him until he could remember where he had met him. Taking the beer over to Marcus, who had stopped at the bottom of the stairs and was openly staring at the young blond woman on the other side of the room.

'Put you eyes back in,' whispered Charles as he poured the beer. 'She's with someone.'

'My God, she is a real looker,' he said taking the glass. 'I see you've met up with Mr. & Mrs Bat then. Any idea where you've met him before?' Charles gave a quick frown and shook his head. 'So where are the other two?'

'I don't know, they were here before. I had to warn Douglas off punching Malone's lights out. I hope your plan is a good one' said Charles slowly looking around the room.

Marcus gave a weak smile and cringed inside. 'Has Douglas told Toby what we saw Malone do?'

Charles shrugged his shoulders. 'I hope not because Toby is a real 'do-gooder'; he'd sort Mooney out for kicking the dog, never mind what he did to the poor old woman.'

A Scottish whoop of delight from the drawing room gave away their presence and the two men followed the sound. As they entered the two other crew members had now set up the balls on the snooker table and it was evident the Scotsman had potted the first ball.

'I'll have thee, Toby. You watch me!' said Douglas proudly putting up his first point.

Toby looked across to Marcus and winked. A few minutes later the Scotsman had slumped into the bench seat by the alcove. 'You should have warned me Marcus, I've just lost a pound to him.' He watched as the young student continued to pot ball after ball with apparent ease.

'It's a good job you found out now and not when you had had a few drinks and the bet was for a lot more.'

'You're right there...'

Marcus went and sat down beside the Scot. 'Look I have a plan to give our fat moon faced friend a little lesson.' Douglas sat up and turned towards Marcus.

'You mean make out Toby here is a crap player and then when the stakes are high, screw him.' Douglas sat back and beamed at Marcus. 'Brilliant. That'll show the little shit...'

'Oh, is it that obvious...' Marcus looked a little dejected.

'Why all the aggravation against Malone?' asked Toby clearing the last red.

A loud gong echoed through the whole building and they heard Malone shouting that dinner was now being served.

'About time,' said Douglas grabbing Charles' arm. 'I'm absolutely ravenous, I've had virtually nothing all day.' He turned to Toby. 'I'll explain about Malone over dinner, but you have to play along with Marcus' plan. I don't think you'll like what I have to say.' Toby looked at the disappearing men quizzically as he placed his cue back on the rack.

Douglas and Charles entered the dining room behind the

young couple, Douglas whispered that they were on their honeymoon and to keep Marcus on a leash. Douglas giggled at his own humour. They took the far end of the long table underneath a huge portrait of a regally dressed woman. Charles looked around for the other two and as Toby came through the door he caught sight of Malone whispering to Marcus in the large hallway. Charles cursed again under his breath. His plan to question Marcus separately and see if their stories tallied had failed; clearly Malone was informing Marcus of their brief conversation. Marcus entered the room and sensed the bat researcher's assistant was watching him and he checked as he passed in front of her.

'Look this is ridiculous. Come on let's all sit together.' Marcus strode round the table and over to the woman he could now barely take his eyes off. Helping her from her seat he led her down to the other end of the table where the rest of the crew were taking their seats. 'Come on,' he shouted back to the other three. 'Get down here and let's be sociable.'

The dinner started off somewhat awkwardly and the young married couple, who were from Holland, found themselves being entertained by Douglas. At one stage he decided to liven up proceedings by taking out his mouth organ and had everyone clapping along with his old navy tunes.

The meal was surprisingly good and the starving Scotsman had managed to acquire second helpings. The flowing wine eased the shyness of even the young bride, who had actually taken quite a shine to the robust Scotsman. Douglas was lapping up her attention and had failed to notice certain dark looks being cast his way by the young groom.

Marcus was totally absorbed with Tamara and apart from the occasional comment to the table he hardly spoke to anyone else. Charles on several occasions tried to get his friend's attention, but he only had eyes for the young woman.

'I just can't quite catch your accent. Where are you from?' asked Marcus eventually.

Marcus looked at her intently but she matched his stare. Marcus loved her eyes.

'It is a long and rather boring story. You wouldn't be interested.'

'Oh, but I am. Come on tell me your life story.' It was then he saw her eyes darken and a chilling look of sadness and pain filled them.

'Can we talk about something else? It is a very long tale, and believe me, it is not that interesting.' She made a sighed and looked away.

'OK, for the moment…' Marcus checked as Malone took away her plate, dropping the cutlery, into her lap. The caretaker went to retrieve them but she quickly pushed back her chair and stood up the cutlery scattering on the floor. 'Don't you dare try that again,' she shouted at him. Malone backed off and scampered towards the kitchen door.

'He tried that one with me yesterday,' whispered Tamara sitting down again and gave a quick glance towards her partner. Marcus gave her a quizzical look. 'Well he dropped the knife and fork in my lap and quite frankly touched me up. He wasn't subtle about it either and Julian had a real go at him. Foul greasy man, he makes my skin crawl.'

'The little bastard! It's creeps like him that give men a bad name,' he continued looking at Tamara, he handed her his napkin. 'I can see I'm going to have to sort out this Malone chap; unfortunately he doesn't leave his vices just to animal cruelty and bullying…'

Tamara stopped wiping the front of her jumper and turned towards him with a questioning look. 'Animal cruelty? Bullying?'

'We saw him kick seven shades out of a dog this afternoon and then…'

Marcus was interrupted as Charles banged his spoon on the table and announced that the occasion called for some ghost stories. Dark storm clouds had now covered the hill behind Kinloch Castle and lights were needed. As the eight diners moved into the drawing room they noticed that the lights would strengthen and weaken irregularly. As Malone brought in more wine, keeping his distance from the two bat researchers, he explained that the lighting system was hydro-electric and depended largely on the flow of water; but the system it seemed was in need of some repair.

The Scotsman started the contest and told a gruesome tale of a ghostly headless woman. His deep resonating voice rose and fell as he told his epic. He finished by describing the beheading of the poor woman by banging the table in front of him so loudly it caused a scream from both of the women. Everyone applauded and demanded more tales.

Malone had come to join the group and had clearly already had quite a lot to drink and he plonked himself down by Tamara. Marcus could feel his muscles tighten. Julian and Tamara glanced at each other and made their excuses and retired. Charles noticed Marcus looked decidedly disgruntled that the young bat researcher had left. A silence filled the room until their footsteps had faded and then a murmur of whispers in the group suggested their retirement was not to get some sleep.

'You lot are cruel,' said Toby. 'I don't think they are anything than what they claim. I don't think they're an item at all.'

'Yes, shut up you lot,' blurted Marcus, a tinge of jealous anger in his voice. 'They're in separate rooms.'

Malone nodded and leered after the departed guests. 'Yes and she can't lock her door…'

'If you so much as go near…'

'What about a game of snooker anyone?' interrupted Charles quickly, jumping up from his seat.

Pat Malone gave an angry glance towards Marcus and then turned to Charles. 'I have spent so much time practising alone on that table that I would even take on Ray Reardon for money. I feel lucky tonight,' he finished giving another quick look towards Marcus. 'Marcus do you fancy a challenge?'

'Why not? Loser buys a round of beers.' Marcus went over to the table and started to set up the balls. The caretaker returned with some cans and muttered that the loser goes and signs the book. Marcus watched as Malone started to clear the table and, noticing the honeymooners and the other two crew members still talking in the main room, he turned and took from his pocket the first miniature bottles of the Vodka. Unscrewing the cap he poured it into Malone's glass as the caretaker was concentrating on setting himself up for another pot. Malone rattled in a red.

'Well Marcus,' said Malone picking up the glass Marcus had just placed near him he took a swig of beer. 'You had better do some potting or you're buying the drinks.' Malone took another sip of beer and looked at his glass. 'Even the beer tastes good tonight.'

Marcus couldn't resist a wry smile and watched Malone sink another ball. When it was Marcus' turn he sent his cue ball completely the wrong way. 'Hard luck, I think you've left me on…' Malone leant forward and hammered in a red and then a colour which put the game beyond Marcus' reach.

'I think you need snookers,' gloated the caretaker.

'OK, Pat I concede.' Marcus gave Malone his glass. 'Come on sink it and I'll buy you another.' Malone didn't have to be asked twice, and emptied it. Marcus took the empty glass and went into the hall way, pouring another can of beer, but checking behind him, he emptied the second miniature bottle of vodka into Malone's glass. He returned to see Douglas taking on the caretaker and placed the beer beside Malone, nodding towards the glass. Ten minutes later the hapless Scotsman found himself sitting on the bench watching his opponent clear the table and Malone, smiling smugly, downed another drink, slamming the glass on the table and wiping his mouth with his sleeve.

'Damn stupid game anyway,' Douglas said trudging out into the hall way to pay for the next round of beer. 'Grown men hitting a few balls around a table.'

'You Scots can talk,' shouted Malone after him. 'You guys go running after a white ball on a walk,' he guffawed. 'Right, is there another challenger?' Malone looked at Marcus hopefully.

'OK,' said Toby rising from his chair. 'I'm not very experienced but I'll give it a go.'

As Toby approached the table Marcus came up to him and when Malone was re-setting the score board he whispered into his ear. 'Lose the first game or so, then raise the stakes and thrash the greasy bastard's arse.'

'My pleasure,' he said grinning back at Marcus.

Marcus went and poured a large glass of wine and presented it to Malone. 'You may need this. This kid is better than us so expect to be humbled.'

The young married couple said their farewells and departed, which caused a sneer from the caretaker.

'I'd give that one a good sorting. Those Dutch birds go like rabbits.' Malone said as he finished setting the balls up. 'Hey, Marcus I'd bet you'd like a taste of her?'

'Pat, you really are unbelievable…' said Marcus shaking his head but forcing a smile at the caretaker; he decided to make his move this evening and to hell with the consequences.

Malone won the first game and turned to Marcus who was now perched on the edge of one of the spectator benches. 'Humbled? It is like taking candy from a baby. Anyone want to make the bet a bit more interesting?'

Marcus could not believe the caretaker was falling for the oldest gambling scam in the book. 'I'll back Toby with twenty quid,' said Marcus nonchalantly and extracted the note from his back pocket. Charles was examining an antique and looked up watching the plan fall into place.

'I'm surprised at you Marcus; I never took you for a mug.' Malone finished his wine. Marcus could see the tell-tell signs of the excess of alcohol as Malone dropped his cue. Marcus looked at Toby and quickly shook his head. 'Let him win again, then nail him on the next one,' he whispered as he passed Toby towards the door.

'Not going to watch me take your money?' shouted Malone loudly.

'Oh yes, I'm just getting more beer to celebrate my winnings,' Marcus desperately trying to smile at the perspiring man.

Marcus returned to see Toby miss an easy pot. 'Hard luck Toby,' gloated Malone as he rounded the table, anxious to make his shot. Marcus had noticed that the Scotsman must have retired and Charles was reading a large leather bound book.

Charles looked up and seeing Marcus nodded at Malone and winked. He held up the book in front of him. 'Marcus this is the game book. My God, I'm surprised there are any deer left. Look, on one day alone they bagged three stag and nine hinds, and there is another…'

'You have to admit Toby, you're just not in the same league,' bellowed Malone as the black rattled down a hole. 'Surrender?' Marcus turned round to see Malone grinning broadly and taking the balls out from the pocket nets. Toby started to speak but Marcus cut across him.

'No he doesn't,' and Marcus pulled out a wad of notes and counted out five twenty pound notes and threw them on the table. 'Hundred quid.' Toby started to protest, but he did not dare look at Marcus in case he smiled.

'You're out of your mind, Marcus. I couldn't possibly take your…' Marcus stooped forward to retrieve the notes. 'OK, alright. I suppose I must keep the customer's happy,' quickly interjected Malone and snatched up the notes.

'So where is your dosh then? Let's see the colour of your money,' said Marcus settling himself down on the leather seat.

'I'll take it off the bar bill,' answered Malone placing the balls into the wooden triangle. Marcus went to protest but remembered the real reason for upping the stakes. The game started slowly and Malone's eyes narrowed as Toby potted a very difficult red to start his break. Marcus looked around and saw Charles was now examining the medicine cabinet in detail. Toby could play so well he even made some of his pots look like flukes. Soon he had Malone needing snookers and the caretaker conceded but only if they could double or quits. Marcus smugly smiled, holding out his hand for his notes.

Malone glowered at Marcus. 'I'll get my money back, don't

you worry,' he muttered and slamming the money on the side of the table he started to set up the balls. Marcus rose and passing Toby whispered not to make it too obvious.

'Anyone for more beer? Oh, I'm just going to the loo as well,' said Marcus leaving the room, noticing Charles still engrossed in the chemical bottles of the cabinet. Marcus pulled the door lightly behind him and strode out towards the toilet. Then he slowed down and looked down the corridor he had been down that afternoon. He shook his head and muttered to himself, 'No, I'm not a ruddy thief.' He turned round but heard Malone shout, 'Get out of that! Oh, if I could pot that little Dutch piece or that bat researcher like that they'd be moaning with pleasure for hours…'

'Little lecherous bastard, well this is for all the girls you grope, women you beat and dogs you've kicked,' whispered Marcus and started to fumbled his way down the corridor clinging to the wall as his eyes grew accustomed to the dark. He saw a candle on a dresser and, using some matches he found beside it, lit the wick.

Marcus felt a surge of excitement and his guilt melted away as his utter dislike for Malone took control of him. He walked to the anti-room at the bottom of the corridor carefully putting his hand in front of the candle to protect the flame. Some faint light was still coming in from outside; Marcus didn't know if was still some remnants of daylight, which was possible at this time of year, or the moon. He thought it would be appropriate if it was the moon, and for a second the effects of the beer made him chuckle to himself. Pulling back the tapestry and placing the candle down, he shoulder barged the panel and it swung back thudding noisily against the wall. Marcus froze. Echoes of voices and shouts were still filtering down the corridor; the game must have become close. He knew he hadn't much time.

Marcus struggled to get through the opening but mustered all his strength and forced himself through only just squeezing into the opening. He pushed hard again and lurched forward falling into the small store room. Just enough light seeped into the room from the tall thin window on the opposite wall and Marcus could make out the outline of the fireplace. His heart leapt as he saw the woman in the portrait seemingly looking at him. He could have sworn her expression had changed to a disapproving frown. He shook his head and picking around some boxes, he knelt down by the hearth and delicately felt the bricks up the chimney.

It was not long before he found the loose brick and grabbing it with his nails shuffled it out. He dropped the brick; he noticed his hands were shaking, but he didn't dawdle any longer and plunged his right hand into the hole. Feeling the canvas bag he pulled it out and heaved a sigh of relief, hesitating for a second. Suddenly the distant sounds of voices had stopped. Panic grabbed him and he picked up the brick and tried to slot it back into position. The brick stubbornly refused to go in. Marcus stood up and placed it on the floor, kicking it behind a box in the corner.

Clutching the bag and its contents Marcus made for the opening. His panic grew as there was still no noise from the distant drawing room. He could make out the flickering candle he had left in the anti-room and pushed himself out of the opening. He felt his shirt snag on something but he didn't care and fell through the small door accompanied by the sound of ripping cloth. He cursed under his breath but scrambled to his feet quickly blowing out the candle and turned, pulling the panel shut, finally sliding the tapestry back into position.

Marcus took a few steps forward and started down the corridor remembering to put the candle back where he had found it. He froze, blowing out the candle, backing into the wall as he saw the silhouette of a man. In an instant he could tell by the wiry hair and its slight figure that it had to be the bat researcher. Had he seen him? What should he do now?

'Marcus,' came a cry from the hallway. 'Marcus. Where the hell are you?' Marcus could hear Charles' voice had a tinge of anger in it. The silhouette suddenly turned and entered the hallway and Marcus could hear them making some pleasantries and the inquisitive Mr. Bat must have gone upstairs. Marcus went up a few more paces and placed the candle on the dresser and put the bag down beside it.

'Charles, I'm bloody well lost,' said Marcus trying to sound a touch drunk and merry.

'Come on, quickly, Malone and Toby are on the final black for the game. Your plan has worked a treat.' Charles whispered the last phrase and turned and went back into the drawing room. Marcus followed trying to wipe his hands clean and to establish what he had ripped getting out of the secret storeroom. He entered just as Malone was bending down eyeing up a long pot on the final black.

'Where the hell have you been?' said Malone standing and putting some chalk on his cue. Marcus was relieved he didn't seem to notice anything untoward with his attire. 'I'm just about to win all my money back,' hissed the caretaker finally taking his eyes off Marcus and looked at the pot he was about to make.

A tense silence filled the room as Malone crouched forward and studied the pot he was about to make. He jabbed the cue forward cracking into the black but it rattled the jaws of the pocket, remaining on the table; he swore an obscenity under his breath. Toby came forward and, giving Marcus a brief glance, lent forward and sunk the black into a pocket.

'Come on Marcus let's you and I play this time,' Malone slurred at the antique dealer. 'I'm sure there is something *we* could agree that's worth playing for.' Malone picked up a full glass of wine and slowly drank it down in one.

'OK, but I couldn't find the ruddy toilet and then I got lost. You set up the balls and I'll pop up to our room and use the loo up there.' Marcus managed to back out of the room without it looking too obvious and he didn't look towards his skipper although he could feel Charles' eyes set on him.

He ran to gather the bag from beside the dresser and coming back to the hallway he strode up the stairs stumbling at the top. He heard a distant female moan of ecstasy from somewhere in the house. Marcus didn't have time to wonder if it was the new bride or Tamara; he just couldn't see her with Julian. He trotted to the bedroom making the floorboards clatter and creak. Marcus slowed and in the end could only manage a lumbering pace as he tried to recover his breath. Putting the light on, he quickly surveyed the room for a hiding place. The shower, he thought. Entering the bathroom he removed the wooden panel on the side of the shower and stuffed the box down by the pipes. Marcus took a few breaths and seeing his reflection in the mirror he saw he had torn his shirt on the right shoulder.

'Damn,' he cursed. He knew he didn't have much time, so he ripped off his shirt and pulled his jumper on. 'Well it is chilly,' he said to himself.

Walking as quickly as he could he re-entered the drawing room to be faced by Charles putting his finger to his lips. Malone had collapsed on one of the sofas. Charles nodded back towards him and motioning to Toby and Marcus he turned out the lights and they tiptoed slowly up the stairs.

'Marcus, you missed most of the fun back there,' said Charles trying to control a laugh. 'Douglas told Toby about the dog and he gave the fat slob a real drumming. The thing is he never noticed. Well done Toby is all I can say. What do think Marcus?'

The two men stopped at the top of the stairs and Toby took the hint and carried onto his room. The two men watched him until he was out of view.

'Marcus, I know you too well; you can't fool me.' Charles had turned to face his friend. 'Come on, spill the beans or you won't get your passage home,' he continued in a quiet, but authoritarian, tone.

'What are you talking about?'

'You and that creep are up to something. I saw you in the dining room this afternoon and then you disappeared with him. However, I also saw you having a little *chat* before dinner. Marcus I can't have stuff disappearing from here, especially in my position, we work with the SNT, you know. Please for once think what it would look like on me.'

'OK, OK, but you're not going to like it!' Marcus found it hard to look into his friend's eyes; Charles gestured for him to continue. 'Malone wants me to be a fence for some of the stuff here.'

Charles lent back on the banister and shook his head slowly, closing his eyes for a moment. 'I hope you haven't agreed?'

Marcus looked away, he wanted Charles to see his sense of unease. 'Charles, you know me. But just a few of these pieces would pay the rent for months and now Dawn's living with me, I… well, I can't resist it. Look, he'll flog them to somebody else if I don't help; at least I will find good homes for them.'

'Marcus, you're a bloody fool. It is one thing being the loveable rogue, but a thief is a thief, and what *you're* going to do is theft, understood? There is no getting away from it, however many excuses *you* conjure up.' Charles was starting to pace slowly up and down the landing. 'How were you going to get them to London?'

'He had got someone with a boat and I was to meet him at Mallaig with my Volvo, or more probably a van…' Marcus kept up with Charles.

'Marcus you are the best friend I have ever had. As a friend I ask you not to enter into anything with this man. Can you imagine if you, and for that matter I, were discovered to have been thieving. It *would not* look good at the V&A, believe me and right now I am on for a promotion of sorts, so leave it, OK?'

'You're right, again, I know. I wouldn't like to cause you any harm. Look Charlie can we get out of here? Strangely this place, and that greasy cretin, is starting to give me the creeps. It has been fun, but let's move on; take me away from temptation, per favore, mi'amico.' Marcus gave Charles one of his special grins.

'Too right we're leaving. Malone isn't going to be happy tomorrow with the headache he will have and he'll also be a couple of hundred quid light. We'll leave early, very early. I'm knackered now so let's go and get some sleep.' Charles looked at his watch. 'Heavens it's nearly twelve o'clock. I'll set the alarm for five thirty.'

'Five thirty? Come on Charles…' Marcus ceased when he saw how Charles was glowering at him.

The two men entered their bedroom and Charles started to undress. 'What about paying the bill?' asked Marcus collecting up the shirt that he had only just discarded a few minutes before.

'I've paid for the rooms and meal, it's just the drinks we need to pay for, but I think he must owe *us* money after Toby had finished fleecing him.' Charles said folding his clothes neatly but a wry smile crept across his mouth. 'Toby was great. Where the hell did you bugger off to?'

'I went to the loo and got lost...' Marcus yawned. 'Anyway I must get some sleep I have some dreaming to do of a certain girl.'

'Yes, you seemed to have hit it off with our bat woman,' Charles tutted. He flung back the blankets, collapsed into his bed, and a few moments later a gentle snore tickled the night silence. Marcus shook his head in disbelief at other people's ability to enter sleep so quickly.

His mind raced and at one point he was sorely tempted to creep into the bathroom and check the jewels, he suddenly thought he hadn't checked if the jewels were in the box. He resisted moving as he knew that would be dangerous; Charles had a knack of waking at inconvenient times. Then he told himself that Malone wouldn't have had the time to return to the secret room in between their meeting and dinner.

He hoped that Malone would not go and check the secret room until they were long gone. Marcus kept telling himself that they weren't Malone's property to start with, so he wasn't really stealing them. Anyway, he argued with himself, the man would possibly have had them broken down into individual gems and sold separately; decimating their true worth. So why was his stomach knotted and he had such a strong sense of anxiety? Something was bothering him and his thoughts were becoming irrational. The sensation of utter cold fear he had experienced when he saw the title of the book, was now creeping up into his conscious mind, like a panther stalking its prey. What he had done was wrong and he knew it but there was something about the jewels that captivated, and at the same time, frightened him.

Marcus fought to remember what Malone had said about a rumour, or a legend, regarding the owner of the castle having an affair with a well-off woman. Then he recalled the old woman; he would have liked to speak to her. On the walk Douglas had also mentioned that in the brochure it had said something about the man who built the castle having worked to bring peace in the Russo-Japanese war at the beginning of the century. There were many artefacts throughout the castle that came from these two countries and now the greasy caretaker comes up with a box of jewels that were clearly worth a fortune. Marcus turned over in his bed; his friend's snoring now becoming slower, rhythmic, but annoyingly louder. What he had stumbled on was spinning in his mind out of control forcing back the impending sleep. Eventually he added the final piece of the jigsaw which he had started to build in his mind's eye. The title of the book with the box of jewels: *The arts, treasures and mysteries of the last Romanov Tsar - Emperor Nicholas 11.*

★ ★ ★

Tamara could not sleep. The noises from the old house and the distant mumbles of voices were only broken by passionate love making in a room not far away. At one time she heard footsteps down the corridor causing the floorboards to creak alarmingly. The thin line of light from the bottom of the door cast shadows in the room, while the wind cried as it tried to enter her windows, rattling them incessantly.

Her breathing was heavy and laboured; her heart beat so loudly she felt the pulse in her ear lobes. "Why now?" she kept asking herself. She had managed to keep any emotional attachment at bay for twelve long, barren years and now in a remote Scottish castle she had met a man, only for a few brief hours, that made her whole body ache in desire.

She knew she would never be able to obtain love until she was free of them and their control over her. She put her trembling hands over her face; the tears didn't come, they never did.

Chapter 5

Charles woke before the alarm had a chance to do its job and he slipped out of his bed, washed, dressed and then woke Marcus. Leaving his friend to shake off his tiredness he went to the next room and shook the other two crew members, whose response at the unearthly hour made Charles smile, but he left them in no doubt that he would leave without them. He returned to his room to be disappointed by Marcus' bed still full and heavy breathing emanating from under the covers.

'Marcus, shape yourself. We'll miss the tide if you don't get a move on.' Charles shouted slamming the door.

Marcus mumbled and he forced his heavy limbs to move. He hadn't been able to sleep and his hope of dreaming about Tamara was replaced by reliving the conversation with her the previous evening in fine detail. He had tried to work out her accent and where she actually had originated from. There seemed to be a couple of accents intertwined. He enjoyed the mystique about her and those eyes; he still had a vision of them. 'What is the ruddy time?' he grumbled to the skipper.

'It's gone six o'clock and I want you to drop me off at the boat first so I can check a few things out. Then you can come back with the tender and pick up the other two. OK?' Charles neatly folded his clothes, placing them in his bag.

Marcus went to the bathroom splashed cold water on his face and was tempted to check the jewels but he was worried in case Charles heard anything. He returned and stuffed all his belongings in his bag and slung it over his shoulder he started to follow Charles out of the room. Marcus suddenly stopped and frowning he turned flinging his bag on the floor. 'Sorry Charles, I'm not feeling quite right I need to go to the loo. It must be that beer last night; I'll only be a minute or two.'

'OK, I'll meet you down stairs,' answered Charles quietly as he left the room. Marcus went into the bath room pulling open the shower panel and for a brief second his heart jumped as he could not see the canvas bag. He desperately plunged his hand into the plumbing and after some rummaging; relief filled him as his finger tips felt the cloth bag. Extracting it he pulled the toilet chain, just in case Charles had returned and stuffed the bag into the wet section of his bag where he kept his dirty linen. 'Nobody will go in there,' he muttered wryly.

Descending the stairs he saw Charles counting up the amount of beer and wine they had consumed the night before. 'I think we are about quits, if you deduct his losses,' said Charles scribbling a few calculations on a scrap of paper.

Marcus went to his back pocket and took out the hundred pounds he had used the previous night. 'Look I don't want to deprive Malone of his livelihood. He can't complain if we leave a hundred quid.'

'My Heavens, are you feeling all right? You hadn't got a good word to say about him last night.' Charles gave Marcus a questioning look but Marcus thrust the money into Charles hand.

'I think the guy is sick and I don't want him coming after us for a measly bar bill do you?' Marcus turned and took a few post cards. 'I'll take a few of these though…'

'You've got a point,' said Charles taking some notes out of his wallet and scribbled a note to Malone. He placed the money inside the honesty book and closed it with a firm slam.

'Good Morning. Are you off then?'

Both men jumped and Marcus turned quickly to see the bat researcher in khaki shorts and a chequered shirt, peering over the banister, his hair had clearly not seen a brush that morning. 'Not very nice weather for sailing,' he continued watching the two men and scrutinising their bags with a long gaze.

'No, cold and damp and not even a great wind as yet but we have to try and catch the tide,' answered Marcus noticing Charles had picked up his bag and left the room. 'We have worked out how much we owe Malone, could you let him know we have left the cash in the honesty book.' Marcus gestured towards it on the sideboard.

'Of course. Where are you off to?'

'Mallaig I think, or if the weather looks OK we might even try to get south down to Iona.' Marcus saw Charles wildly gesturing to him from the entrance hall indicating to follow him. 'Anyway nice to have met you and good luck with the bats.'

The man above him made a small wave now looking slightly disappointed, even a little sad. Marcus followed his skipper outside and struggled to keep up with Charles' pace.

'You don't like him do you?' panted Marcus.

'No it's not that, I just hate being in a position where I can't remember where or when I have met someone. It unnerves me.' Charles splashed through some puddles by the old bridge. 'I just have a feeling about him.'

'Actually you may be surprised to know I rather fancy his assistant, Tamara. Love her name, beats Linda.' Marcus jumped over a pool only to realise Charles had stopped.

'You are totally incorrigible, any port in a storm. Anyway she's not like your usual type. Not much tits and toothpaste about her,' said Charles shaking his head.

'Charles, you go on at me to find a *decent* girl and then when I do you pull me down.' Marcus trudged on sulking. 'Her eyes have a sensual quality and there is a mystical quality about her. Charles I really like her but…'

'But what?'

'She wouldn't give me her number or even where she lived or for that matter anything about herself. I gave her my number though, so I hope she calls. One thing though, she seemed very interested to know who you where and what you were doing here.' Marcus stopped and turned to his friend.

'It's strange because I think I have seen her before as well. Maybe I've met the two of them somewhere.' Charles said frowning.

'Well if you finally get the grey matter to work will you let me know? I would love to meet her again.' Marcus carried on down the path his head slightly drooped in thought.

'Wow, she really has got under your skin, hasn't she?' said Charles following him. 'Hey another thing, did you see the way that Julian chap was staring at our bags this morning; as if he was searching or scanning them with those wild eyes of his.' Charles caught up with Marcus. 'Actually, thinking about it, I *should* search your bag. I suspect you've got a vase or two in there.'

Marcus turned and tossed the bag at Charles' feet cringing inside as he saw the bag loudly hit the ground; he hoped his underwear would soften the blow. 'Go on and search it.' He felt anger growing inside him which quickly dispelled into guilt. He glanced back nervously, half expecting to see Malone chasing after them in a fury.

'Oh for pity sake Marcus, I was only joking,' Charles picked up the bag and handed it back. The men walked on in silence Marcus' guilt gnawing into him. He hated himself for deceiving his oldest and most loyal friend. Marcus slipped his bag over his shoulder and felt the box dig into his flank. He was having serious doubts about taking the jewels. He kept thinking about how Malone would react.

The men arrived at the tender and untied it laughing at their antics in Tobermory. Marcus took Charles over to the yacht where he nimbly jumped on board showing no signs of his injury two nights before. Marcus then returned to the slipway to wait for the others. The skipper opened the boat and started to repair the kicking strap after he had checked the oil and lubrication of the engine.

Marcus meanwhile just sat on the nose of the tender humming to himself and taking in the scenery towards the majestic castle. The wind was starting to increase and he tried to put the jewels out of his mind, even trying to picture Tamara, but he kept seeing the open box and the contents glistening in the badly lit storeroom. What if these jewels *were* really something to do with the old Romanov dynasty? His heart pounded as he went through the possible consequences, apprehension was wrapped in excitement. After a few minutes he made out the other two crewmembers trudging towards him. An urge to replace the jewels cascaded through him but then he thought of the slime ball Malone; he just couldn't bring himself to let that man have them. Instinct told him they spelt trouble and more than a little excitement spicing up his life. Once again Tamara crossed his mind. Wouldn't it be ironic if on a remote island he found his fortune and the woman of his dreams, he thought. Then an idea came to him that if the jewels were worth a fortune he could actually pay Malone off and prevent him becoming aggressive in any way. A warm feeling went through him. Of course that's what he'd do. He smiled to himself and stood up as Douglas and Toby arrived, with Toby yawning loudly.

'What time is this?' said the Scotsman throwing his bag into the dinghy. 'Doesn't Captain Bligh like a nice comfy bed, eh?' Douglas nodded towards their boat. 'At times that man loses all touch with reality. Lord, its cold,' he shivered.

'You know what a stickler Charles is with his tides!' laughed Marcus and pulled the dinghy out into deeper water waiting for the two men to scramble in.

'Well he didn't get them right the other night, did he? Bloody madness, if you ask me,' continued the Scotsman careful not to let the water go over his sailing boots. 'I thought this was supposed to be a relaxing holiday.' Marcus started the engine and they chugged to the yacht. Marcus started to lash the tender to the transom and the other two went below to put on their weather gear. Charles joined him beaming.

'I've fixed the kicking strap and checked the engine, so we're ready to go. Can you do the honours with the anchor?' Charles asked Marcus while starting the engine.

'Yes, of course,' replied Marcus again surprised by a weary tone in his own voice. Charles also heard it and quickly looked at Marcus. 'I'm sorry Charles; I feel a bit grumpy today, just ignore me.'

'Well so long as you and I haven't got a problem…?'

Marcus shook his head and smiled. 'No, not at all. I just feel a bit irritable that's all.' He went forward and Charles followed him.

'Marcus, do I sense a little love sickness in the air?' Charles placed his hand on Marcus' shoulder. Marcus shook his head and laughed.

'I don't believe in love at first sight,' he lied. 'But I have to admit she is in my thoughts a hell of a lot. So no teasing, please, or we will have a problem!' Marcus knelt down and started to fiddle with the windlass. 'You'd better take the helm and move forward a bit,' he said pressing the button on the deck as the windlass sprung to life making Marcus jump.

'OK lover boy,' said Charles making a rapid retreat to the helm.

Half an hour later the four men sat in the cockpit, Marcus at the helm as usual, all holding a steaming mug of coffee.

'That was the strangest night I've ever had,' said Toby thoughtfully. 'You know we should all have at least one night a week where the TV is banned.' He turned to Douglas. 'That was a cracking ghost story, where did you hear it?' he asked.

'Ork, it's all true laddie,' laughed Douglas. 'If you don't believe me, I'll take you to the place where she still roams the passageways on the nights when the moon is full.' The men laughed and for a while their silence was only broken by the thud of waves on the bow plus the creaking of straining rigging. Charles looked up at the mainsail and adjusted the main sheet telling Marcus to keep a steady course.

'Come on Doug, give us a rendition,' shouted Charles suddenly aware of the troubled look his helmsman was sporting. Douglas took out his mouth organ and started to play. He soon tired and the men returned to sitting quietly taking in the view, moving with the roll of the boat. Marcus was particularly quiet, which both Doug and Toby had noted, but they had decided not to interfere or ask any awkward questions. They had also noticed Marcus' interest in the young bat assistant.

The week passed without further incident except Douglas was laid low with stomach problems after a couple of helpings of haggis and chips in Mallaig. Even as they sailed south they could hear his long low moans from the forward head above the sound of the waves hitting the bow.

On the final day they sailed down the Sound of Mull, towards Oban. It was a sunny day with a good breeze. Marcus' quiet mood had continued and it was now starting to greatly worry his old friend. Charles decided it was time to act and establish exactly what was the reason for Marcus' quiet mood; if it was love then it was the first time he had seen his friend like this.

'I am not usually in favour of this whilst we are sailing, but it is such a gorgeous day I think it warrants a beer,' said Charles, coming up from the salon, juggling with four cans of beer. He gave a can to all three and, cracking them open, they toasted a good week's sailing. Douglas went and sat on the gunwales near the bow and let his legs dangle over the side. The sun's rays could be seen drilling down into the dark clear water. 'Toby,' said Charles, 'you can sometimes see porpoises around here, go up with Doug and keep your eyes peeled. Shout if you see anything.' Toby nodded forward and sensed Charles' ulterior motive.

'Isn't it Porpoii or something like that in the plural,' mused Marcus after Toby had moved forward.

'Ah, he speaks,' jested Charles. 'Actually I don't think so. It comes from the Latin; porcus, a pig and piscis, a fish.'

'I knew I shouldn't have asked, I forgot you were fluent in Latin and all sorts of other ancient tongues,' said Marcus with a touch of sarcasm, but a smile started to break across his face. 'Have you enjoyed the week?'

'Well Marcus, I was going to ask you the same question. Ever since Kinloch Castle you have been quiet and, if I may say so, a little off hand and distant with us all.' Marcus looked at the wind indicator at the top of the mast and didn't reply. 'You also seem a bit edgy, not exactly what I would call going through a touch of the love pangs. Is it something you want to talk about?'

Marcus wanted to tell Charles, he really did, but he knew the man standing in front of him and his high set of principles plus his position within the V&A would compel him to return to Rum. Marcus had managed to take a quick peek at the jewels and he was relieved they were as he recalled them in the hidden room. Inspecting them caused his hands to tremble and sent his heart racing. He recognised true quality when he saw it, but they also were troubling him; how was he ever to sell them? A romantic dream of what he was going to do with them formed in his mind and it involved Tamara.

'If you want to know the truth I am having a bit of a struggle with my conscience. Well a couple actually.' Marcus answered as Charles sat down and leant against the bulkhead; a thoughtful look on his face. 'Firstly I feel as if I let that greasy toad down…'

'Why? We paid him the bar bill; why should you feel you have let him down? Is there something else you're not telling me?'

'Let me finish, Charles, please.' Marcus said annoyed at the interruption, while taking a deep breath and ducking down, he checked underneath the sail for any other boats. 'I did promise I would help him sell a few of the antiques and walking out might have unnerved him slightly. I am surprised he hasn't come after me.' Marcus wanted to involve Charles in some way without telling him the truth just in case Malone was waiting for them at the marina.

'Oh, come on Marcus, it's not as if you signed a contract with the man. I can't see him chasing after you just for that and I think you could handle him quite easily. He's hardly a black belt.' Charles watched the helmsman carefully noting Marcus' weak argument had fazed him a little.

'Well, he may feel he has compromised himself.' Marcus picked up his can and took a long gulp cursing his feeble story. He couldn't bring himself to catch Charles' eye. 'Anyway the other real issue is…' A long pause ensued and Charles kept his eyes on the helmsman. 'I left a load of fantastic antiques there. I've told you, just a few of them and I'd have been quid's in. Mooney also seemed very keen to make a few bob and get off the island as quick as he could.' Marcus cast a wary glance at Charles who had nodded. Would he swallow this tale, Marcus pondered just in case Malone was waiting for them in Oban.

'I grant you that you would have made quite a bit of profit out of those antiques, but it's unlike you to be so down in the mouth. You're not having financial difficulties are you Marcus?' Charles questioning look turned to concern.

'No, well, no more than usual. I don't know Charles, I'm also feeling a bit strange at the moment. What, with Toby and Dawn being so happy together and seeing you and Samantha enjoying married bliss. Then there was all that opulence at the castle… I suppose I'm questioning a few things.' Marcus looked straight at the man who had been his unswerving ally and confident in his life; an urge to tell Charles everything suddenly filled him. Marcus took a deep breath but seeing Charles' worried expression he realised it would be more than foolhardy. He'll find a way to move them on and then no one would be any the wiser. He took a sip of beer and continued. 'Well Charles I think I've fallen for that girl Tamara. Dear God, you're never going to believe this but I've never felt like this before, ever!'

'Ahh, so that's it you've fallen in love *and* starting your mid-life crisis…'

'Mid-life crisis. Do you mind! Ruddy hell Charles I'm trying to have a serious conversation here.'

'No think about it. You are starting to question a few things in your life…'

'Charles,' Marcus lent over the wheel, 'you're talking absolute and utter nonsense. If there is anyone here who is having a crisis it's you. Don't forget that idiotic night sail and ghosts.' Marcus felt uneasy at his outburst. 'Marcus Chapman is just having a few thoughtful moments and maybe he wants some companionship as well as love.'

'I think you mean sex…'

Marcus ignored the comment. 'For heaven's sake look at the scenery,' he swept his arm across towards the shoreline. 'Just a few days of peaceful contemplation. That's all. You know I've been restless recently; I'm tiring of London. It's not the place it was. What did your father say? This is God's country. So let's drop it and pass me another beer; I've a terrible thirst on me.'

Marcus' attempt at mimicking an Irish accent made Charles shake his head in disgust and he went below for more cans. Marcus realised he needed to pull himself together or Charles would know something serious was bothering him; he unfortunately knew him too well. Charles had an annoying habit of always being right. Maybe he is going through a mid-life crisis; but in his heart he knew a thief is a thief and there can't be any excuses. He wasn't the loveable rogue after all, for he couldn't ignore he was feeling awful about what he had done. He had been involved in some very shady deals, but never open theft. His problem was how to sell the jewels without any repercussions. If his suspicion was correct the jewels would be very valuable. He must read the book that was with them; even that sent a shiver of fear through him. What if they had been stolen? Then what would he do? He had spent the week trying to devise a plan where he could bring Charles in without letting him know the exact origins of the jewels. Even he would never guess they were from Kinloch Castle and if there was one person who could help him now it was Charles.

They dropped the boat off at a marina near Oban and picked up Charles' Mercedes. It was too late for the long drive back down to London so they spent the last night in a small guest house just outside Oban. As usual, there was too much beer and joviality. Marcus had only managed another brief glimpse at the box of jewels and he was itching to study them properly. He had now decided that he would wait a few weeks and show Charles one of the pieces of jewellery. Marcus had taken many artefacts to him in the past, which he had acquired from Antiqarius, a market of small traders which Marcus often dealt with, just a few doors down from his shop. Charles had many colleagues inside the V&A museum and he was always able to establish their history. Normally they had been virtually worthless junk but he had stumbled on two pieces over the last few years which had made him a pretty packet. If these jewels did have anything to do with the old Romanov dynasty then Charles would find out the whole story. He smiled to himself and knew he could ultimately trust Charles, but only if he never associated them with Kinloch Castle.

Charles had the task of driving them home and he made a short detour dropping Douglas off near Lockerbie for his wife to pick him up. Nearly six hours later he was driving down the King's Road cursing the traffic. 'I can't wait for this congestion charge to be introduced and to rid London of some of these cars,' Charles moaned.

'Firstly, it isn't coming out this far and secondly these are my customers,' replied Marcus. 'Are you coming with me or going back to your own flat?' he asked turning round to Toby in the back seat.

'Look, tell Dawn I'll come round in a couple of hours after I've showered. I think I hum a bit. Could you take me back to my place Charles?' Charles nodded as Toby lifted an arm took a sniff and wrinkled up his nose. 'Listen guys I really appreciate you asking me on this trip. I had a great time.' He slapped Charles and Marcus on their backs. 'You're no way near as bad as Dawn was making out! No, seriously I enjoyed it, especially that night in the castle. Nobody is going to believe me when I tell them.'

Marcus laughed and as Charles pulled outside his small shop he ran to the rear of the Merc pulling out his bag. 'Pop down soon Charles and bring Samantha and the kids. Hell, you're only a few hundred yards away.' Waving to the two men in the car he went up to the door and as he entered he heard the buzzer sound in the small office at the back of the building. 'Coming,' he heard his daughter shout out.

'It's me, I'm home…' His daughter burst into the room and

threw herself at her father, sending him off balance. Quickly looking around, her face showed a flash of disappointment.

'Toby will be round in a couple of hours he needs to freshen up. Sorry it's just me for the moment,' said Marcus a tinge of disappointment with his daughter's priority of men.

Dawn smiled and taking a step back held her nose. 'He's not the only one who needs to freshen up. Phew, didn't you shower this morning.'

'You cheeky whippersnapper,' he said giving her a playful clip around her ear. 'How have you been, everything all right?'

'All right? I've made you a fortune. Look,' the young woman opened her arms and did a half turn in the middle of the shop, looking like Julie Andrews on a hilltop, 'you'll have to get out and buy some more stuff.'

'Ruddy hell, you have done well. Where has everything gone? You didn't give the stuff away,' his daughter pulled a tongue at him. 'I'll suppose you'll want commission next?'

'Actually Dad, it just so happens…'

'Don't push your luck young lady,' he said wagging a finger at her. 'I'm away up stairs,' he continued trying to mimic Douglas' accent.

'Oh, how is Uncle Doug?'

'On really good form as usual! Listen let me go and take a shower, change and we'll lock up and go and get a coffee down the road. My treat!'

'I should think so,' she shouted after him. 'Tied to this shop while you go off having a good time…'

'Stop your harping,' he bellowed down the stairs and throwing his bag into his bedroom he went into the kitchen and poured himself a glass of water. The post was laid out on the little table in the corner and he quickly flicked through to see the usual array of junk mail and bills. Marcus showered, dressed and went down giving his daughter a quick hug. He then wrapped his arm round her waist and led her onto the King's Road, locking the door behind him, he turned westwards towards Chelsea.

They sauntered along chatting about the past few days finally coming to their local café. Dawn told her father to go in and order a coffee as she had to go and buy something from the chemist. Marcus watched her almost skipping down the street her long dark hair flowing behind her. He had not really seen her grow up and was now so happy he was getting to know her. He took a table in the corner and ordered two cappuccinos. A few moments later she rushed in and took the seat opposite. Marcus studied her face as she extracted a bottle of shampoo from a paper bag, studying the small print on the back. He noticed she hadn't any make-up on, but her dark features and olive coloured skin meant she didn't have to. She is stunningly beautiful, he thought, and for a moment he remembered his first wife but then the memories of the rows and arguments caused his body to make an involuntary shiver.

'So what do you think of my fella then?' She put the bottle down and rested her chin on her hands giving her father a piercing look with her large eyes. 'Is he acceptable?'

'Apart from that infernal earring he sports, he is a really nice chap.' His daughter raised one eyebrow. 'I actually think he is a genuinely good man. I knew he was a good pool player but you should see him on a snooker table. He wiped the floor with all of us.'

His daughter smiled and they let the waitress place the coffees down. 'I'm not sure if I am pleased or not. You know, I was hoping to bring a man back that wound you up!'

'You're not that sort,' replied Marcus scooping the froth up with his spoon. 'Charles and Doug both think he is great as well, especially Uncle Doug.' His daughter sat back and Marcus could see her sense of pride. 'He's a bright lad as well. He was telling us about the exams he has to do. Did you know he has to learn hundreds, and I mean hundreds, of legal cases? Sounds boring, but actually he seems to thrive on it.' He watched his daughter sip her coffee, froth sticking to her top lip. 'Charles was telling me that one day he should make a lot of money, once he has done his time with a law firm.'

'Why do you think I am going out with him,' giggled Dawn. 'He's hardly a movie star.'

'You little hussy, I'll tell him…'

'No you won't. Anyway he'll know I was just pulling your leg,' she said wiping her mouth with a serviette. 'He actually reminds me a little of Charles. Studious, a little intense and very principled. Do you know he wouldn't…?'

'I don't want to hear, thank you. Your personal life is just that, personal.'

'Oh, Dad you are such an old prude at times. We'd better get back, it's not good leaving the shop on a Saturday afternoon,' said Dawn glancing at her watch.

'My heavens, what's come over you, or is it that Toby might be back soon,' said Marcus standing and leaving some coins on the table.

Dawn flashed a broad smile at her father. 'It maybe…'

'Dawn, I will give you some extra money for all the work you've done. I'll need to check what price you sold them at first…'

His daughter took his hand and led him out and they walked slowly down the King's Road heading towards Sloane Square. 'Dad, was the sailing all right?' she suddenly asked stopping. Marcus checked and nodded his head slowly. 'You seem a bit distant, sort of pre-occupied somehow.'

Marcus shrugged his shoulders and pecked her on the cheek. 'I'm just a bit tired and I've had far too much beer, that's all.' He left his daughter peering longingly in a small woman's fashion boutique window and went back to his shop. He unlocked and then went upstairs and took out his dirty linen. He felt the canvas bag and the hard objects inside. Looking around his bedroom he searched for a safe hiding place. He had considered using the old black safe in the office below but Charles had scalded him about its security. He had told him someone could get into it using a teaspoon. It may have looked impregnable, heavy and secure, but according to Charles anybody with an ounce of knowledge could break into it. He hadn't told Charles he normally forgot even to lock it. He had decided to put them in the small attic but he would have to be sure his daughter was not around when he did that; so for the moment he put it under his bed pushing it well out of sight. He laughed to himself, no one would think of looking there. He heard the buzzer from downstairs and he went to see a young couple examining one of the few remaining antiques. Marcus went into sales mode…

That evening Toby came round and to their utter surprise he had removed the earring. Nothing was said but Marcus felt a touch guilty. Marcus became impatient as the young couple chatted away as he was keen to examine the jewels in privacy. Finally exasperated at their dithering he gave his daughter some money to go out for a meal. Half an hour later Marcus was finally alone and he went to his room and extracted the canvas bag from under the bed. He cleared the top of his dressing table and, pulling the curtains tightly across, he withdrew the box and book from the bag.

Marcus' heart pounded as he spread the top layer of jewels out carefully untangling a few of the necklaces. He then pulled out the tray and gently laid out the suite of jewels. He was breathing heavily and slowly as he sorted the suite of earrings, bracelet, necklace and ring in the centre of the dressing table. The stones sparkled and Marcus tried to count how many diamonds there were in the necklace but gave up at fifty. He picked up the ring slowly, studying the shank and stones. He had never seen such a large sapphire and the diamonds that surrounded it were almost too big so that they seemed a little out of proportion. He had become a little light headed and sat down unable to take his eyes off the sight in front of him.

'Wow, you've hit the jackpot here Marcus old son,' he whispered to himself. He picked up the necklace, surprised at its weight. For a second he thought about giving it to his daughter on her wedding day. He smiled to himself as he recalled a recent outburst that she would never marry and just live in sin, but that was before her involvement with Toby had become serious. Marcus had always feared that her parents' divorce would leave a scar within her.

Marcus placed his jeweller's magnifier into his eye socket and examined the necklace and then the ring. His hands started to shake at the realisation the stones were flawless and crystal clear. Then he tried to find a hallmark but there were none on the suite of jewels only on the other pieces. He frowned and checked again finally he noticed a tiny identity stamp looking like two letters intertwined. It could have been an 'X' and 'P' or 'R'. Marcus sat back and his hand swept through his hair and over his face when he noticed the monograms on the top of the jewellery box looked remarkably similar. He turned and picked up the book. The title had given Marcus more than a clue to their origins and flicking through the pages it fell open where several leaves had been torn out. He frowned in annoyance. Placing the book down, he picked up the ring again. 'I wonder what stories you can tell,' he said to himself. 'I think I'll have to do some research into you, or better still get Charles to investigate.'

The whole room was bright with the reflections from the jewels. Marcus put the ring down reluctantly and went downstairs to find the old wooden cigar humidor he had bought recently. He eyed the safe again and knew it would be best to put the jewels in there but he was concerned that his daughter might discover them. Returning to his room he put the jewels into their new home and on closing the lid his eyes caught the nasty gash on the front of the original box and for the first time that night he recalled Malone; his sense of guilt returned.

'When I find out more I'll call him and send him a cheque,' he whispered picking up the humidor. He went to a cupboard and pulled out the step ladders and clambered up to the top floor. He placed the ladders under the hatchway and entered the attic. Crawling into the loft he scrabbled over a few rafters; the dusty fibreglass lagging making him cough. He moaned as his knees ached and lifting the light cotton wool like installation he hid the box under the eaves.

Marcus retuned to his room and looked at the damaged fine old box that had housed the jewels. 'I'll get this fixed, clean it up and it should fetch a pretty packet,' he said to the empty room.

Finally he picked up the book, flicked through it again trying to establish what would have been written on the missing pages and wondered why anyone would want to rip them out. He frowned and felt angry inside but decided to study it later and, closing it, he placed in the tightly packed bookshelf above his bed.

Cleaning up he went into the lounge and slumped into his favourite chair; a few minutes later he had fallen into a deep and fitful sleep. A clang of metal woke him with a start. It was the sound of the ladders being brought downstairs, folded up and then noisily heaved back into the store cupboard. He cursed himself for forgetting to put them away.

'Dad, what are the ladders out for?' Dawn said entering the room knocking dust off her hands.

'Oh, I… err… I thought I heard the overflow going…'

'Overflow? Dad you're over tired. I'll go and get your slippers and make you a cocoa and then you should go to bed. You look decidedly pasty.' His daughter went out and round the landing to his bedroom. Marcus closed his eyes and put his head back, why hadn't he finished the job properly he thought to himself.

'Where's Toby?' he shouted after her.

'He was shattered, he was neither use nor ornament tonight,' she said as she re-entered the room, but this time she was quietly stepping towards him. His eyes opened fully to see his daughter carrying and examining the box the jewels had come in.

'Where did you get this?' she inquired. 'It's beautiful. The workmanship is just…'

'Oh, yes I picked it up in a shop; I think it was Mallaig.' Marcus stood up. 'It's a shame it has been badly damaged on the front but I think I know someone who could fix it.' His daughter was studying the box carefully.

'How much did you pay for it?'

'Not a lot, fifty nicker I think. I just liked it and I thought I might keep it.' Marcus took the box from his daughter.

'You keep something? Not a chance,' she jested and went out towards the kitchenette. 'Your usual sugar?' she called back.

'Yes please,' he replied taking the box to his room. His anger with himself growing. He had better start being a little more circumspect now his daughter was living with him. He went back to his room and placed the box in his underwear drawer still cursing himself.

Marcus returned to the kitchenette and chatted to his daughter for a while before yawning loudly and, making his excuses, went to bed. He was pleased his daughter hadn't mentioned the casket again and he tried to think of a plausible story in case she continued to ask about it. He was starting to be concerned about the number of lies he had been spinning over the last few days.

A few days later his fears manifested as Dawn enquired after the box. 'I've had it sent away for repairs. I *was* serious I would like to keep it.' His daughter was standing in the shop right in front of him, her hands on her hips. Marcus felt like a little boy about to be scalded.

'Well Toby doesn't recall you going off and buying any antiques.' His daughter's face hardened a little.

'Well young Toby wasn't with me all the time, you know. Anyway what's all the inquisition about? It's only an old damaged box.'

'That box is not just an old damaged box. It is magnificent, you should get Charles to look at it. Toby thinks you might have stolen it from that castle you stayed at.' Marcus' heart jumped and he held his breath his mind searching for something to say. Dawn saw his reaction and continued. 'I bet you just couldn't resist taking a little souvenir? A memento of your stay? You didn't break into it, did you?'

'Dawn! What do you think I am…?'

'I know you can't help yourself at times, Dad. I've seen how you wheel and deal, remember! Plus you have been very morose since you came back and acting very oddly. So you can see why I am more than a little suspicious as to whether you acquired it with or without the owner's consent. Toby said you went quiet after the night at the castle, or maybe it was a certain lady you met? Come on Dad, I want to know the truth.' She had now taken a pace towards him and Marcus felt almost intimidated by his own daughter.

'Lady? Oh, Tamara,' Marcus said knowing his attempt of casualness was not fooling his daughter.

'Yes, Tamara. Toby said you took quite a shine to her.'

OK, OK, I admit I did have a thing for a woman I met. But we only chatted over dinner and I didn't even get her number. Happy?' Marcus couldn't bring himself to look at his daughter straight in the eye but his relief that the subject matter had changed was short lived.

'And the box?'

'Yes, I did get it from Kinloch. But it is *not* what you think.' His daughter narrowed her eyes expecting the full explanation. 'The caretaker showed it to me and confided he had broken it to see what was inside. It is apparently listed in the contents of the castle, and could be worth a lot. I agreed to have it repaired before the next full audit at the castle.' Marcus was delighted with himself at the credibility of his quick talking.

'So why lie then?'

'That's enough Dawn, I was just trying to protect the guy, and yes, he did try and get me to sell a few pieces for him, but I declined. I told Charles about it.' His daughter started to speak but Marcus raised his hands. Time for some fatherly authority, he decided. 'I don't want to discuss it any more and I'd appreciate it if you didn't mention this to anyone, especially Charles. I'm clearly not very good at lying as Charles picked up something as well.' Marcus made a weak laugh. 'Maybe he is right, I am going through a mid-life crisis.' Marcus sat down on one of the chairs in the shop and looked at people passing the window glancing in.

'Sorry Dad, but it is only because I care. I'll go and make some coffee.' His daughter left and the sound of a French carriage clock's high pitched chime was only just audible above the passing traffic. He had become a very accomplished liar, and the thrill of spinning the yarn was masking how utterly ashamed he was. Marcus vowed that he would move the jewels on as quickly as he could. He had realised he was living in fear of a call from Malone, possibly accompanied by a couple of heavies. For the first time he contemplated having the jewels broken down. He shook his head in self disgust.

Several weeks later Marcus arranged a get together with Charles, Toby and his daughter. Douglas could not make it for the crew's reunion. They met at the Ebury Street Wine Bar and taking a table in the front room by the bar they nosily sifted through the pictures recounting slightly exaggerated sories of the holiday. After a snack the young couple departed and left the two men sipping the remains of a bottle of white wine.

'I'm sorry Samantha couldn't come, she's up to her eyes with work and the kids…' said Charles.

Marcus shrugged. 'Of course! I don't know where she gets her energy from. You know I always thought people who lived in the likes of Wellington Square had a posse of servants.' Charles ignored the remark. His wealth had never been an issue between them. 'How are things at the V&A?' continued Marcus quickly changing the subject. 'You never seem to be home much nowadays.'

'Oh, the usual, desperately trying to raise funds to protect our national heritage. It is a constant struggle keeping tabs on all the treasures we have scattered around the country.' Charles swished his wine around in his glass. 'And you, how's it with you? You seem to have come out of your doldrums a little.'

'Yes, I never heard from Tamara which, to be honest with you, I am a bit surprised about and a touch disappointed. I felt there was something between us…' Marcus smiled sadly.

'You're losing your charm, at long last…' Charles laughed. 'Actually Marcus I could have sworn I saw her a few days ago leaving the V&A.' Marcus sat bolt upright. 'Yes she was in a nice suit and looked every bit the city woman. Nothing like she did at Kinloch.'

'Charles, why the ruddy hell didn't you tell me?'

'I just did! Look to be honest I'm not absolutely sure it was her, but maybe that's where I have seen her before. What are you going to do camp out on the steps of the V&A?'

'Yes, if I have to…' Marcus felt tense and forced himself to relax a little. He had not been able to shake the thought of Tamara from his mind.

'Wow, you really do have it bad.'

Marcus thoughtfully nodded his head.

'I am so glad I have Dawn living with me at the moment. I think if I was alone I would go mad. She is also doing such a good job in the shop, I've been spending all my time buying stuff. No sooner do I buy a load than she has sold it.'

'Bravo Dawn,' replied Charles smiling. 'Should help the finances…?'

'Yes it certainly has but I had to go all the way to Lancashire in the Volvo the other day. Took me ages to get home.' Marcus shuffled in his seat. 'The problem is she has been hinting she doesn't like her course at university and she could help me run the shop.'

'Tell her to get her degree first then she can work with you after that.'

Marcus nodded. 'The problem is she is a *very* strong willed young woman.'

Charles smiled and a silence fell over the table for a few moments. Marcus cleared his throat and spoke.

'Charles I know you've helped me before but can I ask another favour?' Charles nodded slowly not liking the sound of what was coming. He took the bottle of Sancerre out of the wine cooler and topped up their glasses. 'I found this ring in a house clearance the other day,' Marcus rummaged in his pocket and brought out the sapphire and diamond ring. 'It's got a very faint mark on it, but it's almost impossible tell what it is.'

Charles took the ring and then suddenly burst out laughing as he quickly glanced around the room. 'I think we are getting a few odd looks Marcus!'

They both looked around the bar together and laughing they ignored the surprised gazes directed at them.

'Don't go down on one knee.' They both tried to suppress a guffaw as Charles continued. 'It's a fine looking ring. A bit incongruous for my liking, but I suspect there are a few carets in the diamonds alone.' Charles looked closely at the ring. 'Wow, it certainly looks a high quality sapphire and the surrounding diamonds are hardly chippings. Where did you get it?'

'Uhh, as I said a house clearance near Henley.' Marcus tried to hold Charles' look. 'Strange place, must have cost a fortune, but had very little taste although there was an awful lot of stuff left. The family just wanted me to take the lot, rubbish and all, to clear the house. I found it under the bed caught in one of the castors. I was told the contents were mine, so, as far as I'm concerned, it's mine. It took me over two days to leave the house in good shape for the sale.' Marcus could feel his face flush. 'I know what you're thinking but I am quite within my rights. A deal is a deal and believe me normally I hardly break even on a house clearance.'

'I never said a word,' laughed Charles sensing his friend's unease. Charles had extracted his eye magnifying glass from his pocket and was peering through it. 'Well it does look a fine piece; it could be worth a lot. Leave it with me and I'll ask one of the precious stones guys to take a look. The mark looks to be Eastern Russian alphabet so I'll try the EED.'

'EED?'

'Oh, Eastern European Department.' Charles placed the ring carefully in his trouser pocket shuffling it into a comfortable position. 'You never know, one day you'll stumble on an ancient treasure and you could retire to the South of France.'

Marcus made a weak laugh and finished his wine. 'Oh, it is important that I get it back.' He feared Charles had not fallen for his story and he waved towards the bar and asked for the bill but he wasn't too worried as he had come to terms with the fact that he knew he would one day have to tell Charles.

Charles decided to walk home; a worried scowl on his brow. There was something about Marcus' countenance that worried him. He seemed defensive and he showed signs of relief when he had agreed to check the ring. He knew his friend had wanted to tell him something, but for some reason couldn't. Charles had had that feeling ever since the night at Kinloch Castle. He was going to make sure he would find out the whole background of this ring, however long it took, before he would give it back to him. One thing he did know, Marcus had not found it at a house clearance under a bed. Charles sensed that, if his instincts were right, the ring may also cause him and his friend trouble, big trouble.

Charles finally arrived home still in deep thought. A few weeks ago he had been told he was being considered for *Vetustus Fraternitas Antiquitas,* commonly known as the *VfA.* Despite its connotations of an old secret society it actually was an organisation known to a select few within the trade. It was a type of international brotherhood who were devoted to the protection of antiquities from the ancient worlds and stopping the racketeering. One of the ironies, of this society, was that it had been set up by the very museums and countries that had plundered most of those very treasures they were seeking to protect. It was an organisation that sought proactive and diplomatic people. Just keeping your nose clean was certainly no passport into this society.

He stood by his front door with his key in hand and recalled a conversation he had overheard the previous day that Kinloch Castle was being investigated on the quiet. Rumours had been circulating for an age about a lost treasure from the Romanov's, Charles felt the ring in his pocket. He had also recalled that he had seen the bat researcher at work in the V&A, he needed to establish exactly what was going on and why he had been at the castle. He scolded himself for mentioning Tamara to Marcus and he knew this ring could only be something to do with Marcus' change of mood since leaving Kinloch. 'I bet that little so and so stumbled on something when he was there.' He said quietly. 'I'll get it out of him.' Charles opened the door pondering his next move.

Chapter 6

Patrick Malone sat down slowly in the hidden storeroom below the southern tower. He still held the brick in his hand which he had found on the other side of the room, the realisation that the London antique dealer had taken the jewels slowly began to sink in. His hopes were dashed of finally making some money and being able to leave this desolate place. Anger grew and festered inside him; he had become sick to the pit of his stomach. He looked around at the boxes full of porcelain and glassware; he would never be able to tell their worth. His eyes rose up to the portrait of the young woman above the fake fireplace and peered at it through the dusty gloom. He wondered if it would fetch any money, but he doubted it; seeing the jewels she was wearing compounded his anger.

'I'll throttle that smarmy little shit. The *bastard…*' Malone shouted at the room and threw the brick hard against the wall. A thundering echo reverberated through the whole building.

He put his head in his hands and ground his teeth as he thought about the smug Londoner; how he must be laughing with his toffee-nosed buddy. He sat there for ages, fuming and plotting revenge, trying to think what he could do to retrieve the situation. Pulling himself together he stood up as he remembered he had received a call from the mainland that several gentlemen were on their way to the castle from Mallaig. Malone knelt by the fire and once again checked the dark hiding place up in the chimney; still nothing. He shook his head again when he finally recalled who these visitors possibly were. The Scottish National Trust had called him to tell him they were doing a spot audit and to expect them any time now. He let go of the mantle piece and sat down heavily again; his legs so weak they couldn't hold his weight. He had disturbed a small calling card, which had been under the portrait, and it fluttered down to the floor. He lit a candle and saw the Chapman Antiques calling card; his anger welled again but then a smirk emerged across his face. He stood looking at the picture again peering at the jewellery with the aid of the candle.

'I'll kill that bastard; I think I'll pay him a little visit. I'll scare the son of a bitch so much he'll be throwing money at me,' Malone snarled at the picture. 'He has a shop in London so he must be worth a bob or two, and I won't have the headache of getting rid of the bloody jewels.'

'*Malone.* Where the hell are you?' A shout rang out from the top of the corridor making Malone jump to his feet and turning quickly he stumbled over one of the boxes. Quickly he checked his watch. 'Christ and damnation, where has the morning gone?' he cursed to himself. Malone picked himself up and stood rigid for a few moments as he tried to fathom out what to do. The tapestry and the hidden panel were open.

'*Malone.*' The voice was louder and Malone could hear footsteps coming down the corridor. His secret room was about to be exposed. Panicking, an idea manifested itself in his mind and impulsively he followed his gut instinct.

'In here,' he shouted back. 'I've just discovered something really amazing.' Malone's panic had made him surprisingly nimble for his size. In a moment he had taken the picture from the wall and squeezed through the opening, jumping down into the anti-room just as Julian Appleforth, accompanied by two men, entered from the corridor.

'Oh, it's you,' said Malone, slowly puzzled as to why the recent visiting bat researcher had returned, this time dressed in smart clothes and sporting an official looking briefcase. 'I was expecting the guys from the trust for an audit.'

'They are here,' said Appleforth flicking his head sideways at the other two men, 'I'm here to assist them.'

'Assist them? You're not auditing the bloody bats now…'

'I'm here to assist in a thorough audit and search of the entire building. I'm here on behalf of the SNT *and* the V&A museum.' Julian said eyeing the portrait Malone had brought out.

'So you don't study bats then? Why were you here then, spying on people?' Malone placed the picture down and glowered at Appleforth. 'What exactly are you then and who was that woman you were with?'

'Shut up, Malone. As I said I'm here to help these gentlemen from SNT. We need to know exactly what we have here at Kinloch. We also believe there maybe a lot more than the last audit showed. You shouldn't go shouting your mouth off in the local pubs.' Julian Appleforth bent down and inspected the portrait now propped up against the wall. His interest focused on the artist's signature but age, dirt and some damage meant he couldn't quite make out a name. 'Fascinating, you know I just might know who this is,' he said quietly, almost as if thinking aloud. He looked up to see three sets of questioning eyes focused on him. 'I'll have it checked but if I'm not mistaken this could be one of the Romanov princesses. There is an uncanny resemblance about her. Unfortunately, they all came to a rather gruesome end as you're probably aware. A lot of the women however survived the first hail of bullets and…' Julian saw the disinterest in the men's eyes and stood up.

Malone took the few moments of Appleforth's interest in the painting to decide what to say. He felt decidedly defensive and decided to try and bluff his way out of the difficult situation he now found himself. He had a wrenching fear this arrogant man may have a suspicion about the jewels; Malone cursed himself for ever going into Mallaig to drink. He couldn't recall mentioning them to anyone but when he had a few drinks it affected him badly; did he mention them to this man's female assistant one night when he had tried it on with her? He turned quickly to the other men. 'I was about to take the tapestry down for cleaning and I slipped and look…,' he pointed towards the opening in the panelled wall, 'I have found a small store room. It's full of boxes and this picture; I was just bringing them all out. It felt like I was entering an old Egyptian tomb; I can tell you it was a bit scary on my own.'

'I thought you had a helper here,' asked Appleforth.

'She fell recently and is laid up. Lazy old witch, she is more of a hindrance to me then a help.' Malone said avoiding looking towards Julian Appleforth.

One of the other men came across and peered into the opening. 'Well if you have found something you'll make the newspapers,' he said straining to see what was in the store room.

'Make the newspapers! I'd expect a generous reward at least,' Malone said trying to keep the atmosphere light-hearted by laughing a little. He saw Julian give him a suspicious disdainful look. 'Do you want to go in, or shall I bring the boxes out? There is a load of them.'

Appleforth straightened up and took a few steps towards the opening then stepped through the gap in the panels and disappeared from view. Malone's heart was thumping in his chest. Should he follow?

'Have you managed to look in the boxes yet?' asked the first man to Malone as he peered into the opening after Appleforth.

Malone shook his head his attention firmly fixed on the opening. 'I've opened a couple and I think they're just full of porcelain, books and the like.' Still no sign of Appleforth. Malone moved forward and just as he came to the hidden door Julian scrambled out.

'Well Malone, it does actually seem you have stumbled on something.' Julian brushed cobwebs from his clothes. 'I don't believe for a second you stumbled on this today, in fact I am certain you haven't, but it grieves me to say all the contents do look as though they have been there for some considerable time.' Appleforth motioned to the other men. 'Right let's start the audit. I want to be away as soon as we can, and you,' he turned to Malone, 'get all those boxes out of there and place them by this wall. I'll examine them later.'

'Great, thanks a lot, not exactly the response I was expecting for finding a hidden store of antiques!' Malone turned and started to make his way through the opening.

'Malone,' said the second man that until then had not spoken or moved since he arrived. Jack Macquarie had not liked Appleforth the moment he had barged his way into his office the previous day. Jack had called the V&A asking for help, not to be railroaded by this arrogant man from London. He wasn't having him pushing his weight around too much despite his position and credentials. Malone heard authority in his deep Scottish accent and turned his head to look at him. 'Well done for finding all this,' the balding man said giving Appleforth a disdainful glance. 'It *is* appreciated, and when we sort it all out, I'll make sure you are rewarded and your find fully acknowledged. We have to make sure people are comfortable about bringing their finds to the authority's notice. Don't we Mr. Appleforth?'

Julian didn't answer and turned to stride down the corridor. An awkward silence held the three remaining men for a moment before Malone entered the store room. When he heard the other men's footsteps follow Appleforth he sat back on one of the boxes; sweat making his face and hands sticky. He might just come out of this with something, he mused. He had to keep the small bald Scot on his side; that one thought spurred him on.

The audit went on for two days and Appleforth became more impatient and agitated. There were many Russian antiques and trophies but apart from the picture, he had not found anything that could be of real interest to his research. He knew Malone had lied and he was still convinced he had found something else, but the caretaker's keenness to assist them and leave the island had confused him. It also seemed that everything else was in order and the contents of the house had not been plundered. He really wanted to get the portrait back to London and let Tamara and her team have a good look at it. He had also become exasperated that Macquarie now wanted to hold a press conference in Oban; the painting was going to be the centre piece of the find. He cursed the Scot with his quest for publicity and, he suspected, a boost to his own ego. He also knew that yet another weekend away from home would anger his wife especially as he had already missed their anniversary the last time he had stayed at Kinloch Castle.

Appleforth finally decided to play along with Macquarie's plans for a press conference and was totally at a loss as to why he was giving the fat caretaker so much attention and praise. They spent an hour in a large meeting room at The Caledonian Hotel; several of the national newspapers had picked up on the story and the room was full of journalists. What really galled him was Malone standing by the portrait expounding how he had found it and how frightening it had been entering the dark storeroom, alone. Eventually the charade was over and Appleforth told Macquarie he would send someone to help them identify the boxes of porcelain and glassware and he was taking the picture down to London. Jack Macquarie started to protest but knew it was futile.

When Julian finally entered the Victoria & Albert Museum, after the long train journey, he had managed to calm down and decided to call Tamara to tell her to come up and collect the picture for a full evaluation. He had considered telling her to return to Kinloch Castle to evaluate the contents of the boxes, but he knew she would not like this especially with the prospect of encountering the fat caretaker again. She had told him that this man had on several occasions tried to get her alone and once even tried to grope her. Tamara was a cold fish most of the time and he knew that she could look after herself but despite this he thought it would be unkind to send her back alone. Unfortunately it seemed she was away for a few days so he left a message for her to call him as soon as she returned.

The next day he walked into work and entering his office was annoyed to see the portrait was still there. He called Tamara's office only to be told that she had been delayed on her project and it was proving difficult to establish contact with her. It seemed there was another imminent panic situation regarding a potential sale of one of the treasures of yet another one of the landed gentry facing financial problems. He sighed deeply and opened up The Times on his desk. He grunted out loud as he saw the picture of Malone and Macquarie standing either side of the portrait blazoned across the front page. Julian was even more annoyed that he could clearly be seen in the background; something he had tried to avoid. He did not like any sort of publicity, but what really upset him was the headline: *Mystery Portrait found in old castle on the Isle of Rum: "Could be a Russian Princess," claims V&A expert.*

'Bloody fools,' he said slamming the paper down, the thud echoing in the empty office. He didn't want to read the small article below the picture, he knew his blood pressure was already too high. 'Freedom of the press indeed; all they want is sensationalism.' He picked up the phone again and barked a command down the phone to his secretary. He wanted to speak to his assistant no matter where she was, or how busy she claimed to be.

★ ★ ★

King's Road, London

Marcus pulled up in his old Volvo estate outside his shop and quickly went round to the back to offload a few pieces of furniture. His daughter saw him and wedged the door open, glowering back at the occasional car who tooted their horn in protest at the obstruction.

'Get lost,' she screamed. 'I'm trying to run a business here.' Marcus couldn't help but smile at his daughter, attired in tight jeans and top, men found it difficult to confront a beautiful woman. In a couple of minutes he slammed the tailgate and told his daughter he would be back as soon as he found somewhere to park. He eventually managed to slot the Volvo into a space and then return to the shop. He passed a newsagent and the sight of the billboard made him collide with a woman and her pushchair. Wincing and rubbing his leg he profusely apologised but was showered with abuse in a foreign tongue. Marcus turned and faced the billboard again:

Mystery portrait found in Scottish Castle

Marcus entered the shop tentatively and picked up the newspaper and saw the smiling, greasy face of the caretaker. Marcus felt as if a switch had been flicked off inside him. He was paralysed. A few customers tried to push past but he remained welded to the floor.

'Are you all right mate,' called out the shop keeper.

After a few moments Marcus felt himself coming round and he put the paper under his arm.

'Yes, sorry about that, I…' he took out some coins and placed them on the counter and nodding at the shopkeeper he left the shop, totally dazed.

Marcus walked to his favourite café, Giovanni's, his mind trying to reason with the shock he felt. The newspaper felt heavy under his arm as he dragged his feet. He entered the café and sat at his usual table in the corner.

'I'll have a double espresso and put a shot of grappa in it would you?' he barked at the owner behind the counter.

'A bit early isn't it Marcus,' answered the proprietor. Marcus just waved his hand at him and opened 'The Times' fully. Marcus studied the picture and read the short article several times and for a moment a sensation of relief ran through him.

Patrick Malone, the caretaker of Kinloch Castle on the Isle of Rum, has made a spectacular discovery. Whilst cleaning a tapestry, Mr. Malone, discovered a secret panel and storeroom, which had not been used for decades. Sources from the V&A Museum say the most interesting find was an unknown portrait, which may well be of a princess at the time of the last Russian Tsar, Emperor Nicholas 11. Mr. Jack Macquarie, the CEO of the Scottish Natural Trust, was quoted as saying the diligence of Mr.

Malone would be rewarded to encourage others who ever find antiques to come forward and declare them. Mr. Malone said that entering the dark room was a daunting experience but he was glad to help in such a worthy cause. He has since returned to his duties back on the island.

The fortified coffee arrived and Marcus also asked for some water, he thought Charles would be pleased with him; he always had water with coffee. Marcus sat back and picking up the cup, sipped the contents thoughtfully. He couldn't believe Malone would have gone to the SNT, or had he? At first Marcus thought that Malone would have had a handsome payout and would be happy that he had received something legally. Then a seed started to grow in his mind. What if Malone had told the authorities? Then a second terrifying thought struck him. This expert was apparently from the V&A where Charles worked. He suddenly stopped and froze again; his jaw fell open as he could just make out, in the background of the picture, a well dressed version of a person who looked remarkably like the bat researcher from Kinloch Castle.

Marcus put his head into his hands and took several deep breaths, the smell of coffee and liquor filling his nostrils. 'Those ruddy jewels have got to go,' he whispered into his hands. He then remembered the ring he had given to Charles. 'Oh shit, this may stir up a ruddy hornet's nest. Charles is going to be furious.'

'What's that Marcus,' said Giovanni, bringing him the water. 'Same again?' Marcus nodded and stared at the front page laid out on the table, but he was unable to focus properly. A strange sensation filled him of being completely out of control like slipping down an icy piste in a snow storm. His thoughts were curtailed by the familiar face of his daughter looking around the door.

'There you are, Dad. I was getting worried…' She came in and stopped in front of him and picked up the empty coffee cup, sniffing at the remnants. 'A bit early isn't it?'

Marcus folded the paper slowly trying not to bring her

attention to the picture on the centre of the front page. 'Good god, girl. I'm old enough to be your dad,' he tried to joke but his voice squeaked and it sounded like almost a hiss.

'Very funny, but when you've finished we've got to get the new pieces into position; I can't manage it all by myself. We also need to discuss what price to put on them. Come on Dad, let's get going…' As she opened the door she glanced back at her father, who had slumped back in his chair and was looking up at the ceiling. In that instance she knew she would call Charles and let him know about her father's continuing strange behaviour.

★ ★ ★

KGB Headquarters, Moscow 1997

Colonel Andrei Suslov entered his office, passing his assistant; he nodded at him and placed his brief case on the floor by the desk. His morning newspapers were laid out as usual and his assistant hovered around waiting for the daily order of strong Italian coffee and fresh orange juice from Florida. Andrei may despise the West but he enjoyed the creature comforts they afforded him.

'What are you waiting for man,' he shouted at the nervous assistant. 'You know what I have.' He smiled to himself for he would have scalded his assistant, a weak timid boy, if he had dared to anticipate his needs. He took out a file from his brief case and placed it on the desk in front of him, examining it for a few moments before shutting it away in a drawer and locking it. In these days of Yeltsin and his West loving government, a file on Westerners who were corrupt and ripe for approaching now seemed irrelevant. Life was changing rapidly in Russia as greed and corruption meant the old ways were dying quickly. He didn't even trust his new assistant and he certainly wouldn't let him see anything sensitive that went across his desk.

Suslov tensed his jaw as once again his assistant had laid out his papers with all the American journals on top. He quickly discarded them and browsed over the pink coloured Financial Times. His assistant finally arrived with his bone china cup and saucer, matching sugar bowl and a very delicate, ornate silver spoon. A few seconds later he brought the orange juice; a slight froth clinging to the sides of the Waterford crystal. Andrei nodded, waved him away and moved the drinks to the side of the desk.

The Russian Colonel checked the back page of the Financial Times and then placed it to one side. Andrei had a habit of spreading out the full broadsheet of The Times and smoothing out the creases. It was one of his pleasures every morning, drinking good coffee and reading the best of the western newspapers. He enjoyed the tirade of stories about how life was so bad in the West; it never ceased to cheer him up. He picked up his cup and saucer and started to read. The centre picture caused Suslov to recoil back in shock sending coffee all over his uniform. He choked as he saw the portrait on the front page; he instantly recognised the Romanov likeness. A lifetime of pursuing the old royal family meant he didn't have to look twice. His hands started to shake and he could not control the chatter of the cup and saucer. He managed to place them on the desk noticing the assistant sliding a sideways glance towards him.

'Dear god!' Suslov opened the drawer to his right and extracted a large brass handled magnifying glass. Stooping forward he strained through the glass to look at the face of the young woman in the picture. 'Where did she spring from,' he muttered to himself. He turned and barked at his assistant who rose, gave a small bow of the head, and quickly left the room.

Andrei went to a cupboard and pulled out a slim clear bottle. Unscrewing the cap he measured out several slugs into his orange juice and took a large mouthful, it sent an involuntary shiver down his body but the warming liquid soothed him. He picked up the paper and read the article.

'Sir,' a voice came from behind him. His assistant stood there holding a damp cloth and a small white towel.

'Thank you,' said the colonel. Taking the wet cloth first he rubbed the coffee stains and then dried them off with the towels. The young soldier stood tentatively in front of him. 'Go and fetch me a detailed road map of Great Britain.' The assistant took the towel and cloth and turned to leave the room.

Andrei sat down heavily on his chair and once again picked up the paper staring at the portrait. 'My god, it just might be true,' he whispered. His assistant entered the room and placed the large blue RAC map book on the desk. He started to return to his desk when his colonel spoke. 'I will not be needing you today, Mikhail. Go and see that young girl of yours.'

'Thank you comrade colonel, but…'

'Just go Mikhail, in the name of God, just go.' The assistant saluted and left making several glances behind him.

Suslov sat back in his chair and looked at the black and white photograph of his grandfather hanging on the wall in front of him. 'Well Grandfather, it looks as if another Romanov bitch has reared her ugly head again. I thought I'd finished the last one off for good when that impersonator finally died, but no, the book by her bastard husband Manahan continued her story, and now this.'

Colonel Suslov looked proudly at the picture on the wall. To have your grandfather as one of the squad which finally ended the Romanov dynasty had been a true honour to the family and especially Andrei. Like his father before, they had carried on the quest to extinguish any semblance of a direct line to the Tsar, however remote. It had become even more necessary when the likes of Anna Anderson, as she had been known, had come forward claiming to be the Tsar's offspring and rightful heir to the throne. He shook his head as he imagined Yeltsin falling over himself, literally, to welcome back their "rightful" monarch. His body shuddered again. Over his dead body, he thought.

Suslov opened the map book and turned to the pages of North West Scotland. Making a few notes he went to a filing cabinet and unlocked it. Taking out an old leather bound book he flicked through the pages, eventually stopping. He jotted down a number and then placed it back in the drawer. He picked up the phone and pressed a red button on the front before he dialled. A few minutes later he relaxed back in his chair a satisfied smile on his face. He loved putting the wheels of motion into one of his plans, especially when it involved this particular agent. She had been one of his best recruits; he had manipulated such a marvellous hold over her. He started to laugh out loud as he recalled her lying helpless and struggling on the bed and how she had begged for her father's life; best of all, he recalled, was her young sister. How delicious she had been. His uncontrolled laughter now filled the room.

* * *

Kinloch Castle, Isle of Rhum 1997

Malone spent the next day clearing up the mess from the store room, and started preparing for some guests who were booked in for the weekend. He had ordered the provisions and soon he would have to go down to the jetty and collect them when the ferry arrived. It had been decided that the secret room would be made a feature of the castle so he was trying to make it presentable. Malone had still been wondering whether to call up the wretched antique dealer from London and put the frighteners on him. Maybe he could get some money from him; but he was, after all, the hero now. He wondered if it was worth all the hassle now that he had been given some recompense, albeit small; it was legal. Malone checked he still had Marcus' calling card in his breast pocket and, patting it, sneered as he contemplated what he would like to do to the arrogant Londoner.

Malone could just hear the distant toot from the ferry's horn and he quickly went round to the rear of the building to collect the large trolley he used for transporting the provisions back to the castle. He saw all his supplies being offloaded onto the jetty and his heart sank as to the size of the large pile. Just as he approached, the ferry tooted its horn again and started to depart. A person was approaching him, quickly and decisively, from the crofts to his left. Malone checked as he recognised the face instantly and by its expression he knew there was trouble in the air. He recalled the last time they had met and panic filled him.

Malone had no reservations for that night and was further confused that this person wasn't carrying any sort of luggage at all. Why had he been so stupid to upset guests, he thought?

'It's good to see you again…' began Malone but was answered with a curt nod. Malone's fear grew to panic and he decided to make a run for it. He turned round and started to lumber back towards the castle.

Not daring to turn around he managed to make the back courtyard where he stumbled through the door only to be faced by the dog snarling at him. 'Piss off you blasted mutt!' he hissed and kicked out at the dog sending it scampering and whimpering into a corner.

He locked the large back kitchen door behind him, cursing that the old woman would be resting in her bed while he was in danger. He turned quickly and ran, breathing heavily, towards the front door. Just as he entered the hallway he saw the front door was open and he knew he was not alone. His unwanted visitor came out from the shadows underneath the stairs and Malone saw the flash of the long thin blade being taken from its sheath; it was all he needed to see. He turned on his heels, fright producing an inner strength and thundered down the corridor towards the hidden room. His heart was thumping loudly in his chest when he saw the door to the tower. He heard footsteps close behind him and wrenching open the door he slammed it behind him climbing the narrow twisting tower steps, finally stumbling out onto the roof his lungs rasping for air. The footsteps from behind him ceased and Malone turned to see a tight thin smile. He had to do something and quickly; what did this person want? Then he remembered, could he have mentioned the jewels…

'Look I haven't got them. I swear the antique dealer has got them…' Malone backed away from the blade and froze holding onto the low parapet. Malone grappled with his breast pocket and finally brought out the Chapman Antiques card. 'He's got them, please believe me.'

'Them?' His assailant took a step forward and snatched the card.

'The jewels. I told you about them, didn't I? That's what you've come for isn't it?' Malone looked bemused and started to take a pace forward as a moment of courage surged through him as he saw his assailant also looking slightly confused. He made a grab for the card and in a flash the knife was pulled back ready to lunge at him. His panic returned and he stumbled back hitting the low wall. He made an unsuccessful grab for support as he somersaulted backwards into thin air. Malone's body made a sickening thud on the front path. The visitor showed no sign of emotion or surprise, and just stepped forward to see the caretaker lying disjointedly below, his body still apart from spasmodic twitching and a slight movement of the head.

Malone thoughts were only of hatred for the antique dealer who had brought this on him. He coughed and warm fluid filled his mouth as he looked up to see the old woman's face peering out of the window at him. He tried to shout defiantly at her as a faint smile crossed her face; the sound of snarling arrested his weakening thoughts. With his last spark of consciousness he focused on the unblinking steely eyes of the black and white collie. Malone tried to cry out but only a mumble came out as the animal crept stealthfully forward. Sensing the life was flowing out of his tormentor the dog saw the chance to attack. Saliva drivelling from the side of its mouth, it bared its teeth again and braced for the lunge at the prostrate man. The old woman smiled and turned away returning to her bed. She would let the dog have its fun before she called for help.

The visitor watched the dog attack and sheathed the blade cursing. Making quick progress downstairs the assailant pushed through the front door; the collie retreated slightly but was still snarling and growling. Stooping over the crumpled figure of the caretaker, the calling card was re-placed back into the dead man's shirt pocket. The visitor quickly glanced around; apart from the snarling dog no other sound could be heard except for the constant wind rustling the trees and the lap of the waves by the shoreline. Even the seagulls had gone quiet. The assailant stepped over the dead body and trotted purposefully towards the jetty, as the dog edged forward towards the caretaker's body again.

★ ★ ★

V&A Museum, London 1997

Julian Appleforth was, at last, looking forward to a weekend with his family. The last few days had been the typical scramble to raise funds to save a masterpiece from auction. He had become weary of the moans and demands of the wealthy demanding support to protect their own treasures. How they could expect special treatment for the treasures that they had bought on the back of others toil always rubbed against his socialist principles. He started to clear the desk and noticed that the portrait had gone. Tamara had called him and had promised to start a full investigation the following week. He had heard that her attempts to save a Rubens had failed and she had taken it personally; as she always did.

He had agreed that she could take a few days off, and he wondered if it was to visit a sister she had mentioned on several occasions; it seems they were very close. Tamara was childless and she had told him once she loved to play the doting aunt, but then he recalled the sister lived somewhere in Eastern Europe. It pleased him that she seemed so appreciative of his agreement to the sudden holiday, she had even promised to make it up to him; language he had never heard from her before. The woman was a bit of a mystery to him. She had no boy friend and he had once wondered if she had a different sexual persuasion, but this had been dispelled by her quite obvious interest with the antique dealer she had met at Kinloch Castle. Maybe she liked a 'bit of rough' and he sighed; he would never understand women.

He zipped up his document case and checked his watch when the phone burst into life. His secretary had left early so he answered to hear James Pulford on the line. Stammering, as he had never normally would have expected such a high ranking official to speak to him directly, he listened to Pulford in disbelief. When Pulford had finished, Julian acknowledged he had understood and closed his eyes and breathing heavily. He looked at his watch again and decided not to phone home as he knew his wife would be outraged if he called her to say he would be late again.

He packed his briefcase and headed upstairs towards the senior official's office. Why this man would take an interest in Tamara and the portrait was beyond him, but all Julian could concentrate on was how to placate his wife for missing yet another dinner party.

* * *

KGB Headquarters, Moscow 1997

Andrei Suslov listened intently for several minutes, occasionally interjecting a word and nodding his head if he agreed with a point. He scribbled a few notes holding the phone under his chin. In the chair in front of him sat an old man, his watery eyes gazing about him. Andrei sent the occasional smile to his father sitting very still and rigidly on the other side of the desk. He placed the receiver down and taking a deep breath picked up the glass of water in front of him.

'Well father, it seems the plot thickens. My agent has just informed me that the portrait of the young woman, which was discovered in Scotland, is not one of the Tsar's daughters, as I had thought. However, by the jewellery she is wearing and her features, especially her nose, she is actually in all likelihood, a

Romanov of some sort.' Andrei came around the desk and filled up his father's water glass from a large jug. 'It is a bit of a mystery as to exactly who she is,' he continued whilst returning to his chair. 'That's not all, for by coincidence and you know what I think about coincidences, one of the museum's staff has handed in a very elaborate and ornate ring which, it seems, could well be traced back to the Tsar. They believe it could be part of a suite of jewels which was made for a person who was a particular favourite of Nicholas. They are trying to establish whom as we speak.'

'Are you sure she isn't one of the larger family,' said Arsenevich Suslov; his voice strong and clear for a man of his age. 'Christ they all inter-married so much she may be from any of several countries.'

'Well, that's what my contact originally thought, but there is no one that fits her description.' Andrei went and retrieved his notes from his desk. 'Under closer examination they found an inscription on the back of the painting which had been all but obliterated. It read, "Lady Xenia, my dearest love child".' Andrei saw his father choke and his eyes bulged as he made a desperate attempt to cough. 'Father...' shouted the Colonel and quickly rounded the desk to help the old man. After a few moments the old man regained his composure.

'Are you...' muttered Suslov but Arsenevich indicated for his son to be still. Adjusting his position he looked firstly at the photograph on the wall of his father and then back to his son and taking out a handkerchief mopped his brow, dabbed his eyes and wiped the moisture from around his mouth. He then started to talk; his voice weak.

'Your grandfather once told me of a rumour that had been started by one of the Tsar's translators. It was many years before the revolution but he claimed he had been at a meeting where Nicholas had admitted to an Englishman of a love child he had fathered, called Xenia, who, it is believed, also had a child out of wedlock. I can't remember the full account because it was thought this man was a bit of a story teller and was making money from it. Incidentally he paid for his loose tongue with his life. Andrei, there is a file on this somewhere, or used to be.' The old man took some deep breaths. 'Are you sure they think this ring is part of a set?'

The old man's son checked his notes and nodded slowly.

'Oh my god. If the story is true then this and the other jewels were to be some sort of dowry. They were originally called Xenia's jewels but they became known as the *Stones of Conscience.*'

'What? The Stones of Conscience, why were they called that?'

'Oh, how old age confuses the mind.' Arsenevich took a sip of water. 'I believe that the jewels were a gift to Xenia, from the Tsar, but after her death they were given to her child, or more accurately to the father, an Englishman. None of the Tsar's women folk would have the jewels because they deemed them to be cursed hence the name. If I am not mistaken it was history repeating itself, and sounded so far fetched it was unbelievable, but this Englishman took the baby back to England. Andrei you must find the file. There could be a direct descendant to the Tsar Nicholas still out there. I am certain Xenia's mother was royalty as well.' The man looked up at the photograph on the wall and then looked away; his face showing a tinge of shame.

Andrei could read his father's eyes. 'Father, if there is a blood line still out there, then trust me I will not allow it to exist for long. As Colonel Andrei Losif Suslov I promise you I will ensure no Romanov will ever come back to haunt the motherland.' The colonel turned, picked up the phone, and pressed the red button. A few moments later he was in deep discussion with his British agent. Will we ever be rid of these Romanovs, he muttered?

Andrei's father listened to the telephone conversation and watched his son sit back with a satisfied smile when the call finished.

'You seem to enjoy a hold over that person?' He asked slowly.

118

'Believe me Father, she will do anything I ask her, anything…'
Andrei laughed again and went to retrieve his vodka from the
drawer. He did not notice the sadness in his father's eyes.

★ ★ ★

The King's Road, London 1997

Marcus sat in the small office at the back of the shop looking at
the photograph of his daughter as a toddler, with her proud
parents dotting over her. He was taken slightly aback as a tear
formed in his eye. He felt a feeling of isolation, an emptiness that
was starting to worry him. It wasn't soon after this photograph
had been taken that he started to drift away from his young wife.
He hadn't really found anybody since. Many, too many,
unattached relationships, he had insisted on that, had come to
nothing. Then he thought about the young woman he had met
in Kinloch Castle. It was a strange feeling one of longing, not lust.
He just wished he could get to know her better. He sensed a
loneliness within her, how he would love to help. He checked the
clock on the wall, went to the front door and, after unlocking it,
ambled back to his office.

Dawn and Toby had just left for a night away by themselves.
A few months ago he would have baulked at the idea, but now he
thought a night of young love in an old pub in Hertfordshire
would do his daughter the world of good. Dawn had over the last
few months started to take control of the administration and sales
of the shop. At first he didn't like the interference but now he let
her rule the roost. He was looking forward to having the place
back to himself for awhile, and he was determined to do
something with the original jewellery box. What really set his
juices running was the thought of the jewels themselves, still
hidden away in the loft. It made his head swim. He made a mental
note to call Charles to see if he had anything on the ring he had
given him.

His mind wandered back to Tamara when the buzzer sounded and Marcus was brought back from his daydreaming. He entered the room to be confronted by the side-on view of a perfectly proportioned womanly silhouette. The sun was shining and he could clearly see the shape of her fine bosom through the thin fabric of the blouse. His eyes drifted down almost mesmorised by the sight and the skirt that held her buttocks together tightly while slender brown legs were supported by tall stiletto shoes. The style was classical but with a hint of sensuality.

She turned her head and the sun shone through her shoulder length light brown hair making him squint. Her heart raced as she saw Marcus standing speechless and ogling her openly. It had been the first time she had ever dressed to be noticed by a man; the effect on Marcus excited her. She looked away starting to examine a vase.

Marcus squinted in the sunlight and could still not make out the features of her face. 'Good morning,' he said clearing a tightness that had suddenly developed in his throat. 'Marcus Chapman, how can I help you today…'

Marcus had now come round into the shop and then he instantly recognised the woman standing so demurely in front of him, but he just couldn't remember where they had met. She was examining a small vase on one of the old sideboards, which was not one of Marcus' better buys. The woman turned again and flashed her eyes at him releasing a patient and understanding smile. Marcus shuffled and made a polite cough and he felt completely tongue tied. For a moment he sensed the woman was watching him out of the corner of her eye; Marcus thought for a brief second that she looked very like the woman at Kinloch Castle but this woman dressed so much more smartly and wore a little makeup. He wasn't sure it was her but he hoped it was his lady from the island; he felt a weakness in his legs in expectation.

'I am not surprised.'

Marcus was completely bemused by the remark. 'I'm sorry I,

err, didn't quite catch that.' He still couldn't be sure but the slight inflection in the voice made him virtually certain it was her. He also sensed she was playing games with him, but he was rather enjoying it.

'I am not surprised you don't recognise me,' she repeated. This time she turned and faced him and placed her handbag on the table beside them. Then she looked straight at him. Her eyes, to Marcus, were the most recognisable feature of her, and he held her look as a smile of recognition widened on his face.

'I definitely recognise you; how could I ever forget. Although…' Marcus waved his hands at her outfit. 'Wow, you look great.'

'I hoped you wouldn't forget me, I did hope you weren't just flirting with me a few weeks ago,' said the woman turning and surveying the shop. A smile radiated from her and she made sure they made eye contact every few seconds.

Marcus still remained speechless as he took in her beauty. He desperately tried not to stare at her, but he just couldn't resist a quick glance over her figure. Then panic struck as for a moment he had forgotten her name.

'Yes, it was quite a night,' said Marcus taking a step back when suddenly, like a bolt from the blue, her name burst back into his memory. 'Blimey, what can I say? My old man would say something totally inappropriate now like, "you scrub up well".' They both broke into laughter. 'Tamara, I hope you don't mind but I've thought a lot about you since…'

'Slow down Marcus, I'm only here looking at antiques,' but she flashed a sideways glance, matched with a coy look, that made Marcus' heart miss a beat. She spied a small figurine in the display cabinet and bent down a little to inspect it knowing Marcus would be watching every move of her body, especially now her derriere was definitely on show.

Tamara thought he looked in good condition and he had clearly lost some weight, she thought, glancing back at him again making sure he was watching her body sway. She could see him standing there, unable to take his eyes off her. She enjoyed her hold over him and loved his round, open, happy face and those eyes of his were like dark smouldering embers. She felt as if they were searching straight into her soul. She bit her lip trying to pull herself together, cursed her life and the fact that she was with this man on false pretences. She had met a man she liked and now she was here to deceive him, or even worse.

'Oh, what I meant was... I am sorry but women have the advantage of makeup; it does make a difference. In your case, if I may say, a marked improvement...' He stopped, realising what he was implying.

'Oh, I looked a mess did I?' She said straightening up and turning towards him.

'No, no, that is not what I meant, what I meant was...'

'Stop digging yourself a hole Marcus,' she gave him a warm smile leaving Marcus feeling weak at the knees. 'I was a bloody awful mess up there. Uncle Julian wouldn't let me put on even a touch of blusher. So the fact you spent the entire dinner talking, or should I say, chatting me up, was a real compliment and I appreciated it.'

'Ah, good, well you see, I believe beauty is only skin deep,' said Marcus relieved that he hadn't offended her and starting to grasp that this woman did actually fancy him.

'It was a shame you rushed off without so much as a "by your leave"...'

'Ah, yes. Well that's Charles for you. He is a stickler for getting the early tide. Maybe I could make amends and buy you dinner?'

Tamara didn't answer and sauntered over to some more ornaments. Marcus knew his next question had to the right one; he cleared his throat. Time to change the subject he thought. Don't be too heavy. 'Do you have any particular era or type of antiques that you are after?'

'I live in a tiny flat so I collect porcelain figures, figurines, that sort of thing,' she pointed back towards the cupboard, 'but my main interest if Faberge, especially his eggs. In fact that is not

122

strictly true for I also collect anything from Russia from the seventeenth to nineteenth century, but I am, like the Tsars, particularly fond of Faberge, however it is so expensive...' She looked questioningly and lent forward on a chair; a small but tantalising show of cleavage meant Marcus found it hard not to take another glance downwards; this time his eyes lingered on her slightly open blouse. 'I'm also interested in old jewellery, mainly from Eastern European and especially Russian.'

A silence gripped the room as Marcus gazed at her like a love struck school boy; she kept her pose, but eyed the room casually allowing her hair to fall onto her chest hiding the cleavage. Eventually she saw a picture on a table in the corner. She glided over to it, her hips swaying gracefully, and looking briefly back at Marcus her eyes became wide and searching.

'Now this is real beauty,' she said turning and picking up a silver frame.

'Yes, it's Georgian...'

'Not the frame, silly. Who is this girl, or is that a stupid question? She has your eyes, hair and complexion.' Tamara took the framed photograph to the window. 'She is stunning; you must be very proud. Youth is wasted on the young, I think the saying goes.' She looked back at Marcus who was having problems concentrating due to all his senses being on overload. As she had passed him he smelt a delicate fragrance of soap and that warm scent of a sensual body.

He became light headed and finally pulled himself round. 'Yes, that is my daughter, Dawn. She lives with me now.'

'You told me you were single. You men, such fibbers,' she turned towards him supporting a small pout.

'No, I'm...'

'You're divorced, aren't you?'

Marcus nodded. 'A long time ago. I don't count it as a mistake because the result was Dawn, and she is not only a stunner, but a thoroughly good kid as well.'

Tamara took the photograph back and gently placed it on the

table, taking a pace back to check it was central. 'So are you single at the moment, or was that the usual male bullshit?'

Marcus could tell she hadn't wanted to ask such a direct question. For a fraction of a second he felt paralysed like prey, cowering in an open field on hearing the screech of an eagle overhead. His eyes wandered back onto her slim curvy body and he stepped towards he, a wide grin forming on his mouth.

'Yes, very single at the moment and no word of a lie, so you had better watch your step, because I'm hungry for love.' He attempted to sing the last few words. 'It just so happens your luck is in.' Marcus was not going to let her have it all her own way. The woman in front of him raised her eyebrows questioningly. Marcus had started to get his act together and stopped drooling like a frustrated dog. 'But I will have to take you to my bedroom; I have something to show you.'

'I bet you do,' her voice turned suddenly stern and cold, her accent more pronounced. She stood up quickly folding her arms across her. The memory of those nights, so long ago, still haunted her and she was still prone to panic attacks. She mustn't lose her control and she swished her head side wards taking in a deep breath of air. She tried to cover her outburst with a smile but knew it was forced and that Marcus' looked confused and a touch dejected. Not all men are the same she told herself but the thought of going to a bedroom with a man still gripped her with utter fear. They looked at each other for a few moments; neither knowing what to do.

'Sorry, that was totally thoughtless of me, I was only jesting, seriously Tamara. I was actually talking about a fine antique I have just acquired. I didn't mean to offend you and I…' Marcus blushed and shuffled nervously. 'I'll go and fetch it. I'm really sorry Tamara; I really didn't mean any offence. I'm actually quite harmless,'

'I don't believe that for a minute.'

Marcus felt relief in Tamara's softer tone of voice, a lump had developed in his throat and he cursed his forwardness and terrible attempt at humour. He went through the arch, took a deep breath and was about to ascend the steps when he felt her presence behind him. Looking round he saw her smiling and supporting a submissive and apologetic look. She shrugged her shoulders and then caught sight of the old safe in the office.

'Ah, that's where you keep all your booty is it?' She stepped into the small office. 'Wow, that's an antique in itself.'

'Yeah, but a good friend of mine tells me it's about as useful as a chocolate poker.'

Tamara threw her head back and roared. 'Chocolate poker, I love that.'

Marcus felt his heart miss a beat again, as she laughed. She was a real beauty and he had the urge to take her into his arms and give her a long burning kiss; the moment passed. Tamara bent down to inspect the safe and studied it curiously. She stood up and the picture that Marcus had been looking at, a few minutes ago, came into her view. 'This is your wife?'

'Yes, ex-wife.'

'Well, she is beautiful. It must have been a painful break up? Will you tell me all about her and what happened one day?' she turned and flicked her hair over her shoulder allowing her blouse to slightly open again. Marcus controlled his wandering eyes and brushed his hair back with his hand.

'If you really want, but it is the usual story I'm afraid, no real juicy bits, we just met too young. Look I can fetch the antique down, it won't take a tick.'

'No, I'm right behind you.' Tamara followed Marcus upstairs and with every step she felt her muscles tighten involuntarily.

Marcus went round the landing and pointed towards the lounge door. 'You can wait in there if you want, my bedroom looks like a bomb has hit at the moment.'

'No it's OK, I trust you,' Tamara said carefully making mental notes of the layout of the rooms.

Marcus went into the bedroom and rummaged through his underwear drawer taking out the damaged box and handing it to her.

'Why, may I ask, have you kept it in a drawer in your bedroom?'

'Ah, bit of a long story,' Marcus stuttered and placed the box in her hands.

'Oh, it is beautiful. Look at the workmanship on the silver,' she said putting it down on the old dressing table. 'What a pity it has been… She then noticed the monogram on the lid of the box; her heart missed a beat. She was certain it was the same as the ring Charles Ashford had brought in; the sign of the Romanovs.'

Marcus saw her pause but thought it was due to the damaged front. 'Don't worry about that I already have someone who is going to repair it and make a new key for the lock.' Marcus stepped forward and opened it revealing the heavy velvet embroidered lining. 'It's something isn't it?'

'Where did you get it?' asked Tamara taking a small step towards Marcus and their arms brushed against each other.

'I can't reveal my sources,' teased Marcus. 'But let's say a few weeks ago you weren't too far away from where I purchased it.' Marcus suddenly flushed at telling her where he had obtained it. The woman didn't react for a moment and she twisted her torso slightly and brushed her bosom against Marcus' arm. Marcus was mesmerised. 'I also found an old book, first edition I think.' He went to his shelf and fumbling behind the shelf pulled out the book. Tamara quickly looked at it and, noting the title and author, placed it back on the shelf. The caretaker had been right she now knew Marcus had them. She stood gazing at the box but found that she couldn't concentrate as her mind was racing. A thought had ripped through her with such clarity and purpose that she struggled to keep her composure. She took a pace towards Marcus and placing the box down looked up at him.

Marcus could hear his own heart as if it were a drum being beaten on a military parade ground. He mirrored her movement and they stood barely an inch apart as if a magnetic force was pulling them towards each other, their bodies touched slightly. Marcus could feel her firm nipples protruding through her clothes and brushing against his rib cage. He bent his head and their lips brushed. The scent from her body filled his senses and he could hear her breathing, which had quickened considerably, as had his. He lifted his left arm and placed his hand softly on her hip and they made the briefest of embraces searching into each other's eyes.

The sound of the buzzer from down stairs made them both jump. In an instant she flung her arms around his neck embracing him with an intense kiss, which made Marcus grab her waist with both arms pulling her body into him.

'My handbag, it's downstairs,' she said not disengaging her grip around his neck.

'Damn, yes, I must go and see to the customers…'

'Can I take the box?'

'No, I will get it repaired first, and I don't know how…'

'Please!'

'No, but I will make you a promise, when it is fixed properly and you kiss me like that again, then it's yours; I give you my word.'

Tamara gave him a brief peck on the neck and released him Feeling cheated and disappointed they went downstairs together silently; Marcus following behind her, unable to take his eyes off her slim form. She stopped abruptly at the bottom of the stairs and he heard a man's voice. Passing Tamara, he entered the shop to be confronted by two men. Instantly he knew they were police.

'Oh, I was upstairs…'

'Mr. Chapman, Marcus Chapman?' Asked the older one more interested in the woman standing behind the antique dealer.

'I must go, darling,' said Tamara and giving Marcus a kiss on the cheek, pressing herself against him for an instant. She flashed a sultry smile at him and left the shop, leaving the three men staring at her swaying figure, like rabbits caught in a car headlight. She was astonished at the effect she was having on men. She did not mind being dressed like this for Marcus but otherwise she felt cheap; she told herself to go back to her usual style.

When she was out of view the older policeman broke the silence.

'I'm sorry Mr. Chapman is this an inconvenient moment?'

'Believe me, you have no idea how inconvenient that was,' sighed Marcus.

'I'm sorry sir. I am Detective Inspector Dave Hines and this is Detective Sergeant Paul Macleod from the Metropolitan Police,' continued the officer slightly uncomfortable at the situation he had clearly interrupted. 'May we ask a few questions?'

'Of course let me close up and we can use the back office. Marcus went to the door, bolted it and turned the 'open' sign around. He ushered them into the small office while bringing in another chair. He kept thinking which piece of antique he was going to be quizzed on now. 'So how can I help you,' he said settling down.

'Do you know a Mr. Patrick Malone?' The younger man took out a notebook ready to take notes. Marcus became a touched alarmed having instantly recalled the name, but felt he had to tread carefully.

'Err no, well yes, his name does actually ring a bell...' Marcus tried to bide for some time. The only reason they would be asking him about the caretaker would be to do with the jewels, he thought.

The younger man pulled out a glossy print of the portrait flanked by Malone and another man. It was the picture from the Times the other day. The younger policeman pointed to Malone. 'This is Patrick Malone, a caretaker at Kinloch Castle...'

'Oh yes, of course that's Mooney...'

'Mooney?'

'Yes, we nick named him Mooney. I had been sailing up in Scotland a few weeks ago with some friends and we stayed at Kinloch Castle. Why?'

The older man lent forward and glowered at Marcus. 'We found your calling card on his body...'

'Body! You mean he's dead? But how?'

The older detective slowly nodded his head and sat back pleased with Marcus' reaction so far. Hines sensed this man was hiding something. Years of experience meant he could smell guilt a mile off.

'But you don't think I had... Look I gave him my card because he was interested in...' Marcus felt sick and decidedly weak. The two men were sitting impassively in front of him watching him squirm. Marcus closed his eyes and cursed; from sheer heaven to utter hell in a few seconds...

★ ★ ★

Tamara left the shop and walked briskly towards the V&A museum. She ignored the men's eyes trying to watch her surreptitiously while they walked along with their own women. She didn't even hear the whistles and calls from passing cars, or seemed to care that her breasts were joggling noticeably due to her fast pace. She walked through the main entrance of the V&A and made her way to the third floor. She slowed as she walked through the silver section and paused, finally going into the sacred silver and stain glass gallery. She sauntered down past the cabinets, where she had spent so many hours in the past and still marvelled at the exquisite pieces. Breathing heavily she stopped at some of the pieces. If only she could have a faith that could make her produce such beautiful objects; she could sense the love and faith wrapped up within them. All, she had ever experienced was fear, until now.

Tamara entered the National Art Library and, showing her ID card, went through into the far section. A few minutes later she located the book she needed in the index, but it was in the upper gallery, which had been roped off. Returning to the centre section she waited until the warder was looking away. Hitching her skirt up she stepped over the rope onto the metal spiral stairs. Hearing some giggling she noticed a group of students who were admiring a good view of virtually all her legs. She turned and scowled at them making them put their heads down; she was getting sick and tired of her outfit. Scaling the stairs she went along the mezzanine, keeping close to the books to make sure the students below couldn't see her. She found the book and slipped it into her bag just as the chatter and giggling below brought the attention of the warder. He shouted up and was also taken aback at the sight of one of the researchers on the top level. He called up and Tamara came forward and waved at him. The old man quickly looked away in case he could see too much of the woman. Tamara was grateful that some men showed respect.

Tamara gracefully came down the stairs and apologised to the old caretaker who was still blushing a little as he fumbled to untie the rope at the bottom of the stairs; he didn't want her to sense he had actually seen a little up her skirt. Giving the students a withering look she returned to her department and her desk. She sat at her desk totally perplexed. She had been horrified at the effect her new outfit had had on men, but excited about Marcus' reaction. She was also starting to fantasise at how she would have liked Marcus to have been sitting in the library looking up at her. She wouldn't have kept so close to the books. She suddenly swore under her breath. 'Damn, damn, not now, not him…' She felt a tear pricking her eye and she bit her lip and thought about her father and sister. Marcus was cute, but she knew where her loyalties lay. She cursed again and slammed the book closed in front of her, then her body made an involuntary shiver as she remembered she had to call Colonel Suslov.

Chapter 7

Marcus opened the door to his shop. He had been deprived of his passport and a whole afternoon's trading. Dawn would be furious and start asking questions. The darkest cloud though was not the five hours being questioned by the police, or his daughter's impending suspicious anger, but that he had no idea how to contact Tamara. He was furious with himself for not having asked for her number. He had acted like a teenager on his first date, desperately fumbling for words on a dance floor.

Marcus trudged up the stairs still muttering to the empty house. He went into the fridge and searched for something quick and light to eat; nothing took his fancy. He considered opening a bottle of wine and having a liquid dinner, but he could not make light of the situation that was developing around him. How could the police seriously have thought he had killed Malone? He cursed out loud at having left Malone his calling card, but they eventually had to admit he wouldn't have left his business card at a scene of a crime. He was certain they were fishing for something else. They could have easily checked that he had been in London, he remembered freezing when they questioned him about whether had taken anything from the castle. He felt the older detective had spotted his nervousness. He was also furious they wanted his passport, but when he agreed they did seem to soften on him. He should have called his solicitor, but he knew that Dawn would probably find out, as she was very friendly with him. He wanted to keep this all well and truly away from her prying mind.

Marcus went out to a Chinese take-away, but he just picked at it and sipping a can of beer he finally discarded most of the meal and went to bed. He retired to his bedroom and smelt Tamara's lingering scent in the room. A pang of loneliness hit him and he looked at his bed and fantasised for a moment. Then he saw the jewellery box still on his dressing table and picking it up gently placed it back in the drawer. Marcus undressed flinging himself onto the bed and tried to sleep, but he just tossed and turned becoming hot and fidgety. Finally he went to the kitchenette and made himself some warm milk. He smiled at the thought of what his friends would say; the great party king, Marcus Chapman, spent Saturday night with a mug of warm milk. His body fidgeted and so he sat up in bed and reached for the book that had been with the jewels. He was still angry about the torn out pages but then realised it may actually give him a clue as to why the book was with the jewels.

He checked the contents; the section missing was the legend of the missing Lady Xenia. Marcus' mind kept drifting and he could only concentrate on the touch of Tamara's bosom against his arm that morning. He closed his eyes hard and hoped, virtually prayed, she would contact him again.

He attempted to sleep again but sat there looking at the shadows on the ceiling and the rumble of traffic outside. Suddenly he pulled the bed clothes back and picking up the set of step ladders from the store cupboard he struggled up the stairs and setting the steps out he opened the hatch. He crawled to the hidden humidor, which housed the jewels, his knees still sore from his last foray into the attic. Taking them down stairs he tipped the jewels from the top tray onto his bed, and then placed the suite of jewels separately.

He took the humidor downstairs and, after a brief polish, placed it on a table by the window and went into the small study. He then took a few items of stationery from a drawer of his desk and climbed back upstairs. Carefully untangling the diamond necklace and the matching bracelet, earrings and broach, he placed them in a velvet pouch he had found in a house clearance. He then made a mental note to call Charles again and ask what he had managed to find out about the ring. He scrambled up to the top floor and climbed the stepladders and crawled to the far side of the attic. He unwound some tough garden twine and tied the bag tightly shut then inched right up to the external wall. He coughed as the dust and fibres ballooned into the air. His fingers found the wall cavity and he carefully lowered the bag with the suite of jewels down until it finally stopped. Marcus tied the twine tightly around a rafter and disguised it with some of the insulation. Checking his handy work he descended and put the stepladder away.

Marcus took a few deep breaths and then spread the remaining jewellery out on his bed and taking a last look at them, picked up a thick brown envelope and dropped them carefully in. His hands were shaking, he knew someone who would take this lot off him and not ask too many questions. He cringed at the thought of doing what he believed the fat caretaker would have done to them; but things were hotting up and he wanted them out of the way. Marcus sat back and felt solemn. He chastised himself for his thoughts about a man who was now dead. He kept wondering if the jewels had had anything to do with his death. He went down to his office and opened the safe placing the envelope under the papers and other boxes in the safe. He searched for the keys but he couldn't find them and finally he recalled the unusual hiding place for the spare set. He found his reading glasses case at the back of a drawer and extracted the key from the inner lining of the lid. Locking the safe, which made a satisfying hiss as the door closed, he returned the key to his glasses case. Finally he felt a wave of tiredness and he retired to his bed eyeing the phone and willing it to ring; hearing Tamara's voice on the line would be the perfect end to a mixed day.

Marcus woke the next morning in a sombre mood which became darker during the day as the shop remained infuriatingly empty, he hadn't his daughter's touch and now the whole weekend had been a washout for sales. Dawn arrived home in the early evening and it was not long before his daughter started to question him.

'Dad, you've hardly sold a thing. No, I'm sorry, you *haven't* sold anything. What have you been doing?' She had her hands on her hips looking around the shop and even her boyfriend looked on nervously.

Marcus tried to think of an excuse but mumbled about it being quiet.

'Quiet, on a weekend in the middle of the summer season. Come on…'

He watched his daughter and Toby go upstairs and he sat on one of the chairs by the window. Maybe it was time to contact Charles? He he pulled himself up wearily and walked slowly to his office to call him; there was no reply. Toby came noisily down the stairs.

'I'm off Marcus,' he shouted as he put his head round the door. 'You've managed to put her into one of her moods so there isn't any point in me staying.'

'Sorry Toby,' mumbled Marcus shrugging his shoulders. 'I'll lock the door behind you.' Marcus let the young student out and locked the door just as the phone rang. Marcus took several strides towards the office but the ringing stopped. He quickly picked up the hand set but the line was dead; his daughter must have taken the call. 'Ruddy hell,' he hissed through his teeth. 'I can't even answer my own phone.' He waited to see if his daughter would call down to him, but it was several minutes before he finally heard his daughter shouting.

'Dad, where are you?' she said descending the stairs, two at a time; which was a habit of hers when she wore trainers.

'Here in the window, cowering from my own daughter's wrath…'

Dawn came across to him and sat on his lap giving him a big sloppy kiss on his cheek. 'Sorry Dad, I'm very tired, and well you know…, neither of us got much sleep last night…'

'I've told you I don't want to hear about your private life.' He gave her backside a playful slap. 'Well I'm hungry and there is nothing in. Do you want to go and have a quick dinner somewhere?'

'Oh, Dad I'm sorry I'm really bushed. Why don't you go over to Giovanni's and get a nice plate of pasta and a glass of wine.' She lent back and looked at him questioningly.

'Do you know I might just do that?' Marcus picked up his daughter and dumped her on her feet as he rose. 'You're getting quite a size, my girl,' he managed to avoid his daughter's punch at his shoulder. 'Oh, who was on the phone?'

'Wrong number, they wanted a restaurant further down the road.' Dawn had turned and made her way back upstairs. 'I'll see you in the morning Dad; I've got to get some sleep.'

Marcus frowned as he watched his daughter go upstairs. He could tell she had not told the truth about the phone call, she had never been able to lie to him; manipulate him but never lie. He shouted goodnight upstairs and leaving the shop he slowly ambled down towards Giovanni's café.

Dawn waited at the top of the stairs until she heard the front door close and her father turn the key. She then ran to the window in the lounge to watch him amble down the road, his head down. For a second she thought about shouting after him but she changed her mind. He had lied to her, the phone call that evening had confirmed that. Why hadn't her father mentioned he had been questioned by the Metropolitan Police?

Dawn dragged out the stepladder and struggled up the stairs she placed them in position under the attic hatch. Brandishing a flash light she spent nearly half an hour searching the loft but she found nothing there. Brushing her self down she put the stepladder away and went into his bedroom and soon found the silver and wooden box in one of her father's drawers. She opened it but it was empty. She searched his room and then found the old book but found it difficult to extract as it was tightly packed in. She flicked though the pages, a damp musty smell caught her nose and she wrinkled it in disgust. Dawn noticed that the book tended to open at a particular page and realised some pages were missing. She checked the index and frowned at why her father would be interested in a missing Romanov lady.

Checking her watch she went quickly downstairs into the office and tried to open the safe. To her surprise it was locked and even more oddly the keys were not in the usual place; namely in the lock. She recalled her father keeping a set inside the lid of his glasses case; a trick he had learned in the past whilst undertaking house clearances. Seeing her fathers reading glasses case on the desk she opened it and pulled the lining out. 'There you are she whispered to herself,' dropping the key into her hand and kneeling by the safe she struggled to turn the stiff lock; eventually she heard a metallic click and the door opened.

The safe was a jumble of boxes, papers and a few articles but then she saw a heavy new brown envelope hidden at the back. She drew it out already starting to fear what it might hold as it was surprisingly heavy. Once again she checked the clock and hoped her father would have his usual grappa with Giovanni. She started to stand up but a cut out newspaper article fell onto the floor. Dawn sat back on her haunches and read about the death of the caretaker from Kinloch Castle. She packed all the contents back into the safe, except for the large brown envelope, and locking it, placed the key back in the case, then ascended the stairs. The briefest of glimpses into the envelope had stunned her. Still bemused by what she had found she went into her father's room and, almost daring not to look, emptied the envelope onto his bed. Her jaw dropped in horror, then amazement in awe at the beauty of the jewels lying all jumbled on the quilt.

'Oh, Dad what are you up to?' Dawn whispered but her legs had started to turn to jelly and she went down on her knees picking up the glittering jewels. 'I think it's time to contact Charles, Dad needs help,' she said, her voice hoarse. She felt herself starting to cry, she knew something wasn't right and her father was up to something. She had come to really love her father and his odd relaxed ways. The thought of him in prison flashed across her mind; sometimes he just didn't think things through and did the most stupid of things and her tears started to fall. She found the jewellery box and started to place the jewels in it. Then she heard the familiar

136

sound of a key in the front door down stairs. She stuffed the remaining jewels in the old box and turning around put the book back onto the shelf. Hearing her father start to come up the stairs she went to turn the light off but spied the envelope from the safe and grabbing it, just made it into the corridor and up the second set of stairs to her room, shutting the door quietly behind her. She pulled back the duvet and throwing it over her, fully dressed, lay there still clutching the wood and silver box.

'Dawn,' came a whisper from the door and it opened an inch. Dawn didn't move and gave a low sleepy sigh. The door silently closed and the darkness returned. It seemed an age before her father finally retired and she waited a full half an hour before she crept out of bed fumbling for the bedside light. She undressed as quietly as she could and slipped on her nightie, which although was very scanty and didn't cover much, she still wore when she went to the bathroom; she hated dressing gowns. Dawn placed the jewellery box on the bedside table and opened the lid. One by one she pulled out the pieces of jewellery. Even in the dim shadowy light, the gems sparkled. Suddenly she heard the creak of a floor board and thinking it was her father threw the jewels back into the box, diving under the covers, but it was just the movement of the old house.

After a few minutes she sat upright gazing at the jewels, hypnotised by their beauty. She picked up the box and examined it. Then she remembered her father's reading glasses case. Dawn, tentatively at first, pulled at the lining of the roof of the box and it moved. She kept loosening it and finally it came away. Her heart raced as an old letter made of parchment fell out. It had a ribbon with the remains of some sealing wax at one end; it had become dry and brittle with age. Dawn was frightened in case she damaged it so she unfolded the paper as delicately as she could. Disappointment filled her as the writing was totally illegible, most of the letters were unrecognisable. She turned it over and on the back was some writing; English writing. She jumped up and tiptoed to her desk putting on her ark reading lamp.

At the top of the reverse of the parchment was a name and address: *Bruce Longbottom, Lower Bank Farm, Lower Leigh, Lancs.* Dawn wrote it down on a piece of paper. Futher down was more writing but in pencil, which had started to fade: *m. Gilbert Davenport 1927: b 14th May 1930 – Roger Nicholas Davenport.* A bit below this now in black ink and very scratchy untidy writing: *God be merciful; he has the disease.* Dawn blinked as a puzzled frown drew across her face. Finally at the bottom and in a dark bluish ink, which was so badly written it was hard to make out: *b. 31st August 1960 – Ralph Nicholas Davenport.*

'Dawn are you all right?' She heard the creek of a floor board outside her door. 'I can hear you rummaging about; is everything OK?'

'Don't come in, I am not decent; actually I'm naked,' she shouted folding the parchment and placing it back in the box and pushing the lining quickly back in. 'I'll be out in a tick when I can find my nightie…' She scooped the jewellery up and placed it all in the box closing it quietly, she opened a drawer and buried it under her winter pullovers. She went and opened the door and her father clapped a hand over his eyes.

'My God girl, you call that a nightie; it's positively indecent. Go and put a dressing gown on!'

'Tobs doesn't seem to mind…'

'Toby's not your Dad, go and put something on.' Marcus went towards the kitchenette. 'Cocoa?'

'Yes, that would be lovely. Oh, a police officer phoned this evening. He seemed a bit agitated you weren't about, and asked where you were.' Dawn had noticed her father had stopped but had not turned round. 'You've not been flogging dodgy stuff have you Dad?' Her father walked on and did not answer so she pulled on her dressing gown and followed him.

'Dad, are you sure everything is alright?'

He made a feeble smile back at her and started preparing the drinks. 'Yes, just too many grappas with that rogue Giovanni. Do you know, I really missed you not being around this weekend. The place felt like a morgue.' A silence fell and was only broken by her father's movements as he made the cocoa. Dawn watched and wondered when she should confront him with his lies.

'So you're not going to tell me about the police then.'

'Well how can I until I've spoken to them...'

'But he said you had...'

'Enough Dawn, please. I'm tired and I'll explain everything tomorrow.' Marcus' expression had turned dark and he could feel a fury building up inside. Dawn knew when to leave well alone, she could see his darkening countenance.

They sat sipping the cocoa making light conversation until finally she yawned and muttering goodnight to her father made her way to bed. She lay there until she heard the familiar snore from his room below hers; he always snored when he had been drinking. Easing her way out of bed she stealthfully climbed down stairs and picked the phone up and dialled. A few moments later a sleepy Charles answered the phone. Dawn gabbled quietly into the phone, Charles occasionally interrupting her, as he came out of his sleep induced stupor. The conversation abruptly finished when Dawn thought she heard her father upstairs. Dawn finally tiptoed back to her bed, guilt raging inside her that she was deceiving her father. If he was in trouble she was now happy that Charles could come to his rescue; if anyone could help her father, it would be him.

Chapter 8

The darkness concealed the figure dressed in a tight fitting boiler suit slipping effortlessly over the back wall of Marcus' house and dropping silently to the ground. Checking for any sound, the figure kept in the shadows and approached the window of the office. The hard training many years ago now proved their worth for such an exercise. The glass pane was cut and window locks opened in seconds. A small pull of exertion saw the figure climbed through the window and kneel by the safe. A skeleton key was extracted from a back pocket and the safe yielded with little resistance. A loud clunk of the handle caused the intruder's body to freeze for a second; ready to depart in an instant. A long, sheathed silver knife was pulled out of a pocket in the trousers; ready for use. The contents of the safe were quietly withdrawn and a murmured curse preceded as the figure moved towards the stairs.

Not a sound could be heard as Marcus' door opened, his drawers searched and his door closed again with a faint click, not disturbing the sleeping antique dealer. The intruder then climbed the next set of stairs and stood by Dawn's door waiting to hear for any movement from inside. The door opened and the figure slipped in. The room was untidy, a slinky nightie lay on the floor by the sleeping girl, but a pad and some scribbled notes caught the trained eye. The heart jumped when the notes were quickly read, especially the underlined heading. The only sound made was the paper being ripped from the pad. Dawn stirred and turned muttering. The figure backed out and pulled the door to, without a noise. A long night of research was about to begin, but disappointment at not finding the jewels clouded the mind. A flash of anger filled the lonely figure as it strode on. The portrait showed the suite of jewels; they would be worth a fortune to the right buyer; they were a one-way, first class ticket out…

★ ★ ★

The next morning Marcus woke and looking at his alarm clock realised he had over slept. 'Damn that grappa,' he said as he pulled himself out of bed, stopping abruptly at the sight of his open drawers. He looked for the box; it wasn't there.

'*Dawn*,' he shouted climbing the stairs two at a time and knocking on her door before running back downstairs to his office. The sight of the safe door slightly ajar made Marcus take a huge breath in which he seemed to hold as the realisation that he had been burgled began to sink in. Marcus started to feel sick and faint, his mind running riot.

'Dawn, get up we've been turned over.' Marcus bellowed up the stairs as he entered into the shop; all seemed to be in order and the front door tightly locked. 'Dawn for God's sake, get up!' he shouted again and slowly went to the safe. Most of the contents had been placed on the floor beside the safe. Marcus tentatively picked through them, but he already knew the jewels wouldn't be there.

'Dawn, for ruddy sake,' his voice weak and ascended the stairs this time slowly and almost out of breath, he was gasping for air as he burst into her room. Her bed was empty. A wave of anger and disbelief hit him; she must have taken the box with the jewels. He stumbled down to the kitchenette holding onto one of the chairs trying to make some sense of why she would take them; confront him but not just take them.

Starting to fill the kettle he saw her note:

Hi Dad. I felt awful the way I treated Toby. So I've got up early and taken my nightie to cheer him up, <u>he</u> won't object! I'll be back for coffee, Luv Dawnie.

Marcus' guilt fell on him like a heavy wave; how could he have doubted his own daughter? 'Ruddy jewels, they've really turned my life upside down,' he mumbled to the un-listening kettle. He threw some instant coffee in a cup and picking up the phone, dialled Charles' number.

'Oh, hi Marcus,' said Samantha. He could hear a young child screaming in the background. 'Hazel would you put that down… just a minute Marcus…' Marcus heard a brief scalding and more crying. 'Sorry Marcus, we are honoured, we haven't heard from you in weeks, then Dawn calls last night, and now you in such a short space of time.'

Marcus couldn't speak; his throat had tightened. 'Dawn called? Last night?' he finally uttered.

'Yes, last night at some unearthly hour. Charles was actually a little cross as he had received a call yesterday, in the middle of Sunday lunch, about getting to an urgent meeting at the V&A; something quite important is going on.' The background of crying had subsided.

'Sorry Sam, oops Samantha, I didn't realise, but I'll try his mobile later. Good luck with the crying kid,' he tried to laugh, but a sinking feeling that his daughter was now actually deceiving him made him sit heavily back on the stool; he stood looking at the receiver.

'Yes, see you Marcus…Hazel…' He barely heard from the phone before the line went dead. He slammed the phone back on the cradle.

Marcus walked slowly in deep thought into his daughter's room and was tempted to look through her drawers and wardrobe, but he just couldn't bring himself to do it. He trudged down to the office coming to terms with the fact that it now seemed his own flesh and blood was being deceitful. He could see Dawn and Charles together, bemoaning him and what they would have to do to get him out of this mess. By the time he had entered the office he had convinced himself his daughter or possibly even Charles had the jewels. In a strange way he sensed some relief that the jewels were no longer his responsibility but sadness that his dream of what he planned for them had now gone. Then he remembered the suite of jewels he had hidden separately and a wave of relief filled him.

'There is no way they would have found those,' he said quietly.

The room was a little stuffy so Marcus went to open the window and saw the neatly cut hole in the glass and the locks opened. A rush of panic paralysed him for a second and then the realisation that he had actually been burgled made his sickening feeling return. He sat down heavily and lent back with his hands covering his face but he couldn't ignore the shameful guilt which filled him as to the accusations he made against Dawn and Charles. The question still nagged him as to why had Dawn called his old friend late last night. He actually knew the answer: he had been acting strangely recently and she had on more than one occasion said she would call Charles. He now appreciated she hadn't been joking. How was he to tell them about the jewels and then, in the next breath, inform them that they were gone? His mind flashed back to the suite of jewels and he gave a long sigh. He stood and went upstairs taking the step ladders and climbed into the attic. He didn't need to be there long as he quickly found the undisturbed twine and knew they were still safe.

'I need to get that ring back from Charles,' he muttered coming back downstairs and examining the perfect round hole in the glass. 'At least the suite is safe. Plan B here we come...' But who could have taken the jewels? 'Tamara?' He whispered to himself. 'No, please don't tell me she is involved in all this; not her...'Why wasn't he denying her involvement straight away? His instincts were honing in on Tamara.

He sat as his shoulders started to droop as his thoughts analysed that there were too many coincidences about the woman. Then he remembered Saturday morning and scrambling through the papers on his desk, he found the small calling card and dialled Scotland Yard. A few moments later he was talking to Detective Inspector Hines.

'I just thought I would let you know,' he looked at the open safe in front of him and recalled how Charles had called it as good as a chocolate poker. Charles was right, again. 'I was burgled last night. I'm about to report the incident...'

'Was anything taken, Mr Chapman?' The inspector's voice was calm but firm.

'Well, that is the strange thing, there doesn't seem to be,' Marcus felt the tightness in his gut as he lied. 'I haven't done a full inventory as yet, but at first glance I can't see anything missing. They weren't smash and grab, I can tell you that.'

'Why, how did they get in?' came the predictable question.

'That's just it. They cut a hole in the glass; very neat job. Then they must have unlocked the window and finally opened my safe as if it hadn't been locked at all.'

'Was it locked?'

'Yes, it ruddy well was. I will admit I am lax at times but I know I locked it last night. I had put something valuable in it,' Marcus slowed as he felt himself digging a hole. As little information as possible, he told himself, but that was never his style.

'May I enquire what valuables you put in the safe, and if nothing was taken are they still there?' The question panicked Marcus and he started to stutter.

'Yes, they were just a few antique ornaments that I have acquired over the weekend. I put them in the safe in case they got damaged actually; they're not worth an awful lot, but never mind that,' Marcus decided to go on the offensive, 'I would like to ask a question of you?'

'I can guess what it is but, go on, ask away.' The police officer had a resigned note in his voice.

'It is bloody coincidence that you lot interview me about a chap's death hundreds of miles away, when I have many witnesses that can verify I was in London, and then...'

'Mr. Chapman, we were conducting our enquiries and we have to follow up all leads. I have no idea and also see no reason why the burglary had anything to do with the death of Mr. Malone, unless however…'

'Yes, yes,' quickly interrupted Marcus, he didn't like how this conversation was going. 'Unless what?' Marcus was becoming annoyed at how this officer seemed so calm and had the ability to make him say things he really didn't intend to. His next question was to continue the same vein.

'Unless… Are you sure nothing has been taken, Mr. Chapman?' The line remained silent. 'Mr. Chapman, are you still there?'

Marcus felt this man had a hunch he really did have something to hide. Marcus scolded himself for calling this man in the first place; things were getting out of control. 'Yes I'm sure, but I will double check.' Marcus thought it better to leave the door open, just in case. 'You can come up and see for yourself.' Marcus made a note of putting the figurines that he had bought recently in the safe. He had to be totally alert with this policeman. 'Oh, may I have my passport back?'

'Are you going away anywhere?'

'No, not really. I just want my property returned if you don't mind.'

There was a heavy silence and Marcus resisted the urge to fill it.

'I'll file a report for you at this end and I could be over either later on today, but I think it is more likely to be tomorrow. I'll bring your passport then. Will that be OK, Mr. Chapman?'

Marcus grunted an acknowledgement and mumbled a good bye. He resisted the temptation to make a sarcastic remark about it not being urgent, but decided he had already said far too much, mostly to his own detriment.

'Bastard,' he bellowed at the phone as he slammed the receiver down. 'They're so bloody arrogant I could spit…' Marcus knew he was the only one to blame for the fiasco of a phone call. He went upstairs and finished making his coffee, trying to calm himself down. 'Right Marcus, let's just go through all this.' He noticed his hand shaking as he picked up his mug. 'Christ, no wonder I'm shaking I've just lost a small fortune…, and made myself look very suspicious to Scotland Yard. Marcus, why do you always do this?'

* * *

Charles sipped his coffee listening intently to his friend's excited daughter, her concern visible by her blood shot eyes. At times he asked her to stop, slow down and tell him everything slowly; Dawn had to repeat herself several times. Charles made notes of what she had found and the author and title of the book. This especially interested him. The realisation that the call he had received last night from his boss, James Pulford, in a very unfamiliar manner was too much of a coincidence. He had already considered the possibility that the ring he had dropped off at EED had caused a rumpus; the lack of feed back greatly concerned him. It was not beyond the realms of possibility that it had been established that it had something to do with the late Romanovs. The most worrying news was the caretaker at Kinloch had died or been killed. Charles' mind raced as he tried to put all the pieces of the jigsaw together. His friend was a bit of a rogue, and always up for a deal, but he had never taken him as a thief and he was certainly not a murderer. What was unfolding was something completely different; his concern for Marcus had turned to anxiety about his own position as well.

He paid for the drinks and exiting onto Brompton Road he kissed the young woman on the cheek emphasising his insistence that she adhered to his instructions. He watched her go in the other direction towards Harrods and turning, made his way in the direction of the Victoria & Albert Museum. On arriving at his office he checked his phone and found he had two missed calls from Marcus. He started to call him but disengaged and decided to try him later. He needed time to think and to establish why he had been ordered in to see his boss. He decided to visit Marcus at his shop on the way home and have a serious talk with him. This time if his friend didn't tell him everything he would be prepared to walk away and wash his hands of him. He smiled, but he knew he could never do that to Marcus. What was it about him that made him so likeable? Charles was the only one who really knew what went on underneath that charming easy come, easy go facade. 'Well this time I'll beat it out of him,' he whispered his smile fading.

Charles entered his boss's office. James Pulford OBE was a very tall man and quite thick set. He had reached a high standard of rugby and twice represented his country. A large scar above one eyebrow was a testimony of his courage in a ruck. He glanced at his watch in an agitated manner and Charles checked to see he was barely a minute late. He sensed Pulford's disquiet.

'You'd better follow me, you're late.' Pulford picked up a file and would not make any eye contact. Standing up briskly he took a back door from his office. The two men went down several corridors and up three flights of stairs well into the attics of the building.

Charles knew where he was going. It was where, only a few months ago, he had been led there in slightly different circumstances. James Pulford took him to meet the Vetustus Fraternitas Antiquitas, known to the antiquities world and high ranking government officials as the *VfA*. Charles, as many in the industry, knew of this society; it was dedicated to protect the antiquities of all the ancient worlds from racketeers. It was an international brotherhood and although it had never been a secret society; they kept themselves out of the limelight. It had always amused him that although Britain had been one of the leading looters of ancient artefacts for centuries, they now believed it was their responsibility to protect these very same ancient treasures. Their main argument was simple: if they hadn't 'acquired' them they would most certainly been lost or destroyed. In many cases the argument holds, but not all. Several weeks ago he had been told by this 'brotherhood' that he was being considered for an appointment as a member; it was a vital move to his career. Today he was not sure what to expect but he knew it had something to do with the ring Marcus had given him. He was so grateful for the fortuitous meeting with Dawn that morning; it just might save his bacon.

They entered a long thin room with one side built into the eaves of the roof. The room was sparsely furnished except for a long thin table supporting a projector and nearby was an overhead screen. Several men and a woman sat at the end of the table and stopped talking as the two men entered. There were no pleasantries and no one smiled as silence settled over them.

'Charles, you have been brought here on a very serious matter.' Charles now knew his gut feelings were well founded; the faces looking at him were glowering with a disappointed disdain. Thank you, Marcus, thank you very much, he thought. 'A week or so ago you brought in a ring to be evaluated. I understand you obtained this from a *friend* of yours.' Charles went to protest but James Pulford gave him a glare that silenced him instantly. 'In a few moments we are going to bring in the man leading the Eastern Europe Department, but first we want to hear your story. I will be frank with you Charles; we are all very disappointed with what we have been told about your role in this matter.'

Charles took a step forward and acknowledging the group sitting at the end of the table he took a deep breath. He was shaking with fury. What had these people been told, *he* had done nothing improper, in fact quite the reverse. He pulled himself up to his full height and faced the group.

'I am not sure exactly what you have told but I have to say that what I will now tell you should reinstate your wavering confidence in me. I have acted solely to the principles that the *VfA* adhere to.' James Pulford looked a little surprised, but a touch pleased and went and joined the group at the end of the table. Charles noted the softening of the glares he had been receiving.

This all might work out quite well for him; he confirmed in his mind however he would be having more than a few words with Marcus immediately after this meeting. Marcus had some serious explaining to do and he needed to find out exactly what his friend had been involved with and what he actually had in his possession.

Charles described the night at Kinloch Castle, his friend's change of mood and how he was keeping a close eye on him. He recalled the evening when Marcus Chapman had given him the ring and how he thought he was withholding the real truth. He explained the meeting that morning with Chapman's daughter and of her finding the jewels plus the note hidden in the old jewellery box.

'Do you know what was written on the parchment?' asked Pulford becoming excited. Marcus shook his head and James now motioned for him to sit down as the atmosphere in the room had markedly relaxed. Charles sensed the animosity from the group in front of him had disappeared and been replaced with respect; some thoughtful looks were now being thrown at him from the opposite side of the table. He felt the tightness in his stomach ease. There was an interruption as someone entered the room and handed James Pulford a piece of paper that visibly startled him. James drew a hand over his face, exasperation etched in the lines on his brow. Charles looked at his boss questioningly but James motioned for him to continue.

The group waited until Charles had completely finished his explanation and his proposal for a plan of action. He took the opportunity to hint that he believed something was not quite right inside the V&A. An older man at the end of the table nodded towards Charles and leaning forward whispered in Pulford's ear and then turned to Charles.

'Well Charles, we seem to have misjudged you, to put it mildly,' said the older man, 'although I have to say there has been quite a bit of finger pointing going on around here lately.' Charles frowned. The politics in such an organisation had always worried him. 'I would be very grateful if you would allow us a few moments to reflect on what you have said,' the old man motioned towards the door.

'Yes, of course,' said Charles trying not to show his feeling of annoyance at still being excluded from all the facts. He went out of the door and took a seat in the corridor looking out at the dome of the Brampton Oratory; if there was one thing Charles hated was being excluded. It seemed an age before he was called back and now there was coffee and a plate of biscuits in the middle of the table. James stood and poured him a cup.

'I am sorry about asking you to leave; it must have felt quite an insult especially as you have been so open with us,' said Pulford sliding the cup over to him. 'However that will be the last time you will be excluded from any discussion on this matter; we just needed to make sure we were all singing from the same hymn sheet, so as to speak. It seems you are in the thick of quite a hornet's nest and you are best suited to lead further investigations for one very simple fact.' Charles felt warmth flowing through him; he couldn't help but smile at the group and raised a questioning eyebrow at Pulford as a silence continued.

'What fact is that?'

'You can watch your friend, Marcus Chapman, without him knowing. I, or rather we, believe your friend has acquired these jewels on your visit to Kinlock, and possibly has no idea what he actually has in his possession, or rather had in his possession…'

'Had…?'

'Let me finish Charles, please. We believe the caretaker is the most likely person to have given these jewels to Chapman and he likewise had no idea of their true worth. As we said earlier we're about to introduce you to the man heading up EED, but you have actually met him before and, I understand, more recently at Kinloch Castle itself.' James watched Charles' puzzled look as it slowly changed when Charles remembered the bat researcher and how he couldn't recall where he had seen him before.

'Of course, Mr.Bat,' said Charles a smile creeping onto his face.

'Mr.Bat? No this man is called… ah yes, of course. I understand he was under the guise of a naturalist researching the local bat population.' The group laughed and James continued as a stern countenance crossed over him.

'I have just been informed that your friend, Marcus Chapman, was burgled last night.' James waited as Charles took a breath in. 'He has informed the police that nothing was stolen…'

'Oh heavens, but he *couldn't* tell them about the jewels, could he…?'

'Exactly Charles. So it's up to you to find out precisely what the situation is.' James said reaching forward and picking up a biscuit. 'It's not out of the realms of possibility that your friend maybe one step ahead of us by making out they are stolen; he may have an inclination that he has been found out by his daughter… There is something else which we have been discussing at some length as to whether to tell you or not.'

'But I thought you said I would be included…' Charles started to protest as James raised his hand to silence him.

'That is why I am about to inform you, Charles.' James opened a file in front of him. 'Our contacts in Russia have picked up that there has been interest in the discovery of the portrait. Julian Appleforth will brief you with the detail, but it seems that the portrait was of a young woman called Xenia. She was the illegitimate daughter of Nicholas II and is possibly the only remaining blood line of the last Tsar. It is very likely these jewels were hers, or rather part of a dowry from the Tsar.'

'Wasn't there a woman claiming to be one of his daughter's, Anastasia?' Charles tried to recall the story.

'Yes and a few other besides; complete bogus claims, con merchants I believe the term is. Life has however changed considerably in Russia with the collapse of the Soviet system.' James put on some half moon reading glasses and continued. 'There is a department deep inside the KGB whose sole purpose is to ensure that no blood line of the Tsar ever has the, err, the opportunity to make a claim for the throne. The man heading this up is a Colonel Andrei Suslov; his grandfather was one of the troops that murdered the Tsar and the entire Romanov family in July 1918.'

'But why does this illegitimate child have anything to do with Kinloch Castle and that awful man Malone?' Charles was starting to grasp the seriousness of the situation and questions kept firing into his mind, some of an alarming nature. How does Marcus find trouble so easily?

'We believe Malone was an unfortunate a pawn in this. He died recently…'

Charles nodded. 'Is there is a suspicion he was killed? This hasn't got anything to do with a visit by the police to Marcus Chapman by any chance? His daughter mentioned it.'

James turned some pages in the file and nodded. 'Your friend's calling card was found on the dead man's body.'

'Ah, but I was there when Marcus gave him the card at Kinloch Castle. Marcus Chapman is no murderer I can tell you that. He faints when he cuts himself.' Charles tried to smile but was met by silence for a moment. 'So what is going on here then?'

'Unfortunately we do not have all the facts and again we are going on a few titbits that our agents in Moscow have managed to pick up. We also understand Xenia herself fell pregnant and records show she came to England about the time she must have conceived.' James sat back and looked directly at Charles. 'It is believed, or rather, it is assumed that the father of the unborn child was a certain Sir Wesley Henshaw who was assisting in the Treaty of Portsmouth at the time. This Treaty ended the Russo-Japanese War. Henshaw did a lot to save the Russian's reputation, as they had taken quite a beating. He was also the owner and the man who built Kinloch Castle.'

'Yes, I read about him in the brochure and it seems he had been given quite a few gifts from both Russia and Japan; most are still at Kinloch. But what happened to Xenia and her baby?'

Charles was leaning forward and wondering if Malone could possibly have been the last surviving blood line to the Tsar. The thought made him shiver involuntarily, but then he recalled Pulford had said he had been just a pawn. Charles felt relieved.

'Well, Xenia died during child birth and no one knows what happened to the baby; until we received an ominous communication recently from someone inside the KGB itself, based in Moscow. It is claimed that…' Pulford read for a moment, 'that Sir Wesley was ordered by the Tsar to take the child and ensure she is brought up in a proper and suitable manner. Sir Wesley was given the portrait and the jewels which we now know he hid on the Isle of Rum. These jewels were known within the Romanov family as the *'Stones of Conscience'*, due to their purpose, namely placating the Tsar's own conscience. There is a particular suite of jewels that are shown on the portrait that are believed to be worth a king's ransom, or should I say a Tsar's ransom. We believe the ring Marcus Chapman gave you is from this suite. We, however, know nothing about the whereabouts of Xenia's child.'

'Nothing, no leads, no rumours?' Charles searched James' face.

James shook his head. 'We were hoping that there may have been something on the portrait or with the jewels. The portrait has nothing on it to indicate even a name. Our last hope was some sort of identification that could have come with the jewels. Your friend's daughter had stumbled on exactly what we were hoping for; that note she found in the casket, but now it's possible it has been stolen… Let's hope you can come up with something Charles. The *VfA* would be very appreciative if you did, I suspect if there is a person out there who is the Tsar's actual bloodline he or she *may* now be in grave danger, if our prognosis about the KGB's reaction to all this is correct.'

'So do you believe the Russians killed the caretaker?' Charles was just starting to grasp the full picture and their potential dangers.

James looked down for a moment and shrugged his shoulders. 'Malone was killed by the fall, he had no other marks on him. Actually that isn't strictly true. He was attacked by his dog after the fall but that aside it still seems certain it could have been an accident…'

'But you don't believe it was, do you?' Charles was surprised by the tone of his own voice. James nodded and again looked carefully at him as Charles continued to ask questions. 'Marcus' burglary must have something to do with this, mustn't it? Look, I hope you don't mind me saying, but this really is a job for the police…'

'Believe me Charles, our contacts at Scotland Yard have been fully informed and are pursuing their own lines of enquiry. The unfortunate incident at your friend's house has stepped things up a bit,' said James and anticipating Charles' next question he held up both his hands to silence him.

'Look all you have to do is find out everything Marcus Chapman and his daughter know and report back to me as soon as you can.' James face softened. 'Charles no heroics here, we believe there may be…'

'May be what?'

'We'll talk later. Now let's call in our man from EED.' James then lent forward and pressed a button on the underneath of the table. The door opened and Julian Appleforth entered carrying the portrait.

'Julian, this is Charles Ashford,' said James standing.

Charles also rose and when Julian had placed the portrait on a chair he lent forward and shook his hand.

'How are the bats?' Charles smiled at the thin wiry man.

'Ah yes, I'm sorry about that. It seems Malone had been shouting his mouth off in a pub one night and we were alerted by the Scottish National Trust. I was trying to find out exactly what he had, when you arrived with your friends. I couldn't believe it when I saw you and at first I didn't think it was a coincidence, but when I checked with London it seems it was one of those odd turns of fate.' Appleforth tried to brush his hair down. 'I didn't manage to pull you to one side and have a quick word just in case you recognised me. We did meet in March last year at the Egyptian Embassy, don't you remember?'

'Well I remembered your face, but I just couldn't place you… That's why I tried to keep my distance.'

Charles spent some time with Julian and his team and when he had finished he walked slowly back to his office. He had met Tamara and he flushed. He wasn't sure how to tell Marcus where she worked and had regretted mentioning her before; especially now he was effectively spying on him. She also looked a lot smarter than she did on Rum and he sensed from her that she knew more than she was letting on. He decided to quiz James Pulford about her.

One thing was certain he would need to have a long discussion with Marcus and Dawn. He wasn't sure if Pulford knew exactly how close his relationship was with Marcus. He looked at his watch and saw it was nearly lunchtime. He pulled out his mobile and called Marcus but it instantly went onto answer phone. He cursed and entered his office to be greeted by James Pulford sitting and waiting for him. He rose as Charles came in.

'Charles, I didn't say anything before but I must warn you we believe we have a mole in our midst.' James was holding Charles' incredulous look. 'I think this person or persons are feeding information back to the KGB.'

'How do you know…?' Charles felt uncomfortable.

'Believe it or not from our own mole inside the KGB. What a sad and complicated world we live in.' James started for the door. 'Keep this one entirely to yourself…'

Charles levelled a questioning stare at his boss. He sensed his unease.

'Just be bloody careful. It is one thing sending information to the Russians but if the caretaker was, well, you know…'

'Oh shit, you mean someone who is more of a spy…' Charles' head spun. Did he mention his suspicions about Tamara? If Marcus ever found out it would put a severe strain on their relationship; not the time to be upsetting the apple cart.

'No, I am sure it is just me, but for god's sake tread carefully.' Pulford stopped and pulled out a card. 'Call me on *this* number if anything happens. Don't do anything stupid or heroic; leave that stuff to Scotland Yard and the intelligence boys. They are taking a lot of interest in this, which is hardly surprising though I suspect *we* are only seeing the tip of the iceberg...'

Charles took the card and watched James leave the room.

'Marcus, I am going to batter you...' Charles thought as he entered his office. He saw his in-tray and cursed when a memo marked urgent was laid out on the top; he really wanted to go straight to Marcus.

* * *

Marcus' relief when he heard Dawn enter the shop was short lived as she looked fraught and a little sheepish.

'You look awful my girl, the nightie work then?' Marcus tried to be light hearted despite feeling thoroughly dejected. 'No don't answer, I don't want to know.' Marcus continued to make an attempt to laugh; losing the jewels was one thing but he also still hadn't come to terms that his daughter was sexually active. He was relieved to know his daughter hadn't taken the jewels; it was small compensation for the actual loss. 'Well I hope *you* had a good night, I'm feeling positively sick in stomach this morning and I am most certainly in need one of Giovanni's 'pep-me-ups', or I might go up to the Chelsea Potter and have a few scoops.'

'Dad, what's up? You look ashen.' Dawn stepped forward and took her father's face with both hands.

'We've been burgled.' Marcus watched as the horror of his words caused a deep frown across his daughter's brow.

'What, when...? How, where did they...?'

'Don't fret they didn't take anything. They ransacked the safe and I think went into my room and rummaged through my drawers, sad bastards.' Marcus took his daughter's hands in his. 'I don't think they went into your room. Sorry Dawnie, but I need a drink; I'll be back in a few minutes. Could you just check they haven't taken anything from your room? I wasn't inclined to search myself...'

Dawn had already turned and scaled the stairs two at a time. 'Dad, don't go! Wait a minute...' But she heard the buzzer from the front door and knew he had already gone.

She burst into her room throwing her handbag on the desk. Glancing back to make sure that her father wasn't still in the house and had followed her; she opened her pullover drawer. Thrusting her hands into the drawer she felt the hard silver and wood box. Checking behind her again she brought it out and opening it gingerly saw the sparkling contents. 'Phew,' she said to herself. 'Christ, I'd better go and tell him, he's probably in a real state of shock.'

Surveying the room she saw the ripped corner of her pad sticking up. Thoughtfully she went to the desk trying to remember if she had torn off her notes from the previous night. At least she still had the originals she thought and remembered that Charles had asked for the parchment.

Placing the box back into the drawer she heard the buzzer. 'Dad, is that you?' she shouted rushing down the stairs. She entered the shop to be met by a couple, who were inspecting the dining room suite, which had stubbornly remained in the window despite a lot of interest in it. Dawn started to make her apologies but checked herself. It will do him good to stew in his own juices, she thought as she began her sales pitch, and then realising the couple had been in before; she could smell a sale. A few minutes later the door opened again, Dawn glanced up to see a woman, dressed in a smart suit, looking at a vase by the door.

'Excuse me a moment,' she said smiling to the couple. Turning to the woman she asked if she could help.

'Is Marcus in?' Dawn shook her head and realising it was not a customer she tried to get back to her sales pitch. 'Oh, I need to speak to him; it's quite urgent.'

Dawn was keen to close her sale; it would cheer her father up.

'I'm sorry I have customers, but you should find him at a place down the road called Giovanni's. If he isn't there try in the other direction and go to the Chelsea Potter. Can I say who is called…?' Dawn saw the woman close the door gently behind her not waiting for a reply. She was fascinated in what such a sophisticated looking woman would be wanting with her father; but she shrugged her shoulders and carried on talking to the couple now closely examining the dining room table.

★ ★ ★

Marcus was sitting in his usual corner staring blankly into space. The café wasn't particularly busy but Marcus didn't notice. All his thoughts were on who had taken the jewels. He tried everyway possible to clear his suspicions of Tamara. At first he would have preferred to blame Malone, but he was dead and that certainly frightened him. Tamara knew about the jewellery box and he couldn't help but feel she suspected he had something. Why had she suddenly appeared and two days later the jewels were gone? Then he recalled her real interest in the jewellery box. Hadn't she also mentioned she specialised in Eastern European jewellery. He was so besotted with her all he could recall was drooling over her. He shook his head for he had spent the whole day doubting people he really loved. Yes, he had come to accept he had fallen for this woman he had only met twice.

He made a long sigh and then he felt a tinge of warmth as he recalled the suite of jewels still hiding in the attic. He sensed someone had come into the café and was looking at him. Marcus knew it would be his daughter attempting to coax him back home. He smelt the faint aroma of soap and Marcus looked up to see Tamara smiling at him. She wore a smart skirted suit with a cotton shirt and neckerchief; Marcus just gawped at her in disbelief.

'Penny for your thoughts,' she said pulling out a chair and sitting down. Marcus waved at Giovanni, his light headedness had immediately returned.

'Do you want a coffee or something?'

She held Marcus' eyes. 'Hmm, it's Italian here, isn't it? Any chance of a glass of Orvieto, or Pinot Grigio?'

'The lady knows her wines Giovanni,' said Marcus to the owner who had now come across to take a closer look at the woman. 'Two glasses of the Orvieto Classico, per favore.'

'Certo, subito,' answered Giovanni giving his thumbs up to Marcus as he returned to the bar.

'Italians, they're always the same. I bet he's given you a wink of approval…?'

Marcus burst out laughing and nodded. 'You should be flattered, he doesn't give the thumbs up to many girls that come in here.' A pause went into an extended silence but neither were embarrassed nor felt uncomfortable. He let his eyes wander over her and then he held her look. They both started to talk at the same time and laughed as Marcus waved his hand giving the floor to the woman in front of him, he realised he had been staring at her again, absorbing the sight and smell of her. Damn he thought, he should be angry with this woman because she was a suspect in his mind, but recriminations just melted away.

'Well, I left a bit hastily on Saturday. They were police weren't they?' Marcus nodded. 'I won't ask what they were doing, however you don't look the sort that handles questionable merchandise.' Tamara still held Marcus' stare, she felt the impulse to grab and kiss him again. These new feelings she was experiencing excited her; it had been years since she had ever imagined being able to feel like this.

'Ruddy hell, you sound like my daughter.' Marcus laughed and waited as Giovanni placed the two glasses on the table trying to take a sly look at the woman. 'Cheers Giovanni, have one on me.'

'Some of us have to work, thanks all the same Marcus,' he said moving back towards the bar but taking the opportunity to study the woman again. He was surprised this wasn't Marcus' usual type of woman.

'Oh, I saw your daughter briefly before. She was heavily engaged with some customers…' Tamara sipped her wine and suddenly felt she couldn't look this man in the eye. She knew she couldn't go through with her orders.

'That's my girl,' laughed Marcus. 'Actually she is ruddy good at selling. The women trust her and she wraps the men round her little finger.' Marcus took the wine and chinked Tamara's glass. 'Cheers.'

'Cheers,' replied Tamara still not engaging her eyes with his. 'Marcus, may I have another look at that box, it really interests me.'

Marcus looked down slightly bemused. If she had stolen the jewellery then why was she here now? He hoped what he was about to say didn't end this blossoming relationship. The palpitations he was feeling when she was with him had him feeling very young. Did she genuinely feel something for him but…, there was something about her, bordering on sinister.

'Well, I have some really bad news,' he saw Tamara's smile fade. 'I was burgled last night. Bastards took some pretty nice stuff and the jewellery box.'

'They went through your drawers while you were asleep? You hadn't moved the box then from its safe place with your underpants?' Tamara voice had a tinge of sarcasm, but was mixed with astonishment.

Marcus went to speak but faltered. How did she know he was asleep in the room when they were taken? 'No, I hadn't touched it since your visit.' Marcus felt uncomfortable for a moment. There was something in her questions that was more than a friendly enquiry, it was too inquisitive. He took a sip of wine but the vision of her and her scent brought his eyes back to hers. She still failed to look him directly in the eye.

'Marcus what a pity! You must be really sick about it all. What else did they take?' Tamara had lent forward a little and pulled her arms into her body revealing a slight glimpse of her cleavage. This time she looked him straight in the eye.

'You don't want to know,' he said relaxing, as his senses heightened and he was now starting to wonder if he actually could take this beauty to his bed. He was starting to forget about the jewels. If she had them she wouldn't have come back he argued with himself. She did however constantly take the lead which unnerved him and he tried to clear his mind as to what to do or say next. There was an aura of mystery about her and she seemed cool and in control. It was this sense of control he found quite appealing if not a touch frightening, but occasionally she seemed remarkably vulnerable. He already sensed her arrival in his life was nothing to do with him; she was in some way inexplicably linked to the jewels from Kinloch Castle; that he was totally certain of. 'Some pretty lovely stuff has gone, and I mean lovely. Worth a few bob too.' Marcus wanted her and he wanted her now before it was too late. He decided to see if she was interested in him or the jewels. He sat silently holding her look.

'You look as if you need cheering up,' she whispered leaning forward as she moved her hand towards his. 'Do you want me to cheer you up?' Marcus could only nod weakly. She was leading again. 'Don't go away I'll be back in a jiffy.'

★ ★ ★

Tamara went out and into the ladies at the rear of the café. She placed a handkerchief under the cold tap and mopped her brow. She had spent most of last night researching the names she had found in Marcus' daughter's room. She dare not do anything at work as she had a suspicion she was being watched by Julian. The thought of him made her skin crawl.

Her research had shown that Olga had married Gilbert Davenport and they had had a son who was now living in London but suffering from haemophilia B. Further evidence that he was from the Tsar's line. The problem was she had established he too had married and had a son. Eventually she had had to give way to sleep, she couldn't arrive at work looking like a complete zombie. Now she was away from work, without permission, only to find the jewels she suspected Marcus had, were now gone. Her plan was starting to fall apart in front of her eyes. She had to find out whether he was bluffing or not. She felt something for him she couldn't deny it and they had already communicated a lot together without words. Could she trust him? She opened her handbag and extracting her phone, made a call; confirming the room reservation with a credit card number. She put her purse and phone away and saw the sheathed knife at the bottom of her handbag; she gave an involuntary shiver.

Tamara started to shake because the decision she was about to make would change her life; she knew that. She bit her lip hard as she felt the first pin prick of tears stabbing at her eyes. She recovered her composure realising her inner battle; the subconscious will versus the trained mind. Her life had been so empty and then she meets someone who finally unlocks her emotions; but this very person she may have to... her whole body shook with disbelief at her predicament. If she only she could get those jewels she would be able to escape and have a new life; a life where she could finally forget her past. She had watched one man die due to the stones. She so wanted to flee and escape her shackles; but she could never leave her sister and beautiful child in such peril. She returned to the café resigned to the fact Suslov had won again. She cursed.

'Sorry about that,' she said sitting down and taking a sip of wine.

'I was going to send in a search party,' Marcus stopped and saw some redness in her eyes. 'Are you OK Tamara, you look as if...'

'I'm fine, well I'm not actually but I'll tell you about it later.' She tossed her hair over her shoulder and looked at him, her eyes still watery. 'You're not the only one that wants cheering up.' Tamara finished her wine and motioned for Marcus to do the same. 'I've booked us a hotel room. The Grosvenor Hotel...'

'Oh Blimey, a bit extravagant...,' stammered Marcus.

'No, not The Grosvenor House this is a hotel on Victoria

Station. We'll be able to just mingle as one with the crowd. I'd rather not be seen.' Tamara stood and flung her handbag over her shoulder and waited for Marcus to pay. They stepped into the King's Road and Tamara hailed a taxi.

Twenty minutes later they stood facing each other both breathing quite heavily. Tamara finally placed her handbag down by the dressing table and smiled weakly at Marcus. 'I don't know what to do. I really like you Marcus and believe me I have never, ever, done anything like this before. What do you want me to do?' She looked down blushing.

'Nothing, just being here with you is more than I had dreamed of.' He came towards her and placed his arms gently around her, holding her trembling body. 'There is something about you that fascinates me, and if you want to know the truth…' Marcus brought his hands around to her front and not taking his eyes of her, slowly unbuttoned her blouse.

Tamara looked up when he had finished; a moment's silence held them together. 'What? Tell me.' She placed her hands on his waist and gently pulled him towards her.

'I'm not sure about you. I think you genuinely like me but…' Marcus slipped his hands around to her back following her spine down to her skirt. Their bodies touched and swayed gently, their breathing was rapid and deep; Tamara gently started to pull his shirt out of his trousers. 'I am actually rather taken with you, no I'm bloody besotted with you,' continued Marcus as her hands went under his shirt and up his broad back. 'But Tamara I sense you have a past that in someway concerns me. Actually I suspect you have many secrets and you are living a charade of a life.'

Tamara said nothing and she pulled her hands from under his shirt and started to unbutton it. This was the first time she had allowed herself to relax with a man. Like a flower caught in a summer breeze she swayed her body and let her pelvis touch with his. Her resolve was melting and she noticed her hands were shaking so much she couldn't undo his buttons.

Tamara's lips began to part as she started to speak but Marcus bent forward and caressed them softly with his. He brought his hands slowly around the waist then up following the contours of her hips and over her breasts. He took her hands and placed them on his hips as he completed the job she couldn't manage. Gently he slid Tamara's blouse over her shoulders and it fluttered onto the floor behind her. He slipped the two bra straps off and pulled her right breast from the cup. Marcus made a deep sigh and bent his knees so he could suckle the dark erect nipple. Tamara let out a deep moan and brought her hands up onto his head massaging his scalp. Tamara glanced behind her and took a step backwards towards the bed. A loud metallic screech pierced the sensual quiet of the bedroom making them both jump and pull away.

'Damn, that blasted thing,' cursed Marcus as he fumbled in his trouser pocket for his mobile, his loosened shirt getting in the way. Casting Tamara an apologetic glance he finally retrieved it and although he stabbed at the off button, he actually answered the phone. He could hear Charles' voice imploring him to speak to him and for a brief moment he thought about answering Charles' pleas. Pressing the red button and terminating the power he threw it onto a chair by the bed. He undid his cuffs and let his shirt drop down and he took a pace closer to Tamara. Marcus cursed his friend as Tamara had now returned to being nervous and she would not meet his eye. She had placed her naked bosom back inside the bra.

'There you go again.' Marcus said a glimmer of disappointment shadowing his face as her naked breast was covered. 'Just when I think I'm getting close to you… up come the shutters.'

Tamara took a step towards the dressing table and stood still as she could make out the handle of the silver letter opener in the darkness of her handbag. She stopped and turned to him her hands reaching and retrieving the knife, holding it behind her back; skilfully sliding it down the waist band of her dress.

'Go and sit on the bed,' she said slowly. Marcus could see the dusty look of lust forming in her eye.

Marcus didn't argue and sat down on the side of the bed. Tamara took several paces towards him but stopped just out of his reach. Circling him she told him to close his eyes. Marcus obeyed while she slipped the knife under the pillow on the bed. Coming back around in front of him she lent forward and kissed him tenderly. Marcus opened his eyes to see Tamara undoing her dress and letting it tumble onto the floor. Smiling at him she unhooked her bra letting it fall to join the dress by her feet. Marcus sat and gaped at the vision in front of him as his loins starting to stir. He could feel his own blood thumping noisily around his body, every nerve sharpened reading expectantly.

'Oh Marcus I have some secrets, you're right, some terrible secrets.' Tamara took a step forward but couldn't pull her eyes away from his.

Marcus kicked off his shoes and lay back on the bed opening his arms and motioning for her to join him. His disarming smile having the right effect as he saw Tamara remove her last remaining garment.

'Come and tell me everything and, if you do, I just might have a little secret to tell you…' Marcus whispered as Tamara knelt astride him, unbuttoning his trousers.

Chapter 9

Charles toiled over his paper work for an hour but his mind kept wandering back to Marcus and the jewels. He really wished he had been able to see them; just once. Finally he pushed all the correspondence into a file, he couldn't wait any longer, he had to pay Marcus a visit. Quickly leaving the building, he hailed a taxi. He arrived outside Marcus' shop a few minutes later and he went straight in. Dawn was sitting in a chair, writing and looking extremely pleased with herself, a cheque held in her hand. She looked up and smiled.

'Uncle Charlie,' she said standing and pecking him on the cheek but noticed Charles' intense look. 'Oh, it looks as though your day hasn't gone particularly well.'

'Actually it went pretty well, after a rough start,' Charles said looking round. 'Where is he then? All three of us need to sit down and sort this mess out. What was taken in the burglary?'

'How did you know about that?' Dawn placed her hands on her hips. 'Charles, how…'

'Your father has reported it and he *claims* nothing was taken. There again I suppose he could hardly tell the police about the jewels he stole, could he?' Charles came and stood by Dawn glancing towards the office.

'Oh no! Damn it, I should have gone after him and told him. I just thought I'd let him stew in his own juices for a while and then I became involved with a customer... He'll be positively beside himself by now…' Dawn started to make for the door.

'Wow, slow down. Explain yourself young woman. What do you mean he *really thinks* they've been stolen?' Charles said taking Dawn by her arm and turning her to face him.

'I went to see Toby for an hour or so, after I left you, and when I came back he was in a terrible mood and that's when he told me we had been burgled. He stormed out, saying he was going to Giovanni's for a coffee and, I suspect, a drop of something harder. He told me to check my belongings. I went upstairs and the box and jewels are still in my drawer.' Dawn looked alarmed as Charles grip tightened on her arm then a shadow of a smile formed on his face.

'You didn't put them back where he thinks they should be?'

'No, Dad came in last night just I was going though them all and it was all I could do to get back to my room and hide them. Later when he was asleep, that's when I found the note. I told you all of this before. I was going to put them back today, but of course now…' Dawn gave a glance towards her arm. Charles, seeing her look, let go as he realised with a flash of embarrassment how hard he had be gripping her.

'I didn't realise you hadn't put them *back* where Marcus thought they were. You beautiful, clever thing!' Charles kissed the girl on the forehead. 'Is he still at Giovanni's?'

'I don't know, I suppose so, but listen I would have put them back, don't let him think I was trying to hide them.' Charles continued to listen but couldn't help let a broad smile develop. 'Oh by the way,' said Dawn making her way toward the door, 'I had written down the names, or most of them, on a piece of paper. Do you remember?'

'Good, I could do with a copy…'

'Well that's just it. I wrote them on a small pad in my room, I could swear to it, but this morning the piece of paper was gone.' Charles frowned and took a moment to assimilate the new information.

'You still have the original?' he asked. Dawn nodded. 'Great, we need to get to Marcus, come on! I just have a feeling he may be getting a visitor soon.' Charles followed Dawn towards the door.

'Visitor? He's already had a caller about half an hour ago, and I sent her down to the cafe.' Dawn turned the door sign over.

'Her? What did she look like?' Charles now had Dawn by the hand and was marching her down the street.

'Charles! I've got heels on, slow down…'

'Sorry, but tell me what did she look like?'

'She had a very smart skirted suit, long brown hair and large eyes. Not pretty as such but very attractive in her own way. Don't worry, she wasn't Dad's type… Charles, slow down!' Dawn was tottering beside Charles who hadn't slowed at all.

'Oh god, I just hope my instincts are wrong…,' he said as they entered the café with Dawn leading the way to the owner working behind the bar.

'Giovanni, have you seen Dad?'

'Yes, he left here a short while ago. Why?' Giovanni was wiping some glasses and had a smirk on his face.

'He wasn't alone when he left?' asked Charles. Giovanni nodded and went to speak but checked as he realised Marcus' daughter was standing in front of him. 'Speak up man, we need to know,' continued Charles.

Dawn nodded and looked at the Italian with pleading eyes. 'Giovanni, it's really important, please tell us,' Dawn's tone had become more demanding.

'He left with a woman, a quite formally dressed lady about twenty minutes ago. She came in not that long after he had sat down,' Giovanni pointed towards the table. 'They had some wine and then suddenly they were gone. It was pretty obvious to all who can see what they had on their minds… She didn't look his type…'

'Stop the riddles man, what had they on their mind?' Charles voice became terse.

'Oh Uncle Charlie, at times you are unbelievable. Thanks Giovanni,' said Dawn turning and leaving the café with Charles still uncertain what was happening and trying to catch up with her on the pavement.

'What on their minds? My god you can walk fast in heels when *you* want to.'

'Sex Charles, they were leaving for sex. I wonder who she is?' Dawn slowed and turned to Charles. 'You know who she is, don't you?'

'Let's get back to the shop, we need to phone him. Do you know where the photos of the sailing holiday are?' Dawn nodded and as they arrived at the shop; she unlocked the door. 'Go and fetch them while I try and contact your father.'

Charles produced his mobile and pressed a pre-set number. He heard Marcus' phone ring for awhile and then Charles could hear Marcus answer the phone but didn't speak. Charles shouted down the phone telling Marcus not to hang up but it was pointless, the line went dead. He tried again and went straight onto the answer phone. 'Damn, damn. Marcus you bloody fool.'

Dawn came down the stairs with an envelope full of photographs. 'Any luck?'

Charles shook his head and taking the pictures, spread them on the table in the middle of the room. 'If you're right about what those two are up to then, hopefully, I've made a mistake…' Charles found the photograph he wanted; a group of people sitting around a long dining room table. He picked out a woman sitting next to Marcus and pointed to her. 'Is that the lady who asked for Charles?'

Dawn examined the picture and focused closely on it. 'Hair is the same but…' She went into the office and rooted out a magnifying glass. 'Yes, that's her I can tell by the eyes, but she looks so different, I don't think she was wearing any make-up here.' Dawn had now come back into the shop, still studying the picture. 'So, who is she then?'

'She works at the V&A, and she was also at Kinloch Castle the night we were there. Your father took quite a shine to her.' Charles sat down and thoughtfully played with the photographs spread out before him. Dawn stood staring at Charles slowly shaking her head.

'Charles, exactly what happened at that castle? This entire situation just doesn't seem real, somehow. Where and exactly what are the jewels that Dad has and why all the interest…?'

Charles lent back and put his face in his hands. 'I wish I knew all the answers, the whole thing seems to be snowballing out of control. Your damn father has started something this time.' Charles glanced at Dawn, a tinge of guilt filling him for cursing his friend. 'Sorry, Dawn. I shouldn't have sworn. You see, I think your old man is in serious trouble, his wheeling and dealing has got the better of him. That's not all, if my hunch is right, he could be in more than just a spot of bother. I think this lady he is currently cavorting with may have another agenda…'

Dawn frowned and sat by Charles. 'Another agenda?' she asked

'It is only a hunch, and the trouble is, I don't know if she has any accomplices and how high up this bloody thing goes.' Charles was thinking aloud and then he suddenly realised what he had said to Marcus' daughter and pulled himself together.

'Accomplices? How high… Charles what the hell are you talking about?'

Charles stood up slowly and decided to calm things down and change his tack. 'So you reckon they are playing lovers. Well I'm not so sure that they've gone off for a bit of…, you know.'

'Sex. It is unlikely Giovanni would get *that* wrong, believe me.' Dawn stood up and took a pace back as she watched Charles' agitation as he brushed his fingers through his hair.

'OK, OK maybe, but then they, or rather she…'

'Charles, I'm getting giddy with all this. What? Tell me, this is my father you're talking about.' Dawn put her hands back on her hips and glowered at Charles. He didn't notice as his eyes were focused in the distant.

'Dawn, get that parchment with the notes on.'

'Not until you tell me…'

'Dawn I will, but we need to find those people mentioned in the note.' Dawn shrugged her shoulders, turning around, her annoyance obvious, she went upstairs to her room, Charles closely following behind her.

As she passed her dressing table she pointed to the pad. 'That was the pad I used, and I am sure I wouldn't have torn it off like that.' She opened the drawer and pulled out the box but Charles was already studying the pad carefully. He put the pad down when he saw the box.

'Oh my, that is just beautiful.' Charles took the box and sat on the chair placing the box on the dressing table.

'The parchment is in the lining of the lid,' said Dawn leaning forward to open the lid and easing out the lining. 'I was writing the names down when Dad came home. I stuffed it all back in so that's why it is all a bit of a mess. You wouldn't have known anything was there before. It has been very cleverly done.'

Charles gawped at the jewels and Dawn pulled the note out of the lining and turned the box around to face Charles. He picked up a pen and started to copy down the names.

'I think this Bruce Longbottom must have been the family that adopted, or took Olga in and brought her up.' Charles carefully smoothed the parchment out.

'Olga, who is Olga? Charles please!' Dawn sat down heavily on the bed her arms crossed and dark eyes flashing at him.

'Look Dawn we just don't have time now, I think someone's life is in danger.' Charles said slowly but he couldn't resist picking up one of the jewels. 'No wonder Marcus couldn't help himself.' He then pulled out the tray and examined the empty space below.

'Just a minute, Charles. Never mind the jewels for a moment, who is in danger? Someone's life…' Dawn took the jewel from Charles and placing it back in the box and putting the shelf back in position; she closed the lid. 'I want a few answers, now.'

'OK, in a nutshell. This Olga woman is the only surviving bloodline of the last Tsar of Russia, albeit illegitimate.' Charles said his eyes transfixed on the box in front of him. Then he started scribbling down more notes. 'It seems our Russian friends would rather there is no chance of a claimant to the throne coming out of the woodwork.' Dawn's jaw fell open. 'It may well be that these,' Charles squinted at his notes, 'Davenport men could be a target for the KGB; there is no other reason for the interest in the names.'

'Davenport? I thought you said she was a Longbottom…'

'Come on Dawn, stay with me. Olga married a Davenport, and their children were Davenport's, obviously. But look at this note; *God be merciful; he has the disease.*' Dawn watched as Charles continued to examine the parchment. 'Haemophilia was common in the Royal households, especially the Romanovs. It is carried by the female but only the males suffer... But who wrote these notes and why?'

Dawn had closed her mouth and was blankly staring at Charles. 'So we need to find this guy and, I assume, Davenport's son, before...' Charles looked at her and nodded. 'But why are you worried about that woman who Dad is probably bonking the hind legs off? What has she got to do with this? She's hardly your average agent assassin...' Dawn eyes widened and her shoulders slouched a little when she saw Charles reaction to her last statement. He stood up and looked a little nervously at her.

'That's the problem, Dawn. I believe that is exactly what she is. We need to get to these two men and fast. She is probably with your Dad now trying to find out where the jewels are and if she really did the burglary last night...'

'Yes, but Dad really thinks they *have* been stolen. He can't help her and he hasn't a clue about the note I found. So why is she still interested in Dad?'

'Now who is being a bit naïve?' Charles looked up at the ceiling annoyed at his own flippancy. 'Yes of course, of course...' Charles' face started to turn pale as he considered the options. 'So she must believe that he has them because she searched for them last night. It can only be that she wants the jewels as well as any clues to a potential survivor of Olga's. It must have been *her* that took your notes and once she establishes that he really doesn't know where the jewels are, or that he doesn't know anything about the bloodline; she might not have anymore use for him...'

'*Oh Christ, Charles.* She might harm him?'

Charles lent forward and squeezed the girl's shoulder. 'Don't worry about your Dad. I don't think she goes around killing people when they have served their purpose.'

'But didn't that caretaker at the castle die recently…?'

'Let's not jump to conclusions. Anyway, you never know, she might actually like him. They got on extremely well at Kinloch, and thinking about it he told me he did actually *really* fancy her. I've never seen your father so bowled over by a woman.'

'I know we're probably over reacting, but we have to do something. Maybe they've gone to these Davenport men together. Oh Charles, call the police or your people at the V&A. We can't take any chances. Charles please, you know what Dad is like with women, he'll be putty in her hands. She will have the names like we do… Hold on,' Dawn stood and picked up the pad. 'I only wrote the first one down, the elder man, Roger Davenport. Dad returning home last night interrupted me.'

Charles stood staring at the parchment. 'But it won't take her long to find out he has a son. Come on think, think man,' Charles chastised himself. 'If she wanted to just get rid of the last bloodline she would have… Blast my mind is about to explode!'

'Unless she now knows that the first, elder guy,' Dawn looked at the parchment, 'Roger, who is 67 by the way and has this 'disease', lives in London and that she was seeing whether Dad knew where this chap actually lives.'

Charles looked at Dawn thoughtfully. 'That's it, you're a marvel Dawn. We have no time to lose. Hide those bloody jewels.' Charles turned and, picking up the parchment, went to the office downstairs. He took out his reading glasses and grabbed a telephone directory and started to flick through it. 'Oh, bugger,' he cursed as he saw the long list of Davenports. He looked carefully at the note: R.N.Davenport. Charles picked up the phone, and dialled. After many rings it's answered.

'Good afternoon, is that Roger Davenport; Ralph's father?' Charles held his breath.

'Yes, I'm Ralph's Dad. Who's speaking please?'

Charles decided not to alarm this man until he, and his son, were both safe.

'My name is Charles Ashford,' said Charles slowly checking

the date of birth of the son. 'I used to know your son and I am passing through…,' Charles checked the address in the phone book, 'Hampstead and was wondering if I could leave some old university pictures for Ralph, I think he may appreciate them.'

'Yes, of course, I'd like to have a look myself! However I am just about to be picked up to go to a hospital appointment. I am a haemophiliac, I'm afraid, and I am going through a particularly bad phase at the moment; bloody awful disease, but I mustn't grumble. What time were you likely to be passing by?'

Charles checked his watch and tried to estimate how long this man would be at his appointment. 'Well, depending on the traffic it would be around seven o'clock this evening give or take half an hour.'

'Yes, I'll certainly be back by then. My homehelp comes and helps me prepare dinner; she normally leaves about six thirty. I'm sorry, what is your name again?'

'Charles Ashford.' Charles heard the chimes of a front doorbell and someone calling.

'I can't recall Ralph ever mentioning your name… Oh, here's the ambulance. I will have to go, but we can have a chat tonight, any friend of Ralph's is friend of mine.'

'Good, I'll see you later. Oh, Mr Davenport. Does Ralph still live in London?'

'No, no he moved to Belgium some years ago. He lives in Bruges now. He says it's lovely, but with my condition I have never been able to visit him. He has just moved in with a new girlfriend… Give me a moment and I can give you his new address and telephone number.'

Charles waited for several minutes hearing the muttering of people and finally Roger came back to him.

'Sorry about that but they're hassling me to get ready. So he now lives in 52 Verriest Straat.' Roger spelt out the names and gave Charles the telephone number. 'Anyway I must really go now, goodbye.'

'Bye, Mr Davenport, thank you for your time and see you in

a few hours.' Charles underlined the name in the telephone directory and wrote down the older Davenport's number and address. He heard Dawn come charging down the stairs tripping on her heels, she made an expletive.

'Any luck, Charles?' She said poking her head into the study.

'I don't need luck. Hit the button the first time.' Charles took a London A–Z map book and jotted down a few directions. 'Can you drive your Dad's car?'

'No, I still haven't taken my test yet.' Charles looked up surprised. 'Well, I don't need to drive. Dad always drives if we go and pick up any stuff and Toby has his car and he naturally always drives. So, no point really.'

'Right, well we will take the tube. My car is in for a service' Charles sat studying the underground map.

'What? Are we going now?'

'No, *I'm* going at about six.' Charles turned and took off his glasses.

'There is no way you're leaving me here alone. What if that woman realises that the only person who could now have the jewels is me!'

'Or me...' Charles said thoughtfully.

'Heavens Charles, you've spent the last few minutes spooking me enough as it is.' Dawn turned and went into the shop and unlocked the front door before returning to the office door. 'Business has to go on, so until we leave I might as well try and earn a few bucks...'

'Your father should take a leaf out of your book.'

Charles spent the afternoon reading in the living room upstairs. Dawn had shown him the book she had found on her father's shelf. Charles made a call to Julian Appleforth but he had a niggling feeling that Julian was hiding something; he seemed to know about the book and said he would call back when he had located a copy. Charles worried that he seemed to becoming suspicious of everybody. There was one man he could trust, but it turned out James Pulford was in a high level meeting at

Westminster all afternoon and had left strict instructions not to be disturbed. Charles cursed, but he wasn't prepared to talk to anyone else.

He felt alone and a little vulnerable, what if this Tamara woman did decide to see if he or Dawn had the jewels. Should he send his wife and the kids away to her mothers out at Bray? He then tried his friend's mobile again and left a very curt and testy message to call him urgently.

'If you're lying somewhere with blood oozing from you, then it serves you right,' he whispered to himself, but he prayed for Dawn's sake that Marcus would be alright. They had become the perfect father and daughter, he thought. He hoped he could have a similar relationship with his daughters when they grew up. Finally he called his wife and explained he may well be very late and asked her to collect his car from the garage. He didn't want to worry her so he decided not to suggest that she should go to her mothers; Tamara wouldn't dare visit his home. His wife blew a kiss down the phone and told him to be good. Charles could hear the tinge of concern in her voice. Charles shuddered at what she would say if she knew the whole story.

At six o'clock Dawn locked up and Charles could sense her anxiety growing as Marcus had still not returned home.

'He'll be alright Dawn. You'll see.'

'Yes, he's probably lying exhausted in that woman's bed with a huge satisfied smile on his face, while we worry ourselves to death. Sometimes, Charles, he is so self centred it is untrue.' She stood in the living rooming fidgeting and after a few moments went towards her bedroom to change. 'Can we grab something to eat when we are out Charles? I can't be bothered to make anything.'

'Sure, my treat…'

'You're a real sweetie,' she said disappearing up the stairs and closing the bedroom door behind her.

Charles tried James Pulford's number again; still no answer. His confidence in this man was also starting to wane. Surely James

Pulford isn't part of this, he thought? However, he couldn't ignore the realisation there was a doubt creeping into his mind even about his own boss. Suspicion is a powerful and destructive force.

★ ★ ★

Tamara exited the Hampstead Tube Station and walked slowly down Heath Street, checking her map, her long coat flowing out behind her. She felt a certain foreboding at what she was about to do and now her mind was racing to think of ways to escape the circumstances in which she found herself. That afternoon, she knew, had to be a turning point in her life. Time and time again she ran through the whole afternoon's events. Tears readily, for the first time in years, had started to form freely in her eyes; she bit her lip and chastised herself to remain strong. In the space of a few hours she had lain with a man and been at ease, so much at ease. Her heart was heavy because she had finally realised that she had fallen in love and that her predicament meant it could never be.

How could she have even contemplated harming him, never mind killing him; how desperate she had become? But was that was all behind her now? Had she told him too much? Had she finally put the event of twelve years ago behind her? All these questions rushed through her mind becoming jumbled and confused. Marcus had been so understanding and gentle. He had sat quietly and listened just stroking her hair and occasionally giving her a gentle embrace. She had expected her nakedness to result in sex, it hadn't. She never believed a man could be like that, certainly not the likes of Marcus Chapman. Why had she met him now, of all times? Could she really trust him? Showing him the letter opener and telling him some of her story had surely been a mistake. Would he still love her if she told him the whole story?

She carried on down the road, her mind still turning over the days events. So much so she almost forgot why she was there and then she remembered the jewels; they would change everything. Marcus claimed he hadn't got them and she believed him, for she had carefully questioned him; he seemed genuinely upset. So who did have them? It must be the daughter, he had already said that she had been very concerned about him recently. She could be the only one who possibly had the jewels. Tamara decided to pay her a visit, but then she saw Marcus in her mind's eye, and knew she could never frighten his daughter. Anyway, harming Dawn would be the end of her relationship with him; but she must find those jewels, it was her only hope.

She saw the road sign for Netherhall Gardens and her conversation with Colonel Suslov brought her back to the task in hand. Still she fought with herself to turn around and run back to Marcus, but the fear of the Russian Colonel won through, again. How she would love to tell Marcus absolutely everything; she almost had at one point in the afternoon. Her fears for her father, sister and nephew could not be wiped out by one afternoon, and yet... Tamara stopped and took several deep breaths. She felt light headed and rested on a garden wall. She could never wipe from her memory the days Andrei Suslov had kept her tied up in a bedroom. Hatred swelled inside her as she recalled the tight bonds on her ankles and wrists, no water or food and unable to go to a toilet; but most of all his smug smiling face every time he visited. He had enjoyed every minute and watching her fear and utter distress grow. She now doubted the information he had told her about her father; but her main concern was how she could save her sister. She forced the bad memories away and then recalled how she had felt in Marcus' arms. Helplessness absorbed her as she knew even Marcus couldn't rescue her from her torment; he would never understand why she had to continue with her orders. She forced her legs on and continued to argue with herself that the fat caretaker had actually fallen, it *had* been an accident. Would Marcus ever believe her? She stopped once more considering the thought of running back to Marcus, but Colonel Suslov continued to win the day.

Tamara turned a left hand bend and she saw the house in front of her. She checked her bag and the long silver blade lay there ready. Flicking her hair back she put a lighter pace into her step and went to the door. She was about to knock when she saw a shape through the frosted glass coming to the door. Then a shout of farewell as the door opened and out bustled a short, round woman, in a dark blue uniform.

'Sorry luv,' said the woman to Tamara and turned back into the house. 'Roger your guests are here…' The woman turned and left making her apologies saying she was running very late. Tamara took a couple of tentative steps into the hall and closed the door behind her. She had been seen; it would be perfectly acceptable to pull out of this task now she told herself.

'Hello, is that you Charles?' A quivering voice came from a door on her right.

'No, my name is Tamara,' she said entering the room and wondering why he should ask for Charles; which had made her forget to give him a false name. Could it be Charles Ashford?

'Oh, I thought Charles, Charles Ashford was coming. He's an old friend of Ralph's.' The man was trying desperately to stand up and his arms were shaking as he stubbornly continued a task he knew he could not manage on his own.

'Err yes; he is just dropping off some things down the road. I am his girl friend. Here let me help you,' said Tamara now realising Charles would be here soon, so if she was going to act she must do it now. Helping the man stand up she waited until he had steadied himself and then shook his hand.

'I'll make some tea. How long will Charles be?' said the man pointing at two walking sticks which Tamara fetched. Painfully taking a few steps he struggled out into the hallway.

'Tea would be lovely, but I can do it, if you want.' Tamara said quietly, as the memory of Marcus' naked body, while he made tea that afternoon in the room, flashed through her mind. For an instant she stood still, she could smell his warmth and how he had been so calm and reassuring…

'No it's alright. I'm not a total cripple yet. Mind you everyone is treating me as one.' The man stood still and breathing heavily, pointed to a picture on the staircase wall, with one of the walking sticks. 'That's Ralph on his graduation day. His mother would have been so proud…' The old man changed direction and tried to move up the first stair. 'I'll get it down for you.' Tamara saw the house was full of pictures of this man, mainly with many people around him at social functions. Some of them she knew their faces; he clearly knew a lot of celebrities.

'No that's OK, I'll get it. Where does your son live now?' interjected Tamara, but the old man had started to move up the first step; he stopped and looked back at Tamara.

'I told Charles he had moved to Bruges. Didn't he tell you?'

'Oh, yes, he did mention it. I didn't know your son that well; unlike Charles,' Tamara said watching the struggling man in front of her.

'Did he bring the pictures?'

'Pictures?'

Roger was now taking the third step of the stairs, which turned round the corner, and hearing the woman's question he tried to turn.

'Who the hell are you?' he shouted. 'That's why you and this Charles fellow were coming here…'

Tamara instinctively took a pace forward as the old man lost his footing and tumbled forwards crashing into the banister. He let go of the walking sticks and tried to grab hold of anything but his momentum threw him onto the floor, his arms and legs had become loose and heavy as his head thudded hard against the wood floor. He let out a small whimper as he turned to face Tamara. His eyes remained opened and in a few seconds glazed over with his mouth opened slightly.

Tamara looked on in horror stooping forward over the crumpled body. She wet the back of a finger and put it under the man's nose and waited; there seemed to be no movement of air. His mouth opened wider and she went to close his unfocused eyes but her hand withdrew involuntary. The old man had a startled look on his face and Tamara saw blood oozing from one of his ears; his hands twitching spasmodically. Standing, she went round the man and being careful not to touch anything, took a long hard look at the photograph on the wall. Now all she had to do was find the address for the son and she could be away.

A sudden banging made Tamara jump; she initially froze on the spot. Turning and placing her back against the wall she leant forward enough to see two shapes through the frosted glass of the front door. More banging and then she heard the letter box open she recoiled to hear a man's voice curse with alarm. The letterbox opened again this time, a woman muttered a little cry of despair. The crack of the letterbox shutting was immediately followed by receding footsteps. Tamara waited as she heard the two visitors talk loudly and walk away. She waited and saw a few plaques to a charity hanging on the wall opposite. After a few moments she checked her map and, moving swiftly and silently, opened the back door, vaulted a fence and walked down Frognal towards the tube station. She wasn't going to wait to search the house for the son's address.

Forty minutes later she sat in her own flat trembling and picking up courage for her next task. Somehow she had to try and talk to Marcus' daughter, but she had to be alone with her. She undressed and showered and slipping into her old night dress, she lay on her bed. Then she tried to forget about the evening's events and the sight of the dead old man. She started to fantasise about lying there with Marcus, holding him, touching him and stroking his broad shoulders. The image of the old man falling broke her reverie. Tears again started pricking her eyes, but she forced them back and focused on her family, especially her father who she hadn't seen in over twelve years. She had to be strong for their sake, her own desires must be put to one side, yet Marcus kept returning to her mind. Then she remembered something Marcus had mentioned, that he had a secret and something very precious. He had only mentioned it once and she felt that Marcus also wanted to tell her something… It was as if he was planning something as well; just maybe…

★ ★ ★

181

Charles and Dawn made their way through London on the Piccadilly line and then changed to the Northern Line to Hampstead. Dawn put her hair into a pigtail as she hated the grime of the tube. They sat silently as the train rumbled along tossing the passengers around in unison. Finally they arrived and Charles took out his A–Z street map and navigated them to Netherhall Gardens. They arrived at Roger Davenport's house and knocked on the glass front door. No answer.

'Strange, I can't imagine he is still at the hospital. I'll call through the letter box…'

'Give him a few minutes. He has quite a debilitating disease, hasn't he?'

Charles waited a few moments and knocked again, but still no answer, so he stooped down and opened the letter box and was just about to call out when he saw the crumpled figure of an old man at the bottom of the stairs. 'Oh my God.' Charles stood up and took a step back.

Dawn stepped forward and looked though the letter box. 'Oh no it can't be, we are too late,' she cried out softly as she backed away from the door.

Charles had turned and started to walk away. 'Charles, Charles we can't just walk away we must call an ambulance or the police. Charles we can't just leave him!' Dawn grabbed Charles' arm and tried to turn him.

'Dawn I am getting a very bad feeling about all this. Let's get out of here and call an ambulance from the tube station.' Charles took the young woman's arm and pulled her along.

'What about your mobile phone, can't you use that?'

'It will be traceable; I need to speak to a few people about this before I start sticking my neck out.'

'Charles what if he isn't dead, we just can't walk away. He *may* have had an accident; Charles please stop.'

Charles didn't stop and continued pulling her along until they came to a public phone booth just outside the station. All he could think of was how similar this incident was to Malone's death back at Kinloch Castle. Charles stepped inside and ignoring the many invitation cards from various voluptuous looking girls, he rang 999, stated the address and said someone had fallen and needed help then he hung up. They took the tube back to the King's Road. Neither talked or mentioned eating.

Dawn tried to open the door but the key wouldn't budge; then she realised the door was already open. 'I could have sworn I locked it…' She opened the door tentatively and heard the buzzer in the office. Charles went inside first picking up a brass handled poker from the fireplace, stealthfully edging towards the stairs.

'Hello, is that you Dawn?' Marcus' voice could be heard from upstairs.

'Jesus…,' muttered Charles and he replaced the poker while Dawn bounded up the stairs in her usual robust manner.

'Dad, where on earth have you been, we were worried sick.' Dawn took her father in a large embrace. 'You could have called, and why did you not take Charles' call…'

'Slow down, Dawnie. Oh, hello Charles, what are you doing here?' Marcus took his daughter and hugged her back. 'You both look worried sick. Shouldn't I be the one asking the questions?'

'Oh, Dad we have so much to tell you…'

'And Marcus, I believe you have a lot to tell us as well, don't you?' said Charles but Marcus just shrugged his shoulders. Charles frowned and gave his old friend a long stare. 'Marcus it is time you came clean. We know about the jewels and…'

'Oh bugger how did you…, anyway it's all a bit academic now for I have some rather bad news for you regarding those…' Marcus' head drooped and he looked at the floor.

'I am going to pop home and kiss the kids good night and try to explain to Samantha where the hell I've been all day. Dawn you had better brief your Dad about what has happened in the last twenty four hours and put him out of his misery about the jewels. I can't stand looking at that hangdog expression all evening. Oh, and you'd better warn him about his new lover as well, second thoughts wait until I return.' Charles turned and left with Marcus slowly turning to face his daughter.

'I am more than intrigued, Dawn. Pray, put me out of my misery! What has your meddling little mind been up to? What do you know about the jewels and what did he exactly mean by: "my new lover?" Have you two been spying on me?'

'Dad, we know about you and Tamara and never mind what *I've* been up to, you have a lot of explaining to do. Dad, as Charles has said, your wheeling and dealing has put not only yourself, but Charles and I, into trouble. Yes, us!'

'OK stop right there, tell it to me from the top. I'll get some wine, you talk. So did I hear Charles correctly, you also know something about the jewels?'

'Yes, I found them yesterday evening…, but let's wait until Charles is back and then talk.'

'You found them? *You've got the jewels…* You went rooting through the safe…' Marcus first felt a leap of excitement that the jewels weren't stolen and then a flush of anger at the thought of his daughter's deceit.

'Well if I hadn't then you would have lost them and I found *a note,*' said his daughter sensing her father's rising anger. Marcus stopped opening the wine and looked at his daughter with a puzzled frown. 'Yes, I found a note in the lining of the lid of the box. Anyway, I really think we should wait until Charles returns and we can go though it all then, it's quite complicated. But it is possible a man is dead because of that note *and* his son could be next.'

'You have the jewels,' said Marcus but as he thought through Dawn's explanation questions started to explode in his head. 'Hold on, Dawn slow down a bit. Dead? You mean the caretaker…'

As Dawn looked at her father's face her eyes narrowed and her lips pursed. 'No Dad, a man who lived up in Hampstead, who was the son of Olga, the only remaining blood line of the last Tsar. Charles believes that if your new girlfriend has anything to do with it, the bloodline will be ending pretty quickly…' Dawn was out of breath and she continued to hold her father's look.

'Olga? Tsar? Slow down for heaven's sake… Oh, so that was why that book was with the jewels…'

'Yes the book, and did you notice the pages we needed had been torn out.' Dawn took a deep breath. 'I think we should wait until Charles is back. This whole thing is getting a little confusing…' Dawn slumped down on a chair and pulled her hair tie out and shook her head, her long black silky hair flowing loose.

'But what has Tamara to do with all this?' Marcus flushed at asking such a question; he already knew the answer, or most of it.

'Just leave it Dad, wait until Charles gets back, please. I'm absolutely knackered.' Dawn leant back and looked at the ceiling her hair flowing over the back of the chair.

Marcus watched his agitated daughter as she nervously flicked with her nails taking care not to meet her father's eyes. He knew he should never have taken those jewels and he cursed the night they had sailed into the Isle of Rum. Then momentarily he questioned himself, those jewels could also give him a new lease of life. He felt a sense of dejection. If he hadn't taken them he would have never met Tamara and the events of the afternoon and his new found love would never have been. But seeing his daughter in such a state hurt him.

'Anyway, what did happen between you and that woman? Charles was really worried he thought…, well I'll let him explain. Dad you should have taken his call, why didn't you?' Dawn stood up and went into the kitchenette, her father followed along behind her carrying the bottle of wine. She took out a chopping board and cut up some lettuce and tomatoes. She stopped and looked at her father as he stood looking slightly perplexed and glum faced. Marcus placed the bottle down and opened the fridge and took out some chicken and placed it into a frying pan, sprinkling some spices on them. Dawn saw he looked distant and in a world of his own; a world that was clearly of concern to him.

'I'm not sure I want to talk about it right now…' Marcus finally said, as he turned the sizzling chicken over; he was aware

185

of his daughter's eyes boring into him. 'Why is Charles so concerned? She works at his ruddy place; the V and bloody A. You're wrong she isn't involved in all this…' He hated continually lying to his daughter. Dawn finished preparing the salad and pushed her father aside to finish cooking the chicken, she motioned for him to pour the wine. The silence continued as the two of them set the table.

'Did you go and have sex then?' Dawn blurted out, angry that she was the first to break the silence.

'What makes you so sure I went and had…? Oh I suppose Giovanni told you.' His daughter nodded and placed the chicken pieces in the salad. 'Well, as a matter of fact we *did* go to a hotel room…'

'My god if I ever did anything like that, you would go absolutely berserk, wouldn't you?' Dawn shook a French dressing bottle violently glowering at her father. 'Dad look what happened to Mum and you; Christ you hardly knew her when you, well you took her. Now you're doing it again with a virtual stranger and I bet there are many more. It is a pity there isn't a name for a male whore, because that's what you are; a male slapper. I suppose you still believe its OK for a man to put it about, but not a woman!'

Marcus was taken aback by the outburst and the depth of her feelings. There were obviously scars from her knowing she was the result of a first night's lusty encounter. Marcus took three glasses and poured wine into two of them feeling affronted by his daughter's outburst.

'I'm not going to argue, or even disagree with you, because you're right, absolutely right, although a bit disrespectful to your father.' Marcus smiled weakly at his daughter. 'In fact since I left your mother I have been pretty lousy to the women I have met, trust me you don't know the half of it. I am *not* proud of myself.' Marcus continued to look at his daughter and was shocked to see tears in her eyes. 'I have led a thoroughly empty life since then, in fact a very lonely life. However, since you came to live here I have started to enjoy life more, but life still feels empty to me somehow.' His daughter came towards him and took his hands looking squarely at her father, she nodded for him to continue. 'We went to the hotel room and she was nervous, not a shy nervous, but really almost fearful. We did get into bed but...'

'Oh Dad, it's my turn to be embarrassed. This is too much information...'

'You asked, so I'm going to tell you, so shut up for a minute.' Marcus turned and picked up the two glasses handing one to her and taking a sip. 'We *did* get into bed and we *did* lie down together. She was fighting something within herself somehow, as if she had some demons that wouldn't leave her alone. She also told me things that I can't repeat...'

'What! Dad...'

'Dawn let me finish, please. She told me, well, about her life and I need to think about what she said before I can discuss it. I'm not sure she has told me everything, some things she said don't add up. Listen to me Dawn, I have to say I really fancied her the first time we met and the second time she nearly blew my mind, so you can imagine what I was going through. She is no teenager on her first date, but she acted like it. Well, we lay together and cuddled a little but then we started talking...' Dawn threw her head back and looked at her father questioningly. 'I'm telling you we lay and talked and I mean talked. I really daren't tell you what we talked about, but let's put it this way, I suspected she is up to her neck in all this. I told her things I shouldn't have, there was something about her that..., then something very strange happened.'

The buzzer went down stairs and they heard Charles calling out and coming up the stairs.

'Dad, what strange thing happened?' Charles entered the room and stopped at the sight of the father and daughter standing in front of each other in deep conversation and didn't acknowledge him.

'She showed me a type of silver letter opener, a type of knife actually…' Marcus checked himself from going into too much antique detail and made a watery grin to hide his own concerns. 'I've never felt so much confusion and inner pain within anyone.'

'Showed you a …?'

Charles placed a bottle of wine he had brought on the table. 'I presume you are talking about Tamara and the events of the day?' They both nodded but kept their eyes fixed firmly on each other.

'So she showed you a knife?' continued Dawn making Charles check and look towards Marcus.

'Yes, she was intending to… Look I really don't want to talk about that. We never had sex, we just held each other. Ha! I even made some tea for her. Standing there in the all together while lying on the bed was a beautiful woman in all *her* glory, and there I was making a cup of ruddy tea. Gee, I'm really losing my touch.' Marcus let go of her hands trying to laugh but he coughed to hide his shaky voice. 'I think we have really fallen for each other, but then she said that we could *never* be together. Something about her job and she has to go away.' Marcus flushed as he lied to his daughter again. 'She drank her tea, dressed and then, rather oddly she apologised to me, about bringing the letter opener… I couldn't work her out at all.'

'Sorry, but where does the knife fit into all this?' Charles had now joined them by the table.

'She told me she was going to use it to threaten me, but she assured me she would never have used it…'

'Bloody hell Marcus, and don't tell me you believe her?' Charles was now wide eyed and viewing his friend curiously.

'Actually I do, and I repeat, I am not saying any more about this evening, so don't bother asking.' Marcus poured some wine for Charles and the only sound was the humming fridge and traffic from outside.

Charles picked up his glass and nodded at the two in front of him. 'Threaten you. What for?'

Marcus didn't answer but took a sip of wine.

'Marcus I believe she was using you to gain information. I think she is primarily after someone; she was looking for the names of the possible bloodline of the Tsar. I think it is very likely that she is working for the Russians.' Charles looked squarely at his friend who didn't meet his look and he dropped his head. Marcus was confused, but not surprised. Tamara had virtually told him as much. This must have been the part of the story she kept from him. 'Come on Marcus, let's sit down and eat and all tell our stories, slowly and carefully. We need to sort out exactly where we are and more importantly, exactly what we do next.'

The three sat down and Marcus recounted events from his first meeting with Malone to his recent amorous encounter with Tamara. He never mentioned the suite of jewels he had hidden separately and his fantasy to help Tamara. Dawn, a little sheepishly, told how she was concerned about her father and decided to go searching for the jewellery box and finally Charles informed them of the *VfA* and what had happened that morning. When they had finished they cleared the dishes in virtual silence as Marcus opened another bottle of wine; they then retired to the lounge. Charles had now started to write down all the facts.

'Look Charles, that guy Davenport it could have been a coincidence... I know you don't believe in coincidence, but he was an old chap and very ill...' Marcus said after asking Dawn to fetch the jewels and the jewellery box. Charles didn't respond and gave Marcus a thoughtful look. When Dawn had brought the jewels and box back she spread them out on the table and the three could scarcely take their eyes off them. Dawn took the note out of the box for her father.

'I've taught you well my girl,' he said pecking her on her brow. 'So what do you think Charles, do we go to the police and tell them? Otherwise this chap's son may be the next to go.' As soon as he had said it Dawn and Charles looked at him a little astonished.

'Well, if we assume that Roger Davenport was killed then the next target would be his son. I would love to believe Tamara isn't actually involved in any of this, but she is. However she isn't a murderer; I'm certain of it.' Marcus was concerned in case his voice showed his own doubts.

Charles was scribbling down more notes furiously and sat back pulling his hands over his head. 'Sorry Marcus, but I believe she is an agent and capable of anything. It is time to call in the cavalry. I know your feelings for Tamara, but all the evidence does point to her…' He looked at Dawn. 'Although you didn't write down the other son on that pad, we must assume she will establish who the son is and where he lives. The good thing is he lives in Bruges, and fortuitously has recently moved in with his girlfriend; not easy to trace his address, but we have the solution…' Charles picked up the paper with the address and leaning back gazed into the clear liquid in his glass.

'Bruges! Well maybe there is a chance we can get to him first.' Marcus said going towards the television. 'Sorry guys but can I watch the local news?' Marcus picked up the handset and pressed a button.

'Let's just suppose that it is Tamara,' started Charles slowly. 'What if she isn't after the jewels, but as she is working for the KGB, she may have different orders.' The other two turned to him quizzically. 'Oh, I didn't mention before apparently there is a department within the KGB that is dedicated to ensuring no Romanov, or any of the Tsar's heirs, ever comes to light. I think they said the head of this department is the grandson of one of the men who killed the Tsar and his family. Well Tamara did study in Moscow…'

'Yes, she told me. She said they treated her badly,' Marcus stopped and pondered for a moment. Charles looked at him questioningly. 'It was part of her story that didn't quite ring true. At the time I felt she was looking for sympathy, but I'm not so sure now. Charles she is not the archetypal KGB agent I'll swear to it, well not voluntarily anyway. I know they have something over her.'

'Ah, you may well have a point there…,' said Charles studying his notes.

The room went silent as the local news came on the television. The mention of Roger Davenport's name brought them all back from their thoughts and in unison they turned towards the TV.

'There is sad news tonight at the death of Roger Davenport. Mr. Davenport had been stalwart in the charity for haemophilia suffers. He had suffered from this terrible disease himself but he always thought of others first. The London Haemophilia Society said he will be sorely missed and over the past few decades he had raised a vast amount of money to help fellow suffers. It is believed he fell down his stairs; however police want to trace three people who were seen around Mr. Davenport's house this evening, plus the unknown person who called 999. A couple were seen going back towards Hampstead from Netherhall Gardens at just after seven o'clock. He was in his early forties, fair and around six foot tall wearing a sports jacket. His partner was a young women in her twenties and had long dark hair tied into a pony tail. A third female was seen exiting the rear of the house. She had shoulder length brown hair, slim, and wore a long dark coat. The police have asked if these people could come forward to eliminate them from their enquiries.

Now it is...'

Marcus stood up and went and turned the TV off. 'Charles you had better call that cavalry pretty damn quick. This *is* now totally out of our control.' Marcus turned to Charles and was met by the sight of him holding his head in his hands.

'That's the problem Marcus; I don't think I can...'

Chapter 10

Marcus and Dawn stood mesmerised at the sight of Charles his head still buried in his hands. He slowly looked up returning their stare.

'Think about it. If we go to the police we are all going to be interviewed and it will possibly be well into tomorrow before they would do anything. Even the V&A could not come to the rescue quickly enough. Unfortunately Marcus you are right we must assume Tamara *is* seriously caught up in all of this… How long before she, or any of her Russian colleagues, find out where the son, Ralph Davenport lives? These people are very resourceful, you know. If I can find the address then they surely can.'

'Just wait a minute. If he has only just moved to his girlfriend's house I'm not so sure. Anyway for the moment can we give Tamara a little bit of slack? She may well yet surprise us, I've got that feeling.' Marcus stopped and recalled the knife she had shown him. He continued, 'Well I would like to think that her involvement is more information assimilation than, well you know. If it isn't then she deserves everything coming to her. However, I think I know her better than you two…'

'You can say that again,' whispered Dawn a little too loudly.

Marcus ignored his daughter's comments. 'She just isn't the person you think she is.' Marcus saw the look his daughter and Charles were giving him and his stomach muscles tightened; had Tamara completely hoodwinked him?

'Dad, shoulder length brown hair, slim; it just has to be her. That isn't a coincidence and I want to know what else you told her while she sobbed her heart out to you. You're so naive with women Dad; you'd fall for the crying on your shoulder trick without a doubt. I know; I could wrap you round my little finger from the age of three.' Dawn paced up and down the room. 'You told her you had had the jewels, didn't you?' She turned and faced her father.

'I didn't mention I had jewels as such, more on the lines I had had a fortunate find, but then I did tell her that I had been burgled… I'm not sure if she believed me, but at the time I genuinely thought I had been turned over.' Marcus let out a long sigh.

'I believe she thinks the jewels have gone from you, but she may come to the conclusion one of us two has them. Marcus, the *VfA* suspects that it has a mole within the organisation; Tamara fits the bill perfectly. Her priority must be to find Davenport as well. Maybe she's after the jewels for her own benefit? So the only thing left is for us to go and find this Ralph Davenport in Bruges…' Charles said quickly picking up his glass. 'If we don't get to him first, then we could have *his* death on our hands.'

'Oh no, please no more.' Dawn put her head down in desperation. 'You have to go to the police, they will call the Belgium police and they will locate this man and everything will be all right. Look, with all due respect you two just aren't up to this…' Dawn started to shout at them and looking up she noticed they had both reacted as if she wasn't there. 'Are you two listening to me?'

'Have the police still got your passport Marcus?'

'Damn, damn, yes they do.' Marcus sat back thumping the arm of the chair with force.

'Then,' Charles stood up slowly, 'we will have to sail to Belgium ourselves.' Charles and Marcus looked at each other; a momentary sparkle in each of their eyes. 'My father's boat is moored at Ramsgate,' he glanced at his watch, 'if we get away now we will be on the boat in a couple of hours and if we motor all the way…' Charles scribbled a few notes and figures. 'We could be in Ostende by late morning.'

'No, absolutely not! Can you two just for once act with a modicum of common sense, *please*?' Dawn was shaking her head, her hair swirling from side to side, as she sat looking at the two men in total disbelief. 'Anyway what about me? Do you want me to just sit here while you two go off like a pair of swashbuckling school boys?'

'You'll be OK. Even if Tamara wanted the jewels she won't risk doing anything to Marcus' daughter, what do you think, Marcus?' Charles said watching Marcus who nodded in agreement and smiled at his daughter. 'Plus in reality she can only have a suspicion it is you; hardly worth blowing her cover for?' Charles watched Marcus' puzzled and concerned frown. 'We discussed the possibility before, that logically Tamara must realise the only people who could have the jewels are Dawn or I. Anyway I think this is all irrelevant as she will now be after this Davenport chap in Belgium…'

'Thanks for that Charles, but I'm not convinced. Turning up seducing Dad and then brandishing a knife that she claimed she wasn't going to use, sounds like an unstable mind to me…' Dawn was flushed and breathing heavily.

'Marcus, what do you think? Are you up for it?' Charles asked watching Marcus who remained seated, his concern showing in his eyes.

'Sorry Charles, but I think Dawn has a point.' Marcus lent forward towards Charles. 'There is something terrifying Tamara, and what worries me is she may be compelled to do something she will regret. Look, what about those guys you work with at the V&A and that Veritus, or what ever it's called, organisation; surely they can help? We can't go gallivanting to Europe. Would this Davenport chap believe us anyway, or even listen to us?'

'Well I've been trying to get hold of my boss, but I just can't contact him. I'll be honest I daren't trust anybody else regarding Tamara, it is not beyond the realms of possibility that there are others, even our old friend Mr. Bat. Few people knew about the ring apart from Julian and of course Tamara…' Charles looked at his notes and recalled the discussions with James Pulford. He felt an ambitious surge as he considered the consequences if he could manage to rescue the jewels and save Davenport; it would be a real feather in his cap at this early stage of his career with the *VfA*.

'OK, so maybe not the V&A but I've still got that police inspectors card,' said Marcus. 'Hines, I think his name was. He'll listen. I think you're wrong Charles, they can get to Davenport quicker than us, heavens we could give them the bloody address.' Marcus went and put his hand on Charles' shoulder. 'Come on Charles we are hardly Starsky and Hutch let's leave this to the professionals. It's not just a bit of a risky night sailing; it *could* be life or death and the way you calculate tides and navigate, it could be our lives.' Marcus squeezed Charles' shoulder again seeing the disappointment and a touch of hurt, in his friend's eyes.

'OK, give him a call but you may have problems at this time of night.' Charles said continuing to look dejected.

Marcus went down to the small office and called D I David Hines' direct line; he was answered by a voice mail. He then tried the main police number and was told the inspector would not be back until the morning. Marcus pondered on whether to call the main police number but he had started to agree with Charles that if the police were invoved, this altered the situation. Everything would be out of their hands, so he slowly went back upstairs and informed the others.

'I have an idea,' said Charles, standing up and going to the window, his voice rising slightly. He turned to the other two. 'I'll go over by myself, and then you, Marcus, call the police in the morning. You haven't got a passport anyway. At least if they either don't believe you or take too long, I will still be able to get there…'

'How do you know she is going to Bruges? What makes you think she has any idea that she knows he is in Belgium.' Dawn said becoming further agitated and wanting to stop this foolish conversation continuing, especially involving her father. She was faced by two men whose excited expressions had faded and she wanted to end any further talk of sailing to the continent that night. 'You see, you two are getting a bit too excited. Think it through where on earth would she find out…? Ah, I forgot she was at Roger Davenport's house, or so we believe…' Dawn's speech faded out as she thought through the evening's events. 'Damn, the odds are she could have found the address.' Dawn went and slumped into one of the arm chairs.

Charles nodded thoughtfully and looking towards his old friend, he took a pace towards him. 'Marcus we *have* to assume she knows.' Charles said, his excitement returning.

'Well you're a liability on your own, and to be by yourself through those shipping lanes…' Marcus glanced at Dawn who was now looking at her father with wide appealing eyes. Her mouth started to open in disbelief; she now suspected her worst fears was starting to unfold.

'Right,' said Charles. 'That's settled then, there's no time to lose. I'll go and get my weather proofs, and you, Dawn look in the international directory to see if you can find Ralph's address, it will be his old one, but it will be handy to have. It may well be where Tamara is heading for right now. Marcus go and fetch your gear and I'll be back with the car in a few minutes; hopefully Samantha has picked it up from the garage.' Charles strode across the room towards the door, he thought again about what James Pulford would say if he did manage to save the day on this one, and acquire the jewels for the museum. 'Finally Dawn, you will call the police in the morning and then at least we are doing everything in our power to avert further blood shed.'

'You two are completely mad! Do you want to know something…?' Both men turned towards her. 'I'm fed up with arguing with such stubborn people. You'd better not tell Samantha what you're doing, she will go hysterical,' shouted Dawn at Charles as he departed.

The father and daughter looked at each other and not a word was said. Marcus left the room and Dawn could hear him rummaging in the old wardrobe in the spare room upstairs. She went downstairs to the office and made a few phone calls and surprised herself how quickly she managed to obtain a number and an address for an R.N.Davenport in Bruges; the question is whether it was correct.

Marcus came in with his sailing gear and looked at his daughter pensively. 'Sorry Dawn. I shouldn't have taken those jewels. I deserve all this.'

His daughter stood up and gave her father a smothering embrace. 'I think you'll find the word is stealing,' she said standing back and trying to look angry. 'I've found Davenport's old address. I suspect it wouldn't take anybody too long to call and get a forwarding address. You'd better let Charles know.' Dawn closed the directory and looked up at her father wavering at the doorway. 'You two, you've never grown up. Don't worry Dad, I'll call the police tomorrow and hopefully everything will be sorted by the time you two cavaliers get there. I promise I'll do my best.' She stood and took a pace forward and hugged him again. 'Dad, please look after yourself. When you get back I want to know exactly what you did talk about with that Tamara woman. Not what she said, but what *you* said to her?'

'I've told you; you really don't want to know…, and I am *not* discussing it tonight.' Marcus went and put the kettle on.

'Well actually I do. You talked about you, and your life now, didn't you?' Her father carried on preparing a flask of coffee, not daring to look back at his daughter. 'Dad, what did you say to her?' Still her father busied himself, not answering. 'She said a few things which sparked off something in your mind. You said before, that you talked in a way you have never done before. Dad I *am* a bit worried, talk to me, please.'

Marcus stopped and turned his head slowly to his daughter. 'There is something that we had in common, something even I only started to really understand myself when she was talking about *her* life.' Dawn went to speak but Marcus stopped her and carried on. 'I will tell you all about it when we get back; I promise, but not tonight Dawn please.'

'Dad, you're really…'

'No more Dawn; but all I will say is…' Marcus took a deep breath. 'I feel as if I have met a passing ship in the night, I know it sounds soppy or even romantic, but I feel an affinity with her. Something I can't fully understand myself, yet. Trust me I really wanted to board her; metaphorically speaking of course.' Marcus smiled weakly at the young woman in front of him and turned away pouring hot water into the flask. Gathering up his belongings he stuffed them roughly into his bag. He heard a car horn outside and kissed his daughter on both cheeks. 'Dawn, get Toby over here tonight to stay with you, and I want him here every night until we return. Understood?'

'My heavens, ordering me to stay with a man; well that'll be a first…'

'You know what I mean; I don't want any of that stuff under my roof so he stays *in* the guest room; OK?'

'Hey, how long are you planning on being away? You're only going across the channel.'

Marcus picked up his gear and gave his daughter his usual playful slap on her bottom. He left without a further word.

★ ★ ★

Tamara got up early the next morning and walked to a phone booth near her tube station. Calling Colonel Suslov on the special untraceable number always brought back the past. He knew that and took full advantage. She started to perspire and tremble from almost the moment she woke. Finally she got through to him and was treated in the usual brusque manner as he instructed her to which hotel she should use and when to contact him again. She waited until he had finished and then gripping the telephone tightly she told him her position had been compromised. She said it would surely be better if another agent should take on the task of eliminating Davenport's son. Finally she went quiet and the only sound was an oscillating buzz from the phone. Suslov's sneer as he goaded her decision not to finish the task she had been given; typical of her and her kind, he said; she might be suitable for information gathering but she lacked the backbone for real work. He continued to ridiculed her and spit his insults at her.

Andrei enjoyed the power he had over her; he had discovered her weaknesses over twelve years ago and he had massaged them mercilessly. He smiled to himself as he heard her trembling voice and her occasional pleas not to harm her father; she hadn't guessed yet that he already had. As he listened to her he lent back in his chair and recalled her naked body lying on a bed. Her fruitless attempts to untie her bonds only resulted in him tying them ever tighter. Her final capitulation was so sweet for him. The real stroke of luck was discovering her sister, her ultimate Achilles heel.

Tamara bit her tongue as she waited for the insults to finish and finally what he had decided to do; it was the first time she had directly rejected an order. If she had any doubts about her new plans before, they had vanished as Suslov continued to play with her his insults cutting into her like a sharp knife; she shook with fear, but a hatred was now festering and becoming harder to control. Finally Suslov ordered her to take a low profile, he would give the task to a man he knew he could trust and was utterly reliable; it was an old and trusted friend. Tamara didn't have to be told his name she knew who it would be and her blood ran cold.

Petrovich Umglo was the result of a liaison between a Nigerian student in Moscow and a young Russian call girl. The young woman had remained in love and loyal to the African despite him walking out on her when her belly started to swell. Petrovich's hatred for the man, who he still believed deserted him and his beloved mother, could only be matched by his loathing of the arrogant west and its decadence. Tamara's hands trembled when she heard his name mentioned and she felt pity for the poor man in Bruges. He was not only a notorious assassin, but he was renowned for enjoying his profession; his trade mark was slow, painful deaths. There needed to be a new word invented for sadists like him, she thought. She placed the handset down and stumbled to a café nearby, demanding a double espresso. When it arrived she spooned in a lot of sugar, stirring it rapidly she then gulped down the sweet warm liquid hoping it would calm her before she returned to work. Her mind running through her plan of how she could escape the trap she found herself in.

Tamara walked up Exhibition Road and she spotted an unmarked police car outside the Victoria & Albert Museum. Then she saw two plain clothes police officers standing on each side of the door watching the employees as they entered, their eyes scanning for an individual; she knew that something was not right. Her plan would have to start earlier than she had intended. Escape was now her priority; it now looked as if Marcus was never to be.

★ ★ ★

Charles and Marcus made Ramsgate in just over an hour; Charles marvelling how easy it was to travel at the dead of night. They readied the boat and with no signs of anyone around they prepared to slip away from their pontoon unnoticed.

Marcus went along the pontoon and bending over untied the forward warp and heard a splash below him; he caught a brief glimpse of his phone floating downwards. Marcus swore but he knew finding it would be useless so he continued to stow the fenders and warps and came back to the rear cockpit of the French made forty footer.

'I've lost my bloody phone, Charles. It was in my breast pocket and as I lent forward… Damn that's the third phone in as many months.' Marcus busied himself securing the sheets and stowing fenders.

'Well I've got mine…' Charles went to his jacket and checked the pockets. 'You won't believe it but I left my phone in my sports jacket. Blast. Well at least we have the VHF radio if anything goes wrong.'

Marcus stopped and looked at Charles. 'Shit Charles, things aren't going too well. Not only have I been questioned about a man's death in Scotland, I am probably on the wanted list for that

Davenport's death and here I am leaving the country in the middle of the night without a passport. I wonder how many years I'll be put away for this?' Marcus sat down and pulled out a few toffees that had been left from the previous sailing trip. Charles refused the sweet. 'Better get used to them for that is all we have except for the flask of coffee.' The men remained silent until they were well out into the North Sea and for several hours they just sat and watched the stars and took in the sounds and movement of the boat and sea. Finally Charles indicated for Marcus to take the helm and he went down below to check his charts.

'We had better keep our wits about us tonight,' said Charles returning on deck and placing a pair of binoculars on the coach roof under the hood. 'This is a very busy shipping lane.'

Charles sat for awhile surveying the scene and then he picked up the binoculars and scanned the sea. A confusing array of lights dazzled him. Slowly he picked out a navigation buoy, also around them he could make out three large vessels in the far distance. Being back on water and busying themselves with the task in hand had raised the men's spirits.

'Doesn't your father have RADAR on this thing,' asked Marcus genuinely surprised.

'He does normally but it is in for repair. Dad's going away for several weeks later in the summer. He wasn't expecting the boat to be used so he took it in to the chandlers.' Charles continued to survey the horizon through the binoculars. 'If you get too tired put the auto-helm on, with the engine running it will be OK. Blimey, there are a lot of ships around tonight.'

Marcus lent forward and pressed a green button to the right of the wheel console. 'What about fuel? I didn't see you checking that.'

'My father always, and I mean always, leaves the boat full of diesel. But I did have a quick look before when the bosun's locker was open, just in case.' Marcus nodded and sat down easing himself into a comfortable position.

'I'll do this watch Charles and I'll give you a call in two to three hours.' Marcus waved his hand at his friend. 'Go on take a couple of hours kip, you actually look quite exhausted.'

Charles nodded and handed the binoculars to Marcus. 'Call me in three hours and make sure you pass the shipping lane at right angles. These modern vessels are doing well over twenty knots so you'll have to almost aim at them and sneak in behind them, or the next one will be upon you before you say *Jack Robinson*.' Charles smiled at Marcus but it formed into a frown as he surveyed all the lights out at sea, then he retired below mumbling a question of who was Jack Robinson.

Marcus sat and watched the night sky rolling above him. He could make out the navigation light at the top of the mast and the swell made it look as if the mast was stirring the stars. Now he finally had time to reflect. The last twenty four hours had gone so fast. It could not have been just a few hours ago since he was with Tamara? He recalled her undressing; her initial desire and wanting. Then the talking had quickly changed the mood from desperate lovers to something more substantial, something serious, he would never have expected that when they entered the bedroom. He brooded on her story and then how he had alluded to his recent find and although he had never mentioned the suite of jewels he had indicated they were very valuable. Should he tell Charles about it, he pondered? He recalled how she talked about it as if she knew what they were; what worried him was he had told her he had hidden them separately. He had never mentioned the ring and neither had she; he didn't understand why. What really was eating into him was how this woman had just slipped into his mind and soul without him noticing; he really cared about her and already he had plans of how they could be together. How could such a thing happen so quickly? But still the nagging doubt about whether he could really trust her returned and he sighed heavily.

Tiredness started to pull at his eye lids and checking the horizon he quickly went down below and brought up the flask of coffee. He could hear Charles' snores and mumblings of a deep sleep. He poured some coffee, checked his course and continued to brood. Tamara was no killer, he was certain of that, but there was an inner discipline and self control about her that he totally lacked.

He was not as convinced as his daughter that she had used her womanly charms to soften him up. He had never seen such desperation, and sexual desire, in a woman and yet in a moment she had become composed again and virtually walked out on him. She had mentioned something in the past still haunted her; no, she had said it still controlled her. She wanted out of her current life and to find something new. Marcus sensed her honesty in that and it excited him; he too wanted a new start. His search for a new life was due to a boredom gnawing at him as the everyday grind had built up into a wall around him. Her despair may have been from a more sinister source but he knew she genuinely wanted him to know about her plight. 'My god, she was crying for help,' he said to the vast empty sea. Marcus sat back and closed his eyes for a moment trying to recall the sight of Tamara that afternoon.

A blast, so loud, it made Marcus discard his coffee mug and looking up he saw the huge bow wave of a boat heading towards him. Grabbing the wheel he tried to turn it, but it was jammed. Still the bow ploughed towards him so close now he could clearly see the detail of the wave flowing over the red bulge of the lower hull. Suddenly he remembered the autopilot, and hitting the red button, he swung the wheel turning the boat away. In a few seconds the boat was lifted as it rode the crest of the bow wave and behind him was a wall of steel that rose up blanking out half of the sky. At the top of the hull he could make out the tiny head and shoulders silhouette of a man waving madly at him. He caught a few words in the night air of a foreign sounding tongue and for several minutes he motored down along side the wall of steel trying to get some distance between him and the cargo vessel. He could see by the Plimsoll line indicating the boat was empty and the chances were the propeller would be partly out of the water. Marcus was right for as the boat's stern came into view the slow grinding blades of a huge propeller splashed nosily sending sea water in all directions.

Marcus turned and went astern of the vessel letting out a long sigh of relief. To starboard he could make out another vessel steaming towards him and he kept his boat at ninety degrees to it. 'Ruddy hell, that was close,' he whispered, picking up his coffee cup, filling it again from the flask. After a while and with the shipping lane behind him he reset his course and put on the autohelm. Marcus sat back down and watched flotsam and debris pass the yacht.

Marcus shook his head as another wave of tiredness started to engulf him and he stood up and hummed to himself. Taking the binoculars he watched the ships in the distance and busied himself by checking the charts, anything to stop his mind wandering back to that afternoon and not on the job in hand; he had already had a lucky escape. But his mind refused to stop working. He desired Tamara; he knew that now and in a way he had not experienced before in his life. Was it love at last? No, he laughed to himself unconvincingly, that's not for him, but he couldn't dispel from his mind the image of him hugging her naked body. Both of them trembling as her despair flowed out of her. He didn't know what to do. At first she shrugged him away when he put his arm around her, but as soon as he withdrew she lunged at him and buried her face into his neck, but there was no sobbing, just a silence. Marcus looked up and watched the continual moving of the mast; the stars now shining brightly. 'Oh shit! Typical, I fall for a girl who is a raging psycho,' he said and tried to muster a laugh; but all that formed on his face was a frown.

Another hour later as the dawn crept into the horizon, Marcus could hear Charles in the head below. He breathed a sigh of relief and checked the surrounding sea. Charles finally came up the hatch and stretched up touching the boom in the middle of the cockpit.

'Everything OK? You should've called me, it's been four hours.' He yawned and picked up the chart by Marcus' side.

'I didn't want to interrupt your beauty sleep… In the spirit of total honesty we were a few seconds from being turned into matchwood.' Marcus handed the binoculars to Charles who was looking at Marcus with astonishment.'I must have drifted off and fortunately I think one of the crew member's must have spotted us and told the bridge to give us a blast on their horn...'

'Oh, I do recall something in my sleep.'

'Charles, your snoring was nearly as loud as that ship's horn. Anyway, I managed to pull us away just in time. Christ, those ships are big when you're up close. It was empty and the prop was splashing quite a bit and if we had run down the side of the ship and into that thing, it would have mulched us to a pulp.' Marcus moved towards the hatch.'Oh, I dropped some coffee, but I'll hose it down when we are in port.'

'Don't worry it will be fully light soon and I'll throw a bucket of water on it. Go and get some rest you look shot.' Charles formed a weak smile, but Marcus had already gone. A few moments later he re-appeared and came and sat with his back to the bulkhead and looked aft, catching the quizzical look from Charles.

'Actually Charles I'm not that tired now, and...'

Charles checked the sea around him and lent back on a small seat by the helm, eyeing Marcus closely.'I can feel a little bit of a confession coming on. Go on Marcus let it out; shame we don't have a drink on board.' Charles said in a soft manner.

'I've not been entirely honest with you; well *straight* would be more accurate.' Marcus ran his hand over his face and through his hair.'There was something else in the jewellery box, which I have hidden separately.'

'May I ask why?' Charles had wondered why the bottom tray of the box had been empty. The ring he knew was part of the suite and he was about to hear where the rest of it had been hidden.

'Look Charles, this is difficult enough as it is so please let me finish,' Marcus said sternly, but he flashed his friend one of his disarming smiles.'The jewellery box had most of the jewels in the upper tray, but if you lifted it out there was a small compartment...'

'Yes, I had noticed it and wondered why it was empty, oh sorry,' Charles added quickly seeing Marcus' impatient look.

'Well do you recall the portrait of the young princess, Lady Xenia?' Marcus raised his eyebrows questioningly at Charles, who nodded not daring to interrupt again. 'Well she was wearing a suite of jewels, all matching to a central theme. There was a necklace with over a hundred gems, bracelet, earrings, broach and...'

'And the ring!' Charles stood up came and sat closer to Marcus, scanning the horizon as he did.

'Yes, the ring. I didn't think you ever believed that I had found it in a house clearance, did you?' Both men managed a small laugh. 'Well, from the little research I've done, these jewels are worth a small fortune on their own, but put them together and bingo, the price goes into orbit.' Marcus kept his eyes fixed on Charles who had now gone into deep thought.

'Put them together and you can identify quite easily their true origins... Could be difficult for you to move them on?'

'That is exactly what I thought you would say, and I suspect that is going to be my problem?' Marcus threw the skipper another smile but it started to fade before it had formed.

'The ring did cause quite a stir at the V&A and I was at one point suspected of being complicit with you. The department that Tamara is in, the Eastern European Department, was given the ring. It was quickly identified as being from a suite of jewels made especially for the last Tsar, Nicholas II. We suspected that you may have the whole suite...'

'We have suspected...? Charles who exactly is this, *we*?'

'OK, I also haven't exactly been straight with you. The *VfA* have asked me to keep an eye on you and to try and find the jewels and to make sure nobody gets hurt in the meantime. Scotland Yard and a lot of others are all watching this; maybe even MI6...' Charles rubbed his chin nervously awaiting the reaction from Marcus.

'Well it looks as if your, *we,* hasn't done very well on making sure nobody gets hurt, has it?' Marcus lent forward towards Charles. 'So what were you going to do Charles, shop me?'

The two men looked at each other in silence, their faces tense at what was unfolding, both sensing their friendship was being tested to its limit.

'Look Marcus, we have both misled each other because of those bloody jewels, for heaven's sake you nicked them and brought them back to London in my car…'

'I do not regard taking them as theft, well not in the strictest sense of the word. They weren't bloody Mooney's to start with…'

'You know that argument is totally unsound and I still resent the way you put me in a compromising position by having the ring examined, when it was bloody well stolen.' Charles had now lent on the steering wheel and saw the coastline looming closer out of the corner of his eye.

Marcus' head dropped and his fingers combed through his hair. 'Christ Charles, those bloody things have been nothing but a problem from the moment I lifted them…'

'Ah ha, you admit you stole them,' said Charles pointing at him, but to his surprise Marcus slowly nodded his head. 'Do you know what they're called?' Marcus shook his head. 'These "stones of conscience", seem to have a bit of a curse attached to them…'

'Come on Charles you don't believe in all that stuff…' Marcus looked around as the sunlight sparkled on the water around them. 'I didn't really have a plan when I took them, but I do now and for your information it includes Tamara…'

'Tamara, are you mad? Marcus for heaven's sake just think this through a moment… Wait a minute; I think she was the last one to have the ring. Oh bugger, she may even still have it.' Charles turned and faced east. 'Marcus we had better get ready to enter Ostende.'

Marcus stood up and looked towards the harbour entrance growing closer by the minute and lent over and pulled back the throttle lever, killing the boat's speed. 'Do you want to hear my plan?' he demanded. Charles nodded. 'Then sit still for a while, but I can assure you won't like it…'

An hour later the two men stood up both relieved their friendship was intact and Charles held out his hand, 'I'll do all I can to help, but as I said there are limits…'

Marcus grabbed his friend's hand and pulled him towards him and giving Charles one of his bear hugs. 'Charlie, old boy you are a ruddy hero…'

The two men laughed and Marcus pushed the throttle lever forward and took the helm. They entered the busy harbour taking the main ferry channel but bearing starboard just before the fish market. Charles called the Harbour Master on the VHF radio and secured a visitor's berth close to the harbour wall. They cleared up the boat as seagulls screeched over head, disappointed no scraps could be seen on the new arrival. In the distance a chiming bell from the cathedral intermingled with the clatter of horses hooves on the roadway above them.

They finally locked the yacht and reaching the roadway walked past the fish market stalls, bustling with chatter of customers speaking in many languages. Both men would have liked to stop and take in the atmosphere but they knew time was not on their side and as they hurried away they heard the deep throaty horn of an incoming ferry. Walking briskly over the bridge and into the railway station they had to push past back-packing students all wandering around, seemingly aimlessly, as they studied maps. They bought two singles for Bruges and hurried to the platform, fortunately a train was due to leave in a matter of minutes.

* * *

Tamara walked slowly up the King's Road. As she approached Marcus' shop she checked around from a distance to see if there were any surveillance CCTV; none were visible. She tried Marcus' phone again and still it went straight onto the answer phone. She approached the door and her heart sank as she saw the closed sign. Should she ring the bell? Her hand was still trembling as she reached out and pressed the button. She stood to one side and turned away so as not to be recognised until the door had been opened. She did not turn round when she heard the bolts being release but waited until the door was fully open before facing Marcus' daughter.

'Can I help…? Christ it's you!' Dawn screamed and tried to slam the door shut.

Despite Tamara's slim figure she was extremely fit and agile and in one movement she had held the door long enough to slip in. The whole building shook as Marcus' daughter put her whole weight against the door forcing it shut.

'Get out, now. I'll call the police,' screamed Dawn, backing away towards the rear of the shop and taking a sideways step as she recalled the poker by the fireplace.

Tamara didn't move but an instinct made her put her hand briefly in her handbag feeling the cold silver handle. She withdrew her hand, she wasn't about to make the situation any worse; her plan needed Dawn on her side. 'Dawn, please. Will you just listen to me…?'

Dawn abandoned the idea of the poker and made a rush for the office. She grabbed the phone but Tamara closed on her in a moment grabbing the cord yanking it out of the wall.

'Dawn, for God's sake will you please listen to me. I'm not here to cause any harm. I need to talk to your father,' Tamara held Dawn's arms as she tried to control the young woman without too much force. 'Just calm down for a minute.'

'You killed that man last night didn't you,' blurted out Dawn her eyes ablaze with anger, but her stomach tight with fear. Dawn struggled to get away and Tamara decided to let her go. 'You won't get them. You'll have to kill me first.' Tamara stopped for a moment before realising she was talking about the jewels; an image of Malone falling backwards made her freeze for a brief moment.

'Dawn please, I really need to speak to your Dad.' Tamara saw Dawn heading for the fireplace and decided she was not going to be able to reason with her; her visit had been in vain. Tamara made for the shop door and quickly opening it she turned to the girl who was stood with her back to the fireplace, brandishing the heavy brass poker.

'Dawn, you must believe me I'm not here for the jewels I just need to speak to Marcus. If I had wanted to harm your father I could have done so yesterday. Please trust me, your father does...' Tamara made a small step back into the shop hoping she had one more chance of persuading the young woman to tell her where her father was.

'Trust you, do think I'm totally soft in the head? He told me about the knife, I bet you have it with you now.' Dawn had a twisted smile on her face; she made a move towards the woman in the doorway. 'Well I'm not as gullible as my dad...'

'He told you about that? Dawn, I just want to speak to him...' Tamara suddenly felt the tears starting to well in her eyes and a sense of panic filled her. Any glimmer of hope in being with Marcus had now faded and she left the shop taking large strides towards Sloane Square. She opened her hand bag and checked a piece of paper with Charles Ashford's address.

Dawn ran upstairs and dialled Toby's number. When he answered she broke down, sobbing and in a hoarse whisper begged him to come round straight away.

Tamara continued up the King's Road and entered Wellington Square. Checking the number of the house she rang the large round brass bell and waited. She could hear the crying of a child and a door being closed but she waited patiently relaxing her shoulders and forcing out a wide smile as the door opened.

'Mrs Ashford?' said a woman, blinking in the sunlight, and nodded. She supported a young child on her hip, who gazed at Tamara with wide blue eyes while sucking at her thumb.

'Yes, can I be...' Samantha took a step into the door way as Tamara rummaged in her bag.

'I am sorry to bother you,' Tamara said slowly finally pulling out her wallet and pushing the sheathed blade to the bottom out of the bag; out of sight. 'My name is Tamara Nolan,' she extracted a card from her purse and handed it to the woman standing in the doorway. She still found it odd to call herself by another name; she had changed it whilst in school. 'I work for the V&A and I need to speak to Charles urgently, it's about a project that I am currently working on. I have tried his mobile…'

'Well the silly trump has left it here in his jacket. It has been going off all morning. He is so forgetful at times,' said Samantha hitching up her squirming daughter back onto her hip. 'He has had to go away rather urgently. All a bit sudden last night. I don't really know the full story but recently he has been so tied up with various things; I can't keep pace.'

'Oh, that is such a shame. I really needed to speak with him.' Tamara knew how to extract information and started to take a step back. 'Thank you all the same Mrs. Ashford and if I may say you have the most gorgeous daughter. She'll break a few hearts in years to come.'

'Thank you, but she's a real tyke actually. May I keep your card and if Charles calls I will give him your number?' Samantha checked Tamara's card as the young girl started to squirm again and wanted to be let down.

'Yes, by all means. I would be very grateful. It is actually very urgent.' Tamara smiled at the girl and made a small wave at her.

'Oh, you could try his friend Marcus Chapman. He's gone off sailing with him. He's always has his phone on. I've got the number somewhere. Step in a moment and close the door behind you; I don't want Hazel running out.' Samantha turned and putting the child down went to a leather book by the phone in a long hallway. Tamara stepped inside and pulled the door behind her. The young girl continued to suck her thumb and stared at her, a smile forming behind her hand. Tamara wiggled her fingers at her again which caused the girl to run off and grabbed her mother's leg shyly looking back at the stranger. Tamara would have done anything to be the mother of that child.

'Here we are,' said Samantha and scribbled down the number on a notepad.

'Mrs. Ashford, thank you very much. I am so grateful. They've both gone off together have they?'

'Yes, Charles' has taken his father's boat across to Ostende. All very strange to me but you know what men are like…' Samantha tried to take the thumb out of her daughter's mouth but the little girl just shrugged her off.

The shock of Marcus and Charles going to Belgium made Tamara speechless for a moment; she quickly composed herself. 'Oh, I know what men can be like, but thank you again Mrs. Ashford. If he does call could you please let him know I called and tell him I need to speak to him urgently.' Tamara waited until the mother had picked up her child and she opened the door exiting into the bright sunlight. 'Oh, I almost forget. Could you also give Charles this when he returns, just in case I miss him?' Tamara pulled out a small brown box and handed it to the little girl. 'Will you give it to Daddy,' she said smiling at the young girl. The girl smiled and nodded, holding the small package with both hands. Tamara thanked her again and left the house.

She had become light headed and she almost felt as if she would faint. Charles and Marcus must have gone over to find the son, she suddenly realised their potential fate. Tamara stopped by a railing at the end of the square and felt a bout of nausea swelling inside her. Petrovich not only had a reputation for the way he killed, but he took any interference personally, and on many occasion bystanders or the police had paid a terrible price.

Tamara suddenly straightened and started to run towards Sloane Square. Finding a payphone by the Tube Station she dialled her contact number. Suslov's assistant answered the phone and at first would not put her through to the Colonel. She shouted and insisted in such a way the assistant relented.

'Colonel,' she said when she heard the man grunt an acknowledgement, clearly surprised by the strong tone in her voice. 'There are two men who are going to Bruges to warn Ralph

Davenport. Look,' Tamara could now hear her own pleading voice return; it made her hate herself. 'I think I can get there and sort this out after all. Colonel please. Please don't send in Petrovich. Not yet anyway. Look I think I can get the address at this end...'

The deep laugh had a sneer to it. 'How I love you pleading with me, Tamara. You've done a lot of that to me over the years. For a moment, I hardly recognised your voice.' He now roared with laughter, power pleased him. 'Don't worry about it. You're a little late Tamara I have already let him loose. You know how he so likes French speaking girls. He always needs a heavy passionate encounter after he's completed a mission, it was one of his little habits...' Suslov roared with laughter again.

'But Colonel these men are only...'

'If they get in his way then, well you know what will happen to them, don't you Tamara... Actually they may well help him find our young Tsar...' Tamara heard yet more laughter. 'I do hope they're not acquaintances of yours, as you'll be attending a couple of funerals soon...' The line went dead.

She screamed at the receiver causing a passer-by to glance hesitantly into the telephone box. In desperation she called the number again and as soon as the Colonel's assistant heard her, he swore at her, telling her if the she called again she would know the consequences. The line went dead again.

Tamara put the phone down slowly and thought about her father and young sister. Then she felt a welling within her, a feeling of desperation, but also an anger that was not like before; she had reached the limit of her submission. She threw open the door of the telephone box and gulped in the air, coughing with the vehicle fumes. She entered a café ordering a double espresso and when it arrived she picked it up, but her hand was shaking uncontrollably. Tamara tried to take a sip but couldn't and she placed it back on the saucer, the cup rattling for a second. She took several more breaths and lent back, her mind formulating her next course of action. A few moments later she decided she only had one option and she picked up her coffee her hand now steady and with a small smile to herself, she downed it in one. She knew now she had passed a point of no return. Her inner strength grew and for the first time she felt a warmth of self belief flow through her. First, she somehow had to convince Marcus' daughter that her father was now in serious danger, and even worse she would have to tell her it was all her fault. It wasn't going to be easy but she must succeed.

Tentatively she approached the antique shop and, seeing the sign stating it was open, she drew in a large breath and burst through the door. She heard the buzzer and voices from the back room. She stupidly prayed it would be Marcus but a young man came out followed by Dawn.

'You *again.*' Dawn stood and stared at Tamara; a heavy silence seemed to engulf them all; nobody moved. Finally Toby edged towards her his arms out in front of him in defensive style. 'Toby, no. Stay here, we'll tackle her together if she tries anything.' Toby stopped and kept his eyes firmly on Tamara.

'Dawn, you have to listen to me,' Tamara's voice was a little horse and shaky. A glimpse of confusion crossed Dawn's face. 'I've just been to Charles Ashford's house and I know he has gone off with your dad to Belgium.' Tamara still saw the hatred in the young woman's eyes and considered for a moment threatening the couple to tell her what she needed to know; she moved her bag so it was open. 'Please Dawn, you must believe me. Both of them are in serious danger and I have to tell you it is entirely my fault. I tried to walk away but…' Tamara stopped as she felt the prickle of tears starting to blur her vision.

'If you think you can fob me off with a few tears, then you are very much mistaken,' shouted Dawn at Tamara as her own tears returned.

Toby saw Tamara wiping her eyes and quickly he took several paces forward to grab her. Tamara moved swiftly and the blade was out and unsheathed before he had crossed half way across the room. Toby froze and stood absolutely still watching the blade glinting. Tamara took a step back and flicking the open sign over she also turned the key.

214

'Ah, the infamous knife, so you wouldn't ever use it would you…?' Dawn pulled herself up to her full height. 'Get back, Tobs I think this woman knows how to use it,' she said her voice quivering and making a grab for her boyfriend. 'Tears, and then a blade. Do you really think you could fool me? My father is a sucker for tears and a sob story, oh but you know that don't you?' Dawn now pulled Toby back and held his arm.

'I don't know what to say to you Dawn.' Tamara went to her bag and sheathed the knife and turned to the young couple. 'The last thing I wanted to do was be here like this. But you have to believe me; he really *is* in great peril. Dawn, I am not joking, and if I don't go now I'll never forgive myself for what I have done. Dawn I would call the police myself but it maybe all too late. He's the only man that I have ever felt at peace with… The first man I felt could offer me any sort of future happiness.'

Dawn stood her eyes gazing with burning hatred, but there was something nagging at her, something her father had said. Toby edged forward but was tugged back by his girlfriend. Dawn recalled her father had said something the previous evening that she could not ignore.

'Exactly what sort of danger?' Dawn spat out the question.

'Dawn, I can see you hate me, but…' Tamara let her hands fall down by her side and she looked squarely at the young woman. 'I actually love your father…'

Dawn started to let out a loud laugh but it never came. Toby had started to move towards Tamara again but Dawn pulled him back again. 'Christ Toby, just wait will you.' Dawn continued to hold Tamara's pleading but steely look. 'I should tell you to get out and you are just another of his one night stands…'

Tamara stood perfectly still and hoped her apparent complicity would sway the young woman. There was nothing else she could say or do. The tick of a clock and rumble of traffic was all that could be heard. Tamara felt suddenly weak and after a few moments she pulled out a chair from the table behind her and slumped into it.

'You haven't answered the question. Why is dad in such great danger?'

'I am working for a department in the KGB.' Tamara turned to face them, her eyes showing her inner grief and growing desperation. 'I didn't want to but… Look I will tell you everything, but we just don't have time now. There is a man, an assassin, who is at this moment on his way to finally end the blood line of the last Tsar. It should have been me, but I just couldn't do it. I was really only here to gather information…'

'You didn't hang about with that old Davenport man in Hampstead, did you?' interjected Dawn with a disdainful sneer.

'I am not a killer; the man was actually showing me a picture of his son and fell. I'll swear it. Dawn, do you know about his son? That's where your dad and Charles have gone. If they are to have any chance at all I have to find this assassin first. Only I can intercept him, I know his ways… The police will just stuff it up and I'll have it on my conscience for the rest of my life, however long that will be.'

'You're having difficulty with your memory today aren't you? You have already killed another man, but let me guess, that was an accident too. Strangely Dad doesn't think you're a killer, but I most certainly *do.*' Dawn let go of Toby's arm and she took a bold step forward towards the hunched figure of Tamara.

'Yes, I'm afraid you're right in some respects I was meant to get information from them, even threaten to kill, but I didn't.' Tamara made a small laugh. 'I actually thought I could get what I wanted without bloodshed. Both men fell, that's the honest truth. If you only knew what would happen to me, and my family, if I didn't do what they told me… I did try and confide in your father but he couldn't grasp the situation I am in.'

'What about my position. If I give you the address and find that you have had *another accident* with a man, then I am the one who is to blame.' Dawn watched as Tamara slowly stood up and pushed her hair back.

'You're wrong about me, Dawn. I really am trying to save your father, and Charles. God if only you knew… I just want to put a few things right. I had no idea I would ever be asked to get involved in such a situation as this… I was just meant to keep Moscow informed with information, that's all. Yes, I did the training but I never thought I would ever be called upon like this. I have spent twelve years in fear for my father's life and the safety of my sister and her child. Your father is the only man who listened to me he at least tried to understand my hopeless position, I think he felt my own *emptiness*, my utter despair. I felt his too…'

Tamara took one last look at Dawn and picking up her bag, making Toby flinch, she picked out one of her calling cards and laid it on the table. 'Just in case you change your mind,' she said turning towards the door, unlocking it.

'Wait,' cried Dawn. Tamara stopped and stepped back turning towards Dawn, a glimmer of hope showing in her eyes. 'There is something that dad said last night about how empty his life had become, but that he had found you…'

Tamara felt the hope surge through her veins and took another pace towards the young woman.

'I don't know why I'm doing this, stay here,' said Dawn turning and going upstairs. Toby and Tamara eyed each other, the tension between them tightening as they heard Dawn leaping down the stairs with a piece of paper in her hand. 'Ralph Davenport lives in number 52 Verriest Straat…'

'No Dawn, don't give it to her…'

'Shut up!' came the reply from the two women in unison.

'In Bruges. I don't know what sort of mess you're in and I know my Dad's a sucker for women, but there is something he said about you…, and a little bit of my own feminine intuition.' Dawn held back a sob. 'If you hurt a hair on my Dad's head, I don't care who else is threatening you, it will be nothing to the wrath I will bring down on you, even if it takes me the rest of my life.'

'I swear to you that you will not regret this.' Tamara went up to Dawn and held her by the shoulders; Dawn did not react.

Tamara looked her in the eye, her heart pounding fast. 'One more thing. Please do not call the police until I have a chance to find this assassin? Dawn it's important, very important, please.' Tamara continued holding Marcus' daughter, her eyes open with hopeful expectation.

'I'll call the inspector that Dad has been in contact with, this afternoon...'

'Dawn, you must be absolutely bonkers...' shouted Toby starting to advance towards the two women.

'Shut up,' replied the two women, again in unison.

'Thank you,' said Tamara in a faint whisper. 'I'll save your dad for you, if I can. I swear it.' She turned throwing her bag over her shoulder and exited the shop making a dash for the nearest tube station.

After she had gone, both Dawn and Toby each let out a long breath.

'Well you're going to phone the police now, and I am not going to let you wait until this afternoon,' said Toby finally turning to face his girlfriend. 'Why on earth did you ever give her the address is beyond me?'

Dawn's lips started to tremble. Had she done the right thing or had she actually put her father in further trouble? No, she must trust her intuition. She recalled what her father had said the previous evening and despite her feelings towards this woman, she sensed her love towards her father. Soon the tears were starting to flow. Toby came towards his girlfriend, stopped and ignoring Dawn's sobs started to go upstairs.

'Toby, have you ever heard of women's intuition?' Toby stopped and turned a little alarmed by Dawn's severe tone. He nodded. 'Well butt out of this one and let me decide how best to help my dad.'

'Oh come on Dawn...' He saw the look in his girl friend's eye, which silenced him.

'If you want to continue going out with me then I suggest you don't go upstairs and phone the police, because the next thing you will do is pick up your coat and walk out that door.' Dawn had pointed towards the front door and gave him one more glare before brushing passed him and scaling the stairs two at a time.

Chapter 11

Belgium, July 1997

Both men sat quietly for the short train journey to Bruges. The last conversation between them seemed to have sapped most of their energy and Marcus let his eyes close as the train bumped and rocked along. After a few minutes Charles opened up a street map of Bruges and taking out Ralph Davenport's address from his pocket he studied the best route from the train station to his house.

'I've just thought…' Charles whispered at Marcus. 'This bloke may not know that his father is dead.'

Marcus' eyes opened quickly and he turned towards Charles. 'Ruddy hell. We'll have to tell him…, or maybe he has already been told and he is on his way back to London.'

Charles put his head back and Marcus could hear a curse from his lips. 'Why the hell didn't we think of that last night? We should have at least called him to see if he was at home… What is the matter with us? It is possible we're now on a complete wild goose chase. We don't have a telephone between us and chasing after a man who in all likelihood could be back in London totally unaware of the danger he is in. Damn, I'm such an idiot at times.' Charles stopped as he noticed his outburst had caught the attention of a woman on the other side of the carriage. Marcus noticed her interest too and made a quick frown at Charles; both men lent back and silently watched the flat countryside pass by.

Marcus kept thinking about the ring that he was now certain remained in Tamara's possession. He hoped it would bring them together again; his tiredness clouded his mind as he continued to rewind the events of the afternoon in the hotel room with her. He continually analysed what she had said, different connotations kept springing into his mind. Had she be playing with him, or was his instinct right and she really wanted to be with him?

When the train eventually pulled into Bruges station they alighted without a further word and strode towards the exit.

'How far is it?' asked Marcus.

'It's about one and a half kilometres to Davenport's place, I think…'

Marcus noticed a bicycle hire shop just outside the station and he turned to Charles and raised his eyebrows. 'It would save a bit of time…'

'Bloody good idea. Look you stay here and I'll hire them with my credit card…'

Marcus waited, watching Charles pay for the hire of two bikes, and for a few moments he was concerned as there seemed to be a lot of gesturing going on. Finally the attendant went over to the bikes and unlocked two, rolling them towards Charles, who nodded curtly at the attendant and walked back to Marcus.

'Day light robbery! He wanted a deposit that was far more than the bikes are bloody well worth; I should have bought them out right. Listen, I've not got any local money. You stay here with the bikes and I'll be back in a moment,' he said nodding towards a Bureau de Change. Charles handed over the bikes and a few minutes later returned moaning again, this time about the exchange rate for Belgium francs. Marcus passed over one of the bikes and watched as Charles opened the street map and folded it so he could navigate whilst cycling. 'Right I think we go down this road,' he mused, 'I suppose it would have helped if I had bought an English version…'

'Charlie, you never fail to amaze me. Do you mean to tell me you can't read Flemish? It must be about the only language you can't get your tongue round. Oh except Welsh, do you remember at the rugby…'

'Come on Marcus, stop babbling and follow me. It has been

a few years since I rode one of these.' Charles straddled the bicycle and pushed off wobbling precariously as he glanced down at the map. 'What is that saying? "It's like riding a bike…, you never forget." Well I've forgotten…,' shouted Charles; his bike seemingly out of control.

'Come on Charles you're shaping up like a real pansy…'

Ten minutes later they found themselves back behind the station. Charles was getting highly agitated as he had twice nearly collided with a vehicle; he had problems in braking. 'Damn this bike, the brakes are useless.' Charles pulled up and studied the map. 'I just can't seem to get across the main Gent to Ostende canal.'

'Pass me the map,' laughed Marcus and pulled up beside his frustrated friend, snatching the map off Charles. 'Right this time you follow me, just concentrate on keeping the bike on the road.'

The two men cycled through the southern part of Bruges and towards the centre, both marvelling at the building and cleanliness of the place. Finally they pulled into the Market Square which used to be the 'Grand Place' of Bruges.

'Wow, what a place,' said Marcus dismounting his bike and wheeling it towards an area to park bikes.

'What are you doing, we haven't got time for sight seeing? Marcus, come on, time is of the essence.' Charles shouted at his friend.

Marcus placed the bike into a metal parking frame, one of many around the town, and turned to Charles.

'Charles, we've not eaten for over eighteen hours and I've spied a good place,' he said pointing towards a café behind him. 'Anyway we've finally made good time on those bikes. Five minutes won't make any difference.'

Charles started to speak but Marcus had already passed him striding out towards the Café De's Arts. 'Anyway I'm not arguing with you. If you're not coming can I borrow a few francs or better still I suggest you come with me.' Marcus entered the café leaving Charles gaping at him in disbelief.

Charles cursed, but with the smell of coffee and with the sun finally piercing the grey sky, warming his face, he felt he had no alternative but to join Marcus, he was also ravenous. 'I suppose he'll want a ride in one of those horse and carts,' he moaned to himself as he fought to make his bike stay upright in the parking frame. When he turned Marcus was already sitting at a table by the square under a large yellow umbrella and talking to a waiter in a white shirt and long grey apron. Both men were laughing. Charles walked quickly towards them avoiding the clattering horse and cart as it trotted past with several Japanese tourists clicking their cameras at anything and everything. He approached the table.

'Bonjour,' said Charles; the acknowledgement from the waiter was in English.

'Don't panic Charles I've ordered two large cafe latté and Pierre is going to bring out a selection of cakes and pastries. Aren't you Pierre? Oh, don't forget the water. My friend always insists on water with coffee.'

'Oui,' said the waiter and turning to Charles continued, 'do not worry I know you are in a hurry.' The waiter tore of a slip of paper from his pad and placed it under the ashtray on the table; he then hurried off eyeing a girl passing by.

'Sorry Charles, but I am actually almost faint with hunger; it must be all this cycling...' Marcus extracted his sunglasses from his jacket pocket. 'This is one hell of a place. I had no idea how beautiful Bruges is and so many canals. A bit pricey though...'

'Yes, I'm glad you noticed that. Exactly how much is this *selection* going to cost; I only changed a few quid.'

Marcus just smiled at him. 'Lighten up Charlie, nowadays you seem to make life all work and no play...'

'Marcus, it may have escaped your flippant mind but...'

Marcus smiled and throwing a serious frown. 'Just look at that building and the size of the tower; it's something isn't it.' Marcus pulled his sunglasses down his nose squinting in the sunlight at the building.

Charles let out a grunt but he couldn't resist smiling. 'Don't try that one Marcus. You have as much appreciation for architecture as you do in tax returns…'

'Tax returns? What's one of those?'

Charles laughed out loud and he felt the tension in his shoulders relax as he turned to watch the passing tourists and appreciate the view. 'What can I do…?'

'You're a hero Charlie, give yourself a bit of slack.' Marcus said putting his sunglasses back on his face firmly.

Both men sat and waited for the coffees, taking in the view and sounds. Across the Market Platz the horse and traps were lining up preparing themselves for the afternoon tourists. The clacking of hooves over the granite cobbles as their drivers, attired in the traditional straw boaters, chatted while they busied themselves with the harnesses and cleaning the traps. An occasional snort from one of the horses, as they tossed their heads, searching for the last scraps of hay, echoed around the square.

'Actually Charles I wouldn't mind a bit of a tour in one of those horse and traps. Looks quite fun…'

'Don't push your luck. But maybe we'll bring our women folk over and do a tour. I've heard Gent is beautiful as well.' Charles stopped himself realising Marcus did not have a girlfriend at the moment.

Marcus sensed Charles' unease. 'Yes, I think Tamara would love it here…'

Charles quickly gave Marcus a sideways glance and noticed the wry smile.

The coffees arrived accompanied by a large plate of pastries. 'Oh my, we'll never eat all those…, said Charles.

'Don't worry, Monsieur, just take what you want and I'll only charge you for those you have eaten,' said the waiter looking up as the sun went behind a cloud. 'Enjoy the sun now as I believe we will have rain soon. Bon appetite.'

'Merci,' said Marcus to the retreating waiter. 'Nice chap,'

continued Marcus taking a sticky looking round cake. 'Mmm, Charles you'll love these,' he said with his mouth full of oozing syrup.

Charles was already salivating and picked up a small bun with a caramel topping. 'Right eat up, come on Marcus, we *do* need to get going. Can you imagine if we miss him now as we sit here stuffing our faces? It's all very well you being so laid back all the time, but I think you've forgotten Ralph Davenport could *actually* be in danger.'

'Charlie, he'll be alright. You really are one of the world's worriers…'

* * *

Dawn sat upstairs brooding for awhile and tried to call her father again leaving another curt message. Finally Toby came upstairs and kissed her cheek; he told her he had to go. Dawn glowered at him.

'So you'd leave me here with that woman about?'

'Dawn, she is half way to Belgium by now. I still think you should phone the police. And don't…'

'Don't what?' Dawn flicked her hair back over her shoulder as she looked up at her boyfriend.

'Don't ever threaten to end our relationship to get your own way. I am not having it, I believe it is too valuable to gamble with,' he bent down and kissed her lips. She did not respond. 'I have to go, but I'll be back around five thirty, OK?'

Dawn looked away and dismissed him with a wave of her hand. She heard him make an annoyed sigh and go down the stairs. For a moment she felt a panic and wanted to call after him, but she was sulking, and her stubborn streak won the moment. Good relationships should be treated with care, she knew that, especially after experiencing her parent's divorce. The front door buzzer sounded and she heard it close loudly. Toby had departed and her heart sank.

Dawn jumped up and ran down to the desk and found the

card of Inspector Hines. Ten minutes later she had told him very nearly everything that had happened; although she surprised herself that she had not mention the jewels, only the box and the note. She had also not given them Davenport's address, she feared they may bungle the situation and she had more trust in Charles. When she had put the phone down she was flushed and talked to the empty room. 'Oh God, like father like daughter; I'm as bad as Dad. Those bloody jewels have become a bad influence on this family, they make you lie.'

★ ★ ★

Dave Hines listened and took notes as Marcus' daughter blurted her story to him. He would have gone round to call at the young woman's house but his next call was to James Pulford who had decided to make an urgent trip to Bruges.

★ ★ ★

James Pulford intended to go along with Inspector Hines; the policeman was not aware that there was more at stake here than just a man's life. Pulford's sources in Moscow had told him Petrovich Umglo had been assigned a mission in Belgium, a man he already knew. Pulford now knew the target and a chance to ensnare one of the Soviet's most notorious killers was uppermost in his mind. Even the political pressures that were already starting to mount, with the foreign office becoming involved, had to be ignored. He was not concerned that this incident could jeopardise an entire foreign policy with the new post soviet Russia.

★ ★ ★

Tamara had bought her ticket at the airport and sat waiting patiently in the terminal building. Inwardly she was praying the flight would not be late. Her entire life's possessions were now held within her hand luggage. She had wired all her money to her sister and given her instructions on where to meet her on the German border. Hopefully the new and corrupt Russian authorities would be more willing to line their own pockets than stop a young woman escaping from her purgatory.

She was able to make herself inconspicuous as all her make up had gone and she wore a pair of jeans, deck shoes and a loose fitting jumper. She sat with her head down trying to read a magazine but she could not concentrate. She did not see any of the pictures or read any of the articles. It was just a barrier between her and the outside world.

She thought that she would be tailed and in a way she found that reassuring. Since her encounter with Marcus' daughter she had tried to conjure up the perfect plan that would prevent any further bloodshed; except Petrovich's of course. She had considered making sure her pursuers followed her to the assassin and let them deal with him, but that would be nearly impossible; Petrovich was too goodand she feared the authorities would possibly end up making a complete hash of it.

No, she had to face up to him first and alone she knew in herself she was no match for this man but she had no choice. She chided herself to think of a way to destroy the assassin. The only one she could muster was to wing it and to hell with the consequences. She just mustn't fail, but the tremor in her hands showed her deep rooted fears.

The return of the ring might be the gesture she hoped Marcus would appreciate as her genuine sincerity towards him. What a time to fall in love. Tamara was changing she could feel an inner steely strength inside her. She no longer feared death, it would be a sacrifice she was now prepared to accept. Her body made an involuntary shiver as she considered her own demise and her sister waiting forlornly for her. She willed herself on and the thought of encountering Petrovich made her stomach turn. She had only met him twice, and on both occasions he had made her skin crawl. He was the sort of man who undressed you with his eyes and delighted in putting a girl ill at ease.

★ ★ ★

James Pulford sat in an office watching Tamara on a CCTV screen. He had insisted that Tamara was not approached; he wanted to ensure she led them to the Tsar's bloodline and hopefully Umglo. Hines had started to protest but he knew Pulford had other roles within the government well outside his remit at the V&A. He decided to go along with Pulford, to a point.

★ ★ ★

Finally her flight was called and quickly she merged with the crowd as it queued to board. She tried to look matter of fact, almost bored. She didn't make eye contact with anyone. She entered the plane and went to her aisle seat half way down the plane. To her relief two women were already encamped in the inside seats and they hardly noticed her as their inane chatter continued. She willed the plane on as she knew time was not on her side; an air traffic control delay was announced. She closed her eyes in disbelief. Most of the passengers had entered through the forward door but she noticed the rear door was also open. She pulled out her compact and pretended to power her nose using the mirror to check the seats behind her. Just before the door was shut she saw James Pulford and another man, whom she had seen in Marcus' shop last Saturday. Clipping the compact shut she smiled; she wanted them just behind her; a plan of action now formed in her mind.

Fortunately the delay was not as long as first indicated and, on arrival at Brussels, Tamara again stayed in the thick of the passengers as they went to arrivals and baggage claim. Tamara walked straight through customs and headed for the car hire desk. She paid by credit card and signed all the forms before picking up the keys and then heading back to the ladies toilet.

Tamara went into the cubicle and placed her small hand luggage case on the toilet seat. She slipped her jeans and pullover off. Opening the case she unfurled a full length skirt, white cotton buttoned shirt and long jacket. She pulled on some tall heeled shoes and winced at their tightness. She finally extracted a large floppy hat and placing it on her head. She stuffed all her hair into it. The final touch was a pair of large horn rimed glasses. Exiting the cubicle she was pleased to see that the woman in the mirror had no resemblance of the one that had entered the toilets a few minutes before. It was time to test her handy work.

She left the toilets and headed for the exit, passing Dave Hines, who was loitering very noticeably by the ladies. He gave her a cursory glance but looked back towards the toilet doors and checked his watch; she knew she didn't have long.

She went to the taxi queue which only had one person in front of her. A moment later she jumped into the Mercedes taxi and leaning forward she unfolded a wad of notes. The driver was a middle aged Turkish man with a thick head of hair but starting to grey around the temples.

'Bruges, and quickly,' said Tamara unable to resist turning and checking behind her. 'I will need you for the rest of the day, is that OK?'

The taxi driver had taken the notes and counted them, raising his eyebrows. 'For this sort of money you can have me for several days,' he laughed and stuffed the money in his breast pocket.

'The condition is you get me there fast; that money will pay for any fines, understand.' Tamara sat back and placed her hand luggage on the floor next to her. 'I'll also give you a big tip when we get back here later, so don't think about leaving me...'

'I'm yours for the rest of the day. Which part of Bruges are you heading? The centre?'

Tamara noticed the driver was looking at her in the rear view mirror and she nodded. For the first time she noticed the acrid smell of spices in the car which made her realise she hadn't eaten anything all day.

The Turk turned his attention to the road and putting his right foot hard down whenever it was possible to do so with the dense traffic and soon they were on the Brussels orbital road heading back to the coast. Tamara sat back and, adjusting her position, made sure she could see in the side mirrors. Religion had never been part of Tamara's life but she realised that she had been praying for most of the day. She closed her eyes and had the urge to go to a church and ask for guidance...

★ ★ ★

James Pulford sat impatiently in the driving seat of an unmarked car within the compound of the airport police station. He drummed his fingers on the steering wheel and, seeing the approaching Inspector, opened the window.

'Where the hell is she?' he said to the Hines who was panting heavily. Hines shrugged his shoulders unable to get his breath and looked to the two plain clothes Belgium policemen in the back seat. One of them had a laptop computer open and a map was visible.

'We are ready to go,' shouted Pulford. 'Hines where is she? She's not gone to her car.'

'She went into the ladies but never came out. I got a female official to check but there wasn't any sign of her.'

Pulford raised his eyes and motioned for Hines to enter the car while he glanced back at the two men on the back seat. One of them was already dialling into his mobile phone. 'I'll call control...,' he said.

The Belgium had a brief conversation in French and looking forward to Pulford he continued, 'It seems no one has seen her. They are checking the CCTV now.'

James Pulford cursed and slapped the dash board in front of him. 'Christ we had better get on our way to Bruges. She must have…'

'What?' came a shout from the man on the back seat. 'It seems it will take a couple of hours to go through the CCTV.' The man terminated the call.

'I can't understand it. I definitely saw her go into the ladies; I'm telling you she never came out. Shall we check again…?'

'No, get a call to London and see if they've got hold of Davenport. Why the hell doesn't he answer his phone? Oh, and try Chapman's daughter again. I don't believe those two buffoons have come over here not knowing where this guy is. Meanwhile I suppose I'd better get us all to Bruges.' Pulford started the car and crunching the gears lurched forward, the wheels squealing as he headed for the exit. 'We have two options. Go and grab this Davenport chap and keep him safe or leave him there for bait.'

Hines turned and looked at the Director of the V&A with astonishment in his eyes. 'Leave him as bait?'

Pulford sensed Hines agitation. 'Call your boss Hines, I'm leading this investigation now. There is more to this than you realise. If Chapman's daughter is right we just may have stumbled onto Petrovich Umglo *and* while he is actually "on a job"; I've been after that bastard for years.'

Hines continued to look at Pulford. 'You're going to put a man's life at risk…? I'm sorry Pulford but I can't…'

'This is my call Hines.' Pulford ordered the inspector. He turned to the men on the back seat. 'Tell those clowns at the airport to let us know the minute they have anything,' said Pulford waving his hand in a dismissive manner as he headed for the orbital. He had completely underestimated the young researcher from the Eastern European Department.

★ ★ ★

Petrovich parked his car well outside the city on the road to Gent, it would be safer there and easier to get away if things hotted up.

He took his bag out of the boot and walked briskly down Generaal Lemanlaan and over the Gentpoort Bridge. A few spots of rain had started and looking up he saw a heavy dark cloud preparing to release a deluge. He felt the vibration of the phone in his pocket and taking it out, stepped to one side finding a quiet spot by the canal. He didn't say much as Colonel Andrei Suslov briefed him on the changing events of his mission. Smiling, he ended the call; he felt warmth flowing through him. Not only was this going to be a profitable day but he could even be given the chance to 'entertain' the lovely Tamara. He knew she had hated him from the first time they had met; this time I'll give her reason to hate me, he smirked to himself.

He walked through the Market Place and north until he crossed over the canal turning right onto Augustijnenrei. Walking a hundred metres he stopped outside the Europa Hotel. The small family run hotel had been a safe house for agents from Russia for many years. The current owner's grandparents had been Russian and had emigrated to Belgium after the First World War, their loyalties still remained with the mother country. Petrovich took out a Sobrani cigarette and, watching a boat on the canal, inhaled a few large breaths before flicking the cigarette away into the canal.

Petrovich entered the hotel where a tall thin man behind the reception nodded at Petrovich. The assassin waited until the receptionist had finished with some tourists and then came over to him, beckoning the Russian to take a seat.

'Petr, how good to see you again,' he said holding out his hand. Petrovich took it forcing a smile at the man, he hated his name being shortened. 'I have your usual room for you…'

'No, I want the twin bedded attic room at the rear of the building.' The man returned to the reception checking with his room sheet. Petrovich followed him, eyeing the noisy departing tourists with disdain.

'Yes, I'm only half full tonight so the top floor is actually empty.' The man looked up.

'That's good, for I am expecting another person to arrive. An

English woman who will possibly book in as Tamara Nolan...' The tall man nodded. 'She has longish brown hair, average height and quite slim with a slight accent in her voice. I want you to give her the single room next to mine. Do *not* tell her *I*, or anyone else from the organisation, is staying here tonight, do you understand.' The manager nodded again trying not to stare at the scar down the man's face. 'I'd better take the spare keys for both rooms. You keep the main one out on show, as if it's empty, OK. I'd appreciate it if no one disturbs either of us. Is this clear?' The tall man lent over and took two keys from a drawer and handed them to the Russian. 'Good. Is the bar open?' The man nodded again. 'Right go and get me a bottle of Vodka, the best you have...'

Petrovich waited until the man returned. 'Call me in my room if she arrives, otherwise no calls or any disturbances.' He gave the manager one last long hard look as he took the bottle. He then picked up his bag and made his way up to the top floor. He passed a dark haired young maid who gave him a sideways glance. Petrovich stopped and looked at her walking down the corridor. A little plump, he thought, but she would do for later if Tamara didn't show. He smiled as he caught her glancing backwards at him, her face initially lighting up for a brief second as she saw he was watching her. Then as she studied him for a moment she felt fear as their eyes met and she saw the brutal scar; she looked away and hurried down the corridor hoping he wouldn't follow.

Unlocking the bedroom door he checked the room before carefully laying out his clothes and equipment. Picking up a roll of thick carpet tape, .45 revolver and his stiletto knife he went and unlocked the room next door. The single bed was by the window and the eaves came in above it. The bed had a cast iron bedstead and made Petrovich smile as he set to work. Ten minutes later he had finished the preparation and closing the wardrobe door, he returned to his own room. Unscrewing the bottle he took a small sip and placed the cap back. 'I'll keep you for later,' he said patting the bottle.

★ ★ ★

Tamara opened her bag and withdrew her wallet extracting a piece of paper with an address on it. She noted the name of the hotel and the street she then checked her map of Bruges. She was certain Petrovich would now be aware she could be arriving on the scene, so she couldn't rely on an element of surprise. What will he do, she kept asking herself? There was only one way forward now and that was go to the hotel and see how the land lay. He may not even not recognise her in this outfit, if only she still had surprise on her side…

The taxi driver pulled into Bruges and after asking her where she wanted to go, she told him to wait in Esel Straat. He started to protest that he had been duped before but Tamara leant forward and putting her arm over the seat patted his bulging breast pocket. 'I'll be several hours but you must stay here.' She pointed towards a café on the other side of the street. 'If you need sustenance or to use the toilet then go to that café, nowhere else, understand?' The taxi driver nodded but Tamara read his doubting thoughts. 'It's the same again for the return trip, so don't let me down.'

Tamara opened the door and pulling her hand luggage with her turned into Pottenmakers Straat. Finally she entered Augustijnenrei where she could see the flags of the hotel a few hundred metres in front of her. All was going well, almost too well.

She entered the lobby, her heart pounding in her chest. The tall man behind reception looked over to her smiling. Tamara's eyes were scanning the room for Petrovich.

'Good evening madam, can I help you?' he asked as he recognised her description from the Russian.

'I am wondering if you have a room available for tonight, I'm here on business and it has run over…'

'Yes, madam I do believe I can manage a room on the top floor, would that be OK.' The man gave an understanding smile.

'That'll be OK. I was wondering if a colleague of mine was staying here tonight?' she continued in a hushed voice despite a lot of chatter around the lobby area. 'Tall, slim with dark skin, oh and a distinctive scar on his left cheek…?'

'I'm sorry madam, nobody of that description has stayed here,' he said shaking his head slowly.

'Oh, I could have sworn he told me he was staying here.' Tamara watched the man. She didn't sense any nervousness or unease in his manner. She had to trust her instincts.

'Will you be requiring the room for just one night?'

'Yes.' Tamara said trying to decide how she was to going to find Petrovich now. Should she go to Davenport's house? Had they managed to find his address; that seemed unlikely. Maybe Petrovich hadn't arrived in Bruges yet?

'Yes, of course madam. May I have your papers? Do you have any luggage?' He said glancing at the woman in front of him; curiosity consumed him for a moment as he wondered what the Russian wanted with her.

'Err, yes. It's in the car, I'll fetch it later.' she said formulating another plan.

The manager turned and gathered the key off the hook and handed it to her. 'Can I get someone to help you with the bags from the car?'

'No, I'll be fine. I might as well go and see the city while it's light.' Tamara started to turn and leave when the receptionist spoke again.

'If you want to freshen up first the stairs are over there,' he said pointing. 'I'm sorry the lift is acting a little temperamental today.'

Tamara nodded, and smiled she continued out of the front door sensing the man's eyes on her. She didn't see the receptionist pick up the phone as soon as she had departed. She slowly walked a few metres and turned up a service road beside the hotel. A large French window was ajar and she entered them purposefully walking through into the hallway at the back of the hotel where she spotted the stairs. Ascending them she thought through her options. Firstly she needed to contact Marcus so she decided to call his daughter, being locked away in her room

235

would be the safest place to be for now; she didn't want Petrovich springing on her when she wasn't expecting it.

Opening the door she felt some disappointment at the small and rather sparsely furnished room. She sat on the bed and pulled out her phone from her bag ripping the hat of her head, she shook her hair down. She took off the glasses and threw them on the bed and checked the number and called Marcus' home. Eventually Dawn answered.

'Dawn it's me, Tamara.' Tamara could feel the tension at the other end of the phone. 'I'm here in Bruges, but I need to speak to your father, it is vital Dawn please.'

'Well that's just it I haven't heard from him either. Have you found this other guy?' Tamara could hear the worry in the young woman's voice.

'No, that's why I must contact him…'

★ ★ ★

Charles and Marcus headed north east on their bikes, and after the occasional wrong turns, finally came into Verriest Straat.

'This chap's girlfriend can't be short of a few bob to be able to afford a place like this,' shouted Marcus as they spotted the house number.

'This isn't England. Most people rent out here…' Charles started to dismount the cycle and grimaced with saddle soreness.

'Even so it is definitely the stockbroker end of town. Right up your street, hey Charles,' laughed Marcus also feeling the effects of the cycle ride. The house was set in a large garden and only a couple of hundred metres from the main canal. The two men placed the bikes against the railings and went over to the metal gate. There was a security system and Charles pressed the button above a steel casing grill. After a few moments they heard the metallic voice of a man.

'Mr. Ralph Davenport?' asked Charles bending and shouting into the speaker.

'Yes, that's right, who is it?'

'My name is Charles Ashford. I, err we, have just come from London. We need to speak to you on a matter of some urgency.' Charles stood up and looked towards the house.

'Oh, what matter of urgency? This is a little inconvenient as I am just about to leave for London myself. Is this about my father?'

'Yes, and also about your own fate. I would appreciate a few moments of your time as …'

Charles was interrupted by a louder buzzing noise from the lock in the door, then there came a click from the gate and it opened slightly. Both men entered and as they came to the front door it was flung open.

'Mr. Davenport?' said Charles extending his hand. 'I am Charles Ashford and this is my friend Marcus Chapman.' Ralph Davenport shook both men's hands and ushered them in taking them into the kitchen at the rear of the house. 'You said you were just going to London?' continued Charles as they arrived into the kitchen area.

'Yes, I've had a bit of bad news. My father has died from a fall,' Ralph's voice wavered. It was the first time he had used those words. They seemed so matter of fact and callous, but there was no other way of saying it.

'Yes we know, I am sorry and please accept our deepest condolences,' said Charles shuffling a little. A frown crept onto Ralph's face.

'I hope you don't mind me being blunt but who exactly are you?' Ralph's shoulders went down and he stuffed his hand deep into his trouser pockets eyeing the two men.

Charles took a deep breath. 'Ralph; may I call you that?' Ralph Davenport nodded. 'It is a very long story and I don't think we have the time to tell it in its entirety, but for the moment we have come here to warn you that you *may* be in some danger.' Charles lent on one of the kitchen units and looked at Davenport firmly in the eye. 'Our priority is to get you to safety as soon as possible but…' Charles stopped as he realised he had not really thought through all the ramifications of walking into a Belgium police station with a rather incredulous story. He felt uneasy as he realised this man was clearly watching him with surprise and rising trepidation.

'Sorry Charles,' interrupted Marcus sensing his friend's thoughts. 'I think we have no alternative but to tell Ralph everything, if he is going to believe a word we say, especially with his recent sad news.'

Ralph Davenport watched the two men and sensed their own unease. 'Well, surely a brief précis of the situation,' he said glancing at his watch. 'My ferry isn't for several hours yet and actually I do have an open ticket, so if I miss it…'

'Yes, you're right, but first I have a bit of a favour to ask…' Charles looked at Ralph with a sheepish look. 'Neither of us have a mobile and we need to call someone in London, rather urgently. May we use your telephone?'

Ralph nodded and took Charles into a neat study down the corridor and pointed at the phone. 'It's prefix 44 for the UK.'

'Yes, thank you. Err, may I ask how you found out about your father's death?' Charles asked lifting the receiver.

'Yes, my father's home help called me this morning…; my girlfriend is away on a business trip so I thought I'd head back to London.' Ralph went to continue but stopped and turned to Charles. 'You're not police are you?' Charles shook his head. 'You see my dad's home help mentioned that the police are a bit suspicious about his death…'

'I think they have good cause to be…' Charles looked at the receiver and back to Davenport. 'Please let me make these calls and we will give you the whole, somewhat remarkable story.'

'This is to do with my grandmother, isn't it?' Ralph suddenly blurted out.

'Olga?'

Davenport nodded.

'Yes, it is in a way. I work for the Victoria & Albert Museum and I can assure you the police are hopefully on the way as we speak. We became involved because, well as I say we'll explain it all in a minute…'

Charles stopped as Marcus joined them.

'I was wondering what was going on. Charles why don't we call Dawn first, before you speak to Hines? See what she says.' Marcus sensed the unease in the room.

'Yes, I'll call her now…'

'No you won't I'll call her,' said Marcus going up to the phone.

Marcus dialled the number and the phone was answered within a few rings.

'Dad, thank heavens you've called… Tamara has been around not once but twice and she said you are all in real danger and that…' Charles could hear Dawn and snatched the phone out of Marcus' hand.

'Dawn, slow down, slow down. Tamara has been to the antique shop?' Charles shouted down the phone as Marcus looked on in disbelief.

'Yes, and she went to your house…'

'My house, what the hell for?'

'Look Charles, I have this feeling she maybe telling the truth. I can't explain myself but I just have this gut feeling she is actually trying to protect you.'

'Protect *us*. Dawn, she is the one we were worried about harming us…' Charles stopped and glanced a little nervously at Davenport whose expression had now turned from concern to astonishment.

'Charles, she said there is a man, some sort of hit man, an assassin from the KGB who is after Ralph Davenport…'

'KGB?'

'Yes but just shut up Charles for a moment. Get Dad to call Tamara on…, oh just a minute I'll get her card.' The line went quiet for a few seconds; Charles motioned to Davenport for a pen and paper.

'Yes, here is her number,' Dawn read out the number, 'Charles there was something she said about dad, but I think you should speak to her first and then call me back. Charles are you there?'

Charles mumbled that he would call back in a minute or so but he was actually contemplating just making a run for the nearest police station.

'Oh Charles, I called that inspector and told him everything.'

'Good, I think we should get, err, our man, into safety as soon as possible. I'll call you in a few minutes,' said Charles slowly watching Davenport's agitation increase.

He put down the receiver and looked at Marcus. 'Dawn and Samantha have had a visit from Tamara…'

'So I gather if you'd let me finish the call.' Marcus had taken a pace forward and stood by the phone. 'What else did Dawn say?'

'She says she has a gut instinct that Tamara is actually trying to protect us from a KGB hit man.'

The room went silent and Ralph Davenport looked at the two men in front of them with wide eyes. 'What the bloody hell is going on? I think you two had better start talking before *I* call the police. You come bursting in here talking about a KGB hit man, then… Ah wait a minute, my grandmother; she was descended from Russian aristocracy.'

'Yes we know,' said Charles slowly. 'In brief we, or rather Marcus, found a portrait of your great-grandmother, Lady Xenia, who was supposed to be…'

'The last bloodline of Nicholas II…' Ralph stepped back and sat on the arm of a chair. 'So dad was right…'

'What? Did your father know…?' Charles stood looking at the young man.

'Yes. He had a call from an old woman who lived and worked in an old castle on the Isle of Rum…'

'Never mind all this Charles let's get hold of Tamara. Dawn is no fool if she thinks the woman is actually on our side she may well be right. I think we could do with all the help we can get right now, so let's speak to her. Here give me the number.' Marcus put out his hand for the number on the piece of paper.

'I bet that was the old woman we saw being pushed around by Malone,' said Charles thoughtfully.

'Charles give me the number…'

No, I think it would be better if I speak to her,' said Charles turning away from Davenport and pulling the pad towards him, he picked up the receiver as Marcus' eyes blazed at him. The silence was only interrupted by the sound of the number dialling. Charles put the receiver to his ear and waited.

'Tamara. This is Charles Ashford…'

★ ★ ★

Tamara emptied her bag placing the jumper and jeans on the bed. She then put the small case in the corner of the room and her hand bag on the small table by the window. Taking out her phone, her eye saw the handle of the silver knife lying at the bottom of the bag; her body shuddered. She looked out of the window but her view was only overlooking a small courtyard at the rear of the building. She decided that it would be better to try and get the number of the Ralph Davenport, now that she had the address. She picked up the phone but then she smelt the faint whiff of body odour. She frowned and looked around just as the phone in her hand rang making her jump. She looked surprised to see a local number and thought it could only be one person. She answered the phone and waited for the other person to speak. She was surprised it was Charles and not Marcus; she wasn't sure whether to answer.

'Tamara. It is Charles Ashford here. Is that you Tamara?'

'Yes…'

'Where are you? Dawn has told us to call you urgently. What the hell is going on?' Charles was still simmering with anger that this woman had been to his home.

'Look Charles I want to speak to Marcus, but first you must listen to me: you must be careful. There is a man after Ralph Davenport and if you try and stop him he will not hesitate in killing you as well...' Tamara's voice had started to rise, and she checked herself, looking nervously towards the bedroom door; had she heard a creaking floorboard?

'We are with Ralph Davenport now, and all is well.' Charles suddenly didn't like the tone in Tamara's voice. 'We're not at his house though and I am considering going to the police now...'

'No wait; where are you?' Tamara tried to keep her voice low. 'This man is good, and when I mean good, I mean good at killing people. He may even be on your trail now, so keep your eyes peeled for him. I haven't been able to find him. He is a half cast between an African and Russian girl, but he actually has a more Arabian look about him. He has a very distinctive scar down his left cheek...'

'Tamara, what are you talking about a *man?* What sort of man, Dawn says he is KGB...'

'Charles just believe me, he is very dangerous, he's an assassin. I need to get to you before you go to the police, so don't go anywhere with Davenport until I am with you. Please Charles, you have to trust me on this. Tell me where you are and I'll come to you.' Tamara tried to speak softly but her need to persuade Charles meant she had become quite agitated again.

Charles rummaged in his pocket with his spare hand, catching the intense look from both men standing beside him, as they both strained to hear Tamara's side of the conversation; he brought out a receipt and squinted at the name and address across the top. 'We'll meet you at the Café De's Arts in the main market place. It is directly opposite the Belfry Tower on the south side of the square and by one of those bicycle parking areas.'

'Come with Davenport...'

'Not likely, it will be Marcus and I and we'll be sitting outside this cafe in fifteen minutes. Then we want to hear why Dawn thinks we should trust you and exactly who this man is. You say you haven't seen him yet? Maybe he's not coming...'

'Oh, I know he is either here now or will be. OK, I agree; fifteen minutes time at the Café De's Arts in the Market Place; you and Marcus only.'

'Yes, just us two. Ralph will be safe where he is…'

'Charles, can I speak to Marcus? Please…'

Charles handed the receiver over to Marcus giving him an apologetic look before taking Davenport by the arm and leading him back to the kitchen. A few moments later Marcus came in, clearly deep in thought.

'I should ask you what she said, but I have a feeling it might have been personal.' Charles said helping himself to a glass of water.

'It was personal, and thank you for not asking, but she said something… It doesn't matter, maybe I should have let you talk to her about us.' said Marcus in a sarcastic tone, his head drooped. 'Gee, that woman really confuses me… Why did you tell Tamara we weren't at Davenport's house?'

'Come on Marcus we can't suddenly totally trust this woman solely by the gut feelings of your daughter. Let's see what she has to say for herself first. She's not got the best record so far…' Charles pulled on his jacket and motioned for Marcus to make himself ready. 'Ralph, you lock all the doors and windows and do not open them to anybody except us, understood?'

'Yes, but I really feel you owe me more of an explanation. You've stormed in here making out I am in danger when…'

'Right, in short,' said Marcus loudly. 'The Russians have found out that your father and you are the last remaining bloodline; as you clearly already know or suspected. Well Ralph my son, it seems our Russian friends don't like that and they want this bloodline…'

'Extinguished?' said the young man anxiously his eyes widening. 'How are you involved in all this,' he continued looking at Marcus.

'Greed,' answered Charles before Marcus could reply. 'Utter selfish greed.'

Charles glanced at his watch. 'Sorry Ralph, but we really do have to go.' Both Charles and Marcus looked at each other and Charles ignored the angry looks of his friend and nodded towards the door.

'So keep all the doors locked…' Charles finished and moved down the corridor towards the front door.

'Just a minute! I'm going to call the police. I'm not happy about all of this.' Ralph had started to make his way towards the study.

'I don't blame you but please why don't you at least see what Tamara has to say. You're safe here and they don't know your new address.' Charles saw the young man's thoughts waver.

'Who is this woman anyway and why is she here…?' Davenport said switching his look between the two men in front of him.

'Now that is getting to be a long story,' said Charles opening the door. 'A certain bit of romance has also muddied the water…' Charles made a playful punch at Marcus who did not respond and was still smarting at Charles' reply to Ralph's question. 'Lock and bolt the door behind us and check all the other doors and windows; we will use the code word 'Olga' when we press the bell at the gate, OK?'

Ralph Davenport closed the door and the two men heard the click of a lock and then the metal rasp of the bolt before opening the gate. They collected their bikes and made their way towards the town centre. Davenport went to the study, picked up the phone; he held it for awhile hesitating to punch in the numbers and finally replaced the receiver without dialling the police. He made a resigned sigh.

★ ★ ★

Tamara pressed the red button on her phone continuing to stare out of the window watching a pigeon vainly strutting in front of an un-interested female on a flat roof opposite. In the distance she heard a bell chime the hour and she went to check her watch. She never managed to see it.

A hand slapped over her mouth and nose while a punch to her kidney's made an instant wave of nausea engulf her. She was forced backwards and slammed onto the floor; as she fell back she could just make out the features of her attacker and saw the wardrobe door open. She went to kick out one of her legs towards Petrovich but a fierce punch to her face made her limp; somewhere inside she found the will to continue to resist. She desperately tried to shout but she could not take in any air as his hand had pinched her nose and blocked her mouth. The lack of air made her desperate and she bit the palm of his hand making him curse as he withdrew his hand. She sucked in a long breath and tried to roll away when a blow to her neck ended her resistance.

She recovered consciousness as she felt cold water being splashed over her face which shocked her senses and immediately she started to struggle, slowly realising all her limbs were tied fast. She opened her eyes and lifted her head to see Petrovich searching her bag and she saw the empty glass on the floor. He saw her movement but continued to rummage in her bag eventually pulling out her silver letter opener still in its sheath.

'What is this,' he said turning and extracting it from its sheath.

Tamara struggled again and looking around her she found she was tied, spread-eagled on the single bed. Her wrists and ankles were tied with thick tape and her panic returned as she struggled to breath. A piece of tape covered her mouth which had been stuffed with cloth. She could only breathe through her nose and her attempts at screaming were barely audible. She looked down at herself and saw her long skirt hitched up above her knees, her legs splayed out.

Petrovich moved towards her examining the blade. 'Andrei said you had a silver letter opener as a weapon. I didn't believe him, very primitive; now if you want a knife...' Petrovich placed her knife on the dressing table and took out an object from his pocket. He pressed a button and a six inch blade burst out of its handle. 'Now this is a knife and a little sharper than a bit of old silver.'

Petrovich came towards the bed and Tamara couldn't help but fight causing her bonds to cut into her skin. He smiled at her futile attempts. 'I believe Andrie once had you trussed up like this for quite awhile. He told me about it one day when we had been drinking. It seems the Colonel took quite a shine to your sister as well. You should be more careful who you let into your bedroom, mad Colonels and of course don't forget *half casts*. I'll teach you to call me a half cast...' Petrovich's laugh was cold and made Tamara's skin go cold. She tried to speak but it just caused her she feel out of breath.

'So, if I heard you correctly your two accomplices are going to be in a café in the market place in a few minutes.' The Russian looked towards the window. 'Two Englishmen sitting out in a café in this rain; they won't be too difficult to find...' Petrovich laughed again and was now right by the bed towering over Tamara. 'Not sure about the outfit, it doesn't do a lot for you. However...' Petrovich pulled up her skirt up further revealing most of her legs. 'Nice legs,' he said admiring them. 'But you can wait until later. Business before pleasure,' he said, but he checked and put the blade under one of the buttons of her shirt. A slight twist of his powerful wrist sent it flying across the room. Some of her bra and glimpse of cleavage was revealed. He repeated the movement a further three times until her blouse fell open. 'Nice breasts as well, I am going to have a good time later, and afterwards I can tell you how I killed your friend.' He pointed towards her phone. 'It sounded as if you have quite a thing for one of the Englishmen?' Petrovich walked back to her phone, he checked the last number and smiling threw it onto the floor, crushing it with the heel of his shoe.

'You've broken the cardinal sin of this game Tamara. Never, and I mean never, get involved. I'll make sure his death is especially slow as I tell him what I'm going to do to you...' Petrovich laughed as he watched Tamara struggle again and checking the woman's bindings went towards the door. 'Just a little thought to leave you with before I go. I always have the need for sex after a job; just imagine how I'm going to be after three killings.' He checked his gun stuffing it deep into one of his jacket pockets. 'Oh, I nearly forgot.' He went back to the dressing table and picked up his knife carefully pushing the blade back into its handle. Crouching down slightly he checked himself in the mirror and smiled back at Tamara. She tried to scream at him but it just made her throat rasp.

'Wish me luck,' he said to her putting the knife in his pocket and patting the bulge of the gun he pulled up the collar of his jacket. 'It's really started to rain. I can't wait to see those two Englishmen sitting in the rain; I'll be back soon…'

★ ★ ★

Charles had checked the map and they followed the main canal down towards Langestraat, and headed for the centre. After five minutes they found them selves back in the Market place and placed their bikes in the parking frames and walked over to the Café De's Arts; a few spots of rain had made several people head indoors. The waiter who had served them before waved at them and opened the door.

'Two beers please, we'll stay out here if that's OK,' said Marcus trying to smile at the young man. He shrugged giving the two men a puzzled look as he glanced up at the darkening sky.

'Do you think it's wise to drink?' Charles was looking around nervously as rain drops started to thud into the canopy above them.

'Sitting here with nothing in front of us would look a bit strange…' Marcus said also checking the huddled passers-by as they fought against increasing wind and rain.

The beers arrived and after some banter with the waiter the two men sat looking out anxiously into the market place.

Charles checked his watch every few minutes giving Marcus a worried look. All the other customers had retired inside and the two men knew they looked conspicuous sitting in the rain drinking beer.

'I thought it was the mid-day sun Englishmen that were meant to sit out in,' joked Marcus sipping his beer.

Charles ignored him. 'Where the hell is she?' he eventually said. 'I knew we shouldn't have trusted her, she has probably gone to Ralph's house, sensing I was lying. Marcus I didn't think we would have a homicidal maniac after us, shit I'm getting more than a bit nervous, I'm positively petrified. This isn't just a mad idea about a night sail, this is, well you know…'

'Talking of night sailing, if you hadn't gone off at that crazy tangent we wouldn't be here now. Relax; she'll be here anytime now, I know it. If she isn't then something has gone terribly wrong…' Marcus said looking towards Charles, 'What if…' Marcus noticed the frown developing on Charles' face. He had stopped looking around and was looking to his left at the large steps to the Town Hall which were flanked by stone lions. Marcus followed his look and saw a man partly hidden behind one of the lions, his collar pulled tight around his neck, as he kept glancing towards them.

'When I say go, get to your bike and this time follow me. Whatever you do don't look round but keep up with me…' hissed Charles pushing his beer away from him.

'Where on earth do you think we can go…?'

'Now Marcus, come on!' said Charles leaping up and heading for the bikes. Marcus instinctively followed and looking back towards the steps he saw the man, standing behind the far balustrade, stiffen as they made their dash for the bikes. He saw the tanned man looking at him and the light line of a scar marring the contour of his cheek.

'Shit we've not paid,' mumbled Charles as they pulled out their bikes; the men were soon peddling hard past the post office and down a narrow street. Marcus struggled to keep up with Charles hollering at him to slow down while he glanced over his shoulder to check behind them. He saw the man jumping into one of the horses and traps shouting at the driver.

'He's got into one of the tourist horse and traps,' yelled Marcus only just realising Charles had taken a sharp left turn. The men rode through some bends shouting for people to get out of the way. Fortunately the rain had meant the street and pavements were fairly clear. Charles turned right into Philipstock Straat and looking over his shoulder saw the horse and cart hurtling towards them with the assassin that Tamara had described kneeling in the cart looking over the driver's shoulder. Charles realised the driver would possibly have a weapon of some sort pressed into his back. As the street bent to the right he quickly turned left and peddled as hard as he could coming towards a 'T' junction. Pulling on his brakes he turned right, the tyres nearly loosing their grip on the wet cobbles. In the distance they could still hear the steely clatter of hooves.

Marcus wasn't so lucky on the turn and skidded. Charles saw Marcus struggling, braked and yelled at his friend to hurry. Marcus ran and jumped on the bike while in motion; his heart was already racing and he was totally out of breath. A few metres on and Charles took a left, peddling hard down Hoogsstraat, when his eye caught a boat on a canal to his right. He jammed on his brakes and jumped off, having to run as he pushed the bike down some steps towards a path bordering the canal. Marcus skidded again and cursed as he careered heavily into the curb stone.

'Ruddy hell Charles, what the hell are you up to?'

'Come on dump the bike with mine and follow me.'

Marcus pushed his bike down the steps and crossing the road after Charles he saw him fighting with a gate by the canal bridge. Cursing out loud, he leapt over it hissing for Marcus to follow. They jumped down onto a small quayside of cobble stones, a large bush was growing up the wall of the bridge.

'Marcus, quick in here…' Charles ducked down into the shrubbery but squinting up the canal. 'Marcus for Christ sake come on.' Marcus had slipped on the cobbles and struggled to make the bushes just as the horse's hooves could be heard entering the street above them. Charles motioned to him impatiently as the horse and cart started to cross the bridge. Marcus crawled up beside his friend pulling large breaths into his lungs and holding his right knee.

'I'm hurt…'

Charles put his hand over Marcus' mouth and nodded his head towards the loud clomping of hooves directly above them as they slowed. A shout in French finally resulted in the horse being pulled up to a stop. More shouting and Charles had realised the man must have seen their bikes.

'Damn, I was hoping we'd lose him,' whispered Charles as a large barge came closer into view. Then the horse's hooves started again and Charles could only assume that the driver had seen a chance to get away and bolted. The barge was almost level with them as Charles heard footsteps crossing the road away from them and, grabbing Marcus, he yelled at him to follow as he leapt onto the small bow deck. Crashing into the bulkhead he turned to see Marcus landing heavily onto the gunwales, almost falling backwards but he then hit the bridge which catapulted him forward right on top of Charles. Marcus winded Charles as both men let out a rasping wheeze. As they passed under the bridge all the sounds around them echoed and Charles was completely disorientated for a few moments. There seemed to be shouting from the aft of the barge.

'Charles, I'm really hurt…'

Once again Charles put his hand over Marcus' mouth and as they came out of the bridge and to Charles' relief he didn't see their scarred friend looking down at them. They lay flat on the deck getting their breath back and after a few moments Charles rose up peeking over the coach roof of the barge. He saw the Arabian looking man searching furiously and then standing over the discarded bikes, he looked up towards the disappearing barge. Charles immediately dropped his head down. He heard further shouts but could not make out what was being said. The barge chugged along for a few minutes going under another bridge; then the engine revs dropped.

Charles saw they were entering a larger canal and he heard the squeaky toot of a horn from the back of the boat. Grabbing his map from his pocket he scrabbled to pin point where they were. Making a small grunt he pulled Marcus to his feet screaming at him to jump.

Both men leapt into the dark oily water just before they approached another bridge. Their feet touched the muddy bottom and the men quickly swam to the side. The barge chugged past with the helmsman gesticulating at them and shouting loudly. They ignored him as Charles pulled himself up onto the path beside the canal, coughing and spitting out the foul tasting water. He turned, helping his muttering friend, pulling him up onto the path.

'Ahh, my right leg Charles it's bad, really,' cried Marcus as he tried to put his right leg gingerly down and he let out another small cry.

'Ralph's place is only half a kilometre up this road,' he said pointing down Blekers Straat. 'Can you walk?' he asked as he scanned the path back down the canal. No one was following and he sighed with relief and turned to the ashen face dripping in front of him.

'Walk, jump, swim, ruddy ride… I can do it all Charles. You are definitely no longer my ruddy hero…'

'That's my boy, now let's get back to Ralph and call the cavalry in. Dawn told me she has called the police so hopefully we can get away from that maniac and out of this bloody mess.'

'For once I am in full agreement,' said Marcus through his teeth as he struggled to limp along. 'Charles, you are going to have to help me.'

Charles took a step back and lifted Marcus' right arm over his shoulder. 'Marcus, you've probably twisted your knee. Just try and ignore the pain and let's get back to the safety of Davenport's house. No more heroics, I promise.'

'Just ignore the pain… At times Charles you're ruddy priceless' muttered Marcus angrily as he attempted to walk.

★ ★ ★

Tamara felt a huge sense of relief as the door shut behind Petrovich. It was short lived as her panic returned; she had to escape. She knew that if she didn't he would kill the three men

251

and she shuddered at the thought of what he would do to her. She started to tug desperately at the tape binding her wrists but let out a stifled cry as they finally bit through her skin. A dark stain started to soak the tape. She stopped struggling and breathed slowly through her nose looking round the room. She saw her knife still on the dressing table but then she remembered the broken glass on the floor.

Calming herself she tested all the ties; her left ankle was the least tight. She pulled her body over and tried to straighten her ankle and foot. Waggling it and turning her leg she felt the tape tighten as she attempted to edge her leg out but the tape held firm. Defeat led to a wave of dejection which she pushed aside. Attempting to shout through her gag she thrust her hips up and down making the bed jump and bang against the wall. After several minutes of total exertion she had to stop her chest heaving trying to suck in enough air through her nose. Tamara let out a terrified scream and even through the gag it filled the room. Then came the sobs…

The young maid had seen the man with the scar leave with a satisfied smile on her face; she felt her skin crawl and managed to avoid him seeing her. She waited until he had descended the stairs and returned to her duties when she heard the rhythmic thumping from the floor above. Tentatively she ascended the stairs when the thumping stopped and the young woman froze. She started to turn and return downstairs when she heard a faint woman's muffled scream…

★ ★ ★

Petrovich's anger grew inside him, flooding his mind with hatred. How could two Englishmen give him the slip? Even the driver of the horse and cart had managed to get away. He knew it wouldn't be long before the police sirens would be heading his way. He returned to the two abandoned bikes he had spotted from the cart and looking up the canal he saw a head ducking beneath the coach roof of the receding barge. Petrovich picked up one of the bikes and started to cycle down the path but the front wheel had buckled and he could hardly make any headway. The barge was nearly out of view and discarding the first bike he ran back to collect the other cycle.

Petrovich swore as the barge disappeared around the corner of the canal making him pedal harder eventually catching up with the barge as it motored under a bridge and out into a larger canal. He pressed on, crossing over the bridge and, steadying himself, he prepared to pull out his gun; he looked over to see that nobody was on the front deck.

Braking hard, the back end of the bike skidding round, he shouted some French at the man on the helm. He couldn't make out all that the man said but he heard enough, two men had jumped off the boat before the last bridge. Pushing hard down on the pedals he went back to the bridge and soon spotted the muddy patch on the path near the canal. He saw the brown watery footprints off to his left. He carefully put his head around the corner into Blekers Straat and saw, a few hundred metres away, the two men hobbling up the street, one leaning heavily on the other. He cycled towards them when they had just gone out of view and discarded the bike he followed them on foot all the way to Verriest Straat. Keeping well back he saw them stop at a gate as one of the men talked into the intercom and after a few moments they entered the garden.

The summer was coming to its end but there was still plenty of foliage for Petrovich to find cover. He scaled the fence at the end of the garden and used the developing dusk and borders, full of shrubs, to circle round to the rear of the house. He stalked from window to window but could only hear voices from upstairs. Taking off his jacket he placed it on a small window of the back door and jabbing his elbow into it managed to break the glass. He removed the broken pieces remaining in the frame placing them on the ground beside him, and then slipped his jacket back on.

Reaching in, he managed to turn the key but the door still did not move. Petrovich could just see a bolt at the bottom of the door. Voices were suddenly raised and he even heard laughter from upstairs so he shoulder barged the door. It gave way and as Petrovich stood silently listening; the voices continued unabated from upstairs. Petrovich didn't make any sound as he scanned the room.

He moved silently to the inner door and made his way down the corridor as he reached into his jacket withdrawing the gun. He found the stairs and could still hear the voices from above. Time to make his move. He sensed that these men would not be talking and laughing if they believed he had followed them. He also knew that in all probability the men would have called the police, disappointment swept over him as he realised there would be little time for his usual pleasantries.

* * *

Charles helped Marcus as they hobbled along towards Ralph Davenport's home.

Marcus breathed heavily. 'At least we lost the bastard, but what if he…' Marcus tried to turn to face Charles but his friend would not slow or talk. 'Charles what if he has Tamara.'

'Stop gabbling and try to put some effort into walking will you. My god you're a dead weight.' Charles did stop at a junction taking in some deep breathes as he checked the dripping map; passers-by looked at them with surprise. 'We'll get to Ralph's and take his car to the nearest police station. Christ, what are we doing? Trying to play James Bond. Damn it Marcus we could have had a very nasty experience back there. Damn and blast those jewels…'

'Charles,' said Marcus stopping and forcing his friend to turn around to face him. 'You promised me. Look Tamara told me she returned the ring to your house…'

'What is the point if both of us end up dead? Marcus get real, we're getting out of here. I can't believe I actually walked into this mess. We're going straight to the police, no arguments. I should never have listened to you in the first place… Those jewels are being returned. I don't want anything more to do with them.' Charles checked behind them turning away from Marcus flushed face. He grabbed a hand full of his friend's wet clothes hauling him back onto his shoulder. 'Now let's go, Marcus at least try and walk. Did you bring that Inspector's number?' Marcus shook his head. 'Damn, well let's hope James Pulford will answer his phone…'

'I'll never forgive you if you don't let me keep…'

'Just shut up about those bloody jewels, Marcus. I am more concerned about staying alive at this very moment. We also have to try and make sure poor old Ralph doesn't join his father in the morgue.' Charles gave his friend a glaring look. 'You didn't just trip over back there, you, no we, were running for our bloody lives…'

Marcus was about to speak but he knew that once again Charles' logic was hard to argue with. He pulled himself up and tried to move as quickly as he could.

'How much further Charles, I really think I've hurt something…'

'You'll be all right. I think you've sprained your knee, stop being such an old man. Look there's his gate up there.'

'Guess what?'

'I know, I'm now your ruddy hero again…' Charles let out a tired laugh as he placed Marcus against the railings by the gate.

'Well, you're making the right steps towards it…, just promise me you won't tell any one about the stones of conscience,' said Marcus pushing his heads against the railings and brushing his hair back.

Charles gave Marcus a withering look and shook his head then pressed the button by the door; when he heard Ralph he shouted the code name and the gate buzzed. They both stumbled in with Charles helping his limping friend up the pathway. Ralph was already at the door and he let them in quickly locking the door behind them, inspecting the dripping men in bewilderment.

'It's OK we lost him…'

'Him, I thought you went to meet this girl?'

'Well she didn't show and our KGB friend gave us quite a chase. Its OK we shook him off…' Marcus straightened and grinned as a touch of pride swelled inside him at their own antics; he sighed with relief that they were safe.

'Right, that's it I'm calling the police…'

'Yes Ralph I agree, but can I just call my boss first. I have a feeling he, or his contacts at Scotland Yard, may well already be on the way. I hope so at least.'

'You two are soaked. Where have you been? Jumping in the canal?'

'Actually yes,' said Marcus dramatically. 'We jumped onto a ruddy barge and then when our Russian friend was out of sight Charles thought it best to go for a swim…'

'Look come upstairs and get those clothes off.' Ralph indicated towards the stairs. He noticed Charles moving towards the study. 'Don't worry there is a phone upstairs you can use…'

'Good. Marcus you can shower first while I call Pulford.' Charles helped his friend up the stairs and fortunately his knee did seem to be improving. They followed Ralph into a large room where an archway separated the main room from a small anti-room by the door. The main room had a large double bed and a small table with two dining chairs facing inward.

'The bathroom is over there,' said Ralph pointing towards a door and taking a large towel off a rack in the anti-room. 'The phone is by the bed,' he added looking at Charles. 'Look I think I have some clothes that might fit you Charles, but I don't have any for…'

'A fat bastard,' said Charles. Both men suddenly laughed as a surge of relief at finally being safe smoothed away the past hour.

'You are a cheeky bastard, Charles. I'm not that big, I've just got big bones…' Charles made a snort of disgust at Marcus' defence.

'Actually, I do have a baggy tracksuit that might do,' interrupted Ralph.

'Don't you start,' said Marcus peeling off his wet shirt.

Charles had gone to the phone and dialled a number. Soon he was speaking and turning to the other two winked, acknowledging the instructions from the person on the line. Finally he finished and replaced the handset.

'Right, they are already on the way, they'll be here in twenty minutes or so. I told you they would be. Good old Dawn. We have to remain here and don't budge or call anybody. All's well that ends well…'

The metallic click of the gun was unmistakable. All three men turned in unison to face the tall slim man, his dark glistening skin highlighting the long deep scar gouged into his left cheek. He stood by the wall just to the left of the archway and a smile crept across his face.

'You don't lose me that easily,' he said, his smile broadening as he saw the fear growing in the three men's eyes.

Chapter 12

Petrovich's smile faded and his face became impassive; his eyes became dark and cold as he prepared for business. He motioned with his gun for the three men to bunch together over by the table and chairs.

'You,' he nodded towards Ralph Davenport. 'You must be the young Tsar?'

'Tsar? No, I don't know what you mean. These two have got it all wrong, they came bursting in here. I'm nothing to do with any Russian Tsar…' stammered Ralph unconvincingly.

Petrovich smiled at Davenport. 'Shut up, you're talking crap. I think your two friends have led me straight to my mark. You may not know it, my Romonov friend, but it seems you're the last link back to Nicholas the second. It's a shame you won't be able to enjoy your new found status…' He then looked at the two Englishmen. 'Just out of curiosity, which one of you has a relationship with Tamara?'

'You ruddy *bastard*. What have you done with her?' blurted out Marcus his trousers still dripping onto the floor.

'Ah, it's you,' sneered the Russian waving the muzzle of the gun at him 'I knew Tamara didn't have good taste in men, but she's reached rock bottom with you.' Petrovich sneered at Marcus eyeing his naked chest. 'She's a bit tied up right now. Awaiting patiently for my return; laid out on her bed. I have to confess I'm looking forward to entertaining her tonight.'

'Charles, let's rush him. Now, all three of us; he's going to kill us anyway…'

A sharp powerful crack caused the floor boards between

Marcus' feet to shatter, sending splinters into his legs; he cried out dropping onto one knee clutching one of his wounds.

'For fuck sake Marcus shut up,' bellowed Charles as the smell of cordite drifted across the room. Ralph stood frozen to the spot mesmerised by the scene unfolding in front of him.

Petrovich pulled out the reel of tape with his free hand and pointing towards Ralph he spoke to Charles. 'Tie up the Tsar,' Petrovich spat at Charles throwing the tape at him. 'Do it properly if you want to live.'

Charles caught the reel as a sense of relief flushed through him that the Russian had said they would live. 'Yes, of course,' he said taking Davenport, who still had not moved since the appearance of the Russian, and sitting him on one of the chairs he quickly taped his wrists and ankles to the chair. Marcus was still groaning and holding his legs.

'You bastard, I hope you go to hell for this…' Marcus looked up to see the Russian point the gun back at him.

'One more sound from you and it will be you that will see the after-life… Now go and do the same to your friend.' Petrovich pointed towards Charles, who had already sat in the other chair.

'Marcus, do as he says if you want to live. He doesn't want to kill us all…'

Petrovich lowered the gun to Marcus' naked midriff and raised his eyebrows. Marcus struggled to his feet, wincing he took the tape off Charles; neither man caught the other's eye as he tied him to the chair. Petrovich looked around the room but there were no more chairs.

'You,' he pointed the gun at Marcus again. 'Lie down on your fat belly and put your hands behind your back.' Petrovich circled the room checking the bonds of the two seated men and returned to rest against the wall. He showed no signs of perspiring unlike the three men in front of him. Then with his free hand he extracted a Sobrani and taking a lighter he lit the cigarette without taking his eyes off the three men in front of him. 'You should have listened to your friend,' he said to Charles. 'He was right, I'm afraid there is no way I can let any of you live…'

A soft moan from Ralph preceded his head slumping down and he fell sideways crashing onto the floor the chair breaking into several pieces.

Petrovich let out a loud laugh. 'That's aristocracy for you; no backbone.'

Charles frowned for a moment as he saw the Russian eyes focus on the crumpled figure on the floor. 'It's a shame but I don't have time for any games today.' He took the cigarette out of his mouth and flicked it away then he turned his gun towards the prostrate man and took aim. His forefinger started to squeeze the trigger.

Charles was about to shout out when the flash of a silver blade came from the archway and went clean through Petrovich's throat; a bloodied point protruded from the other side. There was a stifled moan but no one moved as the Russian's left hand tried to grapple with the hand that was still holding tightly onto the handle. Petrovich's right arm had dropped as he ceased to struggle, Charles watched in horror the Russian's eyes started to glaze over blood continuing to spurt from his punctured jugular vein.

Petrovich's rasping breaths were becoming fainter and blood dripped from his open mouth. He realised that life was ebbing from him. His knees started to buckle as in his last gasp of life he remembered his mission. He made a gurgling sound and started to straighten his legs, lifting the gun back towards Davenport. He ignored the knife being turned frantically in his neck. His vision blurred as he tried to home in on the figure lying on the ground.

'Marcus grab the gun, quick!' screamed Charles pulling at his bonds.

Marcus had tried to stand up as soon as he saw the knife enter the assassin, pain shot through his body like lightening bolts. He slipped at first but finally managed to lunge forward lashing out at the Russian's wavering hand as he still gripped the revolver. The gun flew out of his hand as Marcus' body crashed into Petrovich; the last of his air expelled with frothy bloody oozing from his mouth.

Marcus rolled away from the dying man letting out a painful cry as Tamara let go of the knife and took a tentative step into the room staring at the body as it slid down onto the floor, leaving dark smears on the painted wall. She stepped over Marcus and kicked the gun across the room then she turned, stooping down over the dead body.

'The blade is stainless steel you disgusting bastard,' she hissed at the dead man.

Marcus pulled himself up, ignoring the pain, as he watched Tamara start to extract her knife. She stopped and took a quick pace back as the Russian's unseeing eyes seemed to be staring directly at her. Her jeans were muddy and her thick jumper was all out of shape and torn in several places. Her left hand was covered in blood and she held it up; horror filled her eyes. Her lips were quivering and her eyes widened but no tears just a distant look that caused Marcus to shudder. Finally she turned to look at him. Marcus couldn't look her in the eye and he glanced back to the gruesome sight on the floor. Tamara's whole body started shaking and she slowly collapsed onto her knees.

'Oh, God Marcus. That's it. They'll come after me now… I have to get away…'

'Marcus cut me loose for Christ sake and check Davenport.' Charles was still pulling at the tape tying his wrists to the chair. 'Marcus come on man, get these things off me.'

Marcus hobbled a few paces forward and helped Tamara back onto her feet. He brought her into his arms and held her tightly for a few moments. He hardly heard Charles' continuing pleas from behind him.

'Marcus! For Christ sake, get me out of these things and check Ralph…'

Marcus turned Tamara round to face him. She didn't cry but was muttering to herself, her arms now limp by her side. Even now Marcus smelt her soapy aroma as he placed his head gently onto the top of hers. Charles had ceased his demands as he watched the sorrowful scene in front of him and he had noticed that Ralph was stirring and started to mutter as he lay awkwardly on the collapsed chair underneath him.

'Are you OK?' whispered Marcus pulling his head away to take a look at her. Tamara kept her head down buried in his chest, her hair covering most of her face.

'*Marcus.*' Charles shouted. 'These bloody ties are really hurting. Ralph's stirring, help him would you...' Charles was now pulling so hard at his ties that blood had started to show.

Marcus shuffled Tamara towards the bed and gently sat her down. As he started to pull away he saw her looking at her blood stained hand and she lifted her face to meet his, saying nothing, everything she felt was in her eyes.

'It'll be alright, you'll see,' he whispered to her. Tamara's eyes were wide and startled, looking helplessly at him as if a pleading child when it had done wrong and wanted reassurance.

'I didn't think I would ever be able to...' She looked down at her hand again.

'Marcus, please... I think they're cutting off my circulation.' Charles' voice had become weak with exhaustion.

Marcus gave a watery smile to Tamara but she was still staring at her left hand, grief etched into her face. He turned and stumbled over to Davenport, kneeling beside him and checking the young man he tried to manoeuvre him into a more comfortable position.

'He's coming round, I think.' Marcus continued to try and move Davenport and looked back towards Tamara who was still motionless, sitting on the bed. He finally managed to turn the man over a little onto his back. 'No I'm wrong, I think he's still spark out.' Marcus looked towards Charles whose face was starting to twitch and contort with pain.

'I need a knife to cut this tape off,' said Marcus looking around the room

Marcus gingerly stood up and limped painfully into the bathroom but came out empty handed. 'I'll try the kitchen,' he said to Charles and started towards the door.

'Marcus.' Tamara's body was still visibly trembling. 'Marcus I have to go before it is too late.' She had heard the repetitive horn of an emergency vehicle in the distance, which started to panic her. Marcus stopped and turning towards her he remembered that the police and Charles' boss would also be here shortly.

'Look it'll be the police..., but don't worry...' Marcus said but was surprised they were arriving with all the sirens.

'It may not be. I asked a maid at the hotel to call an ambulance after twenty minutes to give me time to get here and hopefully intercept him... that must be it.'

Tamara stood up taking a pace towards Marcus. 'Look Tamara this was all in self defence,' his eyes quickly glancing towards the dead body to his right. 'You saved our lives from that bastard,' Marcus now pointing towards the corpse, 'he wasn't going to let any of us live, he made that very plain.' Marcus took her in his arms again and this time she responded by putting her hands around his waist.

'It is not only that Marcus, I have been working for the KGB since I went to university in Russia..., and they have...'

'Shh, this isn't the time...,' said Marcus knowing Charles would continue to be demanding his release. He was right.

'Marcus! Will you go and find something to cut me free,' whined Charles as he had started to struggle again with his bindings. 'You'll have to get the knife from out of his neck. Marcus?'

Tamara whispered into Marcus' ear. Charles watched feeling helpless as Tamara assisted Marcus as they started to leave the room.

'*Marcus!*'

The sound of the emergency vehicle came closer and to Charles' relief Marcus turned to face him still leaning on Tamara as she bent down and picked up her bag.

'Charles, I'm sorry but I am going with Tamara.'

'Marcus you bloody fool. James will sort all this out, I promise you.' Charles desperately tugged at his bonds making him cry out; the emergency vehicle could now be heard only a few streets away

'No time to explain, but please keep to our agreement we made on your dad's boat, I am worried you might renege. Do you promise?'

'Only if you don't run off…'

'Sorry Charles, there is too much at stake for me. I'll be back soon when I've sorted Tamara out…' Marcus limply raised his arm towards his friend.

Charles heard the couple stumble down the stairs and a door slam. He did not shout out, his breath had been taken away by Marcus' exit.

Tamara led Marcus through the gate and the couple managed to stagger down the road just as the ambulance turned into Verriest Straat. They made slow progress as Tamara had to help Marcus' every step. His trousers were now stained with the blood continuing to ooze out of his wounds. Tamara finally set Marcus down on a low wall.

'Stay here, I'll be back in a few minutes. We'll never get away at this speed.' She turned and Marcus watched her run down the street. He felt weak and nauseous. A few minutes later Tamara gave a sigh of relief as she saw a taxi parked in Ezel Straat.

The Turkish driver smiled as he saw her approach but was puzzled by her dirty and dishevelled appearance. At first he thought she was being chased but he noticed she gave him a smile as he approached. 'Quickly, we have to get back to the airport, but first we have to pick someone up.' Tamara jumped into the front seat and gave the driver a very pale and anxious look. Tamara gave directions and they soon pulled up alongside Marcus who was very pale and still clutching his knee. The driver jumped out with Tamara and helped Marcus into the back seat and Tamara slipped in beside him.

'Please get back to the airport as quickly as you can…'

'I very nearly gave up on you,' he said slipping the automatic into drive and taking a right turn to head back to the motorway.

'Yes, thanks for waiting. We were a little delayed…'

She lay back on her seat and turned her head towards Marcus.

'I suppose we have a lot of talking to do, but first…' Tamara lifted her left arm and put it around Marcus' neck and pulled herself towards him laying a long kiss on his lips. 'Thanks for trusting me; I promise you won't regret it.'

'Because of you I have possibly lost my oldest and dearest friend,' he replied quietly as he tried to steady himself while the vehicle swung to the right. 'Don't let me down…'

'I promise.'

The taxi made good time and at the airport Tamara helped Marcus to the car hire compound. Marcus tried to walk but he needed Tamara to lean on, he was becoming quite weak. She lent him against a concrete pillar and took the keys out of her bag.

'I just need to check something,' she said as she opened the car and leaning forward pulled the bonnet lever. She went to the front of the car pulled up the bonnet her eyes searching around the engine compartment. Finally she saw the small metal box taped under the fuse box.

'I thought so,' she whispered to her self and pulled off one of the spark plug leads and slammed the lid down. Jumping into the car she started it up and heard the missing beat of the engine. She got out of the car and looking around, spied an attendant and shouted to him. Marcus watched totally bemused. Tamara then proceeded to engage in a long discussion with the attendant and he left only to return a few moments later with another set of car keys. A few spaces down, car indicators blinked and Tamara helped Marcus into the passenger seat of the new car.

'What was all that about…?' he said trying to push the seat back.

'My car had a tracker on it.'

'A tracker? Who on earth would have…?'

Tamara gave Marcus a knowing look. 'I've been followed ever since I went to the airport. It's Charles' boss and the police.'

'They knew about you all along? But why didn't they help you. That Russian bastard said he had you tied up or something…'

'I managed to give them the slip at the airport when I arrived. It was very nearly the worst mistake of my life…' Tamara said driving out of the compound. 'Right you had better help with the navigating. I need the road to Luxembourg, but first we must find the road for Namur…'

★ ★ ★

Charles continued to stare at the empty archway, he felt like a jilted lover. To his relief he heard the ambulance pull up outside and stopped fighting with his bonds. Davenport had started to come round but he mumbled something and drifted back into unconsciousness.

Charles heard the paramedics shouting from the street. He bellowed back but it seemed they couldn't hear him. Panic filled him for a moment when he realised they may abandon the call, but then he remembered James Pulford and the inspector had said they were on their way. Charles could see the blue lights flashing outside and then he heard another car arrive. Further voices confirmed that his boss had now taken control. Charles let out a huge shout even causing the unconscious Ralph to stir. It did the trick and he could hear the doors down stairs being tried. Finally the stomping of heavy boots on the stairs reassured Charles that his bonds would soon be cut. James Pulford was the first to enter the room and he was immediately confronted by the sight of the dead Russian lying in a large and still growing, pool of blood. Then his eyes cast over the distorted figure of the unconscious Davenport. Inspector Hines followed him in with another suited man and finally two uniformed Belgium police officers.

'Holy Jesus,' muttered Hines as James Pulford finally rested his eyes on Charles. 'What the hell happened here?' he asked taking an unconscious step away from the corpse. He didn't see the satisfied smile on Pulford's face.

'You are not going to believe what has just happened here but first will you cut me out of these blasted things before I bleed to death.' Charles saw Hines extract a penknife and pulling out a large blade approached Charles and began cutting the tape.

Charles stood up as soon as he was free and ripped off the tape letting out a quiet expletive. He rubbed his wrists watching the Inspector and one of the policemen cut Davenport free and taking him over to the bed placed him down.

'They need seeing to,' said Pulford looking at Charles bleeding wrists. He turned to tell the other plain clothes policeman to get the paramedics up here.

Charles walked slowly over to Davenport and turned to Pulford. 'He fainted when the Russian told us he was going to kill us all. He was one hell of a scary bastard…' Charles threw a glance at the assassin's crumpled body.

'Where is your friend?' Pulford asked examining the knife still embedded in the Russian's neck. Charles went to answer but Pulford put his hand up. 'I think Charles, you and I should have a chat before anything else is said, don't you Hines,' James Pulford looked towards the police inspector who was examining the large hole in the floor boards but looked up at Pulford and nodded.

The paramedics came in and at first started to examine the corpse before a bark of command from one of the Belgium officers had them scurrying over to the bed. Davenport mumbled a faint moan as he started to come round. James Pulford nodded his head towards the door and as Charles followed him into the corridor he looked down at the Russian whose eyes still stared vacantly at some distant object. His mouth had fallen open and blood trickled down his chin and onto his shirt.

'Tamara's handy work?' James said, turning and looking at Charles as they reached the landing. Charles nodded. 'So where is she? And what about this Marcus chap? He hasn't gone off with her, has he?' he continued in a hushed voice.

Charles nodded again but this time he turned towards his boss. 'James we would all have been goners if she hadn't got here in the nick of time.' Charles looked back up the corridor to see two of the policemen knelt over the body now examining the letter opener. 'I'm not joking James, that guy was frightening, cool, calculating and focused. Even in his death throws he still tried to kill Davenport. Thank heavens Marcus managed to throw himself causing him to drop the gun. Look James, Tamara must not be punished for killing that animal,' Charles nodded his head back towards the bedroom. She did it entirely in *our* defence.'

'So why did she run, and why did your friend run with her?' Pulford mused starting to make his way down the staircase. 'I think it is not just this episode she is worried about,' James said as they went down stairs and into the damp, but warm night air; their shoes crunching over the broken glass on the floor. 'I wish she hadn't gone on the run. It is not going to make my job any easier nor do her cause much good. I still can't understand what the hell your friend is doing by going with her... God only knows.' Charles just nodded in agreement, but slowly he was beginning to realise the depth of feeling Marcus must have for this woman; he started to be concerned at exactly what were Marcus' plans.

'They can't have gone far. Marcus injured himself when we were being chased and I think he received some splinters when the Russian fired into the floorboards.' Charles said wishing for a moment he hadn't said anything.

'Right, Hines, get those two officers from upstairs and let's start a search at the area'

* * *

The couple had hardly spoken a word since leaving the bloody scene in Bruges. In the taxi they just held their initial embrace and watched the lights flash by. Marcus had drifted in and out of an exhausted sleep. Now they had their own transport, Tamara seemed to have become more focused and had started to talk to Marcus. Marcus was still dazed. He had worried about how Charles was going to react, but sitting close to Tamara and the way she gripped his hand, whilst her thumb gently massaged his

268

fingers, gave him a thrill he hadn't felt for years. The moment was spoilt by his continually nagging distrust of her; he tried to shake the feeling away.

'So what now?' he said hoping that Tamara had everything figured out in her own mind. To his further disappointment she just shrugged her shoulders. 'Tamara we have to talk, we just can't keep running, and I'm sorry but a couple of splinters have gone quite deep into my leg…'

'What do *you* want to do,' said Tamara her eyes now dry and sparkling as she drove into the night. 'I have nothing to go back for and I will certainly be the target for my ex-colleagues in Moscow.' The car slowed as Tamara lost her concentration.

'There's something worrying you Marcus, what is it? You still don't trust me do you despite me leaving the ring with Charles.' Tamara quickly glanced at him, Marcus didn't respond and continued to rub his knee. 'If you don't, you had better leave me now and go your own way. I am most certainly "persona non gratis…"' A sob came from nowhere and she quickly tried to disguise it with a small cough; she focused back on the road. 'You have a business, a daughter and a good social life. You may not be very happy at the moment and feel life is empty, but I have nothing except my handbag.'

'I don't believe you. You're right I just feel I can't trust you. What the hell are you doing working for the Russians? One minute you're sensitive and vulnerable, the next you're cool and calculating. I bet you've got some one waiting for you right now. All you wanted from me were the jewels…'

Marcus could see Tamara's chest heave as she breathed heavily.

'You're spot on Marcus. I did want those jewels and I do have someone waiting for me. Two people actually. I'll drop you off at the next service station, there's one in a few kilometres.' Then suddenly Tamara slowed down and pulled into the hard shoulder ignoring Marcus' protests.

'Shut up Marcus, I can't see through these bloody tears. I need a handkerchief.'

'I thought maybe you were going to dump me here!'

'Maybe I should…'

'Look I am being up front with you, can't you see my side? There is something about you that unnerves me, I can't help my instincts and you have already said I was right.' Marcus saw Tamara pull her handbag off the back seat; the car rocked with the slipstream of passing vehicles.

'My sister and her son are the two people waiting for me. I sent them every penny I had to bribe their way out Russia; hopefully they will be waiting for me on the German border near Regensburg. If not then I'm totally alone. Now's that's emptiness…'

'I'm sorry I didn't know…'

'You're sorry! I came here to save you from Petrovich!'

'Petrovich?'

'The assassin who was just about to kill you all.'

'Look I am really grateful…'

'Let me tell you where I am. I mentioned the other day about how lonely I am and how controlled I felt. For twelve years I have been living in dread of what they would do to my sister and my father…' Tamara sat forward putting her head on the steering wheel. Marcus shuffled over and put his arms around her shoulder ignoring the pain from his legs.

'Look, I'm very tired and after what has happened a bit confused. I think I have fallen in love with you and I'm worried that with all this you could…'

'Be put away for a long time.' Tamara turned her head and looked at Marcus, his face illuminated occasionally by passing head lights.

'No, you killed that man in total self defence, you must see that?' said Marcus quietly and he squeezed her shoulder.

'I went to that house with the intention of killing Petrovich, make no mistake about it. I also went back to Kinloch Castle. I was prepared to kill the caretaker if I had to and the same goes for Roger Davenport. You've fallen for the wrong girl Marcus; they turned me into a person I can hardly recognise myself…'

'What did they do to you? What control do they have over you? Is it your sister? How did you get into such a mess?' Marcus stopped as he felt her shoulder shudder and then he saw the tears dripping from her cheeks. 'Oh Tamara, just tell me...'

'I not sure of the whole story but my father seemingly upset the authorities. He wasn't a communist, in fact he was a republican, well I believe he was also a royalist. How ironic is that. He instigated my interest in the history of Russia. He kept antagonising them and having articles published in the West about the Tsar and how he wasn't as bad as the new Russian history books were portraying him. He advocated re-instating the monarchy.' Tamara let out a long sigh. 'Then I won a scholarship in England which he insisted I accepted. It was a terrible wrench as I was very close to my little sister; my mother had died several years before and I effectively brought her up. At first I was terribly home sick but after a while I loved it in England. So much so I opted to do a split degree in Moscow and London. Then it all went wrong.'

Tamara took in another deep breath and took hold of Marcus' hand. 'We'd better move on, the police will spot us here.' Tamara drove in silence until they came to the service station where she parked the car and, leaning back in her seat, continued:

'I returned home to do a year's study in Moscow. I hadn't seen my father for quite awhile and he had changed. He was bitter and during our first dinner together he just ranted about the Russian government and how corrupt it all was. He told me to go back to London and change courses so I didn't have to study in Moscow as he feared for my safety.'

'Your safety?'

'Yes, he was going to write something which would really upset the Government. So he had already sent my sister away to an aunt who lived in Prodna, near the Polish border. He gave me her address so I could write to her but he told me to wait until the dust had settled. The next day I was meant to meet him but he never turned up. I searched for several days and reported him

271

missing, but nothing. Then one day I was called and told to go to an office on the outskirts of Moscow. They had some news about my father. That was when I first met Colonel Andrei Suslov. Initially he was courteous and civil and asked me about my time in England, but then he started asking me about my father. I actually didn't know anything, but he wouldn't believe me. Suslov then said my father was a member of a dissident group who wanted to end communism and bring back democracy, but he had also advocated a monarchy.

'That's when he suddenly turned nasty and Suslov had me tied to a bed, naked. No food or water; I couldn't move at all. I wasn't able to tell them anything because I didn't *know* anything. They also wanted to 'interview' my sister and I wouldn't give them the address. Fortunately I had hidden it back in my room, but they eventually broke me and I told them where the address was hidden. Marcus you have to believe me I was delirious I just didn't know what I was doing.'

Tamara looked over at Marcus and he responded by leaning forward and kissing her gently on her nose, tasting her salty tears.

'A few days later they took me to a room which had a window looking into another room. It must have been a one way mirror. My sister was sitting in a chair her hands tied behind her back and she only had her pants and a white T-shirt on. She looked so frightened and utterly confused. I screamed to her but she didn't hear me and then it started. A brute of a man started hitting her with the back of his hand. He had black leather gloves on. Her face just…'

Marcus twisted his body and put his left arm around her. 'It's OK. Let's pray she is waiting for you…'

'They kept beating her and telling me what else would happen to her if I didn't cooperate. They also said they would look kindly on my father as well if I did as they asked. I knew then that they were lying but what could I have done? I never heard from him again; and yet I still believe, or maybe it's just a pathetic hope, that he might be alive. So I finished my degree and was trained by the KGB on how to spy for my homeland; a land I barely knew and had now come to hate. They were clever though and they allowed me to keep in close contact with my sister. Once I stood up to them, I really upset them and my sister paid the price, a very dear price. I didn't hear from her for weeks and, then when I did, she wouldn't tell me what had happened to her. Eight months later she gave birth to a baby boy. She says she doesn't know who the father is, it was all a mistake. But I know she is lying to me, they did it to her, I know it. I still believe it was Suslov. So I had to obey them; I had no choice.'

Marcus gave her another gentle squeeze and taking the handkerchief patted her eyes dry.

'I can see why you wanted the jewels. I've got some bad news about those,' he said watching her wipe the tears from her face and look towards him in the dim light of the car park. 'I have promised Charles he can have the jewels and the box, or rather the V&A can.'

Tamara searched Marcus' eyes trying to detect if he was serious. 'Why?'

'They have brought me nothing but trouble…'

Tamara said nothing for a while, her eyes fixed on him. 'Marcus, it has over one hundred diamonds hasn't it, and is part of a suite, isn't it?' Marcus straightened pulling his arm back. 'It's the Faberge suite made especially for the Tsar as a gift to his sister in 1891. It has never been found, but you have it don't you? I checked, the ring is part of the suite, there is no doubt. I gave the ring back to you to show you that you can trust me.' Tamara lent forward and rested her head on the steering wheel again.

'Yes, I do have it…'

'Does Charles know about it?'

'Yes, but I've done this deal…'

'You still don't trust me do you? Everything I have said to you has been the truth.' Tamara's voice was stronger and her tears had stopped. 'What is the deal you have done with Charles? Please don't tell me you have offered to give the suite away as well.'

Marcus shook his head. 'Not exactly, Charles has come out with an idea of how to gain some financial reward. It's a long story…' He looked towards her and raised his hand touching her face. 'What are you going to do now? You wouldn't have planned for your sister to meet up with you unless you had somewhere to go. It just isn't you.'

Tamara signed wearily. 'Ydra. It is a small town on an island in Greece. I went there many years ago and I decided it was perfect for me. I have rented a small apartment and I hope to set up a small business or something and live there. Nobody is waiting for me and I hope nobody finds me, except…' Tamara had moved her head to one side and looked at Marcus. 'It is a quiet place where I can hide with my sister. I am after all now a murderer. Hell, I was actually thinking of possibly setting up a small shop selling antiques…, hopefully with you.'

'I really don't know what to say…'

★ ★ ★

Charles was taken to the nearest police station and for several hours he sat in discussion with his boss and the Scotland Yard Inspector. Charles had wanted to call Dawn to see if her father had contacted her but he knew she would fret when she found out he'd gone missing, and more significantly, with whom. He had also not called home; Samantha would not have appreciated a call in the dead of night which could also have woken the children. Davenport had been admitted to the hospital with concussion and suffering from shock.

'Well it seems your little sailing trip to Scotland turned out to be more than you expected.' James was going through his notes of the past few hours. 'The jewels are still at Marcus Chapman's house?' Charles nodded but aware that James knew more than he was letting on; he seemed quite relaxed about the whole affair.

'What do we do about poor Ralph Davenport? I am assuming that the Russians may try again?' Charles said irritably flicking a pencil to and fro in front of him. He was still angry and hurt that his friend had left him, especially in such circumstances.

'This has escalated and I will have to speak to London.' James Pulford continued to scribble notes. 'Knocking off one of the Russian top agents will cause major diplomatic repercussions, but if the Russians know that Davenport is a *protected* man...' James shrugged his shoulders. 'I just can't see this chap Davenport turning up at the Kremlin and asking for his throne back somehow.' The three men all smiled. It was the first time they had done so that night.

A hum of air-conditioning drowned out Pulford's continued scribbling when the door opened. One of the Belgian policemen came in holding a piece of paper.

'He has turned up.' The officer said, reading from the paper. All three men stood up.

'Alone?' James asked.

'Yes, but...'

'What?' demanded Pulford impatiently.

The police officer checked the piece of paper. 'He was trying to get through the border post into Luxembourg near Arlon, on foot, but was spotted and when approached he tried to get away, but as he is quite seriously hurt he didn't get far..., however he...'

'Get away? What in heaven's name is that idiot up to?' roared Charles. Pulford raised his hand to silence his subordinate.

'However what?'

'Well our men have been through the CCTV and we can just make out a car that we believe to be the one the Nolan woman hired. It seems she had swapped cars a few hours ago. It actually looks as though Chapman was diverting the attention of the border guards in order for her to get through.' The young Belgian folded the paper and stood looking at the three men their faces aghast and silenced by the news.

'Have you sent out a description of the car to the Luxembourg authorities?' James said now becoming agitated again. He dearly wanted to speak to this woman, he could have helped her, if she would let him. He was keen to get to her before the Russians did.

'Yes, but she will probably be through Luxembourg by now, so we have alerted the police in Germany and France.' James and Hines both nodded and the Belgian took his leave.

'What now?' Charles sat back down in his seat flicking the pencil away.

'We wait...' said Pulford walking over to the door. 'I need some sleep.' He opened the door. 'Coming? There is nothing we can do here until Chapman is back and hopefully the elusive Tamara is caught.'

The two other men followed him out and after a few phone calls they were taken to a small, fine old Bruges Hotel near the market place, Relais Bourgondisch Cruyce on Wollestraat.

Charles took his key from the receptionist and asked if it would be possible to have a drink. The receptionist nodded and said the night porter would come over and take the order. 'Can I join you Charles?' said James as they said their farewells to the Inspector. Charles nodded and they ambled together to find a quiet corner away from the reception area.

'What sort of mess is Tamara in and for that matter what about Marcus and I?' Charles watched Pulford carefully, but the man looked relaxed and at ease.

'Firstly, your friend Marcus will have to tow the party line if he wants to get out of this without any sort of unfortunate recourse.' James ordered two large whiskies from the night porter who could barely raise a civil comment, he had been disturbed from his sleep.

'He's not got a passport...'

'Don't worry about that. I'll sort things out. I just hope he doesn't make things difficult for himself, or me. I am assuming you will be able to influence him...?' They fell silent as the drinks were banged down on the table and the man grunted and left. 'Well with a bit of massaging we could make sure your role in all this is looked upon in a favourable light, if not almost a heroic one...'

'Heroic, what the hell are you talking about?'

276

'Well, you'll be the one that discovered the jewellery. I need to think this through as to the actual chain of events…' James had a broad smile on his face and picked up his glass and raised it to Charles. 'I think your role, and mine for that matter, will be viewed well by the *VfA*. One must always look at making the most of every situation.' James took a sip of his drink followed by a small cough. 'I've had better…'

Charles picked up his glass and leaning forward took a sip. He was still smarting about Marcus, but his initial anger had now started to wane. He sensed that whatever was going on between Tamara and Marcus, it was clearly something important. He knew his old friend would not have acted like that without good reason. Concern and more than a touch of curiosity, was now replacing the anger.

'But what about Tamara? She is a killer and worked for the KGB, as an agent…' Charles mirrored his boss by coughing as he drank the whiskey.

'As I said I will do my best. I believe your friend and she are an item.' Charles nodded.

'It seems he really has fallen for her. I can't wait to see what he has to say for himself,' Charles said examining his glass.

'Charles you are aware of the history of these jewels. Lady Xenia was an illegitimate child of the Tsar's and that is what is slightly confusing about of all this. Davenport could never have made a serious claim to the throne. If he did and succeeded there are probably many more people walking around England with more right to the throne than our own Queen.' James smiled at Charles. 'Forensics stated that there was no evidence that Malone had died from unlawful killing, just some superficial injuries caused by being ravaged by his own dog. What a strange situation… I am not entirely certain about the Davenport's situation, but a quick call to the investigating officer said first signs are that he also died from a fall…'

'And Tamara did save us James. That man had every intention of killing all of us, there is no doubt in my mind. It makes me shudder just to think about it.' Charles' body did shudder and made him smile at Pulford. '*She* did actually save our lives so she should be given some leeway…'

'We don't know all the facts yet, but instinct tells me I may be able to sort this mess out. The problem is, will she let me?' James swilled the remains of his drink, slapped his knees and yawned. 'I am absolutely shattered. Time for bed I think.' James rose with a warm smile on his face. 'I can tell you we know a lot more than you would imagine about Tamara and her association with the KGB.'

Charles downed the last of his drink, tiredness starting to blunt his mind. He still couldn't come to terms with the fact that he had been minutes away from being murdered.

'James, I would appreciate it if that this never got out; Samantha would kill me…'

'I can assure you, I want all this kept well under wraps…'

Chapter 13

Colonel Suslov entered his office and was surprised to see his assistant was not at his desk. He frowned and put his case slowly down by the side of his desk. Years of living in fear and trepidation at the heart of Soviet Russia had given him a sixth sense when something was not right. His daily papers were still on his assistant's desk and not laid out as usual. He went back and rummaged through the few papers on Mikhail's desk but nothing looked suspicious. He told himself that his assistant had probably over slept or could be ill, but he sensed things weren't right.

He went into the small kitchen adjoining the sub-office. Opening the fridge and taking out some fresh orange juice. He poured himself a glass and returned to his desk and dialled his assistant's apartment number. No answer. He collected the newspapers and his eyes were immediately drawn to the bottom of the front page of the Times.

Mystery Russian dies in suburbs of Bruges…

Andrei Suslov flicked to an inner page where more details were to be found, but he heard heavy footsteps coming down the corridor. In an instant he had grabbed his brief case and made for the kitchen; there was no where to run. He did not think what he would do or how he could ever escape but his instinct was to run.

The door was flung open and two uniformed men came in baring his exit. Behind them stood his assistant and another man

279

that Suslov recognised, a KGB General who was responsible for internal discipline. Nausea wretched at his stomach.

'Comrade Colonel would you please come with me,' said the man at the rear. Suslov started to speak but he knew any resistance now would aggravate his plight. He nodded and put down his case. Inside was the file on Tamara Nolan and Petrovich. He remembered the file he had been reading yesterday and quickly glanced around, there was no sign of the Davenport file on his desk.

'It is here Colonel,' said the man still standing by his assistant and holding a pale grey file. Several more men had now entered the room and two uniformed men took Suslov's arms and escorted him out of the room. As he passed his assistant he muttered, 'Traitor, you will be known…'

'Quiet,' barked the KGB general. He turned to the men who had now just entered the room. 'Clear everything and shut this entire unit down. Destroy everything.'

'No, no this is insane. I was only doing my job…' Suslov tried to turn to see the KGB general, but the soldiers pulled him along. 'I am Colonel Suslov…; I am the grandson of…'

Suslov's legs were unable to bear his weight, but the two soldiers dragged him. He was taken down a small staircase at the rear of the building and unceremoniously thrown into the back of an old windowless van. The doors were slammed shut and locked. He heard a bang on the roof, the engine fired up and the vehicle lurched forward making Andrei crash backwards in the dark. The crack on his head caused his head to spin momentarily but there was another reason he felt faint. He knew where he was going and he would never see Moscow or his family again. He had sent too many down this road to know what his fate was going to be. He struggled groping on all fours in the dark to find a seat of some sort, but the movement made it almost impossible. He slumped back onto his back and rode the violent movements as the van careered down the streets of Moscow. How had this all happened? He recalled Tamara's telephone calls and surmised that she must have double crossed him and poor Petrovich. 'The bitch,' he cursed.

He tried to recall all the atrocities he had inflicted on her to appease his anger. He visualised her lying on the bed, tied up and desperately begging him not to hurt her, or her sister, how could such a weak individual have had the last word. He cursed her again and closed his eyes hoping his end would be quicker than Tamara's father; the memory of his demise finally brought a smile to the Colonel's face as he went to meet his own fate.

* * *

V&A Museum, late July 1997

Charles knocked on the large wood panelled door and heard James Pulford shout an acknowledgement. He entered carefully cradling the wood and silver jewellery box. He felt excited and nervous all at the same time, the thought of bringing such a find to the V&A would be seen as a real feather in his cap. He had decided to keep his deal with Marcus and worried in case his own slight deception may have been discovered.

Pulford stood and introduced the people around the table. Charles had met most of them before at the previous meetings but this time James Pulford took time to introduce them individually. Everyone was smiling and many couldn't take their eyes off the wooden box that Charles had placed on the table. Coffee was distributed and Charles took his seat, making himself comfortable. He placed his hand lightly on the box and his thumb stroked its front, which had now been lovingly repaired. He could still see Marcus barely able to hand it over to him.

'Well, I see you have Xenia's jewellery box and I hope the jewels,' Pulford said laughing a little and looking at Charles, then he glanced down at the box. Charles nodded and slowly opened the lid. His face began to glow with the reflection of the jewels. He then turned the box to face the group seated around the table. Initially silence reigned and Charles lent forward pulling up the tray to show more jewels in the bottom of the box.

'Oh my!' continued James. He lent forward and picked up a bracelet turning it slowly in his hands. 'It is just exquisite.' James passed it onto a woman sitting beside him and then pushed the box to an older man and motioned for him to inspect.

This man took all the pieces out one by one and inspected them with a silver jeweller's eye glass. After what seemed an age to Charles he finally spoke. 'No doubt about it. These are some of the pieces that were made for Tsar Nicholas ll. I would say from about 1870's onwards. Unfortunately there doesn't seem to be the suite of jewels made specially for the Tsar by Faberge.'

There was a short awkward silence.

'What! Aren't there any more Charles?' asked Pulford slowly, still examining some jewellery.

'No that's all Marcus gave me,' Charles stammered; he was furious with himself that he was showing such nervousness and hence guilt.

'The ring you brought in from Chapman was definitely from that suite.' James Pulford looked across at the elder men. He nodded. 'We also do not seem to be able to trace this ring…'

'I suppose Tamara must have taken it with her,' blurted Charles too quickly then feeling his face redden. Other members of the group were now examining some of the jewels and Charles could sense James Pulford eyes boring into him.

Finally Pulford placed the jewels back into the box still looking admiringly at them. 'Well I suppose all I can say Charles is very well done for retrieving all these…' A hum of approval went around the table.

'James, err may I…'

'Charles, we'll have a chat later, but I would like to say on the behalf of my colleagues here today how grateful we are at the V&A are for this find.' James finally tore his gaze away from the jewels and smiled at Ashford. The older man coughed and looked at Pulford. 'Oh, of course Charles, I almost forgot. The *VfA* have asked me to see if you would formally accept the offer of becoming a member.' The whole group turned their attention towards Charles who was now standing and very flushed. 'There is no induction or anything like that, you will just be part of the world wide fraternity. Oh that includes both sexes,' James attempted a weak laugh as he quickly glanced at the woman by his side.

Charles nodded. 'Yes, I would be honoured. I can't be sure if I can grace you with such finds on a regular basis…' Charles waved his hand at the jewellery box standing majestically on the table. A few polite laughs and Charles sensed it was time for him to go. He couldn't wait to leave the room. Pulford must suspect something and he cursed the day he had agreed with Marcus to help him try and sell the suite of jewels privately. He left the room as a murmur of voices started to gather strength as the jewels were once again being examined closely by all. He descended to the lobby and bought a coffee in the main restaurant; he felt numb. He hadm, for the past few years, been keen to be asked to join the *VfA* and now that it had been bestowed upon him it had been an anti-climax. He felt let down by the informality of finally being part of the organisation but also feared whether Pulford's suspicion he was lying would affect his career.

He stirred his coffee watching the visitors passing him. His thoughts laboured on the silence in the room when the Faberge jewellery and the ring had been mentioned. What was James Pulford thinking? Hopefully that Marcus had kept the jewels without his knowledge, but why did he blush so: damn!

Marcus had been so grateful when he had given him back the ring; even more grateful when Charles had given him a contact to approach. Had Marcus inadvertently compromised his own position? He pushed his coffee away, feeling sick in the stomach, as he contemplated the consequences if this suite emerged in the market place and James Pulford traced it back to Marcus or even him; it could be one of the shortest careers in the *VfA*.

Two months later he was summoned to Pulford's office. Charles feared the worst, he was right to. Charles took a deep breath as he knocked on James' door and entered. The box of jewels was on the cabinet at the side of the room and Pulford was reading a file laid out on his desk.

'What do you think? Shall we display them or not?' Pulford rose and approached the box. 'Might wind our Russian friends up a bit. But…'

'Well we've being doing that for decades…'

'Ahh my dear Charles, but things are changing, for the moment.' Pulford caressed the casket with his finger tips. Another silence fell between them like a barrier. Finally Pulford turned to face Charles. 'Has Marcus Chapman said anything of significance about what happened? Or more importantly has he ever mentioned the Xenia suite of jewels? The so called *Stones of Conscience.*'

Charles watched his boss as he now turned and opening the box picked up a pendant, peering through the large citrine stone surrounded by diamonds.

'Well, we have broached the subject but only superficially. We laugh about the chase and there are a few jokes but to be honest James I don't see a lot of him at the moment. He's not around that much at the moment. When we do talk he tends to avoid any questions, almost ignoring me, especially regarding Tamara. He is very busy and a little distracted but I know the man well; he is certainly brooding on something. One day, when he is ready I'll get the full story.' Charles unease had turned to self preservation.

'Yes, Tamara Nolan went to ground with remarkable ease and your friend *has* been very busy. I believe Nolan had her plan laid out for some time and I think Chapman is in regular contact with her.' Charles couldn't avoid swallowing hard as Pulford came back to his desk and examined the file. 'We've not managed to trace her exact location as yet, but we don't have any real reason to. Anyway when we do I'll leave all that to Inspector Hines.' James watched Charles who felt himself frowning as Pulford talked with a measured and reassured style. Charles nervousness had turned to dread. 'I can confirm that the Malone death has been accepted as an accident, death by misadventure, I believe it's called. Although he was savaged by his dog after the fall, did you know?' Charles nodded. 'Poor old Roger Davenport definitely died from falling down his own stairs. He was very ill and the haemorrhaging meant he died very quickly. There was no sign of anything untoward…'

'But wasn't Tamara there at his house? She could have pushed him…' Charles said stumbling on his words.

'Yes, there is absolutely no evidence that she did anything; innocent until proven guilty. The home help actually could not identify Tamara from the photographs.' James had stopped looking at the file and faced Charles. 'As far as her killing of that Russian agent, that has been a little trickier. The story did leak out, but we managed to suppress any real investigative journalism; you know how they love sensationalism.' James stretched and kept an eye on Charles who still sported a deep worried frown on his face. 'Self defence of others is exactly the same as protecting yourself in the eye of the law, well it is in Belgium. The agent was killed in an act of self defence, and the only thing the Belgium police wanted to do, and our people for that matter, would be to thank Tamara for saving three men's lives. You of course being one of them…'

Charles nodded. 'Yes, and I should be, well actually of course I am, grateful but are we not the slightest bit concerned that we had a KGB agent in our midst? It doesn't make sense to me that you can just brush all this under a carpet and…'

'Charles, be pragmatic. Do you want this whole story being exposed and put under the microscope by the gutter press? The *VfA* do like to keep a low profile even when we have done a pretty good job…' James smiled and raised his eyebrows. 'The Russians lost a lot of their treasures in the revolution and it would be useful with the current thawing of relationships between the two countries if we were to return something to them. The Xenia's jewels would have been perfect for a particular plan that is being discussed. Unfortunately they seemed to have disappeared until…'

Pulford motioned for Charles to sit down. He could see

Charles' was becoming unsteady on his legs. James smiled watching the newest member of the *VfA* slump into a chair his worried countenance pleasing Pulford. 'It seems someone has been touting the suite around…' James continued to study Charles' face. 'It is being done very discreetly of course, but such artefacts will always cause tongues to wag. Do you think Marcus could still have the suite of jewels? It would be a crying shame if they were ever sold to someone who broke them down…'

Charles shrugged his shoulders. Pulford had the ability to ask questions and yet portray he already knew the answer. Charles considered his options; would honesty be the best policy?

Charles made a nervous cough. 'Marcus has been acting a bit strange lately as I said he has been a bit distant, so I can't really make more than an educated guess whether he has any jewels or not. He has also been travelling a lot recently…'

'Yes, we know he takes regular trips to Athens. Does he have any friends out there?' Pulford's tone had a sarcastic note.

Charles felt himself start. Pulford was still having Marcus watched.

'Not that I am aware of…'

'So that could be where Tamara is.' Pulford stood and ambled towards the window, a heavy silence filling the room. He returned to his desk and sat down slowly still in deep thought. 'It must be difficult for you being his oldest friend and all that. I admire your loyalty towards him but it isn't helping the situation.'

Pulford's gazed at Charles with a knowing look. He hoped the younger man would finally come clean with him.

Charles sensed the time had come to be honest but decided to play for time. 'Yes, the whole episode has been difficult but if you want I will sit down and find out exactly what he's been up to. I hope he sees sense…' Charles waited a moment and then started to stand and make his exit when Pulford raised his arm for Charles to remain seated. He swivelled his chair and looked out of the window, indicating the meeting was far from over.

'One bit of good news,' he continued, 'out of all this is, apart from the demise of that bastard Petrovich, it seems the new Russian authorities have disbanded their department that was dedicated to destroying any legacy of the Tsar. So Davenport and Tamara can sleep in their beds at night. It also transpires the man in charge has been removed…' James stopped and swung his chair around to face Charles. 'Just suppose if Marcus still has the Faberge suite of jewels: the stones of conscience. I could offer these back to the Russians as compensation for the loss of one of their agents and we could then keep the other jewels and that marvellous jewellery box, for us to display. If only we could manage to communicate to Tamara that her tormentors had been, well, had left their positions. The luckless Tamara would be able to live a normal life and of course we would have to reward the person who found the jewels; I suspect a worthwhile reward. Do you get my drift Charles? Everyone would be a winner including you and I.'

Charles watched Pulford as he slowly turned his chair from side to side not able to look the man squarely in the eye. Pulford continued slowly. 'There is something that has coloured our perspective, so as to speak, on poor Tamara. She had been put under a lot of duress and had little alternative but to do the beckoning of the KGB; she must have been through hell. So it is such a shame she doesn't know that she could now live her life normally and not in fear.'

Charles finally met Pulford's hard gaze. 'What exactly would this reward be?'

'Well, if Chapman did suddenly come up with the jewels we could reward him with… Let's say he wanted to acquire another shop maybe he would want to go international, a shop on an island in Greece for example. I understand one of the best places for the antiques collectors is on Ydra. Who knows, he may even bump into Tamara stranger things have happened. If you went out there and met her you would be able to put her mind at rest, wouldn't you.' Pulford's voice was light but he supported a furrowed and knowing frown.

Charles felt like a boy in front of the head master. Pulford clearly knew Marcus had the jewels and that he was seeing Tamara on a Greek island.

'I'll see what I can do…'

'Do that, and tell Chapman I don't make offers like this every day of the week. I am certainly not going to barter…' Pulford's eyes were fixed on Charles as he started to stand. 'Do you think you can swing this one Charles?'

Charles went to the door, turning to look back at his boss.

'Maybe a bit of cash as sweetener to set the business up…?'

'Agreed. So, do think you can persuade our Mr. Chapman?' Pulford frowned at the thought of rewarding theft.

'He doesn't really have an option does he?'

Pulford's frown faded and it was replaced with a smile. 'No not really, now you mention it; and *your* misplaced loyalty would also be forgotten…'

Charles left the building walking slowly towards Marcus' shop. He hoped Marcus would not over react when he found out he had been followed and his every move watched. If Marcus didn't play ball they would both rue the day…

Chapter 14

King's Road, London, April 1998

Marcus stood rigid, completely dumbfounded. It was finally happening, he was going to lose his daughter; in front of him stood the man who wanted to take her away. Marcus had known something was up that morning when Toby had asked to see him, and inwardly he had feared it would be to ask for Dawn's hand in marriage; but nothing had prepared him for facing the ultimate truth. Since Toby's call he had started to consider his situation and after the initial fatherly shock he was now starting to see his daughter's marriage as fitting in perfectly with his own plans.

'Toby, I am speechless. Firstly thank you for asking me, I am honoured in today's society. Does Dawn know your intentions?' Toby nodded and shuffled as he tried not to show his nervousness. 'What if I say no?' Marcus tried to keep a straight face but couldn't help himself laughing as he saw the flash of concern on the young man's face. Toby let out a sigh of relief when he saw Marcus laugh and continued the light hearted spirit.

'Then you give me no choice but to elope...' Both men laughed together not sure of quite what to do or say next. Toby broke the silence. 'Marcus we are ready to get married, we have discussed it in some depth.'

'Yes I know you are, but there is one thing bothering me. Where would you live and what would you live on?' Marcus sat on a chair by the window of the shop still watching Toby. 'Ruddy hell, Toby you'll only qualify in the summer...'

'Well that's just it Marcus I have just been offered a really good job in the city. I am starting on a pretty good packet as well.'

Marcus stood up and came over to Toby. 'Congratulations, you certainly worked hard for it…'

'Thanks, and with Dawn working fulltime here with you…'

'Yes, I wasn't happy about her abandoning her course, you know that. However she is doing a bloody good job here. At times I feel almost redundant when I'm in the shop.' Marcus turned and gazed out of the window. 'Does her mother know?' Toby shook his head as Marcus glanced back at him. 'Blimey I am honoured. Damn it Toby, you have stunned me with two bits of information that can only result in one thing. I am sorry but…' Marcus continued to look out of the window, holding the moment and turning towards the young man. '…this calls for a drink. Where is Dawn?'

'Too right… She's waiting down at Charles' house having a coffee with Samantha. She believes you will go ballistic.' Toby turned to go to the office. 'Can I call her and put her out of her misery?'

'No, you can not. I'll do it.' A wide grin had caused Marcus' face to wrinkle. 'I'm going to enjoy this.'

'Marcus please don't tease her too much, she is really nervous about this, please.' Toby gave Marcus a pleading look as he passed him and entered the office.

'Don't worry I'll be gentle.' Marcus picked up the phone and dialled. Charles answered. Marcus bellowed down the phone. '*You're* harbouring my daughter, I believe.'

'Oh hello Marcus, yes she is here. Has Toby spoken to you yet?'

'Ruddy right he has…' Marcus held his breath for a few moments. He could hear Charles' breathing and a rustle of the phone. Charles wasn't the only one listening in. He still held the silence, Charles also said nothing. 'You'd better get her pretty little butt down to the Chelsea Potter, last one there buys the champagne!' Marcus had to hold the phone away from his ear as he could hear his daughter and Samantha squeal with delight. Charles said they were on their way and Marcus put the phone down and turned to face Toby, who was standing in front of him, a wry smile crossed his face.

'That was a bit cruel Marcus,' he said grinning. 'I wish I'd been there…'

'Come on Toby! Do you know at first I thought I had lost a daughter, but you know,' Marcus came up to Toby, 'I've just gained a son.' Marcus started to move but Toby stayed still.

'Marcus, you will not regret this. I am not merely in love with Dawn I am besotted with her. I *will* make her very happy.' Toby finished off with a small nod at his new father-in-law in waiting.

'Bloody right you will.' Marcus laughed making a small jab at Toby's midriff. He stopped and looked at him. 'Actually Toby I know you will. There is something about you…' then they suddenly gave each other a hug and stepped away in embarrassment after a few seconds.

The two men walked down the King's Road and just before the pub they heard Dawn shouting and waving, running towards them.

'Oh, Dad, Dad. Are you alright with it, I mean is it all right, well…'

'Oh belt up girl. I am delighted for you both. I am still worried you're both so young but what the hell… Oh, but no children for a while; I am not ready to be called Granddad yet.'

'Dad, you really are incorrigible…'

'What you've only just figured that out,' said Charles as he came up with Samantha on his arm. The small group went into the pub where champagne was ordered and they stood at the end of the bar as Dawn told them all her plans for when and where the wedding would be.

'Toby says you haven't told your mother about this yet?' Said Marcus unable to disguise a touch of satisfaction in his voice and went around filling everyone's glass.

'No not yet, we are driving to Odiham tomorrow, after we have bought the ring, so no one let it out of the bag yet, especially you Dad.' Dawn said taking a long sip of champagne and eyeing her father.

'What sort of ring are you going to buy? Maybe your father

has something…' interjected Charles with a mischievous smile.

'She doesn't want second hand stuff, do you Dawn?' answered Marcus throwing a stern look towards Charles. 'Anyway I am surprised you can get in anywhere at this late notice.'

Dawn took Toby by the arm and looked towards her father. 'I am lucky there is a free day at the church in the first week in September, and the George Hotel can do the wedding breakfast. I am planning on no more than a hundred or so…'

Marcus choked a little and frowned at his daughter. 'A hundred or so, that is going to cost a ruddy fortune, girl. We don't know a hundred people.' The remaining group laughed and soon another bottle of champagne was ordered; Marcus was resigning himself to an expensive autumn.

Samantha had to leave as the nanny would have to leave shortly. Then the young couple wanted to go shopping in the West End to look for the engagement ring. Soon it was just Charles and Marcus left, now seated in Marcus' usual table in the corner.

'I wish you hadn't mentioned anything about me providing the engagement ring. It's taken me weeks to convince Dawn that I really have returned all the jewels…' Marcus finished his champagne smiling at Charles. 'This stuff is so gassy, do you fancy a beer?' asked Marcus. Charles nodded.

'You know why I brought it up,' he said. 'You've not told me exactly what has happened since you met Pulford.'

'You don't want to know. He gave me a real grilling but then calmly agreed to the purchase of a place Tamara had her eye on in Ydra. How come he seems to wield so much power, it's as if he…'

'It is rumoured he is part of the intelligence service…'

'Oh my God,' said Marcus leaving for the bar and returned supporting two pints.

'Well who would have thought it,' said Marcus still beaming with delight and deciding to change the subject. 'Little Dawn getting married. You've got all this to come…' Marcus sat and watched the people mingling around the bar. Charles raised his glass and checked the beer.

'Marcus, you can't keep changing the subject. I would really like to know how you're getting on with Tamara and what *your* plans are?'

'Well strangely enough I was going to have a chat with you about all that. I appreciate that I am the one that seems to come out of this rather well, except for a knackered knee and some scars. But I'm not quite ready to tell you what I have planned so can I ask you to be patient just for a little bit longer. It will be for the best.' Marcus' mood had become serious and he wore a worried frown. 'I've got to make sure all the bits fit together, but now Dawn is getting settled, it just may all come together...' Marcus said brooding over his beer as if Charles was hardly there. A few moments silence lingered as Charles continued to watch his friend.

'To Dawn and Toby and a damn good wedding.' Charles finally said and took a large slurp of beer. 'Marcus where are those two going to live? Toby will have to be in commuting distance of the city and if Dawn stays working for you...'

'There's only one thing for it Charles.' Marcus whispered studying Charles' face. Charles looked at him quizzically. 'Oh ruddy hell if I can't trust you then who can I trust. Right sit tight Charles because what I'm about to say must *not* go any further and I mean not telling anyone, even Samantha.' Charles suddenly felt like the old times were back as he saw Marcus' eyes become bright and sparkling. 'I know this sounds ridiculous but I have been putting together some plans...'

* * *

Odiham, Hampshire, September 1998

Marcus came out of his room as he heard the church clock strike seven and, attired in jeans and a shirt, he had eyed the morning suit still hung behind the door with a touch of trepidation, he went downstairs for breakfast. Charles was the only other person in the restaurant and Marcus came and sat opposite him and ordered a large coffee.

'Well dear old Linda made sure we had an early night; now I know why I left her.' said Marcus picking up a menu card on the table he studied it and placed it back on the table. 'Actually I'm glad she did. Not the day to start off with a thumping hangover.'

'I still feel a bit groggy even after only a couple of beers. I've become a light weight.' Charles waved to a waitress who had come in from the kitchen and they ordered.

'Look Marcus I have been meaning to say something for a while since you told me what you were going to do.' Charles took a deep breath. 'I know your intentions are good well, very generous actually, but dropping this on her today of all days, her wedding day… Wouldn't it be better after the honeymoon?'

'Charles I've thought about it. Everything will be OK. Trust me.'

'I have this sneaking suspicion that you're doing this for your own reasons, not Dawn's. You know how you like a bit of theatre. Am I right?' Charles was watching Marcus intently as the coffee and toast arrived. Marcus' full English breakfast followed a few moments later.

'Charles, how come you're always right…' Marcus smiled at him over his coffee cup. 'Yes, I am doing it for myself, for Dawn, Toby but most of all to piss Linda off.'

Charles grunted while the two men sat silently eating. Marcus puffed his cheeks out. 'Not sure if I'm up for eating all this lot,' he said pushing the bacon around his plate.

'It'll be good to soak up the booze later,' mused Charles chewing on his toast.

'Charles…' Marcus said finally starting to chomp his way through the full plate in front of him. 'It will be for Dawn's own good and if I do it this way there is no turning back. They can make plans while they're on the honeymoon.'

'Look there is something I have been meaning to tell you about Tamara. James Pulford told me why she had been acting for the Russians…'

'Charles, I know everything.'

'Everything?' Marcus nodded as Charles continued, 'She hasn't been troubled by her experiences?'

'The woman was living in a hellish nightmare, believe me I know more than even your sources could never find out. I have found my soul mate and that is the end of it. The past is the past. Now I am not going to discuss this any further. Just do me one big favour, please,' Charles nodded and waited for Marcus to speak, as he ate a rasher of bacon slowly. 'Could *you* tell Dawn all about her? How she suffered…'

'Oh come on, you should…' Charles saw the look in Marcus' eye and stopped.

'It would be better coming from you, Dawn worships you.' Marcus had stopped eating giving Charles a pleading look. 'I would love it if they could get on…'

Charles bit off a piece of toast. 'OK, but really it should come from you and I still think today is not the time…'

'Thanks Charles, you're a ruddy hero, I knew I can rely on you. Now let's eat up and get going before that ex-wife of mine and her new husband arrive. Heavens he's a bore!' Marcus took a sip of coffee, smiling, his mind wondered as he thought if all went well he could buy a boat one day, Charles had always loved sailing in warmer climes.

'I thought you were getting on splendidly with Linda last night. You were actually being civil with each other…'

'All for Dawn's sake, believe me, come on I've got to try and work out how to get into that blasted morning suit…'

The two men left the restaurant and three hours later Marcus found himself sitting in a Rolls Royce, on the way to pick up his daughter from his ex-wife's new home, he felt trussed up with the tight fitting collar. The car pulled into the drive and the chauffeur was out quickly to open the door. Marcus quickly exited as he saw his ex-wife fling open the front door and holding a handkerchief to her face. Marcus heart jumped and, fearing something was wrong, he started to run towards her when from the shadows he saw his daughter glide out from the hallway.

Marcus checked and gasped. The sun was shining making her dress sparkle; Marcus thought she looked as if she was floating on air. Her olive skin looked radiant against the white dress and her dark hair swept back gleamed in the morning sun highlighted by fresh flowers.

She held a small posy and had a nervous smile as she searched her father's face. 'Do I look alright?' She put her hand up to her the flowers as she noticed him looking at them.

Marcus had come to a stop and he felt his legs were leaden. 'I… I am either looking at an angel…'

'Dad, seriously. Do I look OK?'

Marcus turned for a moment to Linda.

'She is the most beautiful thing I have ever seen. Something good did come out of our relationship, thank you.' Marcus nodded towards his ex-wife which sent her into further floods of tears.

'Stop it you two,' shouted Dawn. 'I mustn't cry, my mascara will run!'

Marcus went over and raised his arm slightly letting his daughter link with him. 'Toby is a very lucky man. You look stunning and I do not say that lightly my girl.'

He led her to the car as the uniformed driver stood holding the door open and helped his daughter and her dress into the car.

'Marcus ask the driver to go for a little detour. We need a few more minutes than you to settle in at the church,' shouted Linda at him retiring quickly inside. The driver closed the car door quietly and returned to his seat turning slightly towards Marcus with a questioning look.

'You heard the woman take us for a five minute gentle drive,' said Marcus. 'As this car has cost me a fortune, I might as well make the most of it.'

'Dad…, behave yourself.' She said making sure her dress was not getting too ruffled.

'Dawn, first of all you look absolutely gorgeous,' Marcus said and he gave his daughter's arm a little squeeze.

'Dad, watch my dress…'

'Secondly, I…' Marcus stopped and thought about what Charles had advised that morning. He was so often right about such things, but not this time. He coughed nervously and Dawn turned to him slightly intrigued. 'I will be giving you, and Toby of course, a small gift later.' Dawn looked at him questioningly; her body a little stiff as she tried to keep her head upright and not knock the flowers in her hair. 'It may come as a bit of a surprise but I want you to know that…' He looked and saw his daughter's large eyes a little moist and could see her struggling to stop the tears already forming. 'Well, it might be a little emotional for you, but I feel it is right as I wasn't there for you when you were younger. If I'm honest I suppose a bit of me is trying to make up for lost time. It just might come as a bit of a shock, that's all.'

'Dad, you don't have to give me anything, and I want to end this conversation now before I cry and I *mustn't* cry.' Dawn squeezed her father's hand.

'OK, not now, but you will not be disappointed.' He looked into his daughter's wide and moist eyes. 'Hey, did I tell you look a million dollars?' He tried to make her laugh. 'Oh, damn did I remember to book the photographer?' They both let out a loud laugh and Marcus saw his daughter's shoulders ease.

The car purred along and ten minutes later they exited into the sunshine with the church bells peeling loudly above them. Dawn's bridesmaids took over the organisation of the dress and Marcus waited until everything was exactly the way his daughter wanted. Then they both looked at each other and in unison took a deep breath and entered the church.

The church was packed and Marcus cringed at the thought of them all coming back to the hotel for the wedding breakfast. The day passed so quickly that Marcus couldn't believe the time had come for him to stand and deliver his speech. Marcus raised himself slowly and deliberately from his seat. He looked down at the two glasses in front of him and then to Charles and, taking a sip of the water, he cleared his throat and began.

'Unaccustomed as I am to public speaking on such occasions…'

Laughter, shouts and friendly insults…

'Well as I only have one daughter, this will be my only chance to say something without being answered back!'

Jeering and more barracking…

'I think my words would be more worthy if I remained within the terminology of the antique world. Therefore this afternoon I have two lots for sale… Lot one.' Marcus pointed towards Toby. 'Here we have a fine example of a Neoclassical, Bun Foot, fine veneered, well certainly today he is, coffer. Why a coffer? Well, the reason he is described as a coffer is the display he showed us on his stag night after attempting to smoke a Monte Christo…, but I'll let the best man explain more.' Marcus picked up his wine and smiled mischievously at Toby and Dawn. Dawn shook her head and frowned back. 'Well to finish off with Lot One I understand he has a weapon….'

Guffaws and calls for Marcus to sit down…

'Yes, I believe he is a self loading, over and under, but alas just a single action machine. Sorry Dawn, but it is true!' The room was now rocking with laughter and even Dawn could not resist but smile. 'Ahh, but the best is yet to come, for I have heard that he has been reported to be a Chippendale…'

Laughter had now been accompanied by heavy banging of the tables

'Lot Two is more of the modern era…'
'Careful Dad, I can still kick in this dress.'
'My apologies for the interruptions, Ladies and Gentlemen.

Lot Two is, today at least and I'm sure you will all agree, lavishly decorated, with some fine inlay and could be described as double breasted...'

Protests and reams of laughter

Marcus had to wait for the audience to settle. 'She has been described as a jewel, well today she is at her most stunningly beautiful...'

More jeers and shouts of encouragement...

'I do however understand that she has a rather unusual and rather difficult to find, hallmark...'

'Dad, that's enough...' Dawn shouted and wagged a finger at him. 'Quit while you're ahead.'

Marcus laughed and put his hands up. He took another sip of wine and as the noise level subsided he let out a small sigh and, as his expression hardened and became more serious; it caused the room to go silent. Everyone was captivated by Marcus as he looked towards his daughter.

'I did warn Dawn in the car to the church this morning that I had something I wanted to give her.'

The muffled clatter of a busy kitchen in the distance was all that could be heard...

'I also warned her it may come as a bit of a shock.' Marcus reached into his inside pocket and extracted something which he held hidden in his clenched fist. 'When Dawn and Toby announced they wanted to marry I did the usual fatherly thing and said; "but where will you live and what will you do for money?" So finally we all agreed that they should use the top floor of the shop for a few months while they looked around for a place of their own. She's made a very nice job of decorating the place even though she would only be living there for a short while. Well, what she didn't realise was she was actually decorating her own home.'

Marcus opened his hand and held up a set of keys. Not a sound could be heard as the realisation of what Marcus had just said started to sink in. Dawn stared at her father and the keys, unable to speak. Marcus stepped up to his daughter and gave her the keys. He kissed her on the cheek and then shook Toby's hand; it was Marcus' turn to have a tear in his eye.

'Oh, I'm not out of your life; I'm going to set up an outlet in Greece. A lovely old town south of Piraeus called Ydra… It's now going to be Chapman and Daughter…International.' Dawn looked at the keys and then up at her father, her tears starting to flow. No words came as the room remained silent.

Charles stood up and was the first to start to clap, followed a few moments later by everyone in the room standing, applauding and cheering as Dawn remained rigid, staring at her father; her mascara smudged on her eyelids and cheeks.

★ ★ ★

Marcus sat cradling his cold beer and looking down to the small beach below him, which nestled in between two rocky promontories. He had had another successful day's sales at the shop. As he had walked up to the small taverna just out of town he had to pinch himself. Life was unbelievable, never in all his dreams would he have thought it would turn out so well.

Shrieks of laughter came from a young woman and her son as they played on the beach below, seemingly without a care in the world. The boy would escape the playful clutches of his mother and run into the sea splashing the woman if she dared to advance into the warm blue water. The game had gone on for awhile and Marcus' gaze changed to the woman's sister sitting beside him. She was smiling watching the horseplay below. Her coffee sat untouched in front of her, deep in her own thoughts. Winter was not far away but the summer had fought off any cold snaps and even this late in the year they sat in shorts and T-shirts.

Marcus sat back. He still sensed the scars had not healed within Tamara's mind. Sometimes she would awake screaming in the middle of the night, lashing out. They had set up their shop in Ydra and it was trading much better than he had expected. Dawn and Toby had visited only two weeks ago and Tamara and his daughter had not only become friends but they gelled so well the business was benefiting. They had even mentioned having children themselves after his daughter's visit, something clearly on the young couple's minds. Tamara had shrugged and thought it maybe too late, even Marcus cringed at the thought of nappies and the continuous demands of a young child.

'Hi Marcus,' said Stamatis as he approached the table. Tamara nodded at him, picking up her coffee she rested on her elbows and continued to look towards the beach.

'Yasoo Stamatis,' said Marcus turning and stretching out his hand.

Stamatis Korfiatis took the hand and as was his way he held it for a long while grinning at his new found English friend. 'You have good time Marcus?' he asked in a thick Greek accent as he pointed towards the beer.

Marcus nodded and shrugged. 'Well it's Saturday and the sun is shining…'

'Marcus, everyday is Saturday to you, heh?' The Greek laughed and tried to catch Tamara's eye but she was engrossed in her own thoughts. 'Where have you been? Everything good?' continued the Greek.

'Yes, everything good, very good. How is it at the bar?' Marcus had turned in his seat to face the visitor.

'Ah, a little quiet… Oh Marcus, I almost forget to tell you, there has been a man asking for you, well actually he asked for Tamara.' Marcus raised his eyebrows and Tamara also turned slowly towards the Greek. 'Yes, a Russian. He said he is an old friend.'

Tamara looked up at the Greek her body tensing at the mention of a Russian. Her eyes focused towards a car parked across the road. She saw the familiar face staring back at her, it sported no expression. She turned quickly in her seat, her heart thumping loudly against her chest.

Both men turned towards Tamara whose sudden movements had startled them. Tamara went to speak but she remained paralysed. Her eyes focused out into the distant blue horizon. A heavy silence shrouded the three of them.

Marcus noticed her coffee cup start to shake. It was barely noticeable at first but within a few seconds her hand shook so violently that the coffee began to spill. Marcus saw her falling sideways and he grabbed her arm just in time to prevent her from crashing to the floor. The cup dropped, shattering loudly and sending the remains of the coffee spreading on the table. Marcus still holding her, pulled her towards him as he came out of his seat; he realised she had fainted. He picked her up and carried her towards a bench supporting a long cushion. Stamatis was stunned and called out for help from the bar staff.

Marcus sat her down, putting her head between her knees. 'Tamara,' he whispered, 'are you alright?' He gently stroked her head as he saw her slowly coming round. After a few moments, with Marcus still having to support her, she raised her head to face him. There were no tears, but her eyes were wide, her pupils dilated with fear.

'Marcus, Oh my God Marcus. It's not over yet...,' she said weakly pointing towards the door of the cafe. 'In the car on the other side of the road...'

Marcus turned, his eyes searching down the street. 'Tamara, there isn't any car...'

Kinloch Castle does exist:

The authors would like to thank the "Kinloch Castle Friends Association" for their assistance and permission to reproduce the cover photograph.

"Kinloch Castle Friends Association" was first established as a membership organisation in 1996 and subsequently registered as a Charity in 2000. The island of Rum is administered by Scottish Natural Heritage but despite valiant efforts the funding was not available to maintain the 100 year old building and the Association was formed.

The 'Friends' aim to work in stimulating interest and provide funds plus human resources to care for the castle now and in the future. Official work parties visit the island several times each year and are rewarded with special privileges that the castle can provide.

You can follow in Marcus and Charles' footsteps and actually stay in one of the Oak Rooms with the original four poster beds! (There is also a hostel with more economical rates).

For further details:

Visitor Services Manager,
Kinloch Castle,
Isle of Rum,
Inverness-shire,
PH43 4RR

Tel: 01687–462037
Fax: 01687–460108